BITE

Wolf turns and jerks his head toward the woman. 'Dolly, you'll sleep with the jeep.'

'We ain't thieves,' the man says.

''Course not,' Wolf agrees enthusiastically, but shoots Dolly a meaningful look. 'Anyway, we should at least get our goods out of the sun.' The townie nods, saying nothing, and Wolf turns to me. 'How 'bout helping us with these bags again?'

Something tells me I should leave right now and pretend I never had anything to do with a strange couple of travelers called Wolf and Dolly. Something tells me a man with a smile like his can only bring trouble. Maybe that something is what normal people call common sense.

But Papa always said I don't have a whole lot of that.

'Sure,' I say. 'Why not?'

BITE

K.S. MERBETH

www.orbitbooks.net

ORBIT

First published in Great Britain in 2016 by Orbit

13 5 7 9 10 8 6 4 2

A CIP catalogue record for this book
is available from the British Library.

ISBN 978-0-356-50770-5

Typeset in Baskerville by M Rules
Printed and bound in Great Britain by
Clays Ltd, St Ives plc

Papers used by Orbit are from well-managed forests
and other responsible sources.

MIX
Paper from
responsible sources
FSC® C104740

Orbit
An imprint of
Little, Brown Book Group
Carmelite House
50 Victoria Embankment
London EC4Y 0DZ

An Hachette UK Company
www.hachette.co.uk

www.orbitbooks.net

For everyone who gave me shit about being an English major :P

I
Show Your Teeth

'Need a ride?'

His grin looks more like an animal baring its teeth. His teeth are yellowed and chipped, with gaps between showing where others have been knocked out. There's something starkly predatory about him, which is the first reason I shouldn't say yes.

The second is I'm small, alone, and unarmed. Any of those could be a death sentence in a place like this.

And there we have the third reason: By 'a place like this,' I mean a torn-up, full-of-potholes road running through the middle of nowhere. It's the only thing marking the landscape for miles. There's nothing but empty desert and the ruins of old cities in every direction. Nuclear war can do that to a place, I guess. But the point is, there's no one around to hear if I scream. Plus, even if someone did hear, chances are they wouldn't give a shit.

The fourth reason is the creepy lady in the passenger seat, who has blue hair and an assault rifle in her lap.

The fifth reason is the red-stained sacks of something-or-other sitting in the backseat.

The sixth reason is ... ah, hell. Need I go on?

I scratch my nose, sniff, and spit. The rumble of the jeep is the only sound in the stagnant air.

It's obvious that getting in this jeep is a terrible idea. A sixteen-year-old girl like me could provide a hell of a lot of entertainment for someone with a sick enough mind. I must look like easy prey, with my ragged clothes and skinny body.

So naturally, my answer is—

'Sure, why not?'

When it comes down to it, I've been walking for days. The soles of my boots are collecting holes. The sand burns my feet during the day, and the world is dark and frightening at night. The sun has left my skin raw and peeling, and when it sets it sucks all the warmth away. I'm down to one can of food and less than two days' worth of water – not enough to make it back to town even if I wanted to go. Lord knows how far I'd have to travel to find more.

This jeep and its driver are smelly, creepy, and very possibly dangerous, but they're my only ticket out of here.

The stranger shows his teeth again. His eyes are hidden behind a pair of goggles too big for his face.

'Hop in then, kid.'

I clamber into the backseat next to the reeking mystery bags, nearly tumbling onto them before I manage to squeeze myself into the tight space between the bags and the door. I place my backpack on my lap, my arms curling around it protectively. It doesn't hold much, just my canteen, one can of food, and a blanket my papa gave me, but it's all I have. I lean back with a sigh as the jeep starts moving. Sayonara, middle of nowhere! I might end up dead and dismembered in a ditch, but it'd be better than wandering aimlessly through this hellhole of a desert.

We pick up speed quickly, and I have to pull down on my beanie to stop it from flying off my head. A few strands of mousy hair poke out from underneath it, and I try to push them under again, but it's no use. I settle for holding the beanie with one hand and resting the other on the side of the jeep. The rank smell of the bags is getting stronger and stronger, making my eyes water. I blink it away and try to ignore it.

My attention shifts to the lady in the front seat, who still strikes me as pretty creepy. She was still and silent the whole time they waited for my answer, but now she turns around. It's impossible not to stare at her hair. It's very long, nearly waist-length, and oddly straight and sleek. I really don't understand how someone could have hair so perfect-looking, or how and *why* her hair is colored electric blue. The color is incredibly vivid in the dust-colored world around us.

She has dark eyes that reveal an Asian heritage, and small lips painted a vibrant red. She's pretty, with a noticeably ladylike figure despite the wasteland garb covering her quite modestly. Her red lips are mouthing something, but I can't make out any words with the wind whipping around me.

I squint my eyes, tilt my head to the side, and give her a vacant stare. She stares back at me for a moment before turning around.

She doesn't try to talk to me again, and neither does the feral man. Apparently they don't care enough to ask where I intend to go. I'm just along for the ride, and that's fine by me. Wherever I'm going has to be better than where I've been.

If I had any common sense at all I'd probably want to stay on edge. But, at this point, I'm already in the jeep. Either they want to kill me or they don't, and I won't get much of a choice in it either way. So I decide to nap. What can I say? It's been a long couple of days.

I wake up with my face pressed against the lumpy garbage bags, and *wow* do they smell. The scent is invading my nostrils, pillaging my throat, and violating my poor brain. I gag and recoil, pressing against the side of the car and frantically wiping my face with a hand that is probably even dirtier. I don't know what the hell is in there, but I don't want it on or near my face.

Once I determine I'm safe from any obscene-smelling substances, I realize the jeep is no longer moving, and my backpack is no longer on my lap. The man and young woman are standing a few yards away from the still vehicle, having a quiet conversation. Neither of them is paying attention to me.

I adjust my beanie and climb out of the car, stretching out my bony limbs one at a time. My back cracks and both of the strangers' heads jerk toward me.

'Err,' I say. The woman still has her assault rifle, and it's now pointed in my direction. I raise my hands and smile nervously. 'My bad.'

She relaxes when she sees it's just me, and the man displays that grin of his again. I notice my backpack in the dirt at his feet. In his hand is what I assume to be my last can of food. Unsurprisingly, it's beans. Despite how sick I am of goddamn beans, my stomach rumbles. But his other hand holds a really big knife that he must have used to pry the can open, so I decide not to comment.

'So you're awake,' the man says through a mouthful of food. He swallows, sighs with unabashed satisfaction, and continues. 'We were about to wake you up, but you looked pretty happy in there. You were drooling a little on the goods.'

I wipe my mouth and feel my cheeks grow hot. He laughs, a hearty and surprisingly genuine sound. He bends down to grab my backpack off the ground and tosses it over to me. I can't resist the urge to take a peek inside, just to make sure nothing else is missing. Once I'm certain that my canteen and my papa's blanket are still inside, I sling the bag over one shoulder and smile at him.

'We found a little town,' he says, jerking his thumb behind him. 'Decided it was as good a place as any to stop.'

'Oh, yeah, great,' I say sincerely. 'That works just fine. Thanks for the ride, mister.'

He laughs again, this time for no good reason I can decipher.

'Right, kid,' he says. 'Mind helping us carry this?'

I glance at the gross bags in the back of the jeep. The thought of lugging them around is far from pleasant. I don't know what's in them, and honestly I don't want to know. But he *did* give me a ride, so . . .

'Sure.'

'Good!' He grins again. 'Don't drop 'em or anything, we're selling this shit.'

I nod and wipe my sweaty palms on my jeans. Right, I can handle that. Probably.

The blue-haired Asian lady has been looking at me intently

this whole time, and it's starting to make me uncomfortable. She has a weird blankness about her. Not a hint of emotion ever crosses her face, and she has an incredibly unnerving stare. It's like looking into the eyes of a corpse. I try to ignore her, but looking at the guy with the savage grin isn't much better. At least the woman combs her hair. The man's is in long brown dreadlocks, and obviously hasn't been groomed in an awfully long time.

The two of them move over to the jeep and start unloading. They pack my arms full first, and I scrunch my nose and try not to inhale too deeply. Once we all have as much as we can carry, we head toward the town.

Or, rather, toward the pathetic collection of shambling buildings we call towns around here. Like most, it's built over the ruins of an old city, and made mostly of crumbling walls and scrap metal. People have patched up half-destroyed shells of rooms with blankets and plywood and whatever else they can find. From the looks of it, no more than a couple dozen townies live here. They peek out of doorways and windows as we pass through the outer limits of town. I see mostly men, a handful of women, and not a single child, which is not surprising. The end of the world didn't exactly encourage people to go making babies left and right, and half of the ones that do get born won't make it past their first year.

I've only ever seen pictures of the great old cities, but it's enough to make me appreciate the sadness of what they've become. I thought the town I left was small and run-down, but now I know the people back there had it pretty good. These people are dirty, thin, wrapped in rags.

Hollow eyes in hungry faces turn to watch us, but they

don't seem overly alarmed. Apparently this place is used to strangers, which is a bit odd. Most of these little towns can go months without seeing a new face. Three strangers arriving would've been a big old affair where I came from, and not a friendly one at that.

We walk for a few minutes, moving into what seems to be the heart of the town, an open space between some of the more well-kept buildings. The man dumps the bags he's carrying on the ground, and the woman and I follow suit. They produce wet thumps and small clouds of dust as they hit. I gratefully suck in fresh air while the other two survey the area. I'm not really sure what my plan is at this point, but these two seem to have some kind of goal, so I figure it can't hurt to stick with them for now.

'Where are they?' the woman asks. Her voice is nearly a whisper, and as flat and emotionless as her face.

'Not here,' the man says, 'which can't mean anything good.'

I eye them, but bite back my question as a townie approaches. He's a tall, wiry, dark-skinned man with a commanding presence and suspicious eyes. He folds his arms over his chest and spits a gob of yellowish saliva that narrowly misses my boot.

The dreadlocked man beside me shoves his hands into the pockets of his ratty jeans, assumes a relaxed posture, and grins.

'Name's Wolf,' he says. 'We've got some goods here. You have anything worth trading for? Gasoline, maybe?'

The townie says nothing. He looks at us, scrutinizes the bags, and looks at us again.

'Might,' he says finally. 'What've you got?' He nudges a bag with one shoe.

Again comes that cruel display of teeth.

'Meat,' Wolf says, overemphasizing the word.

The other man's eyebrows rise.

'Ain't seen that in a while,' he says. 'What's it from?'

'Couple o' wild hogs.'

'Hogs,' the townie repeats. He stares at the bags, his jaw working as if he's chewing on the information. 'Lot of meat for a couple hogs.'

'Fat ones,' Wolf says dryly. 'Look, you gonna trade or not?'

The man pauses.

'Let me think,' he says. He seems to be carefully weighing each word. 'I'll have to look at our stocks. Why don't you lot stay overnight? We'll talk in the mornin'.'

'Meat won't stay good forever,' Wolf says. It's hard to read his expression behind the goggles.

'Meat probably ain't good now,' the townie says, spitting again. I have to hop to the side to avoid this one. 'One more night won't hurt.'

'Fine,' Wolf says. He turns and jerks his head toward the woman. 'Dolly, you'll sleep with the jeep.'

'We ain't thieves,' the man says.

''Course not,' Wolf agrees enthusiastically, but shoots Dolly a meaningful look. 'Anyway, we should at least get our goods out of the sun.' The townie nods, saying nothing, and Wolf turns to me. 'How 'bout helping us with these bags again?'

Something tells me I should leave right now and pretend

I never had anything to do with a strange couple of travelers called Wolf and Dolly. Something tells me a man with a smile like his can only bring trouble. Maybe that something is what normal people call common sense.

But Papa always said I don't have a whole lot of that.

'Sure,' I say. 'Why not?'

II
The Strangers

Carrying the cargo is sweaty work, and by our second trip into town I think I'm starting to smell as bad as the bags. It doesn't help that Wolf is off bartering somewhere, leaving Dolly and me to handle it all ourselves. None of the townies offer to help. Instead they completely ignore our presence. Men rest on rocks or lean against nearby buildings in small clumps, carrying on conversations that fall silent when we get close. And it really is all men; the women have disappeared. So have the elderly, and the incapable. Every single person left lingering outside looks like they could give me a thorough ass-kicking if necessary. I can feel their eyes following me when I turn my back.

'This is weird,' I say in a low whisper. I glance over at Dolly, who keeps her eyes forward. 'Isn't it?'

She gives a minuscule shrug of her shoulders and says nothing. I guess that's as close to an answer as I'm going to get. I sigh and try to ignore the uneasiness creeping up on me. These people did invite us to stay in their town for the night. That alone makes them friendlier than the town I left. Wolf and Dolly would've been shot the second they got within ten paces of the place. These townies are just being reasonably wary of strangers. Probably.

'So, where are you and Wolf headed, anyway?' I ask, trying to distract myself from my nerves. Neither of them has told me anything about themselves or why they're here. They haven't asked about me, either. Come to think of it, I don't think they've even asked for my name. Maybe I'm supposed to assume those are the rules of our temporary relationship, but my curiosity is getting the better of me.

'Nowhere,' Dolly says. I frown.

'So you're just ... driving around randomly? Isn't that kind of ... ' Pointless? Dangerous? A waste of precious gas? I don't even know where to begin. 'Are you traders?' Traders are the only people I can think of who would have any reason to wander like that. Well, and myself, but I have my own reasons.

'No,' she says. I wait for her to continue. She doesn't.

'Okay,' I say. When I was young and my papa left me in our bomb shelter by myself, I used to play a game that involved bouncing a ball off the wall. It always just came bouncing back, but I would keep doing it like I expected something new to happen, or thought a friend might materialize. Trying to carry on a conversation with Dolly feels about as productive as that did.

I shut my mouth and keep walking. I should save my breath, anyway. Even though I'm only carrying half as much as Dolly, the bags are heavy, and the exertion is making me more aware of the hunger in my belly and the tired ache in my bones. Despite that, it's nice to feel helpful.

Back in my old town it was always *Get out of the way, girl* and *Don't you know how to do anything right?* One of the many reasons why braving the wastes alone sounded better than staying.

As we pass one of the rickety buildings, the door bangs open. A woman comes out, dragging a young boy behind her. I guess there are children here after all; they must just keep them hidden away when strangers are around. The woman stomps her way over to a group of men sitting on the hood of a rusted, broken-down vehicle. She speaks in hushed whispers to them, saying something that involves a lot of head shakes and hand gestures. She releases the hand of the boy as the conversation seems to grow more heated. The boy's gaze wanders over to us. As our eyes meet I shoot him a friendly smile.

My smile drops as the kid takes that as a sign to start walking over to us.

'Oh, no. No, no, no,' I mutter. As much as I like children, somehow I don't think this kid is supposed to be near us. I don't want to give the townies any other reason to distrust us. But it's not easy to wave him away with my hands full, and I don't want to raise my voice and draw attention.

I slow down as he gets closer. It's hard to see the kid around the bulky bags I'm carrying.

'Careful, little guy,' I say, stepping around him. 'This is heavy stuff.'

Apparently he's not the sharpest tool in the shed, because he moves away from me and steps directly into Dolly's path. He stares up at her with wide eyes and doesn't move. Dolly stops in her tracks.

'Can I touch your hair?' the boy asks.

'We're kind of busy here,' I say. Dolly doesn't seem like the kid-friendly type, and I don't want to see her go all ice queen on this poor kid. But instead, to my surprise, she drops her bags and crouches down, bringing herself to eye level with the young boy. With several inches between their faces, they scrutinize each other with an apparently shared sense of awe. He raises a hand and touches the ends of her hair with small, chubby fingers. I'm sure his hands are filthy, but Dolly doesn't pull back from his touch. I catch a glimpse of something oddly soft in her face, a crack in her blank expression. She almost looks sad for a moment.

'Mommy said you were bad people,' the boy says, 'but I think you're nice.' He smiles. His two front teeth are missing. Dolly leans close and whispers something in his ear.

A surprised expletive alerts me that the boy's mother has noticed his disappearance. She looks around frantically, homes in on us, and rushes over, her eyes wide and fearful.

'Jimmy,' she hisses, grabbing the boy by the hand and yanking him away. She pulls him behind her and backs away from us. Her suspicious eyes flit back and forth between Dolly and me. Once she's apparently decided we're not going to attack her, she turns her back and hurries away, tugging her son along. 'What did I tell you about talking to strangers?' she scolds him.

With another loud bang, she disappears into the building she came from. The men near the jeep are watching us with a renewed and obviously unfriendly interest. I frown, and glance at Dolly to see if the interaction bothered her, but her face is back to its usual blank slate. She stands up, takes her bags, and resumes walking. I hurriedly follow, trying to match her long strides.

'You like kids, Dolly?' I ask, not really expecting a response.

'Yes.' A straight answer, to my surprise, and when I turn to look at her there's a ghost of a smile on her lips. It disappears immediately when she notices me looking.

'Me, too!' Finally, some shared ground. I smile at her, but she doesn't seem to notice. 'What'd you say to him?'

'To listen to his mother.'

I nod slowly, automatically assuming it to be good advice before I remember what his mom said.

As the day grows later, the townies invite us to share a meal with them. It's good hospitality, especially for a place this small. The idea would have been laughable where I came from. Even after living there for a couple of years, I wouldn't get fed unless I got enough work done during the day.

I'm grateful for the generosity, and yet something about this place is definitely rubbing me the wrong way. Nobody says anything openly, but everyone gives us these weird sideways glances and dirty looks. It's gotten even worse since this morning. Part of me wonders if it's Wolf and Dolly specifically they're suspicious about, but since I arrived with them and have stuck with them since getting here, it's a little late for me to try to distance myself from them.

Since Dolly is watching the jeep, Wolf and I are alone. The townies light up trash can fire pits, place sheets of metal over the tops, and set aluminum cans of food on top of those. They cluster around the trash cans as the sun sets and the day's warmth slips away. Wolf and I stand apart from them. I can barely feel a hint of heat from this distance, and have to rub at my arms to keep from shivering. However, the smell of the meal cooking reaches us just fine, and my mouth waters at the distant memory of hot food. I haven't eaten anything but cold beans for days.

But the looks from the townies sour my stomach. They all look incredibly pissed off as soon as they catch me looking. I can read the accusations in those stares: *strangers, untrusted, unwelcome.* I'm particularly familiar with the latter. In the wastes, you have to fight for your right to exist.

'Are you sure we were invited?' I ask, turning to Wolf and trying to ignore the stares. My stomach churns with a familiar discomfort. I didn't leave my last town just to become an unwanted mouth to feed again. At least Wolf doesn't seem to mind my presence.

''Course I am.' He continues staring at the food. He pulled his goggles down around his neck when the sun set, and his eyes are sharp and intense without them. I shrug and look down at my boots.

As the townies start passing out cans, clumps of people shift into a messy line. I watch as Wolf walks up and completely ignores them, bypassing the line and snatching a can of food without a moment's hesitation. I attempt to follow in the wake of his bravado, but only make it two steps before someone bumps into me and sends me stumbling.

I look up to see a gaunt-faced townie scowling down at me. His eyes are hard, his lip curling derisively.

'Sorry,' I say automatically, as my brain tries to work out where the hell he came from. All of the other townies were by the fire pits, so why was this guy behind us? Was he watching us? My uneasiness deepens, and I swallow hard.

'You ain't supposed to be here,' he says.

'Huh? Wolf said—'

'Not him. *You.*' He jabs a finger into my chest. I back up, rubbing at the spot and staring at him. 'What are you doing with them?' he asks me.

'Umm, well, it's kind of a long story—'

'Scrawny little thing like you,' he says, stepping closer and bringing his face down to mine. I'm uncomfortably aware of how much bigger than me he is. Would the other townies step in if he tried to hurt me? I doubt it. 'Think you can just wander into town and help yourself to our food?'

'I thought—'

'You thought wrong.' He puts a hand on my chest and shoves, sending me stumbling right into Wolf.

'Is there a problem here?' he asks.

I never thought I'd be so happy to see his crazy grin. I scamper behind him and stay there, eager to have a shield from the townie. The man stares at Wolf for a long few seconds. Wolf barely looks at him; he's focused on the can of food in his hands, which he's slowly opening with a knife much too big and sharp for the task. Metal grates harshly on metal as he peels it open. The townie's jaw is clenched, a tic jumping in his cheek. He looks like he's dying to throw a punch. But just when the tension seems taut enough to snap, he shakes his head and walks away.

I let out a low whoosh of breath and step out from behind Wolf.

'Well, I'm sure glad I didn't show up here alone,' I say,

forcing a laugh. Wolf shrugs nonchalantly, raises his can to his mouth, and takes a big gulp. My mouth fills with drool at the sight, and I realize with a sad twist of my stomach that there's no way I'll be brave enough to get food for myself now. Wolf lowers the can and notices me staring.

'What?' he asks, wiping his mouth with the back of his hand. 'What is it? Why aren't you eating?'

'Oh, uh, I'm not that hungry,' I say. 'I just ate ... the day before yesterday.'

Wolf rolls his eyes.

'Do I gotta do *everything* for you?' he grumbles.

Before I can protest, he shoves his can into my hands.

'Let me show you somethin', kid,' he says. He walks over to the townies and casually cuts into the front of the line again. He grabs a can, grins at the man passing out food, and saunters back to me. 'See? It's that simple.'

Apparently he doesn't notice the death glares and murmurs that follow. Though, at this point, it's probably more accurate to say that he doesn't give a shit.

'Well, that's easy for you to say. You're—' I pause before the word *scary* leaves my mouth. 'Umm. You have a really big knife.'

'Oh, this?' He looks down at the knife, which he's currently using to pry open the second can of food, and chuckles. 'This ain't nothing. Now eat your damn beans before they get cold.'

Of course it had to be beans. I suppress a sigh and take a sludgy gulp of the familiar food. At least they're hot. I scarf them down as quickly as possible and swipe a finger around the can to collect the last remnants.

Once I'm done, I watch Wolf. He eats slowly, which is

strange. Most wastelanders eat as quickly as possible, not only because we're starving half the time, but because we're afraid someone might take our food. The way he eats shows that he's not worried about either of those problems. It says a lot about him, and raises more questions, too. I can't help but wonder about him and Dolly. Who are these people? Where are they from, where are they going, and why did they stop to pick me up?

When he finally finishes eating, he notices me looking and exhales an exaggerated sigh.

'What do you want now?' he asks.

'Oh, I, umm.' I consider the whirlwind of questions in my head, but bite my tongue. 'I just wanted to say thanks. You didn't have to do that. Get me food, I mean.'

''Course I did,' he says. 'I took your last can, didn't I? Fair's fair.' He shrugs. 'Anyway, you're with us – for now. And we look out for each other.'

I'm not really sure what being 'with them' means for me, and the pointed 'for now' is a little worrying. Still, I guess it's going pretty well so far, seeing as I've got a belly full of warm food and avoided getting shoved around by that townie.

'Sounds good to me.'

'Good. 'Cause you've got first watch tonight.'

He turns and walks away. I smile at the back of his head before setting off after him.

III
Sharks

'No idea what you're flapping your gums about.'

I awaken to the sound of a voice nearby. It's just past dawn, judging from the light. I'm sprawled out on the ground, twisted up in my papa's blanket, but the spot Wolf slept in is now empty.

'You sayin' this is all coincidence?'

There's another voice. Both are marked by open hostility, and gradually rise in volume.

'Yeah, that's exactly what I'm saying.'

Wolf's lazy drawl alternates with the low rumble of the townsman. They must be only a few yards away.

'Stop bullshittin' me.'

A heavy silence falls. Even though I'm not involved, I can taste the tension in the air. Several seconds of silence pass, and a new sound fades in: footsteps, headed in my direction. Wolf's face enters my line of vision, his dreadlocked head bending down toward me.

'Eavesdropping?' he asks.

'Well, kind of, I guess.' No sense in being dishonest.

'Heh. So you know we're leaving?'

'Now I do.'

'Good. Get up.' He prods me in the side with one foot.

Apparently I'm along for the ride again. I don't mind at all. As if yesterday wasn't strange enough, with the atmosphere this hostile, I don't want to be left here alone. While tagging along with these strangers isn't a great option, either, I'd rather be out on the road than stuck here. It's actually nice to have a reason to get up. When I was by myself, it wasn't always so easy. I'd sometimes lie there for hours trying to think of a reason to keep going, and mostly coming up with reasons not to.

Not that it's ever really *easy* to get up. Even now I feel like I could sleep for another week or so. Being run out of town by pissed-off townies is not exactly how I like to start my day. Plus my feet still hurt, I'm down to one day's worth of water, and I have absolutely no idea where I'm headed next.

So?

That's what my papa always said on the long trek across the wastes after we left our bomb shelter, looking for somewhere new to live. 'I'm thirsty,' I'd say. *So?* 'My feet hurt.' *So?* And then he'd look at me expectantly.

'So I carry on,' I mumble, sitting up. Luckily Wolf isn't paying enough attention to give me shit for talking to myself. Instead he's staring away from me, sucking his bottom lip between his messed-up teeth. He almost looks worried, which makes *me* worried. If the guy with a big-ass knife is concerned, that means it's definitely time to go.

Despite the sense of urgency, I take the time to carefully roll up my dusty blanket and place it into my backpack before

I stand. I have to take care not to step on the bags of meat surrounding me.

'So why are we leaving?' I ask.

'Thought you were eavesdropping?'

'Only kind of.'

'Well, you did a shit job of it.'

'Not a lot of practice,' I say with a shrug. Following his lead, I start picking up bags. Today the smell has increased tenfold, and the bags squish against my chest as I lift them. There's no way this stuff is still edible.

'S'pose not,' Wolf says. 'Well, the gist of it is that there have been an awful lot of disappearances over the last couple weeks, so of course they're inclined to blame us.' He rolls his eyes exaggeratedly. 'That, and some suspicious strangers showed up a couple days ago. They're convinced we knew 'em or something.'

'Oh,' I say uncertainly. 'Well, *do* we know 'em?'

'And what's more,' he continues, 'the townsman seems to be implying we not only killed the missing locals' – he pauses as he lifts a particularly full sack – 'but *then* we might've come and tried to trade with the very town they came from.' He turns and winks at me, grinning devilishly. 'But that would be a fucking stupid plan, huh?'

'Uh, yeah,' I say. 'Yeah, it would be.' Wolf seems way too unconcerned, and the whole thing is starting to feel a bit fishy to me. Still, right now, I just want to get the hell out of this town, so I'll keep my mouth shut and roll with it. Anyway, I have to get to work picking up our reeking cargo, because Wolf's arms are already full. He starts walking away as I hurry to finish gathering the rest.

'Get to the jeep when you've got everything,' he calls without turning around.

I nod, look over my shoulder, and falter. The townsman is standing only a couple of yards away. He's watching me. His dark arms are folded over his chest, jaw set, body tense. The other townies are gathered in clumps near him. Some of them carry weapons, metal pipes and rusty knives and the like.

Shuddering, I turn around and speed up my efforts. I need to scram, and fast. But without Dolly there's more to carry, and Wolf didn't make up for much of the slack. That leaves me with a hell of a lot to juggle.

I stack up the bags, forcing them into one big pile, and lift it with a grunt. My scrawny arms can barely fit around it all, and my muscles tremble with the effort.

One step. So far, so good, although my eyes water and my arms burn.

I take a second step, and the bag resting on top begins to teeter precariously. I stuff my face into the bags in an attempt to steady them. The stench is overwhelming: rotten and raw.

I take a third step, moving as carefully as I can, and the bag falls. The wet smack of impact stops me. The rest of the pile doesn't follow the first one's tumble, but that doesn't improve the situation much. What the hell am I supposed to do now? If I want to pick up the fallen bag, I have to set down the rest and start over. A second bag falls as I hesitate.

'Need some help?' a voice asks, and a chorus of angels somewhere sings to accompany it. It's the townsman. I crane my neck to see him walking toward me.

'Uhh, sure,' I say. Though the sudden kindness from him

is strange, I don't really have any alternatives but to accept his help. 'Thanks!'

He crouches next to the fallen bags and pauses, hand hovering over one. Suddenly he pulls out a knife and drags the blade down the length of it. The fabric rips loudly and easily. A mass of moist red meat begins to ooze out of the tear, spilling sloppily into the dirt. There's no skin or bone to be seen, just a mound of wet, raw meat.

And, oh God, the *smell*. It hits me like a slap to the face. I choke on the putrid air, gagging.

'What the hell did you do that for?' I ask, my voice squeaky with surprise. Ignoring me, he plunges his hand into the puddle of meat and sifts around. I find myself filled with inexplicable apprehension, and some very explicable disgust, as I watch. He freezes, and gradually withdraws his hand, now in a closed fist. He unfurls his fingers one after another.

Resting in his hand is a bloody human finger.

'Shit,' I say.

Oh, holy goddamn *shit*.

'Sharks,' he snarls, turning a burning gaze toward me.

Sharks.

People will do a lot to survive. Everyone in the wastes understands that. Scavengers, thieves, whores, raiders ... everyone knows they're just trying to stay alive. But even in the desperate, lawless world of the wastelands, sharks are hated by all. They practice the last taboo, the one globally acknowledged evil, the act too immoral and repulsive and unfathomable to be accepted: cannibalism.

The bags tumble from my numb arms, toppling one by one and smacking against the ground. I hold on to the last one, sticking it out in front of me like a shield, but I hastily drop it as I remind myself what's inside. The townsman rises to his feet, knife clutched in his hand.

'Stop the others!' he roars, and the townies scramble to obey. 'I'll take care of *him*.'

He takes a step toward me.

'Actually, I'm a gi—' The glint of his blade reminds me how very unimportant that is right now. I step back, raising my hands palms out. 'Wait, wait, just hold on a second here—' He continues his advance. 'I'm no shark! I'm not even with them! I mean, sure, I got here with them and all—' And I was about to leave with them, too. *Shit*. This really does not look good for me.

My foot catches on a rock as I back away. I stumble, pinwheel helplessly, and topple over. I hit the ground hard. The townsman is just a few feet away now, knife raised and face twisted in a righteous fury, ready to avenge all of the crimes against humanity he thinks I've committed. Aw, hell, I always knew I was gonna die over something stupid. I squeeze my eyes shut.

There's a sudden roar, a rush of movement. My eyes fly open just in time to see a familiar jeep hurtling at the townsman.

He dives for safety, arms outstretched, and lands belly-up on the dirt several feet away from me. The jeep flies past. Chest heaving, he rises again. Knife still clutched in his hand, he turns and lunges toward me, but the jeep is already making a sharp turn.

His eyes bulge as he turns to face the oncoming vehicle, and—

Crunch.

The driver, Dolly this time, drives back and forth a few times to ensure he's well and truly dead, while Wolf whoops appreciatively from the passenger seat.

Disgust and gratitude fight for control of my mind. On one hand, I just saw someone die – messily. On the other, he *was* going to kill me. I guess I'm not really sure how I should feel right now, so I save my judgments and stand up.

Wolf extends his hand from the nearby jeep, grinning.

'The hell you waiting for, kid?'

As if this is perfectly ordinary. Then again, it could be for them. I hesitate, letting my gaze drift to the townie's body and then quickly dragging it back to Wolf. Do I really want to stick around two people who could do that to a man and grin about it? Scratch that – two *sharks*? I'm not really sure. Then again, it's either these two sharks or a mob of angry townies at my heels, and the sharks have been quite a lot nicer to me. They even came back for me.

'You saved me,' I say, the statement rising at the end into an almost-question. 'Umm, thanks.' I step forward to grab his hand and pull myself up, but Wolf shakes his head.

'Get the cargo first!'

Or maybe they came back for that. My nose wrinkles, but I stifle my disgust and start heaving sacks into the jeep. If they're my ticket out of here, I'm not complaining.

A few bags into the job, a loud bang nearly makes me jump out of my skin. I whip around to see one of the townies in the distance, pointing a gun at me.

'Aw, calm the hell down, kid. There's no way he can shoot us from that far away,' Wolf says.

I nod shakily and toss in another bag.

There's another bang, and then the unmistakable sound of a bullet sinking into the ground just a few feet to my left. I freeze, wide-eyed.

'Then again, I could be wrong,' Wolf says. 'It happens occasionally. Get in.'

I hop into the backseat and burrow into the pile of bags, just moments before the jeep jerks forward and we roar toward freedom.

IV
The Mob

'No, no, not that way!' Wolf is shouting. 'We gotta drive through – for fuck's sake, not *toward* the townie with the gun!' He lets out a long string of swear words that don't make much sense when used together, followed by 'Oh, shit, they're gonna shoot for our ti—'

The jeep swerves. Bags slide and thud, and I find myself crushed by them. A loud crash, and the jeep shudders with the impact of hitting something heavy. The engine whines with the struggle, a pathetic sound lasting only a few seconds before we jerk to a stop.

My head spins. I gasp for air. Someone grabs me by the shoulder and drags me out of the jeep, only to drop me on the ground again. I pry my eyes open to see Wolf. His lips are moving, but my brain is too jumbled to make any sense of the words or bring myself to move. He gives up on me, rummages through the jeep, and pulls out a ragged duffel bag.

I manage to drag myself to my feet as my ability to think returns. We seem to have crashed inside one of the ruined buildings. A makeshift covering of sheet metal and cloth lies crushed under the jeep's wheels.

'Staircase!' Wolf barks. I turn in a full circle and a half before locating the barely intact stairs. Wolf is already clambering up them. I take a step forward, skid on loose gravel, and fall flat on my face. Groaning, I rise up to my knees, shaking my still-spinning head in an attempt to clear it. I'm distantly aware of shouts and howls from outside. The townies are closing in. I will myself to move, but with my vision swimming and my legs shaky it's hard to get my body and mind to cooperate.

A hand closes around my arm and yanks me to my feet.

'Come on,' Wolf says gruffly. 'You lookin' to get torn apart by those townies or something?' He half-carries, half-drags me up the stairs. By the time we reach the top I've regained my sense of balance.

The second level of the building seems on the verge of collapse. The roof is torn off and the wooden floorboards are smashed up and unsteady, with a big chunk caved in to the left of the staircase. The wall across from us gapes with holes, letting sunlight and sound pour in. I dash over to find a relatively safe spot against the wall and peer out. It provides a clear view of the street below.

Townies are swarming the building. They look thirsty for blood, nothing like the hollowed-out, passive folks from yesterday. Their dirty hands are full of weapons – some makeshift, some very real and deadly. One of them aims a gun at my head as he spots me. I duck down to the shelter of the wall.

Wolf searches through his duffel bag, whistling something

off-tune. Dolly looks as calm as ever as she scopes out the approaching townspeople.

'Quite a few of them,' she says tonelessly.

'Yeah,' Wolf says, similarly unaffected.

'Some of them have guns.'

'Yeah. Since when do townies have such big-ass guns?'

'Maybe they took them from the others,' she says, shrugging.

'If they're not dead already, I'm gonna tear those bastards apart for not showing up.'

'What bastards?' I ask. They ignore me. The more I try to make sense of this situation, the more bizarre it gets.

'You can always trust Pretty Boy to screw up a job,' Wolf says, shaking his head and grimacing. 'Townies closing in?'

Dolly peeks out and quickly recoils. A rock flies through the space her head occupied.

'Yeah,' she says, casually flicking a strand of blue hair out of her face. 'Armed. Some with guns.'

'No worries,' Wolf says. That wild grin is back. He pulls a shotgun out of the bag and turns to face the staircase. 'Mine's bigger.'

The townies announce their arrival in an awful cacophony, raucous howls and shouts bubbling up the staircase. I cringe at the noise. They sound like a pack of starving animals, all shreds of civility gone.

Wolf stands directly in front of the stairs, the barrel of his shotgun aimed at the doorway.

'Dolly,' he says, inclining his head toward the duffel bag. 'Arm yourself and the kid. I can handle the first few.'

Amazingly enough, there isn't a hint of nervousness in his

voice. If I stood alone against a pack of angry townies, I'd shit myself. In fact, I'm pretty damn close right now. Yet somehow Wolf doesn't seem concerned.

While Dolly grabs the bag, the first townie stomps up the stairs. He's alone, testing the waters. He's either very brave or very stupid for doing so . . . or maybe completely mad, which is what it looks like. His eyes are way too big and bright, his teeth clenched in a violent grimace. He looks like the human equivalent of a rabid dog, except he's armed with a gun instead of tooth and claw.

He pauses at the top of the staircase and turns his wild eyes on us. Wolf calmly aims. The man takes one step, pointing his gun at Wolf's head, and the sound of a gunshot drowns out the mob below.

The townie's face shatters and his body tumbles down the stairs. The crowd's yells subside. I blink rapidly, feeling as though the image is imprinted on the back of my eyelids. So fast, so sudden, and a man is dead. Bile rises in my throat, and I swallow it back.

'Have I mentioned how much I love close-range gunfights?' Wolf says cheerfully. 'What a mess. A fucking beautiful mess, y'know?'

Actually, I'm kind of wishing I could go back and unsee that happening. Point-blank shotgun blasts to the face aren't really my thing. But there's no time for me to dwell on that gruesome image. Dolly kneels next to me with the bag, head bowed, long hair nearly covering her face. She pulls out two pistols, ensures they're loaded, and stands. One dainty foot nudges the bag toward me in an open invitation. I peek inside.

It's full of weapons. There are guns of all shapes and sizes along with boxes of ammo. No wonder Wolf went out of his way to grab this. Stuff like this is *valuable* nowadays. With a collection this size, it's obvious these two have done a lot of traveling, and a lot of raiding, too.

I let out a low whistle and sift through it all, trying to choose one. This one looks too big, I doubt I could even lift it. And this one looks way too small! Bullets that size couldn't do much damage, could they? Not a single one of these feels right. And how am I supposed to know which ammo to use?

In the background, the roar of the townies is rising again. We don't have much time. I imagine them egging each other on. With the way they've looked at us since our arrival, the hate in their eyes ... we must be like fresh bait to them. However this ends, it won't be with peace.

Footsteps on the stairs announce the arrival of more townies. I look up from the weapons as three of them burst into the room. One is instantly taken out by Wolf's shotgun, but Wolf has to pull back to reload. The two remaining men home in on me, crouched on the floor and completely unarmed. Their faces light up at the sight of such easy prey. These two don't have guns, but they do have knives. They manage to take about two steps before Dolly shoots from somewhere behind me.

Compared to Wolf her shooting is beautiful. She kills like it's an art: two bullets at once, two clean shots, splitting their skulls open like eggshells and erupting in a mess of brain matter on the other side. They're gone before they hit the ground.

'Nice shooting, Dolly,' Wolf says. With his gun loaded again, he moves back to his former position and places one foot on top of a body.

'Yeah!' I agree enthusiastically. It draws Wolf's attention to me, and he frowns.

'And where the hell is *your* gun?'

'Umm . . . ' I glance between the bag and his face, smiling awkwardly. 'Is this a bad time to mention I've never used one before?'

'Oh, for the love of—' Wolf cuts himself off and scowls. 'Just grab a gun! You aim, you pull the trigger, brains go flying. Easy.'

Dolly mumbles something.

'Right,' Wolf says. 'Don't forget the safety thing.'

'Safety thing?' I pick up a random gun and stare at it in bewilderment.

'Yeah, you know, the—' A townie comes into sight, and Wolf blows his face off. 'The safety thing!'

The townies are getting louder outside. My heart pounds faster and faster as I scrutinize the gun, unable to make any sense of it.

'Goddamn,' Wolf says, and for once he seems to feel a flicker of concern. 'Dolly, we're going to need some explosives. This kid is obviously useless.'

'I'm right here,' I mutter under my breath, though I know it's true. Dolly tears her eyes away from the doorway and looks through the bag again. She moves hastily, but her face is still completely blank.

'And by the way, I *do* have a name,' I say, raising my voice. 'It's—'

Dolly interrupts me by shoving something into my hands, saying something too soft for me to catch. I drop the gun and grab it, surprised. The shape and texture are odd, unlike anything I've ever felt before. I open my hands and stare.

A grenade.

She did *not* just hand me a grenade. I freeze, eyes locked on the explosive, which I'm sure is about to blow my hands off in a matter of seconds. Holy shit, I can't even shoot a gun; how did she *possibly* think I could handle a grenade? I've only ever seen them in pictures, but I know damn well what they can do. Time slows down. My breath quickens and my heart beats a million times per second. Even the yelling of the mob fades into the distance, my breathing somehow louder in my ears. Nothing matters except the grenade resting in my hands. My brain whirs, attempting to come up with a course of action that doesn't involve me splattering into a thousand bloody bits.

After a moment of frozen panic, instinct kicks in. I turn and hurl the thing toward the far wall. Thankfully, it sails out one of the holes rather than bouncing back to me.

I turn around, feeling triumphant, and Dolly's dumb-founded expression tells me I just screwed up. It's the first time I've seen actual emotion on her otherwise impassive face. It changes from shock, to disbelief, to unmistakable anger before returning to a stony, controlled state.

'Did you just throw away our last grenade?' she asks, her voice low and toneless.

'Well, I wasn't going to hang on to it!' I tell her defensively. What did she expect?

'You have to pull the pin before you throw it.'

She's still staring at me.

'Pull the ... what?'

'It won't work unless you pull the pin.'

That would explain the lack of an explosion.

'Where are those explosives?' Wolf yells, turning around to glare. Dolly points at the wall behind us.

'Out there,' she says.

'And what the fuck are they doing there?' he snarls. She points at me.

'Kid!' He looks about ready to rip my throat out. 'Are you *really* this stupid, or are you just fucking with us?'

'Seriously, I have a name!' I say, pointedly ignoring the rest. 'Like I was trying to say, it's—'

I'm drowned out by the sound of townies coming up the stairs. A *lot* of townies. All three of us turn back to the doorway, and the two who aren't miserable failures raise their guns.

A clump of townies spills into the room all at once. A few are taken down by some well-aimed shots by Wolf and Dolly, but they don't have time to reload before others are upon them. I scramble into a back corner and crouch there with the gun I have no idea how to use.

Wolf tackles the closest man and brings him down with a thud. He smashes the butt of the unloaded shotgun into the townie's face, hitting him repeatedly until he goes limp. Two others are on him almost instantly. He disappears beneath them.

A few bodies are already on the floor near Dolly. She has a crowbar and is attempting to hold back the crowd at the doorway, while the mob outside seethes and writhes like water about to boil over.

Despite Dolly's best efforts, it's already too late. Wolf doesn't seem to be faring well with his two attackers, and another man is lunging at me.

I dash for the window on my hands and knees, but a hand closes on my backpack and yanks me back. I scramble for a hold, scraping my nails against splintered wood. It's useless; he has me. As I turn, I recognize him – it's the man from last night, the one who shoved me. His mouth spreads in a gap-toothed grin as he meets my eyes. The hand that doesn't have a viselike grip on my pack is holding a broken bottle, the jagged edges glinting cruelly.

When I reach for the gun, the townie gives another vicious yank, pulling me away from it and closer to the sharp edges of the glass.

An explosion drowns out my screams.

The building shakes. The man lets go. My eardrums nearly burst.

Everyone is disoriented from the blast, stumbling and blinking. Wolf gains his composure first and takes advantage of it, pulling down the two townies he's been tussling with. Spurred into action, my former captor grabs a hold of me again. I kick out desperately. This time I dislodge his grip and crawl away on my hands and knees. As I search for an escape route, Dolly steps between me and the townie. Armed with a crowbar, she looks like the closest thing to a miracle I could expect right now.

I peek around her legs and see the man smirk.

'Pretty thing, ain't ya?' he comments, leering at Dolly. 'Come on, little girl, you can't fight me.'

One crack to the side of the head is all it takes to prove him wrong. Unsatisfied with that, she bends down and beats the crowbar into his skull until blood pools around him. I can't look away, my eyes wide open and locked on despite the nauseous churn of my stomach. Finally Dolly stops and turns to me, pale face flecked with red. She offers me a bloody hand.

'Thanks,' I squeak, pulling myself to my feet. Wolf is up as well now, and looks very satisfied despite the blood streaming from his nose and a gash on his head. The room is still, aside from us. Strangely, gunfire continues down below.

'Phew!' Wolf wipes a hand across his forehead, pushing his matted hair back. 'Now *that* was a good fight.'

I don't even know what to say to that. Instead I ask, 'So . . . uhh . . . what exploded?'

'Not the grenade you wasted, that's for sure.' I wince at the reminder. 'But otherwise . . . haven't got a clue.'

'The jeep?' Dolly suggests.

'Let's hope not.'

Wolf leads us down the stairs, which are blackened from the explosion and thoroughly decorated with townie guts. I have to step over detached limbs and disfigured torsos to get down. I feel nothing; numbness stifles the emotional responses struggling to fight their way out of me. I almost feel like I'm watching the scene through someone else's eyes.

At the bottom of the staircase the mob is dispersing. Injured townies are scattered on the ground, howling in pain and nursing wounds. The remainders sprint or limp off to safety. I see the mother and son from yesterday in the distance, hightailing it out of town, and am thankful they didn't end up involved in this mess.

Amid the dead, dying, and deserting stands a single figure, who raises a hand to greet us.

'Pretty Boy!' Wolf exclaims.

And *damn* is he pretty.

V
The Aftermath

I'm not the kind of girl who gets all flustered about boys. But, then again, the wastelands have a serious shortage of boys like this. It's rare enough to find someone who isn't missing a few teeth, or a few fingers, or maybe their sanity. Everyone's missing something or other. For me it's probably wits, and for *this* guy ... well, he's not lacking anything in the looks department, that's for sure.

'Pretty Boy,' as Wolf referred to him, is dusty and tired-looking and has a smear of blood down the side of his face, but beneath that he's still ridiculously attractive. He has high cheekbones and long eyelashes and beautiful hazel eyes. Sure his nose is a little crooked, most likely from being broken a couple times, and his dark hair is tousled and dirty, but I'll be damned if it doesn't just add a hint of roguish charm to his otherwise perfect looks.

As he walks toward us, he holsters his gun in his belt and winds his way through mangled corpses with an effortless grace. I, on the other hand, trip over a severed arm as I stare.

'Am I late to the party?' he asks with a grin. He shoots

me the briefest of glances and I avert my eyes. I'm suddenly aware of my sunburnt face and boyishly short hair.

'Yeah,' Wolf says, and spits. 'Just a little.'

He punches him right in his pretty face.

Pretty Boy reels from the impact, loses his footing, and trips over a nearby body. He falls to the ground hard, holding his face. I gape. Dolly laughs quietly from somewhere behind me.

'What the hell, Wolf?' Pretty Boy wails from the ground, still covering his face with both hands. 'Why do you always have to—'

'Where the fuck were you when we showed up? Do you know how much shit you got us in?' Wolf shouts at him. 'Do you have to screw up *every* job?'

'I didn't ... It wasn't ... I swear ...!'

'Shut up.' Wolf grimaces and turns in a circle, surveying the messy scene around us. 'Where the hell is Tank?'

Pretty Boy pulls his hand back from his face, double-checks that his nose isn't bleeding, and stands up. He takes a few steps back, putting some distance and a corpse between himself and Wolf.

'He's coming,' he says, his voice sullen. 'Slowly.'

'Fat bastard,' Wolf says with a wry smile. 'Ah, I missed him. Dolly isn't much company.'

'Is that why you picked up the stray?' Pretty Boy's eyes shift to me. I smile awkwardly. He looks back at Wolf.

'Yeah, well, we needed an extra hand.' Wolf looks at me and shakes his head. 'Damn near got us killed, though.'

'Sorry,' I say.

'What? How?'

'The little shit tossed our last grenade out the window.'

'Sorry,' I repeat sheepishly.

'Well, that explains a lot . . . ' Pretty Boy gives me another, more curious look. 'Lucky I was there to find it, then, eh?'

'Very lucky,' Wolf says, his tone implying a lot of unfortunate consequences that would have happened otherwise. I try to pretend I'm not terrified.

'Boss, I'm here!' An unfamiliar voice bellows out of nowhere. A few seconds later a dark-skinned stranger comes into view, plowing toward us at a slow jog. When he finally reaches us, he leans over with his hands on his knees, wheezing. 'I . . . made it . . . sorry . . . is everyone dead already?'

This guy is *huge*. He must be at least twice my height and width, with broad shoulders and a thick torso. It's difficult to tell whether all of the extra padding is fat or muscle, but either way, it looks like he could snap my spine like a toothpick. His face is scarred and hard, but the smile he shows us seems genuine, teeth whiter than I'd expect.

'Tank!' Wolf's greeting is considerably friendlier than his one to Pretty Boy. He walks over and gives the big man a slap on the back. 'Good to see you, buddy. And yeah, everyone worth killing is smeared across the ground, sorry to disappoint.'

'Damn,' he wheezes out. Only when he finally catches his breath and straightens up does he notice me. 'Who's the little one?'

'Hi,' I squeak at him nervously. Standing up, he's the biggest man I've ever seen in my life. 'I'm—'

'Just some kid we picked up,' Wolf finishes with a shrug. 'We needed some help.'

'So what do we do with him now?' Pretty Boy asks.

'I'm a—'

'Not much meat on the bones, wouldn't make much of a meal,' Tank says, his face hard as he looks down at me. I force out a laugh and hope he's joking.

'Might be useful,' Wolf says, scrutinizing me. 'Or might not. Who can say?'

'I can be useful,' I say, desperate to get a word in. I really don't want to end up a meal. And if I *could* make myself useful to these guys, with their jeep and all those guns, well . . . my days of being afraid and hungry would be over. They might be a little bit crazy, but with them on my side, even I might manage to stay alive out here in the wastes. I stare at Wolf, seeking acceptance, my mouth opening but unable to find the words to convince him.

'I want to keep it.' Dolly steps up behind me and lays a hand on top of my head. 'Let's keep it.'

'It?' I repeat, confused. I guess I should probably be offended she's referring to me like some kind of pet . . . but, in the end, being a pet is better than getting left behind or becoming dinner.

No one says anything. Tank is hard-eyed, Wolf skeptical, and Pretty Boy, I notice nervously, has his hand on the gun at his hip.

Wolf breaks into a grin and the tension snaps like a twig. Everyone else relaxes the moment they see the all-too-amused look on their leader's face. Tank gives an easygoing smile, followed by a booming laugh.

'Okay, Dolly, fine. We'll keep it,' Wolf says. He walks over and punches me in the shoulder. What he probably intends as a light tap sends me reeling. 'Welcome to the crew, kiddo!'

'Um, thanks.' I rub my shoulder and smile. 'And just so we're all on the same page, I'm a girl.'

'Whatever,' he says. 'Someone get the jeep. Let's get out of this shithole.'

VI
The Crew

We make camp a few miles out from the massacred town, with a fresh supply of dead townies to chop up and sell as 'hog meat.' After seeing how terribly awry it went, I wonder how often this plan works, but I figure it's best not to bring that up. At least we now have the gasoline Wolf was looking for, toted by Tank from the town coffers, and plenty of canned food. Listening to the way Wolf boasts and brags, it's as if the mission was a great success.

As for me, I'm most excited by the fact we have ample food, not to mention a fire. Everyone else seems amused by my delight, but I don't care. I've had too many long, dark nights spent shivering because I was too afraid of what flames could bring. When I was with Papa we had to be cautious about fires, and when I was alone they weren't even a remote possibility. Now we make camp out in the open and build a roaring bonfire. When I suggest it could cause trouble, Wolf laughs.

'We *are* the trouble, dumbass,' he tells me.

That's when I remember the guns. And I finally feel safe, safer than I ever have before.

I sit close to the warmth of the flames while the others enthusiastically sift through the loot we collected. Wolf finds a new pair of boots that fit him almost-right. Pretty Boy finds a broken but shiny pocket watch, which Dolly promptly steals from him. Tank finds a rusty knife, which he tosses down at my feet.

'Wolf says you can't handle a gun for shit,' he explains with a good-humored smile.

'Oh, wow!' I pick it up and turn it over in my hands. Underneath patches of rust, the blade glints in the firelight. It's small, but it's sharp. I tuck it away into the side of one of my scuffed-up boots. 'Thanks!'

Soon it's time to eat. I knew it would come eventually. I tried to steel myself, but still, it's rough. At least they did the slicing and dicing back in town, so most of it is unrecognizable, but the smell still gives me an odd combination of repulsion and hunger. My brain knows that what they're cooking used to be a person, but really, it just smells like meat. The last time I had real meat was when my papa found a dead rat and attempted to cook it. It didn't turn out well.

This, on the other hand, actually looks really … tasty. After days of beans, the sight and smell make my mouth water.

I look away from the spit on the fire and try to busy myself by sharpening my knife on a rock. It doesn't seem to do much, but it distracts me from my hunger. When I glance up, I see Wolf and Pretty Boy standing together with their heads bowed conspiratorially, both looking in my direction. I quickly look down again and pretend I didn't notice.

Still, when Wolf sits beside me with a chunk of cooked meat in his hands, it's hard not to pay attention. The smell wafts toward me tantalizingly, and out of the corner of my eye I see him tearing into it with a vehement hunger. I slowly turn my head, even as I will myself not to, and see that what he's holding is clearly a human arm.

To my horror, my stomach lets out a loud rumble.

I turn away, face reddening. Wolf laughs.

'Hungry, kiddo?' he asks.

'Nah,' I say weakly.

'Like hell you ain't.' He leans over and holds it out in offering. 'Here, have some.'

'Uh,' I say. 'Um. Well.'

He's looking at me expectantly. I fumble with my words, not even sure what I'm trying to say.

'I don't know . . . if I . . . I just . . . uhh.' I look back and forth between the meat and Wolf's hideous grin. My hands flutter in some vague gestures that communicate even less than my words do. 'This is kinda, uh . . . '

'Just try it,' he suggests, and shoves the meat into my hands.

I glance around nervously and, of course, everyone is watching me. Dolly is blank-faced, Tank grinning broadly, and Pretty Boy curious. A sudden weight descends on my shoulders. I realize that this moment could be important, that I'm being judged by the group.

I turn the meat over in my hands, looking at the way the grease glistens in the firelight. I swallow my excuses and try to smile.

'Well,' I say. 'Papa always said don't knock it till you try it.'

My teeth brush against the meat – and I stop as a wave of revulsion rises up in me. I can't bring myself to bite down. I can't stop thinking about how this hunk of flesh used to be a person.

The silence around the fire thickens as I lower the meat. I hold on to it for a few seconds, trying to decide if I want to change my mind, before I hand it back to Wolf.

'Sorry,' I say. I hunch over self-consciously, biting my lip. I wonder if this is the part where they kick me out and leave me behind in the dust. Or, more likely, put a bullet in my head and be done with it.

Wolf looks down and sighs heavily. I watch him, my shoulders tensing nervously, not sure what he's going to do. A moment later he abruptly looks up and grins.

'What'd I tell you guys?' He holds out a hand and gestures to the others. 'She didn't eat it. Hand over your shit.'

I look up, frowning, and realize that the spotlight is no longer on me. Everyone is looking at him. Tank groans and tosses over a glass jar half-full of what looks like jam, which Wolf hoists triumphantly. Pretty Boy sullenly produces a metal flask from his pack and hands that over as well.

'Not fair,' he complains. 'You really had to give her an arm?'

'Thanks, guys. Pleasure as always.' Wolf stuffs the new goodies into his pack and smirks, giving a mock-gracious bow of his head.

'What's going on?' I look around the circle, trying to make sense of what just happened. 'You guys aren't . . .' Going to kill me? 'Upset?'

'Nah,' Wolf says. He's chuckling, looking very pleased with

himself. 'More meat for us. We always bet on whether or not the newbies will eat. And Pretty Boy is always wrong.'

'One day someone's gonna do it, and I'll win big,' Pretty Boy says.

'Nope. You'll forever be the only one who was fucked-up enough to eat the first time.'

I stare at Pretty Boy, surprised. Out of the lot of them, I definitely wouldn't have expected him to be the one who took to cannibalism so easily. He shrugs.

'I thought they would kill me if I didn't,' he says by way of explanation, not quite meeting my eyes. I nod. I thought the same thing, but there's no point in saying that.

'And he puked it all up about thirty seconds later,' Tank says. 'Waste of good meat.'

'And you bet that I would eat, too?' I ask, looking over at him – or, rather, at his protruding belly, because it's rather intimidating to stare at his scarred-up face.

'Well, look at you. Scrawny little thing, I figured you must be hungry,' he says. Despite losing the bet, he's smiling, his tough face softened by good humor.

'Joke's on you, big guy,' Wolf says. 'She ate yesterday. I made sure of it.'

'So you rigged it,' Pretty Boy says. 'Asshole.'

The three of them devolve into bickering over the fairness of the bet. I watch, half-amused and half-disturbed by how lightly they view the whole issue. A tap on my shoulder startles me out of my thoughts. I look up to see Dolly, who wordlessly hands me a can. The top is already half-opened for me.

'Oh,' I say, surprised. 'Thanks!'

She stares at me. It seems like she wants to say something, but she merely turns and walks away. I smile at her retreating figure before raising the can and taking a sniff.

Beans.

After everyone finishes eating, the camp settles down and I relax into a state of sleepy contentment. Maybe I shouldn't feel so safe, considering I'm surrounded by cannibals who just decimated the population of a small town, but I do. It's pretty clear they have no interest in killing me at the moment, and it's hard to feel too concerned with a full belly and a warm fire. Matter of fact, I'm starting to nod off as the exhaustion of the day hits me.

A pair of fingers snaps in my face, jolting me awake.

'Hey, you,' Wolf says, waving a hand in front of my eyes. 'Go to sleep already. You've got second watch.'

'Umm, okay.' I rub my eyes and yawn. The fire has died down to glowing embers. It looks like Dolly has already fallen asleep, curled up on the ground near where Wolf was sitting. Tank is setting up a spot close by, while Pretty Boy is sitting near the fire and has a peeved expression that tells me he got stuck with first watch. I'm about to dig out my blanket and find a flat spot on the ground when I realize they still haven't bothered to ask for my name. 'By the way, I've been trying to tell you, I'm—'

'Nope!' Wolf practically shouts so I have no chance of talking over him. 'No names.'

'Huh?'

'Most people who join us don't last long,' Tank says. He states it like someone might comment on the weather.

'Like Sticks,' says Wolf, counting off on his fingers. 'Three days, that one. Or Snake Eyes. One week, I think. Or Bluebird—'

'I liked Bluebird,' Pretty Boy says, sighing.

'You liked her tits, you mean. Anyway, the point is, we don't use real names.'

'Oh,' I say. 'Okay. So, who should I be?'

Wolf grins.

'That's obvious,' he says. 'You'll be Kid.'

VII
Trouble

I wake up with the barrel of a gun in my face.

It takes my foggy brain a few seconds to register the danger. As soon as it does I snap awake, sitting up and scrambling back in the dirt. The gun follows, never losing sight of its target.

I keep my eyes locked on the gun, and only then think to look at who's holding it. I feel sick to my stomach, thinking I'll look up and see Pretty Boy or Wolf ready to pull the trigger. I slowly raise my eyes, letting my gaze climb from a hand to an arm to a face . . . a crooked and cruel face I don't recognize. It's almost strange how relieved I feel that it's not one of the crew.

Wolf swears loudly from behind me. Careful not to make any sudden movements, I swivel my eyes from side to side to take in the situation. Dolly and Tank are also being held at gunpoint, Tank on the ground and Dolly crouching like an animal ready to pounce. Pretty Boy is on his knees with his hands behind his head, though nobody is actually pointing a gun at him. And Wolf, I can only suspect, is as tied up as the rest of us.

The fire has burned down to dully glowing embers and the sun is just starting to rise. We almost made it through the night without any trouble. I try to keep in mind that Wolf said we are the trouble, but that's hard to believe right now.

'Who the hell was on watch?' Wolf asks. ''Cause I am going to kick their ass.'

'It was you,' Dolly says flatly.

'Aw, shit. I take that back about the ass-kicking.'

'Shut up,' the man above me growls. He's a stooped guy with missing teeth and a face peeling from sunburn. He jabs me in the forehead with the gun. 'Nobody move.'

He takes a few steps away, still keeping the gun pointed in my direction as he makes his way around our campsite. As his attention shifts to the jeep, I sneak a glance at Wolf. He's on the ground, held down by a hulk of a man with a wide-brimmed hat. Wolf looks over at me and raises his eyebrows. Maybe it's a signal, but I have no idea what he's trying to tell me. I shrug at him helplessly and he rolls his eyes.

'What the fuck is this?' the man checking out our camp asks. I look over to see him drop a bag, chopped-up townies spilling out as it hits the ground. He recoils, covering his mouth. 'Well, looks like we caught ourselves some sharks, boys.'

'Hey, hey, isn't there a bounty out for sharks?' one of the others asks. 'From them guys out by the radio tower?'

'Only if we bring 'em in live, I think.'

'What do they want with live sharks?'

'Don't know, but that's how it is. We could take the jeep, but still, too many of 'em.'

'So we shoot a couple, bring in the rest.'

'Waste of good money.'

As the men eagerly discuss their prize, their attention falters. I look back at Dolly and notice her slowly reaching for her boot, eyes locked on the man above her. She's so close – but so is his gun, and if he happens to look down at her . . .

I don't think, I just spring up and barrel toward the man pinning Wolf down. I ram into him at full speed. It has all the effectiveness of a pebble against a boulder. But when I wrap my arms around him, he's forced to let go of Wolf and stand, trying to shake me off. He lets out a furious bellow.

'Keep it under control, Kid!' Wolf says, and he's gone. I can't tell where or why or what's happening. The man has taken to spinning wildly and trying to tear me off him with his huge, clumsy hands. Everything is a blur of motion, and all I can do is cling. My grip slips. I dig my fingers in like claws, but I can feel myself losing my hold bit by bit. When the man stumbles and falls, he flings me off.

I hit the ground like a sack of meat. I'm instantly sprawled out on my back, the breath knocked out of me and the world still spinning. I suck in air and look to the side. The huge man is already stirring, head turning in my direction. I flip onto my stomach and crawl away. I block out all the noise and chaos around me, vision tunneling, searching for anything that can help me – a person, a weapon, anything!

I see the jeep. I propel myself toward it on all fours and worm underneath.

Though the noise rages on nearby, I feel safer in the cramped darkness underneath the vehicle. I allow myself a moment to breathe, closing my eyes and resting my forehead against the cool sand.

Something cold and sharp pokes the side of my throat.

I hold my breath and raise my head agonizingly slowly.

'Pretty Boy?'

'Kid? Ah, hell, you scared the shit out of me.' He pulls the knife back, gripping it so tightly his knuckles turn white. He eyes are wide and his chest heaving. 'What are you doing?'

'Hiding. There was this big guy . . . I got away, but . . . wait, why are *you* hiding? Don't you have a gun?'

'Just get out!'

'What?'

'I'm hiding here, so go somewhere else!'

'But I—'

We shut up as a pair of boots appears next to the jeep. We look at each other, and back at the boots. The man outside falls to a crouch with a grunt. One large hand reaches underneath the jeep, groping around near Pretty Boy.

Don't move, I mouth at him. He's focused entirely on the hand moving closer and closer to him. It brushes his arm.

He lashes out with his knife, severing two fingers. The man yells and recoils the hand, but his other one shoots under and grabs me by the leg.

'Pretty Boy!' I squeak imploringly, reaching for him. He pulls back, his face cold. I'm yanked out from my hiding place, hands full of nothing but sand.

I end up upside down, held by one ankle and swinging helplessly through the air. I catch glimpses of things happening around me as I swing back and forth: Wolf struggling with someone in the dirt, Dolly chasing a wounded man,

Tank on the ground and motionless, Pretty Boy wriggling out from beneath the jeep. My heart surges at the latter, but he runs in the opposite direction.

'Help!' I yell, still trying to find something to hold on to as the man carries me away. 'Pretty Boy! Someone! Help me!'

No one does. And when I turn my head, it's all too clear where I'm being carried: the fire. Along the way he grabs a container of gasoline.

'Oh shit,' I say, mind going blank with panic. 'Oh shit oh shit oh shit.' I squirm like a worm on a hook. The man looks down at me and grins.

'Into the fire, little monkey,' he says, gleefully swinging me.

'I'm not a monkey!' I wail. I latch on to one of his legs and cling there, wrapping both arms around him.

He stops, grunts in annoyance, and swings the gas can at me in an attempt to dislodge my hold. One glancing blow hits me on the ear and makes my head ring, but I refuse to let go. He drops the can with a curse and grabs one of my arms with his injured hand.

I act instinctively and bite down on the bloody stubs of his fingers.

Howling, he drops me, and I get a face full of sand. I taste dirt and blood. I force myself onto my hands and knees, shaking.

A bang deafens me. The raider stumbles, disbelief spreading across his face as red blossoms on his chest. He almost catches his footing again, but another gunshot goes off and a new wound appears near his heart. He crashes down into our still-smoldering fire pit, and struggles for a few moments before lying still.

Footsteps approach. Wolf prods me in the side with the barrel of a gun.

'Y'all right, Kid?' he asks.

'Yeah. I'm okay.' I pat myself down to verify, checking for injuries and finding nothing substantial. I look up at him. 'Thanks for saving me.'

'Eh, just didn't want you to get all the glory.'

I laugh breathlessly and he offers me the barrel of the gun, which I use to pull myself to my feet. My mouth tastes like severed fingers. I spit a couple of times, which doesn't help.

'Damn, that was a mess,' Wolf says.

'Yeah ... and what was that about a reward for sharks?' I ask.

'Y'know, I've been hearing rumors along those lines for a while now,' he says. He pauses for a moment, thinking, and then shrugs. 'Eh, well. Sounds like a problem for later.'

He walks off, and I look around to survey the damage. Tank is still on the ground, but stirring now. Wolf crouches beside him, laughs, and pats him on the shoulder, so I figure he's all right.

Dolly appears beside me, moving too close like a little kid who doesn't understand what 'personal space' means. Her face and clothes are stained with blood. It's hard to tell how much of it is hers. I stare at her. After an awkward moment she holds out her hand, clutching something. It takes me a few moments to recognize the dirty piece of fabric as my beanie. I don't even remember losing it.

'Oh, wow, thanks,' I say. I shake it out and put it back on. Dolly says something I don't quite catch.

'What?'

She leans closer. I step forward and wrap my arms around her, automatically assuming she's looking for a hug or something. The way she stiffens up immediately informs me that I was wrong about that. After a brief pause she pats me on the shoulder awkwardly, and I pull back, a little embarrassed. But once I let go, she offers a smile for a brief instant before moving on to inspect the bodies of the raiders. When one moves, she shoots him in the face. I look away, grimacing.

'Anyone seen Pretty Boy?' Wolf yells from Tank's side. I point in the direction I saw him going.

'He ran off,' I say.

''Course he did. Always runs when things get too hairy. Dolly, find him.'

Dolly gives the raider's body another kick and dutifully runs off, gun in hand. The sight gives me a flicker of worry for Pretty Boy. I do my best to stifle it, remembering how I almost burned to death while he ran away. Taking a shaky breath, I walk over to the jeep and sit down for a much-needed rest. My heart is still pounding and my hands trembling as if my body hasn't realized I'm out of danger yet. Tank lumbers over and sits next to me. We smile wearily at each other.

'What a way to wake up,' I say.

'I've had worse,' he says, chuckling.

'I don't even want to know.'

'Really, I'm mostly disappointed I got knocked out so early. As soon as the fight broke out the guy hit me over the head with his gun, and then . . . next thing I remember is waking up to a bunch of dead raiders.' He lets out a long sigh. 'Missed the whole damn fight. Again.'

Before I can respond, Dolly marches back into camp with

Pretty Boy in tow, gun in one hand and a fistful of his hair in the other. She shoves him in front of Wolf. He stumbles for a few steps before catching his balance, and slowly raises his eyes to Wolf's face.

'Well, glad to see you're all okay,' he says with a flicker of a smile.

'Shut up.' Wolf waves at him dismissively before turning to me and Tank. 'And you two, get off your lazy asses!'

'Seriously?' Tank groans, hauling himself to his feet. I follow.

Wolf shades his eyes with a hand and looks toward the sun, which is just starting to peek out over the distant mountains.

'Time to move out,' he says. 'The day's just getting started.'

VIII
Heating Up

'Well, the jeep's wrecked.'

'How wrecked?'

'Very,' Tank says, shutting the hood with a bang. 'Looks like it took a gunshot too many.'

'Damn.' Wolf begins to pace, running his hands through his stringy dreadlocks.

'You can't fix it?' I ask, turning my head from side to side to watch him. I'm in the broken-down vehicle next to Pretty Boy, where we were seated and ready to take off until it failed to start. My hand brushes against his leg and I jerk it away with a whisper of an apology. He doesn't seem to notice.

'What? No. Do I look like a fucking mechanic to you, Kid? Don't be stupid.'

'Oh. Sorry,' I say sheepishly. He doesn't respond, but Tank ruffles my hair.

'I might be able to if I had the right tools, kiddo, but I don't,' he says.

'So what do we do now?' Pretty Boy asks. He only glances

at me once, and looks quickly back at Wolf. He hasn't looked me in the eyes since the fight.

'We get a new one, obviously.'

'Where from?'

'Ahh . . . ' Wolf stops pacing and stares into the distance. I picture rusty gears turning in his head. After a moment he snaps his fingers, triumphant. 'We go see the Queen!'

'And how do we get there?'

'Stop asking stupid questions, Pretty Boy.'

'Who's the Queen?'

'Same goes for you, Kid.'

Dolly produces a rolled-up piece of paper from a pack and holds it out to Pretty Boy. As he unfurls it, the others gather around him. I join in, peering curiously.

'Is that a map?' I ask. I can't read a word of it, but I recognize the shapes of mountains and roads.

'Again with the stupid questions,' Wolf says. 'Of course it's a damn map. See, it's got all the towns and shit.'

'Wow.' This piece of paper holds more of the world than I've ever seen, not that it means much. Before I left town, I knew other places like it existed, but certainly not their locations or names. 'You guys made this?'

'Got it off a caravan,' Pretty Boy says.

'So you stole it?'

'It doesn't count as stealing if they're dead,' Wolf objects.

'I think it still counts if you killed them for the map . . . '

'I never said *we* killed them,' he says. 'And no. That would count as looting, ain't that right?'

'Isn't that worse than stealing?'

'Whatever.' Wolf silences me with a wave of his hand and

gives Pretty Boy a rough nudge. 'Where are we off to, then?'

'All right, well we just came from—' Pretty Boy slides his finger over the map and taps a small black mark. 'Here. It was called Steelforge. So now we should be just around here.' He moves his hand up.

'Is Bramble on there?' I interrupt. He looks up and meets my eyes briefly.

'Yeah. Of course.' He points it out. It looks like it's only a stone's throw away from Steelforge. It felt like so much longer when I had to walk most of the way.

'That where you're from, Kid?' Tank asks.

'Well, I—'

'I don't give a shit about Bramble. We want to see the Queen,' Wolf urges impatiently. I shut up.

'Right. She's up here.' Pretty Boy points.

'Fuck, that's far,' Tank groans. 'All that on foot?'

'We won't make it,' Pretty Boy says. 'There's no way. We might have enough food, but definitely not water.'

'We have to make it,' Wolf says. He regards the map with pursed lips, and then indicates a town sitting between us and our destination. 'What's this one?'

'Blackfort,' Pretty Boy says. 'I've heard of it. Not very friendly.'

'So if we raid Blackfort on the way, we can make it to the Queen, yeah?'

'Well, we can follow the road ... but, again, there's the water.' He shrugs. 'Hard to say.'

'Great.' Wolf claps his hands together and grins. 'That's the plan, then.'

'Wait, but—'

Despite Pretty Boy's protests, the others begin prepara-
tions. As Tank siphons gas out of the jeep and Dolly searches
the raiders' corpses, Wolf gathers up some makeshift packs
and tosses them out, shouting orders about how to divide up
supplies. I rush to follow his directions, and Pretty Boy joins
me. Each of us gets a small ration of food, a jug of water,
and some stuff worth trading: gasoline, first aid supplies,
weapons. I stuff everything into my backpack, my blanket
tucked neatly beneath it. This time they even give me a gun,
after a lecture from Wolf about how I better keep it pointed
far away from him. Having a real weapon tucked into my
waistband is both exciting and nerve-racking.

'I hope you know what you're doing, Wolf,' Pretty Boy
says, weighing his portion of water and looking uneasy. 'This
isn't much.'

'Oh, cut the whining. We've made it through worse.'

'Yeah, and usually someone ends up dead.'

'Well, what a coincidence. I've been looking for an excuse
to get rid of you!' Wolf says cheerfully, clapping him on the
back. Pretty Boy looks even more nervous. 'By the way, Kid,
I don't suppose you can read?'

'Nope, sorry.'

'Damn shame. Relax, Pretty Boy, we still need you
around.' Wolf grins at him. 'And don't think I didn't notice
you pocketing the map. Hand it over. That's way too important for you to carry.'

Pretty Boy looks as if he might argue, but another look
from Wolf silences him. He purses his lips and pulls out the
map. Wolf takes it, gives him a shove that may or may not be
playful, and tosses the map to Dolly.

'Well, guess we're as ready as we're gonna get,' he says, and we're off.

It doesn't take long for the going to get rough. Everyone sets off in good spirits, talking and joking, but after a few hours the sun is directly overhead and the heat beats us into silence. The light brings the wastelands to life, and soon heat radiates from both above and below us. The cracked asphalt of the road becomes too hot to walk on, so instead we walk alongside it. The sand is hot, too. I can feel it through the thin soles of my boots, and if I pause for more than a second it feels like my feet are being boiled in them.

The landscape remains the same in every direction. There's nothing but dry, empty sand marked only by the occasional old building. The mountains in the distance never seem to get any closer. It's easy to lose yourself in the wastes. When I was alone I feared they might swallow me, especially with bad memories behind me and Lord-knew-what ahead. I now know why the wastes can make men mad. There are crazies that live in the emptier parts, wild and hungry like packs of dogs. I had a brush with them once with my papa, and I still have nightmares about it.

Traveling is easier with company. The others carry on with determination and purpose, and I follow their lead. I plunge forward, one foot in front of the other. Despite my best efforts, soon I'm panting and sweating and lagging behind, unable to match the pace of Wolf and Dolly. I end up beside Pretty Boy.

He stares ahead without acknowledging my presence. One hand brushes sweaty hair back from his face, and he groans a wordless complaint.

'Umm,' I say after a few moments. 'I'm not, uh, mad at you or anything. Just so you know.'

He looks at me sideways and away again, hesitating before he speaks.

'Why would you be?'

'Well . . . ' I bite my lip. 'You did, you know, kind of run off and leave me to die.'

'Ah. Right.' He pauses again, and I sneak a glance at him, not sure if he intends to continue. He clears his throat, still not looking straight at me. 'Yeah. I guess I did. Sorry about that.'

'Oh, no big deal.'

'It's just kind of how things are, you know?' He doesn't sound sorry at all.

'Yeah, I guess.' I think about how Wolf came back to save me in the end, but don't say anything. Wolf is a bit crazy, after all, so maybe Pretty Boy has the right of it.

'Well, I'm glad you didn't end up dead, if it means anything,' he says, and smiles at me. His smile is slightly crooked and way too charming for a guy who almost let me die earlier today. I blush and promptly feel like an idiot for doing so.

'Uh. You, too?' It comes out an uncertain squeak. I don't know how to deal with a boy who smiles at me like that.

'Thanks,' he says dryly. 'You're probably the only one.'

'That can't be true!' Sure Wolf gives him a lot of shit, but he's still clearly a part of the crew.

'Yeah, Tank might miss me.' He looks over his shoulder at Tank, who has fallen even farther behind than us. 'Hey, fatty! Would you miss me if I was dead?'

''Course I would! Who would I make fun of?' Tank shouts

back. We slow down and he huffs and puffs to catch up with us. Sweat runs down his face and stains the armpits of his shirt, but he looks cheerful. He cuffs Pretty Boy around the neck, and Pretty Boy yells about the stench before wiggling free.

Having Tank around lifts the tension, and Pretty Boy visibly relaxes.

'So, Kid, how old are you?' he asks.

'Uh, sixteen. I think.'

'Oh, wow. You really are a kid, aren't you? Everyone used to call me young, and I'm eighteen.'

'Shit, how do you guys keep track?' Tank asks. 'I haven't got a damn clue.'

'That's 'cause you're an old man,' Pretty Boy says, earning himself another cuff.

'Papa told me I was born in the winter, right 'round when it starts getting cold,' I say. 'That's how I keep track.'

'Your papa?' Tank asks. 'He still around?'

'Nope,' I say. 'Dead. For a long time.' I didn't see it happen, but I know it to be true. The town took me in and left him out in the wastes. No one makes it long alone. I later wondered if the townies even really let him leave, or if they just shot him when I was gone.

'I was born on April twelfth,' says Pretty Boy. 'Not that it means anything, most of the time. The Queen knows those kinds of things, though, so I can check up on it from time to time. She usually gives me a present.'

There's that name again. Seeing as Wolf isn't around to tell me to shut up and stop asking questions, I try again.

'So who is this Queen person?'

'You've never been?' Pretty Boy asks. I shake my head. 'Ah. She's called the Queen of the Wastes. Nobody is really sure how she started off, but now she lives in this big mansion with a ton of guards. She runs this place called the Crossroads. All of the trading routes of the main caravans cross there.'

'Why?'

'Water, mainly. She lives right next to a river, and has a way to make the water drinkable. So people trade her for it, and now she has just about everything you could ever need. Traders buy and sell her shit along their routes. And people like us, too. Raiders, I mean. Sharks. No discrimination as long as you have stuff to trade.'

'Wow,' I say. It sounds big and important, definitely more so than anywhere I've ever been. 'I didn't know anyone like that existed. I guess I never thought about where the caravans get their supplies.'

'Yeah. She's a powerful lady. And a rich one.'

'So you guys go to her a lot?'

'Whenever we get a chance. She has a lot of stuff that's hard to get anywhere else.'

'It doesn't hurt that she has a thing for Pretty Boy,' Tank butts in.

'Shut it,' Pretty Boy says. 'She likes Dolly, too. Dolly used to work for her.'

'What do you mean, used to work for her?' I ask. They exchange a glance. 'Like, a bodyguard?'

'Not exactly,' Pretty Boy says. 'She was . . . ' He trails off, looking nervous. I follow his gaze to see Dolly staring back at us. She studies each of us for a few long seconds before slowly turning back forward.

'That is just not normal,' Pretty Boy mutters under his breath. 'God, she's creepy.'

'She just doesn't like you,' Tank tells him.

'No, no, it's not just me! Once we went into a town as partners, you know, scoping out the place. And it was the one and only time, because nobody wanted a damn thing to do with us. Thought she might be less sketchy than the rest of you, but nope, not even a little. There I was trying to be friendly and get them off their guard and shit, and Dolly would just stand there with that face of hers, just staring and not saying anything and . . . ugh, it was bad.' He shakes his head.

'I think she's nice,' I say.

'Well, she likes you,' Pretty Boy says. He almost sounds jealous. 'For whatever reason.'

'She does?'

'Seems like it.'

I look ahead at her, scrutinizing the back of her long blue hair. As if on cue she looks over her shoulder again, meeting my gaze. I smile, and she blinks and looks away.

'See? That's about as friendly as she gets,' Pretty Boy says, watching with a wry half smile. 'If I ever tried to smile at her like that, she'd break my nose.'

'Again,' Tank says.

'Right. Again.'

'She broke your nose?' I ask.

'He deserved it.'

'Shut up, Tank.'

'But I thought you guys were all friends,' I say, confused.

'Friends?' Pretty Boy laughs. 'You have a lot to learn, Kid.'

I don't understand, but his condescending tone bites

enough to make me stop asking questions. We walk along in silence, the only sound our ragged breathing. It hurts to inhale. My mouth and throat are already as dry as the sand we're walking on, and the hot air burns. My tongue feels thick in my mouth, as if even that is coated by dust, and my lips are starting to crack and bleed. I finally cave and pull out my water flask. I take a short gulp and quickly cap it again before I chug the whole thing.

It doesn't even take the edge off my thirst. The water is warm and goes down as thick as paste.

Soon enough even Wolf and Dolly are beaten down by the heat, and they slow enough to allow all five of us to walk side by side.

'You know,' Wolf says, 'it's days like these that really make me appreciate humanity.'

His comment is met with silence. I assume everyone, like me, is trying to work out how that makes any sense.

'The fuck?' Tank finally says, effectively summing up my own thoughts.

'I'm serious. I mean, look at this place. Look at this fucking world we live in.' He sweeps his hands in a broad gesture, indicating the expanse of wastelands around us. 'It's unlivable. Or at least, it should be, you know? And yet here we are. I bet most of you weren't even alive before the war, huh, Kid? Pretty Boy? Little post-bomb babies raised on radioactive milk, that's what you are. Probably shouldn't even be possible.' He lets out a low whistle and shakes his head. 'People just do what they have to do, like always. Ain't nothing that can kill us.'

'Like cockroaches,' I say.

'Right. That's deep, Kid.' Wolf laughs and abruptly stops walking, cracking his back. 'And this cockroach is about ready for a break. One hour, everybody eat and piss and do whatever else you need to do.'

The first day is long and rough. By the time we stop for the night, seeking shelter in the broken-down shell of a house, my water canteen is dangerously close to empty. Judging by the way the others check their flasks and mutter and pore over the map, I'm not the only one. It's frightening how much water I consumed in a day.

Wolf doesn't want to risk a fire after this morning. We eat a quick, cold dinner and I spend the night squeezed between Tank and Dolly, with my blanket wrapped around me and my backpack as a pillow. I have trouble falling asleep with water weighing on my mind.

Still, curled up and staring at the dark sky through the holes in the roof, I think back on all the nights spent on my own and know this is so much better. Ever since my papa was swallowed by the wastes – maybe even at the end of when we were still together – I've felt a constant ache of loneliness. Even though Wolf snores and Tank smells and everyone's a bit crazy, somehow I feel like I belong here. I finally fall asleep with that thought in mind, and it makes everything a little more okay.

IX
Death Sentence

'Wake up, lazy fucks!'

The voice cuts through the fog of sleep and wakes me. I keep my eyes squeezed shut and my blanket wrapped tightly around me.

'No, not yet,' I groan and roll onto my side, trying to hide from the sun. Hands yank my blanket off me. 'Hey!' I stand up slowly, rubbing my eyes and yawning. Wolf's grinning face steps into my line of sight, and a hand smacks the side of my head and sends me staggering.

'That enough of a wake-up call for you, Kid?' he asks. I shake my head to clear it and give him a weary thumbs-up. At least this is better than waking up to a gun in my face. He returns my blanket, and I pack it up. 'Good, good. Let's get going.'

Everyone except Wolf looks as tired as I feel, but they all trudge onward so I have no choice but to follow. I shoot Pretty Boy a sleepy-eyed smile. He smiles back, which makes my stomach do a flip and helps me keep going.

I feel more awake after we've been traveling for about an

hour, when the last coolness of the night has leaked away and the sun seems intent on roasting us where we stand. Today is windier than yesterday, but the hot air blowing at us gives little relief. Instead it only fills my eyes and mouth with gritty sand. I feel dry and dusty deep down to my core, but resist the temptation of my canteen. I refuse to be the first one to take a drink.

'So . . . ' My voice comes out rough and unfamiliar. I cough and clear my throat and try again. 'So, what's the plan once we get to Black . . . Blackrock?'

'Blackfort,' Pretty Boy corrects.

'Yeah, that one.'

'Right, a plan,' Wolf says, as if it had just occurred to him. 'We should reach it today, so I guess that would be a good idea.'

'How do you guys usually do this?'

'Eh, well, we send in two people to scout, make sure the townies aren't going to chase us out with pitchforks on sight or nothin', trade some of our shit for their shit . . . '

'Who does the scouting?' I ask.

'Always Pretty Boy, because he's good at bullshitting if nothing else, and then whoever else has got nothing better to do.'

'It'd be better if you let me go alone,' Pretty Boy says. 'All the rest of you ever do is make my job harder.'

'Ha, ha, let you go in alone? So you can fuck us over and leave? No way in hell.'

'And after you scout, then what?' I ask, not wanting them to veer off track.

'They meet up with the rest of us, and if it seems like a

good target, we raid the place.' He shrugs. 'Kill some people, take their stuff, you know, the fun part.'

'Okay . . . ' It doesn't sound like the most well-thought-out plan, but I figure they've been doing it for a while so I'm in no place to question it. 'Wait, so, what happened at that town back there?'

'Well, that time everything got a bit screwy.'

'How do you mean?'

'Pretty Boy fucked it up.'

'I did not!' He throws his hands up in exasperation, shaking his head. 'Tank and I got there to scope it out, and they were suspicious from the start. I don't know, the area was a shithole, maybe we looked too well fed or something. We had to get the hell out and camp nearby. Seriously, I thought they were gonna string us up there and then.'

'So why did you and Dolly still go there?' I ask.

'No choice. The jeep was almost out of gas so we had to just roll with the plan. But hey, it worked out all right.'

'Except we ended up losing the jeep for the gasoline,' says Pretty Boy, 'so we're still fucked.'

'Aw, lighten the hell up,' Wolf says.

'We probably don't have enough water to make it to Blackfort, and even if we do they'll likely as not shoot us when we get there. We look like a bunch of crazy raiders.'

'But we *are* kind of a bunch of crazy raiders, aren't we?' I ask, confused.

'It's usually not so obvious,' Pretty Boy says. 'It's vital that we trick them into thinking we're harmless. So as long as we look like this, we're screwed.'

'Shut up, you're pissing me off,' Wolf says.

Pretty Boy falls into a sulky silence. He grabs his flask off his hip and takes a swig of water, which makes my heart surge. Finally, I can take a drink without feeling too guilty about it.

'Hey, don't get all moody on us now,' Tank says to Pretty Boy as I break out my canteen. 'It's just Wolf being Wolf.' He reaches over to clap him on the back.

Allowing myself a tiny sip of water, I'm far too focused to pay attention to anything else. It's only once I've finished my paltry drink that I notice everyone else has stopped walking. I turn around, about to ask what everyone is staring at, but as soon as I look their way I know.

Pretty Boy is standing with an arm outstretched, a look of shock on his face. On the ground is his water flask, with the last of it draining out into the sand. The dirt takes it in as hungrily as any of us would; just like that, it's gone.

He unfreezes and falls to his knees, snatching up the canteen and placing it upright. As an afterthought he desperately scoops up the wet earth in his hands, as if he could take the water back from its clutches. But as the dirt sifts through his fingers it's already drying, disappearing as if it was never there.

Pretty Boy sits back on his heels and stays there. Everyone is dead silent. I screw the top back onto my canteen, suddenly afraid of it falling from my hands.

'What the hell did you do that for?' Pretty Boy asks after a few seconds, his voice shaky. He glares at Tank with red-rimmed eyes.

'I didn't do anything!'

'You fucking knocked it out of my hands!'

'I didn't – I didn't mean to! Come on, Pretty Boy, you know I would never . . . ' Tank looks horrified.

'Well as it stands, I don't . . . ' Pretty Boy sucks in a deep breath. 'There's no way I can make it to . . . ' He looks up at Wolf with his lower lip trembling. 'Wolf, please.'

'What do you want me to do?' Wolf asks, his face and voice hard. He's more serious than I've ever seen him, both the humor and ferocity absent, and it frightens me.

'I don't—' He gestures despairingly, the words dying in his throat. 'I mean, it wasn't like I just *dropped* it—'

'I saw.'

Pretty Boy opens his mouth to speak again. Wolf holds up a hand to silence him. He sighs and pushes his goggles up, leaving a streak of sweat and dirt behind. His face is stony as he rubs the bridge of his nose, and after a few seconds he slides the goggles back into place and looks up at Tank.

'Tank, give him your water.' The sentence falls as final as a guillotine.

Tank doesn't argue, but I can see his hands shaking as he hands it over. Pretty Boy drops his empty flask and takes the new one from Tank's hand, clutching it against himself.

I stare at my feet. The silence feels thick, and I'm struck by the impression that all of them are strangers again.

Wolf turns back to the road and starts walking again. Dolly follows first, and then Pretty Boy, and then me. When I look back I see Tank picking up Pretty Boy's empty canteen and checking it for any drop of water before tossing it away again. He follows the group even more slowly than before, and nobody but me looks back at him.

*

As the sun saps our strength and the sand grows hotter, it's impossible not to notice how far Tank is falling behind. Wolf and Dolly exchange meaningful looks. Pretty Boy looks at nothing but the ground and doesn't say a word. His eyes are red, but dry.

I keep glancing back at Tank. He's struggling, sweat streaming down his body and chest heaving.

The next time I look back, he's stopped, his eyes closed. I look frantically at the others.

'Guys, wait, Tank is—' Nobody stops walking or so much as glances at me. 'He stopped, shouldn't we wait . . . ?'

'No,' Wolf says without turning around.

'No?' I stop, staring at their backs as they continue to move forward.

'He's not gonna make it, Kid,' Wolf says. 'We keep walking.'

Keep walking. Carry on. It's what I have to do, what I've always done.

I will my feet to move, telling myself this is the way things have to be, yet somehow I can't bring myself to. The idea of leaving Tank behind makes me feel sick. I remain motionless, all too aware of the others moving farther away every second.

But I can't continue.

I turn and walk back to Tank. He opens his eyes and gives me a weary half smile.

'Hey, Kid, it's okay,' he says.

I offer my canteen to him.

'What are you doing?' he asks.

'Take it.'

'No way.'

'Come on, it's fine, you can have the last of it,' I say.

Forcing myself to crack a smile, I add, 'It's not like I'm thirsty or anything, anyway.'

He chuckles, but still hesitates; I give him an encouraging nod, and only then does he take the canteen and down the rest of it. Even I have enough common sense to know we're both screwed at this point with no water between us. Still, I can't regret it. I couldn't have lived with myself if I left him behind.

'Thanks, kiddo.'

'Yeah.' I start walking again, and Tank comes with me. 'I mean, we're friends, right?' I add.

'Friends,' he repeats. He smiles in a sad way and puts an arm around my shoulders, giving them a gentle squeeze before releasing me again. 'Yeah, I guess so.'

We catch up to the others, and nobody breathes a word to either of us.

It takes a while for it to sink in, but eventually I realize I'm going to die. I mean, I always knew it would happen, and probably sooner than later, but it feels too soon. Maybe it always does. I never thought it would be like this, though. All the rules my papa taught me about survival keep running through my mind. Trust no one. Eat anything edible, even if it's gross. And always bring enough water to get there and back again.

I force myself to keep pressing on, but I feel myself growing weaker. Every step is a little harder, comes a little slower than the one before it. My vision blurs. I do my best to focus on Pretty Boy's back in front of me. I cough, and my breath comes out as dry as sand.

Pretty Boy's silhouette warps. I can't tell if it's a trick of the sunlight or my own hazy vision.

'Guys, I—' I stop to cough again. My voice lowers to a raspy whisper. 'I don't know if I can ...'

I trail off. Nobody answers or even looks at me, or maybe I didn't even really speak aloud. Maybe my brain is boiling in my head. Maybe this is how people become crazies. Even as my thoughts melt, some survival instinct keeps me plowing forward. *Carry on*, I tell myself. Keep moving. Always.

It's not enough. Whiteness creeps up on the edges of my vision. I feel distant, as if I'm watching everything through a screen that is beginning to blur with static. My head feels hot and heavy.

'I don't feel good,' I murmur, or maybe I don't. Everything goes white.

I don't realize I'm on the ground until I hear voices above me. The sand must be hot, but I can't feel it. I can't open my eyes, either.

'Is she dead?' Dolly's soft voice.

'As good as,' Wolf says. 'Dolly, no, don't poke her. She's out.'

'Get up, kiddo.' There's Tank's voice, closer than the rest. A hand shakes me and I will myself to move, but I can't.

'It's no use. Come on, Tank,' Pretty Boy says. 'We should be close now. You can probably make it.'

'Then I'll wait for Kid to wake up.'

'It's her own fault.' Pretty Boy sounds irritated. 'You'll both die if you stay.'

'We need to get moving,' Wolf says, 'or we're all dead.' A brief pause; a shuffle of feet. Footsteps fade away.

'Don't be stupid, Tank!'

'Tank?' Dolly again, even quieter than before. 'They're both staying?'

'Looks like it. Let's go.'

'Seriously, man? Seriously? I can't believe this shit.' Pretty Boy's voice wanes, farther away. 'You're an idiot, you know that? She ain't worth it.'

Then there's silence, and a hand on my arm again.

'Get up, Kid,' Tank says. 'We have to find some shade, at least.'

'I'm so tired,' I say, the words barely audible. *So?* My papa's voice whispers on the edge of my mind.

'You have to get up,' says Papa – no, Tank. But I can't.

I shake my head, and feel my grasp on the world slipping. I find relief in the stillness.

X
Wastelands

I dream of water, and wish I could dream forever, but I don't.

When I wake up again, my thoughts go immediately to the raw, dry pain in my throat, and then to the realization I'm moving. I peel my eyes open. The sunlight hurts. I see only the sky at first, and then, as I move my head, Tank's face. He's carrying me.

'Are we dead?' I ask, voice cracking.

'Don't think so, Kid,' he says wearily. 'Too thirsty to be dead.'

'Makes sense,' I say. I cough and run a dry tongue over my cracked lips. 'Where are we going?'

'Blackfort.'

'We won't make it, they said.'

'We're gonna try.'

I don't know what to say, and speaking hurts my throat anyway, so I shut up. Tank manages to continue for only a few minutes more before he stops. He carries me into the shade behind a boulder, where the sand isn't quite so hot. He sets me down and sinks to the ground.

'Just a little break,' he says, leaning back against the rock and closing his eyes. His breath comes in shallow wheezes. 'Wake me up in ten minutes.'

I'm ready to pass out again myself, but my instinct screams *no*. If I let myself go here, I won't wake up again. I force myself to stand and take a few shaky steps away from the resting spot. It's not like I haven't been here before, this awful dehydration and exhaustion. One of the last days with my papa, I asked for a drink and he told me there was nothing left. I remember that sinking feeling, that fear, that certainty I couldn't go on. And yet, I survived. It's kind of what I do.

I shield my eyes with a hand and survey the wastelands around us. Off in the distance I see the remnants of a building. There isn't anything more promising, so I force myself to stagger in that direction. Wind whistles around me, and I cover my eyes to shield them from the dust.

In the ruins there are a few metal cans lying around. I snatch them up eagerly, but only end up burning my hands on the hot metal to find them empty. I kick the cans aside and continue searching, opening ruined cabinets and drawers. I'm too weak to open some of them myself, and the effort saps my breath. Everything is empty. The place has been ransacked already.

I see movement out of the corner of my eye. The sight makes me gasp and whirl around, nearly falling over in the process. And there it is, sitting on the table: a lizard.

'What the hell?' I mutter, placing a hand on my chest to steady my racing heart. Of course there are still animals running around, but they're rare, like humans. We just have more of a tendency to clump together. I can't remember the last time I saw a little creature like this. My first thought is it's cute enough to keep as a pet. The second is wondering if I could stay alive by drinking its blood. I almost laugh . . . and quickly become somber, thinking harder about it. It seems worth a shot.

I inch toward the tiny creature, slowly raising my hands.

'Hey, little guy,' I attempt to coo, but it comes out raspy and disturbing. I sound like a creepy old man. 'Come here, buddy.'

I lurch forward and grab for it. My hands clamp down on empty air. The lizard is gone in a flash, nimbly skittering away before I'm even close. I stay frozen, and despair flows over me like a wave. I would probably cry if my eyes weren't as dried out as the rest of me.

'Well, this is it,' I say aloud. 'I'm gonna die.'

I sink to the ground and flop onto my back, accepting my fate. My head hits harder than expected. The action is accompanied by a strange clanging noise. I slowly raise my head and bring it down again. *Clang.* It's a hollow, metallic sound, definitely not the kind usually produced by either my head or the sand.

I sit up, feeling only dull curiosity at first but soon filled with realization. Almost afraid of feeling too hopeful, I wipe the sand away and dig down to what's hidden beneath: metal. I recognize this kind of hatch in the floor instantly. It's exactly the kind my own home had. It's a bomb shelter, just like the one I grew up in.

Once I reveal the edges of the hatch I try to pull it open, but it refuses to budge. I uncover more and more, fingers searching for a weakness or opening. Finally I find the latch, and the lock that goes with it. The lock is heavily rusted, but not weak enough to break with my bare hands. I take off my backpack and grab my gun, pointing it toward the lock.

I'm stopped by a vivid mental picture of the bullet ricocheting and killing me. It seems *far* too much like an appropriate ending for my mess of a life, and I lower the gun again. I take the safer option of using the butt of it. I beat at the lock, smashing the gun into the rusty metal as hard as I can. When nothing happens, I hit it again, and again, and again. I carry on until the dry skin on my knuckles cracks and bleeds, and keep going.

'One more time,' I mutter to myself when my arms feel too weak to continue. I raise the gun and bring it down again, hard, the contact vibrating up my arms. Nothing. I suck in a breath through my teeth. 'One more . . . ' My hands bloodied and stinging, I strike again.

The lock breaks. Panting, I move the broken metal aside. I dig my hands underneath the hatch and pull, struggling to lift the heavy metal. It swings open to reveal a staircase. Only hints of sunlight pierce the depths below, but I don't have time to waste on being scared of the dark. I plunge downward. An awful smell is drifting out, bad enough to make me light-headed, but I hold my sleeve over my mouth and nose and continue downward.

The shelter is small and cramped and dark. I fumble along the wall, unable to see anything but fuzzy silhouettes. My hand catches a switch, and dim fluorescent bulbs flicker to life.

'Oh, wow,' I whisper. The place looks a lot like the one I grew up in. If not for the stink, it might feel like home. Better yet, the walls are lined with shelves full of supplies. I see cans of food, bottles of medicine, bandages, soap, and, best of all, *water.* One shelf is full of dusty bottles of it. I rush forward and grab one, hands shaking as I struggle to remove the cap.

I've never tasted anything so good. The water is lukewarm, but still refreshing after the heat. As soon as I've had a taste my body screams for more, and I can't stop. I down an entire bottle in less than a minute, and am reaching for another when I remember Tank. I shove several bottles into my pack and turn to clamber up the stairs.

Then I notice the body.

It's off in a dim corner of the room, sprawled across a cot on the floor and mostly decayed. I've seen corpses rot incredibly fast in the heat, but underground it's cooler, so it's hard to judge how long he's been dead.

I take a few tentative steps toward it, noting the stain of blood on the mattress and the gun hanging limply in the body's hand. Locked up alone down here, it must have been suicide. So many supplies, and he killed himself.

I don't want to admit it to myself, but I can think of plenty of reasons why. My gaze shifts to another cot next to the body. This one is empty. My brain churns out possibilities. The shelter was locked from the outside, so maybe his companion left intending to return, and never did. And this man could have waited, and waited, and finally got tired of waiting. My stomach twists as I remember long days and nights of wandering alone. Living in town was just as lonely.

I bend down and touch the corpse's hand. The others would probably strip his body for loot, but I can't bring myself to.

'Sorry, friend,' I say quietly. 'Sorry you got left behind.' The loneliness reminds me I have a living friend to get back to. I shake off the sadness and half-run up the stairs.

I find him resting against the boulder with his eyes closed, completely still.

'Tank!'

His eyes open slowly. He smiles, looking tired and half-dead.

'Hey, buddy, we're gonna be okay!' I say. I drop to my knees and let my backpack fall to the ground, bottles of water spilling out. I see disbelief cross Tank's broad face, followed by joy, and he grabs and uncaps a bottle. The water spills across his face and down the front of his body in his eagerness.

'Holy shit,' he says once he's finished the bottle, life seeping back into him. 'How did you find this?'

'I was trying to catch a lizard,' I say. 'I found a bomb shelter full of stuff. There's first aid kits and food, too. Oh, and a dead body.'

'Damn,' he says, shaking his head. 'I can't believe ... Where the hell did you *come* from, anyway, you crazy kid?'

'Oh, you know ... around. Same as everyone.' I shove the rest of the water bottles into my pack, smile brightly, and stand up. 'So, are we going to Blackfort?'

'You still want to meet up with the others?' he asks. He drags his bulky body up with visible effort.

'Of course!'

'They left us to die, you know.'

I shrug.

'It's just the way things are, ain't it?'

'But you wouldn't leave me.'

'Well . . . ' I kick at the dirt and shrug. 'Maybe I'm not as smart as the others, I guess?'

Tank laughs, a great booming laugh that makes me smile.

'Well I like you just the way you are, Kid.' He ruffles my hair and grins. 'Let's stock up at this bomb shelter of yours, and then we can go find the others.'

We spot Blackfort from a distance, and my dread of the place only grows as we approach. It becomes more and more clear this town is no Steelforge, and a far stretch from Bramble or anywhere else I've been. A fence runs along the perimeter, sharp metal spikes reaching toward the sky. Inside it is the usual shamble of poorly made shelters amid a mess of crumbling buildings, but even so, it's off-putting. It looks bigger than other towns, the ragged edges of ruined buildings making intimidating silhouettes against the horizon. I'm not sure if it's the memory of the last town or the one I came from, but the sight makes me uneasy.

'You think we'll find the others here?' I ask Tank, trying to shake my nerves.

'Hope so. 'Course, they could have taken off already.'

'And then how will we find them?'

'We won't,' he says bluntly.

The town looms closer. The sun is setting, and its dying rays make the fence shine like knives. The wastelands are deceptively friendly at sunset, when the heat is dissipating and the chill of night hasn't set in yet. It almost seems more appealing to stay out in the wastes rather than venture into the unknowable town. I remember what Pretty Boy said about the place: *not very friendly.*

Flickers of light appear within the gated town, fires starting to ward off the night. They grow larger as we approach, until finally we find ourselves at the entrance. There are two armed guards standing outside. My heart starts to pound.

'What if they won't let us in?'

'They'll let us in. Relax.'

'What if they only let me in and make you leave?'

'What? Why would they do that?'

'I don't know,' I say, even though I definitely do. My chest feels painfully tight. I don't want to be alone again, especially not now, when I've finally found real friends.

'*Relax.* And just in case,' Tank mutters as we approach, 'if we see the others, pretend we don't know them.'

'Why?' I ask, but by then the guards have noticed us. We stop in front of the guards and I resist the instinct to run when one of them points a gun at me.

'What's your business here?' The guard sounds like he's deliberately trying to make his voice deeper. He leans close to me and puffs out his chest, but Tank stands bigger and broader than the two guards combined. I scoot closer to him.

'Trading,' Tank says, his voice a growl. It's far from the jovial tone he uses with me. I almost forgot how intimidating he can be. I put my hands on my hips and plaster on a solemn face, trying to be as frightening as I can be at just over five feet tall. The guards smirk, deflating my posturing and my pride.

'And what would two ragged waste-rats have to trade with *us*?' one of them asks, mocking.

I look at Tank. He nods. I remove my backpack and show them the inside, filled to the brim with clean bottles of water. The guards each take a turn peering in, their hard faces revealing nothing, and mutter to each other.

'Might be that there's more where this came from,' I say, 'if we can work something out.'

They confer again, and one of them gives us a sharp nod.

'All right. Are you two armed?'

I look at Tank again.

'Of course we are,' he rumbles. 'And we're going to stay that way.'

'Then keep 'em put away. Act like a threat and you'll be treated like a threat, you hear?'

We both nod.

'In with you, then.'

They unlock the gate and allow us in. One of the guards accompanies us. As they shut the gate I nervously realize this is the only way in or out. The gate has closed around us like a bear trap. I swallow hard and stay behind Tank as we follow the guard into the depths of the town.

On the inside, Blackfort looks much like any other town. It's the same collection of ramshackle buildings with their crumbly parts patched up. But torches light our path, and the streets are empty. Not only does the town have a fence, but guards patrol the perimeter and stand watch at the entrances of the bigger buildings. As we pass through the center of town, I see something that strikes dread deep within me: a wooden post with a noose hanging from it.

'We hang troublemakers here,' the guard says proudly, noticing my interest. 'Ain't worth the ammo of a proper shooting. Matter of fact, we've got a few lined up for an execution tomorrow.'

'That so?' I ask, my voice squeaking. I risk a peek at Tank.

'What are they in for?' Tank asks, with considerably more composure than I can muster up.

'Cannibalism,' the guard spits out with disgust. 'Damn sharks wandered into town earlier today, but we were ready for them. Matter of fact, we were warned specifically about 'em.' He looks over his shoulder at us and grins. 'Maybe you can come watch the hanging at sunrise.'

Oh, shit.

XI
The Rescue

I stay as calm as possible while the guard escorts us to a room for the night. It's tiny and outfitted only with two sleeping cots. He promises we can speak with the mayor in the morning, and informs us that there's a guard right outside. *Just to be safe*, he assures us. Normally I would be giddy over such safety, but not now. The guards, the fence, the capacity to take in strangers: All of it says a lot about Blackfort, and it isn't good news for us. Whoever is in charge has total control over everyone here, visitors included. The idea is terrifying to me. Somehow I imagine the fence isn't only for keeping people out.

Once the door is closed I allow my panic to set in. I sit on one of the hard cots and put my face in my hands.

Tank paces the length of the cramped room, stirring up dust.

'He said they were warned about them,' I say, recalling the guard's words. 'What does that mean?'

'I don't know,' Tank says. 'Last town was ready for us, too. Something's going on.' He continues to pace. The whole thing gives me a headache just to think about – but more important than that is the problem currently at hand.

'So what are we going to do?' I ask, raising my head to look at him.

'I don't know,' he says again. He stops pacing and sinks onto the cot across from me. 'I just look scary and kill people, I don't make plans.'

'Shit,' I say. Plans have never been my strong point, either. I pull my knees to my chest and hug them, trying desperately to think of something. I'm stumped, and evidently so is Tank; we sit in silence as time ticks onward.

'We should eat,' Tank suggests. His stomach rumbles as if to second the notion. 'Maybe it'll help us think better.'

We dump out the contents of our bags. Along with the dry remains of the food we took for traveling, we each gathered a few cans from the bomb shelter. Some of them were labeled, not that it's much use to me. Tank can read at a very basic level, bits and pieces he was in the process of learning before the bombs dropped, but after scrutinizing some of the cans he admits the only word he knows is *beans*. We each take a can.

Without any utensils it's hard to eat, and I have to drink from the metal container. I end up spilling an unfortunate amount down the front of my already-dirty shirt. The beans are cold and bland, but they fill up my stomach. Tank adds some townie-meat for taste, which bothers me less than I'd expect. He gulps down another couple of cans after I'm done.

With my belly full and a bed beneath me, it's difficult to resist the urge to pull out my blanket and sleep my troubles away. My brain is so tired it hurts to think.

'Got any ideas?' Tank asks.

'Not a clue.'

'Me neither.'

I sigh and lean my head against the wall, picking at the peeling paint with one idle hand. I wish Wolf was here with his wild ideas that always seem to work out in the end.

'You know,' Tank says, 'maybe we shouldn't do anything.'

'What?'

'It might be impossible to save them, and we would just be risking our asses for nothing.' He shrugs. 'Might be better to just cut our losses.'

'No way!'

'You're being stubborn, Kid. They'd do the same.'

'I don't think so,' I say. 'I mean ... the water issue was one thing. They would've died if they had waited for us. But, when there's a chance ... I think they'd give it a try.' I think about it. 'Okay, maybe not Pretty Boy.'

'Definitely not Pretty Boy,' Tank agrees. 'I mean, he and I get on all right, but I know he'd never risk his ass for me. For any of us.'

'Why does he stay with you guys, anyway?' I ask. 'Couldn't he just leave one night?'

'He's ... ' He pauses and searches for the right words. 'He's, you know, one of us. He may not act like it sometimes, but he is. Just like the rest of us, probably too screwed up to make it with everyone else. He's just better at hiding it.' His face hardens suddenly. 'You remember that, Kid, all right?'

'What do you mean?'

'What I mean is ... ' He sighs and shrugs. 'What I mean is even though he's my friend and all, that doesn't mean I trust him. None of us do, and you shouldn't either. Okay?'

'Okay,' I say, though I don't quite get it.

'Anyway, back to the rescue plan, if you're sure about that.'

'Ah, yeah.' I scratch my head. 'Do we even know where they're keeping them?'

'There was a building near the noose with a few guards outside. It *could* be a jail,' Tank says.

'How many guards?'

'Two or three.'

'Think we could handle them?'

Tank shrugs.

'If we take them by surprise? Probably. But gunshots will bring others running.'

'Aw, shit, you're right.' I sigh and press my palms against my eyelids, trying to ward off a steadily building headache. 'What if we just hit 'em over the head with something?'

'Could do. I think I packed a crowbar.'

'And I could get a ... a rock or something,' I say. 'And then ... ' Then, who knows. I try to picture it: the two of us, knocking out the guards and busting into the jail. We would need a key, but one of the guards would probably have it. We'd grab the key, release the others, and fight our way out. I wouldn't be so scared of taking on the guards with the others on our side. It seems like a decent plan to me.

'Well, do you have any better ideas?' I ask Tank.

'Nope.'

'So I guess that'll have to do.' We don't have the time to construct anything more concrete. The guard said the hanging would be at dawn, and I'm guessing we should hightail it out of here before the whole town is awake.

'We have to take care of the guard here, first.'

'Oh, right. Shit.'

'Go distract him, and I'll come do what I do,' Tank says. He sifts through his bag and pulls out his crowbar. The metal is stained with rust and what looks like old blood.

'Oh ... you mean, like, *right* now?'

'When else?'

I guess he's right. Still, I feel nervous. I try to fight back my fear as I sling my backpack over my shoulder and head over to the doorway.

I glance at Tank, take a deep breath, and walk out.

The guard is leaning against the wall across from the doorway. He stands at attention as the door opens and fixes a pair of mean eyes on me. I smile nervously.

'Where do you think you're going?' he asks.

'I ... gotta piss,' I say. I move out of our doorway, leaving it partially open, and take a few steps toward the stairwell leading out of the building. I try to act nonchalant, but my movements feel stiff. The guard turns to follow me, putting his back to our door.

'Oh.' He almost loses interest, but regains it after a second glance. 'So why are you bringing your bag?'

'Uh,' I say. I try to think of something smart, but my mind fails me. 'In case of ...' I start, and then stumble over my words. 'In case of trouble?'

'Won't be any trouble,' he says. 'We have this place on lockdown.'

'Right, well, umm,' I say. I can feel my face turning red. 'I still need it.'

'Why's that?'

I gape like a fish. He stares at me.

'None of your business!' I blurt out, not knowing what else to say.

'Actually, it is,' he says. 'I'll come keep an eye on you.'

'No!' I say quickly. His hand is now resting on the holster of his gun. 'It's . . . I need the bag for . . . ' I pause, stutter, and finally come up with something. 'It's . . . girl stuff, you know?'

'Girl stuff?' he repeats incredulously. We stare at each other in silence. His face changes as he understands, gradually shifting from fierceness to embarrassment. 'Oh,' he says. 'You mean . . . Oh.'

'Yeah,' I say. My face is probably purple by now, and his is reddening as well. 'So . . . '

'Fine, fine, off with you then. Hurry up or I'll come looking.' He makes a shooing motion at me. Out of the corner of my eye I see our door sliding open, and Tank's bulky form emerging. Realizing I have to stall a bit longer, I try to grab his attention again.

'Where should I go?'

'Oh. Right. If you leave this building, the latrines are that—' He turns to point, and comes face-to-face with Tank. 'Way?'

Tank grabs the guard's head and slams it into the wall. He crumples to the floor without so much as a cry.

'Let's go,' Tank says. I nod, exhaling a breath I hadn't known I was holding in, and follow him outside.

We make our way toward the execution square, dodging behind buildings whenever someone approaches. It's hard to shake the feeling we'll be surrounded by guards at any moment. I try to stay calm and follow Tank's lead, moving when he moves and waiting when he waits. Eventually we find ourselves around the corner of the building Tank mentioned.

'Can you tell if it's actually the jail?' I ask. He shrugs. I shrug back.

'As good a bet as any,' he says. He fishes his crowbar out of his pack. I search around on the ground until I find a decent-size rock. 'I'll take the guard on the left,' he says.

'Got it,' I say, straightening up. As my arms shake I wonder if I should have picked a smaller rock, but it's too late.

Tank holds up three fingers and counts down as I try to steady my grip. *Three. Two. One.*

Tank turns the corner and charges at the guards. I raise the rock above my head and follow. The guards are too surprised to pull their weapons. Tank plows into one of them and knocks him off his feet, and I fling my rock at the other before he can react.

It falls short of its mark. *Very* short.

The guard turns toward me with an incredulous look, and I curse and fumble for my knife. As soon as I get it out of my boot I run to attack, but it's not fast enough.

'Intruders!' the guard bellows, his voice echoing as loud as a siren in the quiet town. 'In the execution square!'

'Sh-shit!' I plunge my knife toward his stomach, but he grabs my arm and twists it, making me cry out. The knife falls. I desperately kick at his shins as he reaches for his gun.

'Heads up!'

I duck. The crowbar whistles through the air above my head and slams into the guard's chest. His grip on my arm goes slack as he falls.

I scramble to pick my knife up and turn to Tank, panting for breath.

'Well, so much for secrecy,' he says, and reaches into his pack for a gun. I shove the knife back into my boot and do the same, retrieving the handgun that Wolf gave me. It feels strange and unfamiliar in my hands, and I fumble to find a way to hold it that doesn't seem awkward.

Tank and I bust through the door to the building, guns ready.

We find a small, bare room which is very clearly *not* a jail. There's only a table and a chair, with a lone woman sitting behind it. She's middle-aged and plain-faced, and her expression upon seeing us is more skeptical than afraid.

There's an awkward pause as we all stare at each other. It's hard to say who is more surprised by the situation.

'Who the *fuck* are you?' the woman asks.

'Uh,' I say. 'This . . . isn't the jail, huh?'

She stares at me.

''Fraid not, hon,' she says. 'This is the mayor's office.'

The door opens behind us and the room floods with guards. I look around and count three, seven, *nine* guns total pointed at us.

Tank and I simultaneously let our weapons drop and raise our hands in surrender.

The woman, who I now assume is the mayor, lets out a derisive chuckle at our expense.

'Oops,' she says, grinning. 'Looks like someone made a mistake.'

'We really should've thought this out better,' I whisper to Tank.

'Tell me about it,' he mutters back.

'Now, let's get you two to that jail you were looking for.' The mayor motions to the guards. 'Take 'em in with the others, boys.'

The jail, as it turns out, is the place *next to* the mayor's office. It's a stout building that smells like sweat and piss. The guards jeer at us as we're marched down a row of cells. Many of them are full. Some prisoners beg for release as we pass by, some rattle the bars and shout vulgarities, and others stare at us with dead eyes. I've never seen a jail this full. The town I came from shot troublemakers on sight, so the jail only held the occasional drunk who needed to cool off. Chaining people like this somehow feels worse. The sight of so many prisoners makes me angry in a way that surprises me. I suddenly find myself wishing we had taken down a few more guards before ending up here, and hoping we'll have another chance to crack some heads.

They lead us back to the very end of the row, a dark and lonely corner where most of the cells are empty. One, however, is very much not so.

'*Please* let me out of here!' a familiar voice says. An arm reaches through the bars, clutching at a guard's leg. 'I don't belong with these psychopaths, I swear, this is all just a big—' Pretty Boy turns his pretty, pleading eyes to us and cuts off abruptly. 'Oh, fuck.'

'Hey to you, too,' Tank says grimly.

'Mayor's right,' one of the guards says. 'Looks like this is the big guy who was supposed to be with them.'

'What about this one?' Another one of them points to me.

'Dunno. The broadcast didn't say anything about an ugly little boy, did it?'

I sigh.

'Nope. Ah, well, might as well toss 'im in. If he knows them, reckon he deserves a hanging.'

They open the door and shove us inside. Wolf, Dolly, and Pretty Boy are all sitting on the dirty floor, the latter as far from the others as he can manage to be. With Tank there, the five of us can barely fit. As the door slams behind us I squeeze into the corner next to Pretty Boy.

'Oh, it's a miracle, you guys are alive,' Wolf deadpans. 'Thank the Lord, we're saved.'

'Don't start,' Tank says. He sits with a groan. 'We tried.'

'No, really. I'm thrilled. Now we can die together, a big fucking happy family.'

I sigh and let my head rest on the cold metal bars, staring up at the ceiling.

So much for our big rescue.

XII
Prisoners

When I wake up, sunlight is streaming through the bars on the window.

I blink at the light and slowly regain my bearings. I realize I'm slumped against Pretty Boy's shoulder and quickly sit up. He looks at me with hollow eyes.

'You drooled on me,' he says.

'Sorry,' I whisper, my face heating up. 'On the bright side, we're not dead yet.'

'Clearly,' he says. He squints at the window. 'I stayed up all night, thinking they would be here any second.'

'You didn't sleep at all?'

'No. I figured if I was about to die . . . ' He chokes on the word, his eyes watering. 'I want to at least be awake for my final moments.'

'Yeah . . . ' I say, trying to think of something meaningful enough to redeem myself for drooling. Nothing comes to mind. I attempt a joke instead. 'Wouldn't want to wake up dead, right?' He gives me a completely unamused look. I sigh. Something about Pretty Boy always turns me into a bigger idiot than usual. And some stupid part of me still desperately wants him to like me, despite his issues and the fact we hardly know each other.

'Say, Pretty Boy,' I say as that sparks a thought. 'Would you mind telling me your real name?' If there was ever a time for it, it'd be now.

He looks over at me, stares silently for a long moment, and shakes his head.

'What's the point?' he asks dully.

Before I can respond, the door to the jail opens and the mayor enters with a handful of armed guards. They come down the dim and cramped hallway directly to our cell. Pretty Boy sits up straighter next to me, and Dolly awakens at the sound of footsteps. Wolf stirs soon after her, and wakes Tank with a kick. I find myself scooting closer to Dolly for protection.

The mayor glares down at us behind the bars.

'Well, looks like it's your lucky day, sharks,' she says. 'Your execution has been postponed.'

Nobody speaks. I hold my breath, unsure if I should be grateful or if this will be a new, worse development.

'Turns out you're wanted at the radio tower,' she says. 'Alive.'

'Where the hell is that?' Wolf asks.

'You're not in a position to be asking questions,' she says coldly. 'All you need to know is that you're being transported.'

'Why?' he asks.

'I said you're not—'

'And who wants us?'

'You—'

'How are we getting there?' he asks. 'How long will it take?'

The mayor stares at him, unblinking. Wolf breaks into a grin.

'Aw, I'm just fucking with you. Let's get going, I'm tired of sitting around.'

She turns a stiffened back toward us and gestures to the guards. They unlock the door with a creak. I recoil, but there isn't enough room to make it far. A man grabs my arm and pulls me to my feet.

'Tie them up,' the mayor commands.

The guard forces my wrists behind my back and binds them with rope, pulling it so tightly I can barely wriggle my fingers. The others get the same treatment. Pretty Boy whimpers pathetically as they tie him. At least I'm holding it together better than him.

They push us along in front of them, a line trailing out of the cell and through town. A small crowd has gathered around the execution square. Disappointed by the lack of a hanging, they jeer and throw things at us as we're herded past. Wolf shouts insults back at them, far too entertained by the entire situation.

Just outside the gate, a truck waits. It's a bulky, durable-looking vehicle with a sizable back compartment, probably used for transporting goods.

'Well, hell, looks like we got ourselves first-class treatment,' Wolf says. 'Mighty kind of you. It'll be nice not having to walk everywhere.'

The guards ignore him. They push us forward and into the back. I'm not tall enough to climb in without the use of my arms, so one of the guards lifts me up and tosses me inside. Once we're all in, they shut the doors. It's nearly pitch-black inside. I can only see silhouettes of the others.

When my eyes adjust, I see the compartment is filled with crates of supplies: food, water, and other goods. I guess that includes us. If Blackfort is willing to comply, they must be trading for something valuable. The thought gnaws on the corners of my mind, and I think back to when we were attacked by raiders. They mentioned a reward, too. Someone's definitely out to get us, but who? And how is it that wandering raiders and the town of Blackfort both know about it?

'I don't understand what's going on,' I mumble, looking at Wolf for answers.

'Don't look at me,' he says with a shrug.

'Has this happened before?'

'What, facing imminent death? Yeah, all the time.'

'No, I mean being transported like this.'

'Oh, right.' He pauses to think. 'Nope, don't think so.'

'Well, what do you think about it?'

'I'm just glad not to have a noose around my neck, ain't you?'

'I guess.' I lean against a crate, letting my head loll back.

My efforts to rest are undermined when the truck starts moving. The engine makes a god-awful roaring sound as it starts up, and continues to growl unpleasantly. The compartment shakes and shifts as we move, making me slide around on the floor. So, no sleep for me. I sit up and look around at the others.

'So ... what are we gonna do?' I ask. Nobody answers.

I sigh and shift, stretching out my legs and trying to better position myself so I won't slide so much. When I look down at my outstretched boots, a realization hits me.

When they put us in jail, they took away our weapons and my backpack, but they didn't search me very thoroughly. Perhaps because I don't seem like much of a threat – which is a valid assessment – they didn't bother to check inside my boots . . . which means I still have my knife.

I squirm around in vain attempts to dislodge it. As it turns out, it's not such an easy task without being able to use my hands. I awkwardly wiggle one way, and another, and stick my foot in the air and shake it, but nothing happens.

'You gotta piss or something, Kid?' Wolf asks. When I look up, everyone is staring at me. I blush.

'Err, no,' I say. 'It's my knife. I think I still have it.'

'Well, shit, get it out then!' Wolf says.

'That's what I'm trying to do!' A frustrated sigh escapes my lips. I abandon all dignity and stick both feet in the air, flailing them with all the effort I can muster up. *Finally* the knife falls out, and narrowly misses hitting me in the face. It clatters onto the floor just beside my head.

'Nice technique,' Wolf says. I ignore him, and push myself up to a sitting position. I slide closer to the knife, trying to grab it with my bound hands.

Just when I'm finally close, the truck makes a sharp turn. I topple over and slide across the floor to slam against the opposite wall. The knife slides, as well – and ends up just beside Pretty Boy.

I look at the knife and up at him. A look I can't identify flashes through his eyes, and I remember what Tank said about not trusting him. If he got free, would he even help the rest of us?

'Aw hell no,' Wolf says from the other side of the truck. 'Don't even think about it, Pretty Boy.' He starts to scoot over, fixing him with a hard gaze. 'Slide the knife to me.'

Pretty Boy bends over, reaching for the knife. Wolf scoots faster, face screwed up in determination. Just as Pretty Boy is about to grab the knife, Wolf launches himself at him, head-butting him in the chest. The air goes out of Pretty Boy with an audible *oof* and he collapses with Wolf on top of him. The knife skitters away.

'Get off of me!' Pretty Boy yells, attempting to wiggle free.

'Give me the knife!'

'I don't even have it!'

'You guys are both being idiots,' Tank says. 'Calm your shit and stop making so much noise.'

Rather than heed his advice, Wolf does his best to beat the crap out of Pretty Boy despite his lack of hands.

The truck swerves suddenly and sends everyone tumbling. I crash into the side of the compartment once more, slide back the other way as the truck swerves again, and end up sprawled across Dolly's lap. She looks down at me with a slightly alarmed expression as I wiggle helplessly. The others are similarly entangled in a heap of limbs. The truck stops.

'The hell just happened?' Wolf asks, still half on top of Pretty Boy. The latter tries to say something, but with his face pressed against the floor of the truck it's hard to decipher it.

'The truck stopped,' I say.

'Very helpful, Kid, as always.'

The growl of the engine cuts off, and so does our

conversation. In the silence I hear doors slamming as the guards exit the truck, followed by the crunch of footsteps.

The truck doors swing open and sunlight pours in.

'What are you idiots doing?' the guard asks, scrutinizing us.

I notice the knife glinting conspicuously a few feet away. I try to slide a foot over to cover it, but unfortunately the movement only captures his attention. He climbs into the compartment and snatches up the weapon.

'Ah, trying to escape, eh?' he asks, smirking and dangling it from one hand. 'No such luck, sharkies.' He turns around and yells to his partner. 'Found the problem yet?'

'Tires are blown. We got spares?' a voice answers from outside.

'Yeah, I'll get 'em. Find out what we hit, would you?'

'Got it.'

Meanwhile, the guard uses my knife to cut a length of rope off the supply crates.

'Just so you lot don't get any ideas . . . ' He reaches down, forcibly pushing and pulling the pile of us apart. It's hard for anyone to retaliate much, bound as we are. I squirm around until I manage to flip onto my stomach and crane my neck, trying to see what he's doing to the others. I can't tell what's happening, but it sounds like a struggle.

I can finally see when the guard moves: He's used the rope to bind Wolf and Pretty Boy back-to-back.

'No fucking way,' Wolf growls. Pretty Boy looks horrified.

'Good luck escaping now,' the guard says, grinning. He's about to give the same treatment to Tank and Dolly when his partner returns.

'We have a problem,' he says.

'Yeah?'

'A big problem.'

He turns to him.

'What is it?'

The guard outside holds something up. I see the glint of sun off of metal, blades sharp as fangs. My stomach twists as I realize what it is: a strip of road spikes.

'This wasn't an accident,' he says, his face paling.

'Shit.' The guard lets the rope drop and stands, reaching for his gun. 'Raiders on the trade route. We need to get the hell out of here, and—'

Gunfire interrupts his sentence, and the guard standing outside falls with a choked cry. The man inside stares, slack-jawed. In the distance I hear whoops and catcalls and shouts, growing closer by the second. It doesn't just sound like raiders. It sounds like crazies.

'Untie us,' Pretty Boy begs. 'Please. Please. Don't let me die tied to this maniac!'

'For once I agree. It would be fucking embarrassing,' Wolf says.

The guard ignores them. He runs to the back of the truck and grabs his injured companion, hoisting him up. He slams the doors shut behind him and bends down to assess the damage.

'I'm fine,' the wounded man gasps, while the blood leaking from him says otherwise.

'I can treat his wound,' Pretty Boy says. 'I can help. Untie me.'

'Shut up!' the uninjured guard yells. He rips off part of his shirt and ties it around the bullet hole, his sloppiness revealing he has no idea what he's doing.

Outside, the noise draws closer every second. Soon it's clear they're just outside, and there are a lot of them. Fists and weapons rain down on the sides of the truck, the sound exploding like gunfire inside. I flinch as something hits the wall just beside my head. Since the truck doors open from the outside, I know they're messing with us, toying with their prey before they go for the kill.

'Just listen to me. *Listen.* There's no way you can fight all of them,' Pretty Boy says, speaking like he's trying to coax an animal out of hiding. 'If you untie us, we can help. We won't tell anyone you let us free.'

The guard hesitates. As his ailing friend loses strength and consciousness, he seems to consider the offer. He reaches into his pocket for the knife.

The doors to the truck burst open. Noise rushes inside, cackling and jeering filling the truck. There's a mob outside. Faces swim in my vision as they clamber to get inside. I scoot away and press my back against the crates. The guard pulls out his gun and fires wildly into the crowd outside. Few of them react, and they cackle madly as their companions fall. For every one that goes down, another two spring up. They look wild, faces crusted with dried blood, skin peeling from sunburn, scraps of clothing hanging off their lean and scarred bodies.

These aren't raiders like Wolf's crew. They're madmen who know nothing but mindless violence. Sometimes the wastelands swallow men up and they don't come out the same. Whether it's the radiation or the heat or something else, their minds are just broken.

Panic surges in my gut as a memory hits me: hiding in an abandoned building with my papa, a pack of crazies right outside. I never saw them, but I heard them as they screamed and jeered. Papa held one hand over my mouth. The other held a gun, and it shook. I had never seen him shake like that.

They didn't find us, but another traveler wasn't so lucky. She screamed all night, just yards away from our hiding spot. Papa had to put her down himself, after the crazies had left her writhing in the dust.

I drag my mind back to the present as the mob surges forward and into the truck, a swarming mass of crazed faces and reaching arms. The fallen guard goes first, swallowed by greedy hands. The second guard is next. He tries to fight back, gun firing several times. It doesn't make a difference. He disappears with a scream.

I catch a glint of something on the floor and recognize my knife, forgotten again. I wriggle my way toward it. Luckily, the mob seems to be temporarily distracted with their new playthings. I can hear the guards screaming, and try to ignore my rising panic as I grab the knife. I saw frantically at the ropes on my wrists. The knife is slippery in my sweaty palms, but the rope gradually thins.

I can only hope it will be fast enough. The mob's blood-thirst won't be sated for long.

'Pass the knife, Kid!' Pretty Boy hisses from behind me. 'Hurry!'

'It's hard,' I huff out, struggling with my nearly numb fingers. Finally, the knife saws through and the ropes go slack. Blood rushes back into my hands.

I get on my hands and knees and crawl to the closest person: Dolly. I hack at the ropes binding her, ignoring the pins-and-needles sting as feeling returns to my fingers. I'm not fast enough.

A hand closes on my leg, and I'm yanked backward too quickly to scream. The knife clatters out of my hands, and I catch a glimpse of the horrified faces of the others as the crazies drag me away.

XIII
Crazies

I'm in a sea of writhing bodies. I find myself pulled and pushed, choked by the reek of blood and sweat. Hands tug at my clothes, my hair, my skin. Nails like claws drag across my arms and leave bloody trails. I open my mouth to scream, but can't even hear it through the noise around me. It's a huge pack of crazies, at least a couple dozen from what I can see.

I use my bony elbows to jab around me. It's enough to grant me open air. I try to run, but a leg catches me in the knees and sends me tumbling. My face hits the dirt. The mob cackles as they drag me back.

Fists and feet pummel me, but never steel. They don't want to kill me yet, they just want to play with me. The thought is not reassuring.

I notice a flash of Dolly's blue hair amid the chaos and fight my way in her direction. I shove my way through the crowd until she's within sight, and struggle to stay there as the mob surges around me.

'Pretty, pretty,' a man says, leering at her. He runs a hand down the front of her shirt and tugs, ripping the fabric. Dolly's eyes flash dangerously.

A second later, a knife is buried deep into the man's eye. He screams and Dolly yanks it back out, slashing at others nearby. The man stumbles into the crowd and they laugh at him, shove him to the dirt, excited by the sight of his blood. Several jump on the weakened man, tearing into him with knives and teeth.

I try to move closer to Dolly, but someone grabs me by the hair and yanks me back. Another hand clamps on to my arm and pulls me in the opposite direction. A vicious tug-of-war ensues. They tug me one way and then the other until it feels like I'm going to be ripped in half. Finally the hand on my head loses its grip, pulling out some hair in the process, and I stumble forward. The hand releases me, and I fall to my knees. Dolly is gone. I'm surrounded by grinning, mad faces.

A creature barely recognizable as a woman crouches next to me, serrated knife in hand. I stop struggling as she lightly presses the tip of the blade against my wrist. The steel ghosts its way up my arm and neck while I cringe. She rests the flat of it against my face.

'Eyes or tongue?' she asks, breath reeking of rotten meat.

'Um, neither, please,' I squeak out, trying to breathe as little as possible.

She smiles too wide, showing a nearly toothless mouth.

'Tongue it is,' she says. She shoves her free hand into my mouth, and I choke on the taste of blood and dirt. Before she can grab my tongue, I bite down as hard as I can. My teeth break the skin and she screeches wildly. She yanks her hand back and the knife swings down toward me.

I catch her wrist with my free hand with the knife just inches from my face. We strain, unmoving, neither of us strong enough to overpower the other. The woman is stick-thin, but her anger and savagery lend her strength. The knife inches closer to my face; soon it's just a centimeter away from my nose.

I wrench my other hand free just in time. With her knife about to sink into my skin, I instinctively jut my hand out to stop it. The steel cuts deep into my palm, and pain shoots all the way up to my elbow. I force her back, she yanks the knife away with a snarl – and the blade catches my little finger, slicing it clean off.

I stare at the stump where my finger used to be as blood begins to gush out. Luckily the woman with the knife is just as distracted as I am, though by something else: Tank charging into the fray. With his hands tied behind his back, he barrels into the crowd, knocking people down left and right. He goes down quickly but takes several others with him, crushing them beneath his weight.

I take advantage of the distraction and scramble to my feet, holding my injured hand against me and shoving people aside as I make my way back to the truck.

Wolf and Pretty Boy are in the crowd as well. They're still tied back-to-back. Wolf seems intent on following Tank's lead and rushing into the mob, while Pretty Boy is trying to run in the opposite direction. They lurch back and forth, neither of them able to get anywhere.

I force my way through the mob of crazies, weaving between them and darting under their legs. Everyone is distracted enough by the others that I can slip by and reach the truck. I pull myself into the back, panting, and crouch beside the boxes. My hand has gone numb, but blood is still spurting. And my finger ... my finger is gone. Where my pinky used to be is just a bloody stub. I stare at it, wiggling my other fingers. It's strange, as though I can *feel* it still there, but it's gone.

And the others are still out in that awful mob. I have to do something. I refuse to run away and hide like Pretty Boy would. But what can I do? My knife is gone. I have nothing.

My heart sinks as I hear the crazies approach, their loud and barely human voices signaling their arrival. The crazies don't even speak properly, only using guttural noises and broken phrases to communicate. I hear 'the small one' and 'blood' and 'kill' as they approach. Everything else is unintelligible, but none of it sounds pretty. I squeeze between two boxes, trying to hide without losing my view of the outside. Three of them are approaching. Luckily, none of them are armed; unluckily, they could easily kill me bare-handed. Desperate, I grab some cans of food out of a box, cradling them in one arm and poising to throw with my uninjured hand. As soon as one of the men climbs into the truck, I send a metal can flying at him.

It sails right past his head. He looks surprised, then cackles madly. The next can catches him right in the teeth and sends him stumbling backward. He falls.

Not waiting for the next one, I take my ammo and run, jumping out of the truck and past them. I stagger precariously for a few steps before catching my balance, and take a look behind me at the three men. They stare at me. I throw a can at them, catching one in the shoulder, and take off running. Shouts and howls follow me.

I run as fast as my scrawny legs can move. My path loops around the perimeter of the truck, marked with an occasional pause to launch a can of food behind me. I run around the truck once, twice, three times, gasping for breath and wondering how I haven't been caught yet – and a man steps into my vision, growling like a dog. I skid to a stop, turn in the other direction, and collide with one of the guys who were chasing me. I stumble and fall. The remaining cans spill from my hands.

One of the men grabs at me, but I dodge his grip and roll sideways – and keep rolling, until I reach the truck. Not the most graceful exit, but it'll do. I tumble under and crawl into the darkness, panting for breath.

I'm not alone down here. For one moment I expect it to be Pretty Boy hiding again. Instead I find one of the guards. It's the one who was shot, and apparently he isn't quite dead yet. He raises his head, eyes dull, and points a gun in my direction, but it's halfhearted. After a moment he lets his head and weapon fall again, and sighs wearily. His head droops back, as if he exhaled the last of his energy.

I crawl closer and ensure his eyes are closed. When he doesn't respond, I snatch the gun out of his hand. His eyes flutter open and he looks at me again, but does nothing.

I retreat, half-dragging the gun. It's a huge, heavy assault rifle, not at all like my handgun. When I crawl out from beneath the truck, I try to hold it like I know how to use it.

The three crazies from before are still there, waiting. One of them grins at the sight of me.

'Gun?' he says, jerking closer. 'Ha. Ha, ha. Too big for the little boy.'

'As if,' I say, trying to sound confident. I pull the trigger.

Bullets spray wildly, mostly hitting sand as I stumble from the recoil. Somehow, miraculously, I manage to hit the man. He falls with a snarl, blood streaming from multiple bullet holes.

I try to keep my tough face on despite the growing pain in my injured hand. My hand and the gun are slick with blood. Breathing heavily, I point the barrel at the other two slack-jawed crazies. They take off running. I give chase, blood pumping, giddy to be the hunter for once.

I stop as I spot the huge mob of crazies. I *could* point the gun into the crowd and go wild, maybe mow down every last one of them, but the thought makes me queasy. And with my luck I'd probably gun down my friends, too.

'All right!' I yell, trying to make my small voice carry over the noise. It doesn't work. 'All right!' I try once more, still to no avail. Frustrated, I raise the gun and fire into the air.

This captures their attention. The crowd quiets down, hungry eyes on me.

'I just want my friends,' I say, 'please.'

The crazies jeer and hiss. Someone throws a bottle that narrowly misses me.

'Dolly?' I search the mob for signs of her shocking blue hair. 'Dolly!'

She shoves her way out of the crowd. She's limping, blood running down her leg, with her clothes torn and her hair in wild disarray. She's still clutching my knife.

'Are you okay?' I ask, although clearly neither of us is. She silently hands my knife back. I wipe it off, put it back into my boot, and place the gun into her more capable hands. For a moment she stares at it, looking even more dazed and distant than usual. She slowly looks back at the mob of crazies. Some of them are circling closer to us now that I haven't opened fire immediately. A frightening look comes over Dolly.

'Wait,' I say. 'We need to make sure the others are—'

The burst of gunfire is shockingly loud. I drop to my knees and clap my hands over my ears. A mess of blood and horrible screaming follows. The mob falls one after another. They don't even attempt escape. Some of them lunge at us; they drop like flies. Bodies pile up. After a few seconds, I squeeze my eyes shut.

When the gunfire dies, it leaves a hollow silence. Dolly is still jamming the trigger, producing dull clicks. I hesitantly open my eyes.

There are bodies everywhere, mounds of them, and *messy* bodies. Sometimes it's hard to tell where one ends and another begins. I fight the urge to vomit. There's no time, because there are still others left, more than I expected.

As the remnants realize we're out of ammo, they grow bold again. They approach us, grabbing weapons from their fallen comrades. One of them beats two metal bars together, the harsh sound ringing out louder and louder as he draws closer.

'Shit,' I say. *Clank.*

Dolly holds out a hand. *Clank.*

'Knife.' *Clank.*

I hand it over, shakily rising to my feet again.

Clank.

Clank.

Clank.

'Stay close,' Dolly says, and they're on us.

She slits the first man's throat before he can touch her. Blood gushes out like a fountain, splattering all over my face. A kick forces the next one back, followed by a swift elbow to one behind her.

The man with the crowbars comes for me, grinning with bloody teeth.

'Dolly!' I squeak as the first crowbar whistles toward my head. I barely duck. Dolly reaches over me and stabs him in the chest before he can use the second. Two men grab her from behind as she yanks it out again. They pull her backward and separate us.

I drop to the ground, grab a crowbar from the dying man, and swing at the nearest pair of legs. With a resounding *crack* to his knees, he falls. I rise to my feet and flail wildly with my weapon, keeping them at bay. My injured hand is slick with blood and it hurts to clutch the crowbar so tightly, but I ignore it.

I swing at one of the men holding Dolly and he stumbles back, howling. She shakes off the other and we stand back-to-back, both gasping for breath. There's still a ring of crazies around us. They seem endless, coming one after another.

'Too many,' Dolly says, echoing my own thoughts.

'What do we do?'

'Get the others.' She jerks her head at the pile of bodies.

'And if they're already dead?'

She shrugs.

Crazies lunge at us from all directions. Dolly darts forward, cutting down one man and breaking through the gap in the closing circle. I run after her, the mob on my heels.

'Tank! Wolf! Pretty Boy!' I yell, frantically searching for

any sign of them. Someone groans to my left. As I turn my foot catches on a body. I fall hard, coming face-to-mangled-face with a corpse.

I squeak and sit up again, only to feel my head hit warm flesh. I look up to find a man standing over me with a bloody meat cleaver.

Shit. I spin around and bring up my crowbar. His blade collides with the bar, metal screeching. He pulls the knife back and I scramble away before he can swing again. I crawl over bodies, trying to ignore the wet squish and discomfiting warmth of them. When my hand hits something moving, I recoil in surprise.

The mound of bodies shifts and swells. A familiar face pokes out from the mass.

'Tank!' He doesn't look good. There's a gash on his forehead and his torso is covered in knife wounds. At least he's still conscious, though, and it looks like he wasn't shot when Dolly went trigger-happy.

'Kid! Get me the fuck out of these ropes!'

'Right, right,' I say, looking around for something sharp. I set my crowbar down in favor of a piece of broken glass. I accidentally grab it with my injured hand and grimace at the immediate sting. I pass it to my other hand and start sawing at Tank's bindings. My grip on the knife keeps slipping, hands shaking and slick with blood.

'Watch out!' Tank yells before I can finish. I throw myself to the ground and hear something *swoosh* through the air above my head. Looking up, I see the man with the cleaver has caught up to me. I reach for the crowbar, but he kicks it aside.

As he comes at me again, I dive between his legs and scramble behind him. He whirls around to follow. Behind him, Tank strains at his ropes. After a few seconds of struggle, he breaks free. He grabs the crowbar and looms up behind the unsuspecting man.

Before the crazed man can slash at me with his knife again, Tank grabs his scrawny arm with one hand and twists it. The cleaver falls to the ground. A few cracks and crunches later, the man falls, lifeless. Tank grabs my hand and pulls me to my feet.

'You all right?' he asks.

'Mostly.' My hands are still shaking. I try to steady them. 'Are you?'

'I'll be fine.'

'The others . . . ?'

He points behind me. I turn to see Wolf, Dolly, and Pretty Boy, all thoroughly beaten up but mostly intact. Dolly and Wolf are armed now, and making short work of the remaining crazies. Pretty Boy isn't helping much, but the other two are doing just fine on their own. The crazies may have numbers and crude weapons, but they're no match for my friends.

'Looks like we're okay,' I say.

'We're lucky it was crazies. Real raiders would've sliced us up before we got untied.'

'Looks like the crazies sliced you up pretty good.'

'Eh, nothing serious,' he says nonchalantly. Behind me, I hear a particularly loud *thud* of impact, followed by a nasty squish. I try not to imagine what's happening. Tank continues, apparently oblivious. 'Shallow cuts, mostly. They were just trying to fuck with us. Thought we were easy prey.'

'Big mistake.'

'Damn right.' He looks down at his torn-up body and grins. 'I'll have some good scars. Think I'll look scary?'

'You already do!'

He laughs heartily.

'How 'bout you, any good battle wounds?'

'Well, umm ... ' I hold up my hand and wiggle it, displaying my missing finger.

'Holy shit, Kid!' Tank exclaims, staring.

'It's pretty ugly, huh?' I stare at it for a second, then let my hand fall to my side. As the thrill of the fight dies off the pain is growing, a throbbing pain that shoots up my whole arm.

'I can't believe that bitch cut my finger off,' I say.

Tank chuckles and slaps me on the back.

'You're gonna be fine, Kid.'

He turns to watch Wolf and Dolly at work, his expression unchanging. I do the same, wincing at the brutality in the way they pick off the last of the crazies.

When that's done Wolf props a baseball bat up like a walking stick and leans against it, breathing heavily.

'All right, guys,' he says loudly.

'You okay, Wolf?' Tank asks as we walk over to them. Dolly moves among the dead, hunting for weapons.

'All right,' Wolf repeats. He looks more disheveled than usual. He's covered in blood, dripping from his dreadlocks and down the front of his shirt. It's hard to tell how much of it is his own. He pushes up his goggles and glares at us. '*All right*. You know what? I am *sick* of this. I am sick of being pushed around and tied up and all of that shit! Come on, people, we're supposed to be the bad guys! What the fuck is going on here?'

He casts a furious look around at the lot of us. Nobody speaks. Pretty Boy abruptly bends over and vomits. Wolf shoots him a disapproving glance and continues ranting.

'Well, I'll tell you what. It ain't gonna happen again. No fucking way. We are gonna find out who the hell these assholes trying to get us captured are, we are gonna find the fuckers, and we're gonna kill 'em. You got that?'

'Got it, boss,' Tank says. I give a thumbs-up, and Dolly nods, looking very pleased with a pistol she found. Pretty Boy says nothing.

'Good,' Wolf says. He slides his goggles down and gives the nearest body a kick for emphasis. 'Now, are either of those Blackfort guards still breathing?'

Dolly locates one of them crumpled on the ground nearby. He never made it far from the truck. She walks over and kicks him. When he groans, she shoots him.

'No,' she says.

'God damn it, Dolly, I wanted him alive.'

'Oh.'

'Fucking hell, nothing ever goes according to plan.' Wolf sighs and pushes his dirty hair out of his face. He looks genuinely irritated for a moment, but soon breaks into his usual grin. 'Fine. We'll follow the original idea and head to the Queen. Load up the bodies; she's never opposed to buying some meat.' He gestures to the truck with his bat. 'And I get to drive.'

With the tires changed, the bodies sliced up and piled in the back, and my injured hand half-assedly bandaged, we all squeeze into the seats up front. I'm squashed between Tank and the door, with my backpack on my lap – we found it stored in the back with all the other stuff.

Wolf, using the key taken off the dead guard, starts the truck. He grins at the obnoxious rumble of the engine.

'This is a big-ass truck,' he says, looking satisfied. *'Almost as good as killing people.'*

He slams his heel on the gas and the truck lurches forward, nearly throwing me out of my seat. The tires bump as if going over something heavy, and only then do I recall the guard beneath it. *Oops.* Probably best not to mention that.

Despite my exhaustion, it's impossible to sleep with the engine snarling and Wolf driving like a madman. The truck threatens to topple at every sharp turn, which only excites Wolf. I hold on for dear life and stare out the window, watching the wastelands go by.

XIV
The Queen of the Wastes

After we've been driving for a while I notice something strange: other vehicles. It's rare to see even one on the road, with gasoline so scarce, let alone this many. They come from all directions as smaller roads merge with ours. Some are big supply trucks like ours, while others are smaller jeeps and transports. A few are bulky, scary-looking war machines, crudely adorned with spiked tires and built-on weapons. One has a rotting body tied to the hood, a gruesome warning to all who see them coming.

'This is the crossroads,' Wolf yells above the engine. 'All roads lead to the Queen, they say.'

As the road thins, the vehicles are forced into a single-file line. Progress slows until we stop, forming a winding line outside of a gate. We end up boxed in by gigantic raider trucks.

'Couldn't someone attack us and steal all our stuff?' I ask, peering at the truck in front. I can barely see through their blood-streaked window, but I think someone turns to look back. I duck down quickly.

'I guess,' Tank says. 'Queen's protection doesn't apply until we're inside the gates.' Seeing the look on my face, he adds, 'You'd have to be crazy to try it, though.'

'Well, I've considered it,' Wolf says, 'so keep your guns ready, boys.'

So we do, and I keep a wary eye out the window, but nothing happens. The line inches forward until we reach the gate.

Wolf attempts to roll the window down; it jams, not budging. He hits it. Nothing happens. After a few tries, he shatters the window with his bat.

The gatekeeper barely blinks as glass rains down around him. He's an older man with a shaved head, a missing eye, and a big gun. He wears all black, with the emblem of a golden crown stitched messily onto the front of his shirt.

'Wolf,' he says, his expression souring.

'Been a while, eh?'

The man nods stonily.

'No trouble,' he says. 'You know the rules.'

'Yeah, yeah, and you know me . . . '

'No trouble. I mean it.' He waves us through.

Wolf drives considerably more carefully as we pass the gate. The Queen's place looms up ahead, growing steadily until I find myself in awe of its size. It's a giant building, one of the largest mostly intact ones I've ever seen. It must have been someplace fancy and important before the bombs dropped. Now chunks of it are crumbling, with sections of walls missing, windows broken, and paint coated in dust and rust. Old glamor still shines through in glints of gold and careful architecture. It's somehow both awe-inspiring and horribly sad. It also gives me a hint of the same nervousness Blackfort gave me, but I try to quash it with the reassurance that Wolf and the others trust this woman.

Wolf pulls into a vast expanse of space designated for vehicles. There are rows and rows of them lined up. The Queen's men wait on the edges of the lot, waving people in to organized rows and keeping an eye on everything. Wolf parks under the directions of one of them, and gives another truck a bump to the side that seems entirely intentional. The Queen's man scowls and flips us off. Wolf goes to talk to him as the rest of us wait.

'Wow,' I say, staring up at the monster of a truck parked next to us. 'Don't people worry about these getting stolen?'

'The Queen's men keep everything under control,' Tank says. 'They look after the vehicles and tally up your goods. If anything goes missing, the guards are responsible.'

'And what if the Queen steals 'em?'

'She can't,' he says. 'If she did, the whole system would fall apart. She needs people's trust.'

'I guess that makes sense.' The whole thing seems awfully organized for the wastelands, but I suppose the Queen has the power to do it. 'What's she like, anyway?'

'Oh, you'll see soon enough,' Tank says with a chuckle.

Pretty Boy sighs exaggeratedly, his face twisting in distaste. I wait for an explanation, but before they can speak, Wolf is back.

'All right,' he says. 'Business taken care of. Let's go see the Queen. Hopefully she has some nice presents for her old friends.' He grins and sweeps a look over us, pausing on Pretty Boy. 'You keep her nice and happy for me, got it?'

'As always.' Pretty Boy sighs, shakes his head, and walks toward the building. 'Lord, I need a bath and a woman ...'

'And a meal,' Tank adds as the rest of us follow Pretty Boy's lead. 'And some whiskey.'

'Some better bandages would be nice,' I say wistfully, looking down at my injured hand.

'You whiny bastards,' Wolf says, and laughs. 'Don't worry, we'll get everything we need. Safest place in the wastes, this is.'

We enter the building after the guards' approval. They don't allow the larger weapons into the building, but we're able to keep our knives and smaller handguns.

The room we step into is huge and mostly empty, with tall ceilings that make me feel very small. A massive set of double doors is directly ahead, with other doors to either side. Everything is very white, though that changes when we come in trekking dirt and blood. I'm painfully aware of how out of place we are in the clean room. We're all wearing torn, dirtied clothes and nursing multiple wounds. We look terrible, and probably smell worse.

And this place is trying so hard to be fancy. There are paintings on the walls, delicate-looking vases, even a few semi-crumbled statues. It's attempting to look elegant, but the decorations look strange with armed guards everywhere and dirty wasteland folk heading in and out of the building.

'Wait here,' says a guard. 'The Queen is coming to greet you.'

'Well, shit, makes me feel pretty special,' Wolf says.

'Doubt it's for you,' Tank says, and glances at Pretty Boy. 'Don't even start.'

'No need to get shy, lover boy.'

'I'm not her fucking—' Pretty Boy cuts off abruptly as the double doors swing open, and replaces his scowl with a very wide, very fake smile. 'Ah, the Queen herself. What a surprise!'

The Queen swoops in elegantly. She has a guard on either arm, both ruggedly handsome men with the crown icon stitched onto their clothes. I can't help but stare. She looks like someone who was once beautiful, and hasn't yet realized that beauty has long since faded. The wastelands age people fast, making their skin sun-spot and shrivel – but still, she looks *really* old. An overly lavish, too-long black dress hangs awkwardly on her thin frame. Heaps of gaudy jewelry adorn her neck and wrists, glinting and clanking as she walks, and her face is slathered with makeup. Her hard eyes remind me of the power she holds. As she draws closer I straighten up and smile politely with the others.

She throws her arms around Pretty Boy and plants a wet kiss on his cheek, leaving a red smear. The smile melts off his face and his lip curls in disgust, but he fakes another smile in the time it takes her to pull back and look at him again.

'Ahh, Wolf and the crew,' she says in a croaky voice. She speaks oddly, with some kind of lilting accent that sounds over-the-top and forced. She pats Pretty Boy on the shoulder before scrutinizing the rest of us. After a moment she erupts in an overly loud cackle, a sound that clashes with her pseudo-elegant appearance. The laugh soon descends into a coughing fit that lasts several seconds. Everyone waits for it to pass. 'It's been too long, darlings,' she says finally. 'Though I've been hearing an awful lot about you recently.'

'That so?' Wolf asks, pleased with himself.

'Sounds like you've been quite busy.'

'As always. Spreading joy and goodness around the wastes.'

'I bet you have.' She laugh-coughs again, and the sound grates on my ears. As if locking in on my discomfort, she turns her shrewd eyes to me. 'And this must be the new one I've been hearing such *interesting* rumors about.'

'Kid,' I introduce myself, trying not to crumple under the attention. 'And, umm, despite what you've probably heard, I'm a girl.'

'So you are.' She doesn't take her eyes off my face, and I squirm under the scrutiny. I scuff the heel of one boot across the floor, leaving a streak of dirt behind. 'Well, I can see why there was a misunderstanding,' she says, and cackles some more. I blush. 'A bath would do you some good. All of you, actually.'

She touches Dolly lightly on the arm. I expect Dolly to give her typical blank stare in return, but instead she smiles. Tank and Wolf receive only customary nods, and the Queen turns around with a swish of her dress.

She walks back the way she came, her bony hips swaying and her dress dragging on the tile.

'Clean yourselves up,' she says over her shoulder, with a wink at Pretty Boy, 'and I'll treat you to dinner. We can catch up then.'

The sound of the doors closing booms in the quiet room.

As soon as she's gone, Pretty Boy leans against the wall with a groan. Tank laughs and claps him on the shoulder. I feel a little overwhelmed. She swept in and out so quickly it was hard to get a read on her.

'She seemed even weirder than usual,' Pretty Boy says, shaking his head.

'Yeah, seems like the ol' hag is losing her marbles a bit,' Wolf says. 'But we need the supplies, so be a good boy and keep her happy. If that means spending the night with her, do it.'

'Let's hope it doesn't come to that.' He looks sickened by the thought. I sincerely hope it's not an actual possibility. Even with her age aside, the Queen seemed a little *off* somehow.

Wolf lets out a hearty guffaw and turns around. He sets off down one of the hallways leading out of the room.

'Well, you heard the lady. Let's go, boys. Kid, you go with Dolly. See you at dinner.'

I turn to Dolly to ask where we're going, but she's already walking away in the opposite direction of Wolf. I hurry to catch her. She walks quickly, so I have some trouble keeping up.

'So you know the Queen?' I ask. She glances sideways at me and doesn't say anything. 'You used to work for her or something, right?'

In response, she only speeds up. I fall behind despite my best efforts.

'Nice talking to you, too,' I grumble under my breath. I follow her around the corner and into one of the rooms.

Suddenly there are naked women everywhere.

And I do mean everywhere. There are at least a dozen people stuffed into this room, and not a single one aside from me and Dolly is fully clothed. The air is warm and steamy, but it doesn't actually conceal anything. I'm not sure if I should cover my eyes or run out of the room or what. Did we take a wrong turn? I freeze in place and stare down at my boots. Somehow no one else seems the least bit fazed by this, least of all Dolly.

She notices I'm not following her after a few steps, and turns to give me a confused look.

'Why isn't anyone wearing clothes?' I ask, dumbfounded.

'Bathing room,' she says, as if that explains everything. Now that I've gotten over the initial shock of excessive nudity, I can see the baths set up around the room. Still, it seems weird that everyone is so comfortable being naked.

Before I can ask any more questions, some of the other women notice Dolly. To my surprise, a lady with long red hair squeals and throws her arms around her like they're old friends. Two blondes who look like twins come over to say hello as well. Dolly smiles.

'Dolly! It's been ages!'

She nods silently, still smiling, her icy exterior thawing in their presence. The redhead's eyes slide to me.

'And is this your little friend?'

Dolly nods again.

'This is Kid,' she says quietly. 'Do not be alarmed, she is a girl.'

'Of course she is.' The woman walks over and tweaks my nose, which I would be more comfortable with if she was wearing a shirt. I try to keep my eyes on her face. She grins, showing a gap between her front teeth. 'I'm Ruby. And I don't see how anyone could mistake you for a boy, you're far too cute!'

'Really?' I've been mistaken for a boy so many times it almost feels odd to be called a girl.

'Of course! Not that I blame you for hiding; it's dangerous to be a girl in the wastes. But not here!'

She grabs my hand to pull me, and jostles my stubby once-finger. I yelp. She lets go instantly, an apology on her lips.

'Sorry,' I blurt out before she can say anything. 'I, umm, hurt my hand.' I hold it up to show her. She gently takes my hand for a closer look, murmuring sympathetic words.

'We can find help with that, too,' she says. 'But first, clean up.'

I don't really have a choice in the matter. The ladies strip me and dunk me into a big metal tub of water. I cover as much of my body as I can with my hands, but nobody even seems to pay attention to it. It seems it really is no big deal here, and after a few minutes I manage to stop feeling so self-conscious.

The baths are filled with river water heated by a fire. It's too hot at first, and I feel like I'm being boiled in it. Warm baths are an oddity to me. Both in the bomb shelter and in town, I made do with the occasional cold sponge bath. I find an actual bath less pleasant than expected. The sting of soap reminds me of every scrape and cut I had forgotten about, and many of my old scabs bleed freshly afterward.

After scrubbing my skin raw, the Queen's ladies give me fresh clothes: a dress. It's plain and nothing too frilly, but still painfully feminine for me. I can't even remember the last time my legs were bare. It makes me feel vulnerable to show my prickly stick-legs and scabby knees to the world. Dolly is coaxed into a dress, as well. Hers is even worse than mine, a white and puffy thing with a big bow on it. She really does look like a doll. Actually, she looks far more natural in it than I do.

Despite my discomfort, it's hard to complain when everyone is being so nice. Even when they take my familiar beanie and clothes, with the promise to return them after a wash, I keep my mouth shut. I don't let them take my backpack, though.

'So do you all work for the Queen?' I ask, uncomfortable while the blondes fuss over my hair and the redhead bandages my injured hand.

'That's right, miss,' Ruby says.

'What do you do?' I ask. She glances at Dolly and doesn't say anything.

'Look pretty,' one of the blondes deadpans.

'And sweet-talk,' her twin says.

'And *entertain*,' the other one adds.

Ruby winks. As it dawns on me, I feel my face heat up. They all burst into laughter, except for Dolly, who remains stoic.

As I walk with her to dinner, feeling weirdly clean, it hits me that Pretty Boy said Dolly used to work for the Queen. And she *knew* those women. And if they sell their bodies for a living, then . . .

My thoughts whir and tumble with that idea, and I have to force myself to act normal and keep my mouth shut as we walk to meet up with the others.

The boys are freshly washed and dressed as well, although it appears Wolf hasn't let anyone touch his dreadlocked hair. I resist the urge to swoon over Pretty Boy, with his hair still dripping wet and all the dirt washed off his handsome features. For once he notices me as well, doing a double take when he sees me.

'Wow, Kid,' he says. 'You almost look like a real girl.'

'Uh, thanks,' I say with a blush. It's pretty close to a compliment. He leans closer, smiling slightly, and I stare up at him with wide eyes.

'So, you had some freckles under all that dirt,' he says. 'Cute.' He raises a hand as if to touch my face, and I'm bright red between that and the fact he called me *cute*, but then Dolly walks directly between us and shatters the moment. Pretty Boy steps back, and so do I, and by the time she passes through it's gone. I blink uncertainly at the back of Pretty Boy's head as he turns to talk to Wolf.

There isn't time to dwell on that, though. I wait for the others to distance themselves and grab Tank's arm. Taking the hint, he slows down so the two of us fall behind the rest of the crew as we walk through the Queen's dwelling. The overly fancy decorations and endless doorways pass by in a blur.

'A while ago, Pretty Boy said Dolly worked for the Queen once?' I ask in a low voice. He nods. 'So when he said . . . did he mean Dolly used to be a . . . a . . . ?'

'Yeah,' he says in a quiet voice, not needing to say the word. My eyes go wide.

'B-But, that's so . . . *she's* so . . . ' I glance up at Dolly, who is oblivious to our conversation, and shake my head in disbelief.

'Weird, yeah. She's different now.'

'How did she go from that to *this*? Why'd she quit?'

'She, uh, got pregnant.'

'Dolly has a *kid*?' It takes serious effort to keep my voice down.

'No,' Tank says. 'Not anymore.'

It takes a few seconds to sink in. When it does, I let my grip on Tank's arm go slack. He pats me on the back and moves ahead to join the others. I lag behind, head reeling as I sort this new information into place.

I'm not given much time to process, because there's already new material flying my way. The room we enter next is huge and lavishly decorated and very, very white. The walls are painted white and adorned with paintings, the tile is white and clean, and the long dining table is covered in a lacy white tablecloth. I feel guilty entering the room. My very presence must dirty the place, even after having my first bath in months. I stick close to the others so I feel less out of place. They all look bored, but I stare around in amazement.

'This place always makes me want to break something,' Wolf mutters.

'Please don't,' says Pretty Boy.

'Aw, shut up.'

Moments later the Queen enters, wearing a new dress, this one a ridiculously puffy and lacy monstrosity that matches the red of her lips. She sweeps across the room with two guards shadowing her every step. One pulls her chair out. The Queen even sits in a grandiose way, gracefully falling into the chair and crossing one leg over the other. Wolf and the others sit across from her, and I hurry to follow suit. I catch myself sitting with my legs open, remember I'm wearing a dress, and hastily squeeze my knees together.

'I'm so happy you came to join me today,' the Queen says, batting absurdly long eyelashes.

''Course we made it,' Wolf says. 'It's free food, ain't it?'

'And we're *very* grateful,' Pretty Boy adds quickly, coaxing a smile out of the Queen.

Silent men set food before us, so much food I can hardly believe my eyes. I thought the crew had it pretty nice as far as food goes, but this is a *feast*. Along with heaps of white rice, there's a colorful selection of corn, peas, and other stuff I don't recognize. I avoid the beans and mix a variety of stuff together on my plate before digging in. I even try a weird little fish that Tank calls a sardine.

I notice out of the corner of my eye that the Queen makes one of her men taste everything before she eats it. Odd, considering it's her own food, but I'm too busy stuffing my face to care. The food is just too good, and there's so much of it.

The meal even comes with real plates and utensils. The plates are cracked and stained, but they look like they could have been nice once upon a time. I try eating with a fork, but when that gets too frustrating I grab two spoons instead and stuff my face like a starving animal.

'So,' Wolf says through a mouthful of food, 'I've got some questions.'

'Yes?' The Queen stops eating and raises her eyebrows at him. No doubt she notices that he's eating with his hands and making quite a mess of the fancy tablecloth, but she doesn't say anything.

'What the *fuck* is happening around here?'

Silence falls as the Queen stares at Wolf. I become very fascinated by my plate.

'I'm afraid I'm going to need more clarification.'

'Why's everyone out to get us all of a sudden? We were at, uh, one of those towns—'

'Blackfort,' Pretty Boy supplies.

'Right-o, that one, and they fuckin' arrested us the second we walked into town. And *then*, instead of hanging us, they said they was gonna transport us somewhere.' Wolf stuffs another bite of food into his mouth and leans back in his chair so it threatens to topple over. He points his slightly bent fork at the Queen, gesturing for her to speak. 'So ... what the fuck?'

'Ah,' she says. She delicately sets down her utensils and folds her hands on the table, her long nails stark red against the white tablecloth. 'Yes. I'm surprised you haven't heard yet. There's been a bit of an ... upheaval, so to speak. Times are changing, Wolf.'

'Changing how?' His voice lowers to a growl, as if he's offended that anything could change without his explicit permission.

'The return of law, and order, and authority,' she says. 'Or so he says.' Her lips twist, something dark flashing across her expression.

'*Who?*'

'He calls himself Saint.'

'Pff,' Wolf scoffs. 'Sounds like an asshole.'

'Law in the wastelands?' Pretty Boy asks. 'How?'

I keep eating and pretend not to pay too much attention to the conversation, but my interest is caught. I steal glances at the three of them between bites. Dolly and Tank seem content to stay out of it.

'Saint has secured a radio tower,' the Queen says, looking at Pretty Boy rather than Wolf. 'And from there he's managed to spread his message and solidify his control.'

'So he talks to the towns that way,' Pretty Boy says, and nods thoughtfully. 'That's why everyone's ready for us.'

'Yes, there's a description of your little crew out on the radio waves, and a hefty price on your heads. He's after sharks, and you're well-known enough for him to target you specifically.'

'But not to kill us?' Pretty Boy asks. 'They've been trying to capture us alive.'

'Yes, yes, for a reward. That's another part of what he's trying to do: trials and all, just like the old days, rather than shooting anyone straightaway.'

'And what's your take on all this?' Wolf asks, pointing again with his fork. The Queen turns to him, her thin lips pinched together. She glances at the utensil, then at his face, and smiles insincerely.

'You know me, Wolf. I stay neutral.'

'Well, we can't afford that.' He drops his fork and leans back in his seat again, placing his boots on the table. 'So what do we do then, eh?'

'What *can* we do?' I ask, unable to keep myself out of the conversation any longer. 'This seems bigger than us.' My place in the world has improved significantly since I started tagging along with Wolf and the crew, but the idea of going against someone like Saint still seems overwhelming.

'Nothing's too big when you've got enough explosives, Kid.' Wolf grins, suddenly confident and fierce.

'You want to blow the place up?' Pretty Boy asks, his eyebrows drawing together.

'Damn straight I do. I'll explode the shit out of it.'

'You want to blow up a radio tower,' he repeats slowly. 'That's your plan?'

'Seems like the most obvious solution,' Wolf says. Tank and Dolly nod along with him.

'Well, count me out.' Pretty Boy throws his hands up. 'I've signed up for a lot of crazy shit with you, but I'm not along for this.'

'Like shit you ain't,' Wolf says. I look back and forth between the two of them, a spoonful of food held halfway to my mouth.

'Who says it's such a bad thing, anyway? A little law in the wastelands? A world where our lives aren't threatened on a daily basis?' Pretty Boy shrugs. 'What's wrong with that?'

'People like us ain't got no place in a world like that.'

'People like *you*.'

'Oh, fuck you. You and your uppity bullshit. Just because you can play nice and pretend you ain't like—'

The Queen slams her silverware against her plate. The loud clang silences everyone. When she has our attention, she plasters on a sickly sweet smile.

'As lovely as it is to listen to you bicker,' she says, 'I'd prefer if you did not do it *here*.'

'Whatever, I'm done.' Wolf takes his feet off the table, and his chair comes down on the tile with a heavy thud. He stands, stretches, and sends the Queen a lazy mock salute.

'I'll expect compensation for what I've told you,' the Queen says coldly.

'Right, right. I've got a truck full of shit to trade. We'll work it out.'

He leaves, the sound of his footsteps echoing in the silence left behind him. When he slams the door shut, Pretty Boy quickly smiles at the Queen.

'Thank you for your hospitality,' he says, his politeness an abrupt change. 'Really, we appreciate it, though Wolf is too crude to say as much.'

The Queen waves a hand dismissively, still frowning. I glance at Pretty Boy and detect a hint of nervousness. If his sweet-talking isn't enough to win back the Queen's good mood, that can't be good.

'We'll be off to our rooms, then,' Pretty Boy says. 'No need to bother you any further.'

He stands up and pushes his chair in, and the others hastily follow suit. I scarf down a few more mouthfuls of food and scamper after them. As we leave the room I cast one last glance back at the Queen. She's still seated at the table, hands folded in front of her, head bowed so her face is obscured.

When the door shuts, we stop and look at each other.

'Well,' Tank says, 'let's hope Wolf is in a good enough mood to buy us some liquor.'

XV
Alcohol

Wolf is in a decent enough mood by the time we find him. He has plans to meet with the Queen soon, but tells us we're welcome to help ourselves to some booze in the meantime. The cost will be subtracted from whatever deal he works out with the Queen.

'None of the girls, though,' Wolf says, pointing a finger at Pretty Boy. 'They're expensive as shit, and we can't afford it right now.'

'Seriously?' Pretty Boy asks, looking pained.

'I mean it. We need the credit for big-ass explosives.'

Pretty Boy lets out a long sigh. Tank, I can't help but notice, looks similarly disappointed. I look away from both of them and try to push back my discomfort. I really don't want to think about either of them with the Queen's ladies . . . though for very different reasons.

Everyone cheers up soon enough when we get our hands on the booze. It's a big, plastic container with no label. The liquid inside is a deep red-brown.

'Ahh, cheap-as-shit whiskey, just the way I like it,' Tank

says. He takes a hearty drink and passes it to me. Just a whiff of it is enough to make my eyes water, so I pass it on to Pretty Boy, who plugs his nose and takes a swig. As soon as he swallows he starts coughing.

'Holy shit, worse than I remember,' he chokes out, and hands the bottle to Wolf with a grimace.

'As tempting as that is,' Wolf says, giving the bottle a sniff, 'I'm about to meet with the Queen, so . . . '

'Sounds like a good excuse to drink,' Tank says.

'Yeah, actually.' Wolf grins, raises the bottle in a cheers, and takes a long gulp. 'That's fucking disgusting,' he says, still grinning, and hands it back to Tank.

'You drinking, Kid?' Tank asks.

'Um, I don't think so.' From what I've seen, drunkenness never leads to anything good.

'Aw, why not?' Wolf asks. 'Loosen up.'

'I've never really drunk before.' The bottle ends up in my hands again, and I stare into it uneasily.

'I bet you'd never hung around sharks or shot someone before, either,' says Wolf. 'And look how far you've come!'

'Well, if you put it like that . . . ' It still doesn't sound appealing at all. But everyone is staring at me, so I figure it's worth a try. I raise the bottle and take a tiny sip.

The taste hits me like a truck. It's god-awful, and the burn in my throat is worse. I start choking as soon as it goes down and nearly drop the bottle. Pretty Boy grabs it out of my hand while Wolf slaps me on the back.

'Good girl, taking it like a champ,' Wolf says. I'm coughing too hard to answer. Eyes tearing up and throat burning, I wonder why the hell anyone would put themselves through this torture. Even when the burning recedes, I'm left with a nasty aftertaste. The heat in my belly is nice, though.

'Well, I better be off,' Wolf says. He snatches the bottle out of Pretty Boy's hands, takes another long swig, and lightly punches me on the shoulder. 'Have fun, guys. But not too much fun.' He pauses to whisper something in Dolly's ear, and he's gone.

'So now what?' Pretty Boy asks. He holds on to the bottle, taking small but frequent sips.

'Now we have fun,' Tank says, putting an arm around his shoulders and stealing the bottle from his hand.

We wander the Queen's mansion until we find a promising room. It's a big dining hall, but not as stiflingly luxurious as the one where we dined with the Queen. This room is more understated, with wooden tables and chairs adorned with crude carvings and stains. It's full of traders and raiders and other wasteland wanderers, many carrying bottles of liquor like us. It seems like this is the place to mingle. Some sit in small groups and speak in lowered voices, having the kind of conversations that stop whenever someone draws too close. Others seem much more relaxed. Cards and dice are strewn over the tables, with rowdy groups playing games and shouting at each other. Often it's hard to tell if they're having fun or about to break into a fight, but since there are no weapons out I assume the former.

We attach ourselves to one of the groups, which is playing some sort of card game. The guys play while I watch and try my best to follow. Dolly stands behind my chair and dutifully watches our surroundings. One man attempts to speak with her, and she responds with utter silence and a devastatingly cold glare. No one else tries to be friendly to her.

A whirl of noise surrounds me. I watch the game go by without understanding it, and listen to Pretty Boy chat with traders. He has a gift for striking up conversations, talking with strangers as if they're old friends.

'Hey, weren't you one of Big Ben's crew?' he asks the man to his left, a thick-necked, red-faced guy with a shaved head and facial piercings. 'Whatever happened to him?'

'Saint,' he says, spitting the word like a curse. 'Got a hold of him and most of the others a few weeks back.'

'Really? Damn.'

'Radio said they were all executed a few days later,' the man says, shaking his head. 'Fuckin' Saint. We can't touch anything as far up as Sniper's Gorge.'

'Well, shit. It's the same out in Blackfort,' Pretty Boy says. He pauses, looking thoughtful, and then lowers his voice. 'He's expanding fast. The Queen isn't threatened by it?'

'Maybe, maybe not,' the raider says. 'But between you and me, she ain't really in a position to do anything about it. Old bitch isn't doing so well. Especially with that cough she's got, and the way she's been acting . . . she's pretty fucked.'

Pretty Boy looks suddenly nervous, glancing around the room.

'Few months ago, one of her men might've shot you for saying shit like that,' he says finally, relaxing when it's clear nothing is going to happen.

'Heh, yeah. Few months is a long time.'

I hang on to the conversation, but when their talk turns to the game they're playing, I lose interest. With nothing else to do, I take small drinks from the bottle whenever it's passed my way. It never tastes *good*, exactly, but it seems a little less awful with each sip. Maybe I'm getting used to it, or maybe it's slowly killing my taste buds. Either way, I keep drinking and keep to myself.

It's interesting to observe what's happening around me when there's such a strange variety of people in the room. There are traders trying to sell their goods, men and women selling their services as bodyguards or bounty hunters, raiders like us enjoying a danger-free day. The Queen's women slip among them selling *their* wares, and from what I see, they're a hot commodity. I'm in no place to judge; everyone is trying to get by.

It feels so nice not to have to worry about danger or dehydration or where I'm going to sleep. The Queen's palace really does feel like a safe haven. I'm happy to sit and drink and let sleepy contentment wash over me.

I'm startled out of my little bubble when one of the men playing slams his fists down on the table. The illusion of peace shatters like glass. Conversation ceases as he rises from his chair. It's the man Pretty Boy was talking to earlier, and he's even more intimidating standing up, towering over everyone at the table.

He points a beefy and accusatory finger at Pretty Boy.

'You goddamn cheat!' he shouts, causing heads all around the room to turn. The circle of card players is tense and motionless aside from him.

'What are you talking about?' Pretty Boy asks. He doesn't cower away like I'd expect, instead staying in his chair and tilting his chin up to look the man in the eye. Maybe the liquor lent him some courage. The raider stares down at him, scowling, his face turning nearly purple with anger.

Behind us, I notice Dolly is holding a knife that I'm *sure* wasn't in her hand until a few seconds ago. She doesn't even raise her eyes to the standing man, but casually twirls it in her hand, a clear threat. He notices, and begins to sink back into his seat.

And then there's a gun in his hand. I can't even tell where he pulled it from. As my head jerks toward him, the world takes a few seconds to catch up. I may have had a bit more to drink than I thought. Maybe for that reason, it's hard to keep up with what's happening. All I know is within a few seconds, literally everyone has a gun in hand ... except me.

I clutch my bottle tightly and shrink down in my seat, wondering if I should slip under the table and hide.

'I didn't *cheat*,' Pretty Boy insists. Though he has a gun in hand, he's halfway out of his chair, as if he has yet to decide whether he wants to fight or run. He teeters, eyes flicking around the circle. 'And even if I did, what would it matter? We're just playing for fun, aren't we?'

Even with alcohol slurring his words, his go-to reaction is to try to talk himself out of trouble. I glance around to see if anyone is convinced, and find only unreadable faces. Aside from my friends, the other four men playing cards don't even seem to be together, and nobody is sure where to point their guns. One of them, looking absolutely baffled by the situation, rapidly switches the barrel of his gun between Pretty Boy and the other man.

The humor in the situation strikes me and, to my horror, I feel laughter bubble up within me. I can't fight it; no matter how serious the situation may be, it looks pretty ridiculous. I let out a loud laugh before I can stop myself, and slap a hand over my mouth.

Everyone's eyes move to me. Again I wish I could disappear.

The pierced man who started it all starts to grin, and then to guffaw. He slides his gun into the back of his pants and sits, gesturing for the game to continue. Everybody relaxes and the weapons disappear. The game resumes. In the aftermath I notice Pretty Boy surreptitiously slide a card into his sleeve. Tank reaches over and ruffles my hair, giving me his big, good-natured grin as he takes the bottle from my hands.

'Well, this feels lighter ... how much you been drinking, Kid?'

'Enough,' I say with a smile, and he laughs.

Soon I start to think perhaps it was more than enough. I grow more and more nauseous as the alcohol hits me. It's hard to focus on anything or talk to anyone. My vision blurs and spins, and everything looks hazy.

'I think I'm gonna go to bed,' I say eventually, not even sure who I'm telling. If I'm going to be sick, I don't want it to be here.

I push out my chair and stand, only to immediately stagger as the world tries to slide out from beneath my feet.

'Whoa.' I grab on to the nearest solid object for support. It turns out to be Dolly, who shoots me a confused look. 'Ah, sorry.'

'You all right, Kid?' Tank asks. He grabs my arm and steadies me.

'I'm fine. Just, uh . . . '

'Drunk,' Tank says.

'Yeah, maybe that.'

'How many fingers am I holding up?' he asks, raising a hand. I squint as my vision blurs.

'Is that a trick question?'

Tank chuckles.

'Really though, Kid, you can't just wander around here alone. It's not safe.'

I wave him away, shaking my head.

'I'm fine, I'm fine, I'm fine.' My nausea hasn't receded, and upchucking seems like a serious threat. 'I really gotta go.' I shake off his grip and slip away, making my unsteady way through the crowd. I accidentally bump into several people. Unfamiliar faces swim in the air around me, some angry and some amused. I wander through a cloud of sweet-smelling smoke that almost makes me gag. It feels like I'll never find the door with the whole room tilting and spinning. I can't even remember which direction I'm heading and where I came from.

Finally I find the door. I fumble with the knob before bursting into the open hallway outside.

As the door shuts behind me, it's like turning off all the sound with a switch. The quiet is instantly relieving. I pause to take a few deep breaths of air that isn't laden with the smell of sweat and alcohol and smoke. I want to curl up on the floor here, but the thought of a bed keeps me going. I only make it halfway down the hall.

'Hey, Kid, wait up!'

I turn toward the voice sluggishly, trying to find its source as the hallway lurches in my vision. It's a struggle just to stay on my feet. To my surprise, it's Pretty Boy coming toward me. His feet are almost as unsteady as mine.

'Hi?'

'Hi,' he replies with a crooked smile. He stands strangely close to me, his hand resting on my lower back. I don't understand. My mouth opens and shuts uncertainly.

I don't realize I'm moving backward until I hit the wall. I think maybe I stumbled, but then understand he must have pushed me there. His hands are on my hips all of a sudden, bunching up the fabric of my dress and exposing more of my legs. His face is very close to mine, his breath warm and heavy with liquor.

'What—' I start to say, and his mouth covers mine.

Getting kissed by him is not at all like I thought it would be. I've never been much for romance, but I know this is wrong. It feels wrong. It's too much, his tongue in my mouth and his hands all over me, his touch sloppy and rough. He tastes like that awful booze and it makes me nauseous all over again. His body presses hard against mine, but it doesn't make me excited like I'd expect. I feel like throwing up.

I stand there stiffly for a few seconds, not sure how to react, before placing my hands on his chest and pushing him away.

'What's wrong?' he asks, hands catching my wrists.

'Umm,' I say. I try to form an answer, but it's hard to even form thoughts. My brain feels hazy and my tongue clumsier than normal.

'I've seen the way you look at me,' he says, slurring his words. 'I know you want this.' He smiles, his eyes crawling down my body.

'I don't feel good.' I try to turn away, but his hold on my wrists prevents me from escaping. Nausea bubbles up through my stomach and into my throat. He leans close, letting go of my wrists and putting his hands on my body again.

I vomit all over him.

He releases me instantly, taking a step back and looking down in horror at the chunky mess.

'Holy fucking shit,' he says, his voice filled with disgust.

'I'm sorry,' I say. I just want to sit down and maybe cry. I turn away from him and walk in the direction I hope my room is in, but Pretty Boy grabs my shoulder and spins me around. I nearly fall over.

'I just want to go to bed,' I say, struggling to break free of his grip. 'Please, I don't—'

He shoves me back against the wall with a frightening force, knocking the wind out of me.

'S-Stop it!' I yell.

'You little bitch, you think you can—'

He stops. There's a knife at his throat. Moving very slowly, he takes his hands off me. He raises them in the air and the knife retracts.

It's Dolly. I'm not even sure when she got here, but I'm relieved she did.

'Don't touch her again,' Dolly says, giving Pretty Boy an icy look.

'I wasn't—' He gestures wildly, taking a step back. 'She was coming on to *me*—'

'Don't. Touch. Her.'

Dolly slashes near him with the knife. He stumbles and falls on his ass.

'This is bullshit,' he says. 'I didn't do anything.'

Dolly takes a step toward him and he scrambles backward on the floor. She turns to me next, and I try not to flinch under the coldness of her gaze even though it's not meant for me.

'Thanks,' I say, my voice shaky. 'I'm ... going to go to bed now.' I resume walking. After a moment Dolly falls in step beside me and taps me on the shoulder. She jerks a thumb in the opposite direction. I nod and turn. Dolly follows, and neither of us looks back at Pretty Boy as we head to our room.

As soon as we arrive, I go for my backpack and pull out my papa's blanket. Clutching it tightly and inhaling the familiar smell, I flop onto the bed face-first. I still feel sick and confused and upset, but I try to stifle it. When I look up, I find Dolly staring at me.

'Are you okay?' she asks.

'Yeah,' I say. 'Better since throwing up.' It's true, the world isn't spinning so much.

'That's not what I meant,' she says quietly.

'I'm fine.'

She blinks at me.

'Okay.'

'Okay,' I repeat, and turn away from her. Exhaustion swallows my whirring thoughts, and I fall asleep with my face pressed into my blanket.

XVI
Betrayal

When I wake up, my head is pounding and my whole body hurts. I taste old vomit in the back of my throat. A groan escapes me and I raise my blanket over my head, trying to will myself back to sleep. It takes me a while to realize the pounding sound isn't coming from inside my skull. Someone's knocking at the door.

Bleary-eyed, I lower the blanket and look around. The sunlight coming through the room's sole window is nearly blinding. I can barely see Dolly standing beside the doorway, a knife in her hand. I stare at her.

'What are you doing?' I ask croakily. It is way too early for her to have a knife already.

'Trouble,' she says.

'What? Why?' I sit up, wincing as my stomach rolls. 'Already?'

'Wolf isn't here. That means trouble.'

'How do you know he's not with—'

'He said he'd be here,' Dolly says, cutting me off. 'And he's not. Trouble.'

I'm really not in the mood to deal with trouble right now, but the knocking is insistent and Dolly seems pretty confident that some bad shit is about to go down. I drag myself out of bed, roll up my blanket, and grab my pack. I fumble around until I find my gun, and place the blanket inside.

'What kind of trouble?' I ask, glancing over my shoulder. Dolly shrugs. I stand up, reach to put my gun into the back of my pants, and stop as I realize I'm still wearing a dress. 'Aw, shit. There's no way I can fight in this.' I search around for my old clothes, but there's no sign of them.

'No choice,' she says.

I heave a sigh and nod. When she places a hand on the door, I hold the gun behind my back in what I hope is a subtle way.

The door opens.

Rather than a host of armed guards like I was expecting, I find myself greeted by the face of the red-headed woman I met yesterday: Ruby. She's wearing clothes this time, albeit scanty ones that strongly accentuate her womanly features. She shows her gap-toothed smile and holds up a tarnished silver tray.

'Brought you ladies some fresh water,' she says cheerfully, 'and your old clothes. Though you look much cuter in that, miss!'

I'm too tired to respond. Dolly puts her knife away and steps out from her hiding place behind the door. The red-head squeaks at her sudden appearance, but quickly covers her surprise with a smile.

'Hey there, Dolly.' She glances from her to me. 'You okay, miss? You look sick.'

'Hangover,' I answer hoarsely. I may not have experienced it before, but I've seen the symptoms enough times to be familiar with them. Now I understand why my papa hated being woken up in the morning.

'Well, drink up, that should at least help a little.' She sets the tray on the bed and gestures to the water. I pick one up. My mouth is as dry as the wastes, and the water looks tantalizing.

'Don't drink that,' Dolly says. She shuts and locks the door behind her.

'What? Why?'

Dolly doesn't answer, and advances toward the red-haired woman. The knife is in her hand again. Ruby retreats, raising her hands palms out.

'Whoa, Dolly! What are you—' She cuts off with a squeal as Dolly holds the knife to her throat.

'Where's Wolf?'

'I don't know what you're—' Dolly presses the knife closer, drawing blood and a whimper. The woman loses her composure, eyes filling with tears. 'T-The Queen has him! That's all I know!'

I gape dumbly, still holding the glass of water.

'What do you mean she has him? What's going on?'

'She betrayed us,' Dolly says.

'But she can't do that! Isn't she ... what do you call it? Neutral?'

'She's supposed to be.' Dolly glares at the woman. Her furious eyes are all the more frightening in her icy face. 'Why is she betraying us?'

'I don't know!' When Dolly's expression darkens, Ruby

starts to cry. Her tears leave gunky black trails down her face. 'I swear, that's all she told me! I was just supposed to come here, a-and act like everything was normal—'

'Please tell me there's not something wrong with the water,' I say, looking longingly at the glass in my hand. Ruby bites her lip and looks away. I sigh. 'Aww, man, I'm really thirsty . . .'

'Why?' Dolly asks.

'She didn't tell me!' She can barely speak through her tears.

'I think she's telling the truth,' I say, feeling a pang of sympathy. 'You're not going to kill her, are you?'

Dolly looks over to me, back at her captive, and pulls the knife away. The woman sinks to the floor, whimpering.

'No,' Dolly says. 'We need a hostage.'

'You really think that'll work?'

'Ruby is very valuable.'

'Dolly, you can't do this to me!' Ruby wails. 'This is crazy! Do you know how many guards the Queen has?'

'It doesn't matter.'

Ruby stares at her with wide eyes.

'What the hell happened to you?' she whispers. 'How did you end up like this? With *them*?'

Dolly ignores her. She turns and tosses a stack of clothes to me.

'Oh . . . right.' I turn my back to them and change into my normal clothes, trying not to think about them watching me. It's a huge relief to feel covered up again. Still, I shove the dress into my backpack in case I need it later.

'Dolly, you don't have to do this,' Ruby pleads. 'Just go to the Queen, I'm sure she'll take you back. And she can protect you from this . . . this . . . crazy shit!'

Dolly looks down at her, eyes ice-cold and pistol in hand.

'I don't need protecting anymore,' she says, and points the gun at Ruby's head. 'Stand up, hostage.'

When the woman doesn't comply, Dolly grabs a fistful of her hair and pulls her to her feet.

'Stop crying,' she commands. Ruby takes a few moments to compose herself, wipes her face with an already-dirty handkerchief pulled from the front of her shirt, and blows her nose. 'You will lead us to the boys' room,' Dolly says. 'And I will stay very close to you with my gun. You will not yell or raise any alarm.'

Ruby nods. Her lower lip trembles, but her eyes don't spill over again.

'Good,' Dolly says. She hesitates, and adds, 'I don't want to hurt you, but I will.'

Ruby says nothing. Dolly presses the barrel of the gun against her back, keeping it held low by her own hip so that it will be hard to spot. Ruby takes a deep breath and stands up straighter. She picks up the tray. Though the rest of her is well controlled, her hands shake, making ice clink against glass. The sound makes my mouth feel drier than ever.

Dolly nudges her with the gun and she starts walking. I shove my gun into the back of my pants, grab my pack, and follow them.

We make our way down the first hallway without trouble. But when we round the corner, we run into two guards standing in front of the doorway to the main hall. They exchange a glance and stare pointedly at Ruby. She slows as she approaches them.

'Good morning,' Ruby says. I can't see her face from where I'm standing, but I imagine it as fake-cheerful as her voice.

'Morning,' one says. 'Where you taking these two?'

'To see the Queen.'

'Why's that?'

'Her orders.'

They glance at each other again.

'Last I heard, her orders were—'

'They've changed,' Ruby interjects. I notice her make an effort to steady her hands on the tray.

A few tense moments pass. Finally one guard nods and opens the door, waving us through. Dolly carefully angles the gun to hide it from their sight as we pass. I smile at the man holding the door, and he squints at me suspiciously.

There are more guards in the main entrance, more than yesterday, and they all stare as we pass. Thankfully, none of them stop us. I'm sweating, perspiration spreading across my brow and beneath my arms. I try very hard to act normal as we cross the room, and find it increasingly difficult. It's like I forget how to walk normally as soon as I start paying attention to it, and awkwardly shuffle along behind Dolly, smiling weakly at every guard we pass.

We cross into another hallway. This one is empty of every-thing but a few paintings on the wall.

'Calm down,' Dolly tells me.

'Calm? I am calm.'

'Then why are you making that face?'

I drop my attempt at a smile and wipe a hand across my forehead.

'Did you see all those guards?' I whisper to her. 'We're so screwed.'

'We'll be fine.'

'How do you know?'

'We have a hostage. And the guards won't want to kill us.'

'They won't?'

'The Queen wants the reward. So, she wants us alive. Yes, Ruby?'

Ruby says nothing. Dolly pushes her forward and we resume walking. She stops in front of one of the last doors.

'Here,' she says. Dolly jerks her head in my direction. I nod, sidle up beside them, and knock on the door.

'Yeah?' Tank's voice comes from within. Relieved, I push through the door. Dolly and Ruby slide in behind me, and we shut the door behind us.

The first thing I notice is Pretty Boy, kneeling on the floor over a bucket. He doesn't look up, and continues retching into it with an unpleasantly wet noise. He seems to have cleaned the vomit off his shirt, at least. Tank is crouching beside him and patting him on the back. He looks bleary-eyed, but not ill like Pretty Boy.

My cheeks color as broken memories of last night dart through my mind. My stomach churns, and I try not to let my eyes linger on Pretty Boy for too long.

'What's going on?' Tank asks, noticing Dolly's gun and Ruby's terrified expression. He straightens up and puts on his tough face. 'Who's that? Where's Wolf?'

'We're in trouble,' Dolly says flatly, ignoring his questions.

Tank stops asking them. With a resigned and entirely unsurprised expression, he leaves Pretty Boy's side and lifts his heavy-looking bag onto the bed. He starts pulling out weapons and laying them on the bed: a crowbar, a gun, and a few knives of various sizes.

'So what are we gonna do?' I ask. 'We can't actually fight them, can we?'

'Not much of a choice,' Tank says.

'You've got to be kidding me,' Ruby says. 'Do you know how many guards the Queen has?'

'A lot, I'd bet,' Tank says. He shoves the gun into the side of his pants and a sheathed knife through one of his belt loops.

'You people are insane.'

'We get that a lot,' Tank says cheerfully.

Someone knocks on the door.

Everybody freezes in place, even Pretty Boy leaning over his bucket.

'Yeah?' Tank calls out after a second.

'A message from the Queen,' a man's voice comes from outside.

Tank and I draw our guns. Then there's a lot of nudging and whispering and meaningful glances as we try to decide who should open the door. Eventually Dolly pushes Ruby forward. She hesitates, gives Dolly a long, searching look, and slowly swings the door open.

'Ruby?' The man outside, a broad-shouldered and grim-faced guy wearing the Queen's emblem, looks confused. 'What are you—' His eyes slide past her and spot the rest of us. He reaches for his gun.

The second his hand is on the holster, Dolly and Tank fire simultaneously, reacting faster than I would have thought possible. The bullets whiz just past Ruby's head and bury into the guard. One only skims him, but the other, likely Dolly's, goes through his left eye.

The body falls. Ruby screams, loud and horrified like someone who's never seen a man die before. The quiet that follows makes me realize how loud the gunshots and screaming must have been.

'So much for subtlety,' Tank says. He bends down, grabs Pretty Boy, and throws him over his shoulder like a sack of meat. 'Gotta move, now!'

'No,' Pretty Boy says, struggling frantically. 'No no no no, just leave me here, I'll meet up with you guys later and . . .'

Tank neither acknowledges his words nor makes any move to set him down.

'What's the plan?' I ask. Dolly grabs Tank's pack and the gun off the dead man.

'Find Wolf,' Dolly says. 'Kill everyone in our way.'

'I like that plan,' Tank says. 'Shoot anything that looks dangerous. Don't hold back, Kid.'

'Me?' I gulp and nod. 'Got it!'

'Good. Let's go.'

We move out, guns ready. Tank carries a complaining Pretty Boy over his shoulder. No guards are in this hallway yet, although the curious faces of other guests poke out of rooms to see who's shooting who. A few guns point at us out of narrowly cracked doors. We rush past them and through the door to the main entrance room.

There are six guards here, all of them armed, and they stop abruptly when they see us.

Dolly holds her gun to Ruby's head, yanking the woman against her so she can't escape. She says nothing, but her hard stare communicates the message well enough.

'Where the hell is Wolf?' Tank asks, his face hard.

The guards hesitate for a split second. Then one raises his gun, and Tank opens fire. I take his cue and do the same, firing wildly in the general direction of the guards. The sound of gunfire booms in the huge, empty space of the room, filling it all the way up to its sky-high ceilings. One guard stumbles into a wall and slides down, leaving a streak of red on the white surface. Another goes down with a bullet to the chest, and a third is incapacitated by a hit to the leg. Three down, but we're not fast enough to kill the others in time.

Our group scatters as they return fire. I dive behind the nearest statue and crouch there. Bullets bite into the already-crumbling marble, sending chunks crashing to the floor. Dolly shoves Ruby aside and drops to the ground, firing back at the man with his gun trained on her. Her bullet splits his forehead before he can loose another round. Tank drops Pretty Boy on the floor and charges the remaining two guards. He rips the gun out of one's hands and smashes him over the head with it. The guard reels and falls; Dolly shoots him the second he moves to stand.

One left. I level my sights on his head. Our eyes meet for a moment, and his mirror the fear I'm feeling. I hesitate. Before I can react, the man turns and fires at Tank. Tank jolts and stumbles, obviously hit – but runs forward again, heedless. He grabs the last standing guard by the throat and lifts him up with terrifying ease. He slams the man into a nearby statue, and skull hits marble with a *crack*. The sound echoes sharply. Tank smashes the man's head against the statue once, twice, three times, and lets the body slump to the floor.

The last remaining guard is still on the floor and clutching his leg with one hand. He points his gun in Tank's direction, his hand trembling. After only a moment he lets it drop and raises both hands in surrender.

The room is still.

I creep out from behind the statue, which is now missing half its head. The one Tank was using as a weapon is dripping blood, and all the paintings are splattered with red and bullet holes. The white tile shows every splotch of blood and brains. A pool is leaking out from the man with the bashed-in head, collecting in the cracks between the tiles and slowly spreading across the floor.

Dolly climbs to her feet, brushing herself off. She points her gun at Ruby without even glancing in her direction. She freezes where she is. Tank leans against a wall, breathing heavily.

'I am way too hungover for this,' Pretty Boy groans from the floor, clutching his head. He doesn't seem to have moved since Tank dropped him.

'Are you okay, Tank?' I ask. I step over a couple of bodies on my way over to him and pause to take the gun from the still-living guard, who cringes away and makes no move to stop me. 'You got shot, didn't you?' My stomach knots with guilt. If I had taken that shot, I could've prevented it.

'No big deal,' he says. 'Guy was scared, missed anything vital.' He holds up his arm and shows me the hole in it, up near his shoulder. I wince. 'Clean through, no problem.'

'Wow,' I say earnestly. 'You're so brave.'

'Nah, just been shot a lot.' He smiles at me, but his face hardens again instantly as he turns to the remaining man. He walks over and shoves the barrel of his gun into the cowering man's face. 'Where's Wolf?'

'W-With the Queen,' the man answers quickly, not even trying to act tough.

'*Where?*'

He doesn't answer, but looks at the huge set of double doors directly across from the entrance door.

'Okay,' Tank says. He shoots the man in the head.

Ruby lets out a loud sob. I realize with a guilty twist in my gut that I'm not even bothered by things like that anymore. I've grown used to it, mostly. Maybe I couldn't shoot a man while looking him in the eyes yet, but a random death no longer has any effect on me. I guess I really am becoming one of them: a raider, a shark. For a second I feel conflicted, but a swell of pride overwhelms the uncertainty.

Tank turns to the big set of double doors. He yanks on the handle, but of course it's locked. He raises one leg and gives it a hard kick. The room booms with the noise, but the door barely moves. He stops and stares at it contemplatively, scratching his head.

'Well, I'm out of ideas,' he says.

'What do we do?' I ask. I catch myself looking around for Wolf before remembering he's not here.

'Move,' Dolly says from behind me. I take one look at

her and scamper out of her way. Tank doesn't take long to follow.

She opens fire the second we've moved, an assault rifle jetting out a stream of bullets. I instinctively duck behind one of the barely intact statues. I peek out at the door from my hiding place, watching as bullets pepper the wood. At first they don't seem to have much effect, but as Dolly unloads relentlessly, holes start popping up. Soon bullets shred the wood like paper, making the doors look more and more flimsy. She doesn't stop until she runs out of bullets. The doors look worn down, but they're still standing. She reaches for a second gun. Tank stops her.

'I got this,' he says. He walks over to a statue, crouches down low, and lifts it off the ground with a grunt of effort. Obviously straining, he waddles over to the doors. He plants his feet, pulls the statue back, and swings it forward like a battering ram. It blows through a whole chunk of the already-weakened wood. A second blow makes half of one door fall, leaving an entrance big enough for any of us. Tank drops the statue, and bits and pieces of marble break off as it thuds to the floor.

'There we go,' Tank says triumphantly. I creep out and peek through the hole, but not much of the room is visible. All I can see is an expanse of empty white tile. I'm too afraid to actually stick my head through.

The others seem similarly hesitant about stepping in, but soon we don't have a choice. The sound of footsteps and voices comes from first one, and then the other door, and then from the entrance as well. Guards are coming, and a lot of them. The only way out is forward. Tank drags an unwilling Pretty Boy up from the floor and pushes him through, and the rest of us file in one by one, Dolly dragging Ruby along at the rear.

We step into the Queen's throne room.

It looks like a much, much larger version of the entrance room, with the same stark white tile and pompous decorations. I notice, with a sense of baffled amusement, that all of the decorations here are obviously modeled after the Queen. The numerous statues and busts bear a striking resemblance to her, minus the wrinkles and other not-so-appealing parts, and the paintings depict her posing dramatically and dressed in her over-the-top fashion. Several of them are done in a crude mockery of older styles, mimicking other paintings I've seen in the building. Even I can tell they're pretty poorly done. They're embarrassing to look at.

'Well, well, well,' comes the Queen's voice, and I tear my eyes off a disturbing half-naked portrait of her to face the real thing. She's seated on her throne at the head of the room. There's a huge painting behind her, showing a younger version of her swathed in a fancy dress and sitting on a golden throne much larger than life. The real Queen seated on her real throne, a rickety old wooden chair, looks sad in comparison, like a balloon with all of the air squeezed out.

Next to her, suspended upside down, is Wolf. He's all tied up, ropes holding his wrists and ankles together, and another keeping him swinging a couple of feet off the ground. The rope is attached to a hook on the wall that must have been made for this very purpose. There's a huge bruise across his cheekbone and dried blood around his nose, but he doesn't seem seriously injured. He groans when he sees us.

'You idiots *would* barge right in here,' he says. 'And what the hell is the plan now, dumbasses?'

As if on cue, a ring of guards surrounds us. They emerge from behind plants and statues, from the corners of the room where the dim lighting made them hard to notice, from everywhere. I turn back to where we came from, but within seconds the room behind us is full of more guards. They step through the hole we made and force us into the empty space in the middle of the room, right in front of the Queen and her throne. There are dozens of them, all with guns trained on us, and most of them have weapons bigger than ours. Pretty Boy immediately raises his hands in surrender. The rest of us hesitate, turning around and trying to figure out where to point our weapons. There are too many targets to choose from. I finally settle on one man directly ahead of me and aim at the center of his forehead. My hands don't shake, though my heart is pounding.

This time, I won't hesitate.

'Give it up,' the Queen says. Her lips are curled to the side in a smirk, her long fingernails tapping against the armrest of her throne. 'You know you don't have a chance.' She folds her hands on her lap and smiles an irritatingly self-satisfied smile.

'You betrayed us,' Dolly says. I glance at her; her fingers are clutching her gun so tightly that her knuckles are turning white. The Queen turns to her, still smiling.

'Of course I did,' she says. 'Saint's new world is coming whether you like it or not, and I intend to survive in it. A partnership with him is exactly what I need to start my new life.'

Wolf starts to laugh.

'Start your new life,' he says mockingly between laughs. 'I think you mean desperately attempt to stay relevant.' He grins at her. 'And if you think you can take us in alive,' he says, 'you seriously fucking underestimate us, bitch.' One of the Queen's men hits him across the face with his gun. It looks and sounds like it hurts, but Wolf only continues to laugh.

'He's right,' Tank says. 'You can let us go, or you can kill us. We ain't gonna let anything else happen.'

'Wait a second,' Pretty Boy says. 'I didn't agree to—'

Tank elbows him to shut him up. The Queen locks her eyes on Pretty Boy and smiles.

'Oh, darling,' she says in a voice that makes my skin crawl. 'I don't intend to lump you in with the rest of them, you poor thing. Come here, I'll keep you safe.' She spreads her arms wide and beckons to him.

Cold dread grows in my belly. I can't bring myself to look at Pretty Boy. He'll take the deal, I know he will. Anything to save his own skin, as he's demonstrated time and time again. Everything is falling apart. The Queen has Wolf, and soon she'll have Pretty Boy, and then what do we have left?

Not a chance.

'Don't do it, man,' Tank says quietly. I finally dare a glance at Pretty Boy. He looks like someone who was staring down a shotgun barrel and just realized it's out of bullets.

'Well,' he says, 'your highness, I've always . . . ' He takes a step forward. Tank reaches out to grab his arm. Pretty Boy pauses for a second, the two of them exchange a look, and Tank lets him go. He takes another step toward the Queen.

An explosion shakes the building. Silence falls, and everyone freezes in place. This room is still intact, but it sounded close.

'What the actual *fuck* was that?' the Queen asks in a low growl, dropping both her dramatic flair and her accent. She gestures impatiently to her closest guards, who rush out through the double doors we destroyed. The rest of her men stir uneasily. The Queen only sits up straighter and glares at us, her composure returning. 'Whatever you sharks are trying to pull, it's not going to work.'

'What are we trying to pull?' I whisper to Tank. He shrugs. I look at Dolly, who also shrugs. 'Did we do that?' More shrugs.

Wolf is laughing again.

'I tried to tell you, your *highness*,' he says mockingly, 'that this would backfire on you. Everyone knows you've been losing it, and the second you turned on us, broke your own rules, you were bound to—'

'Shut up,' she snaps. 'And secure the rest of them. What are you idiots doing?'

The Queen's men close in around us. We pull into a tighter knot, all back-to-back. Dolly yanks Ruby closer to her and jams her gun into the side of her head. Ruby closes her eyes, trembling.

'Don't move any closer,' Dolly says.

'Oh, Dolly, sweetie,' the Queen says with a grating, half-coughing laugh. She lazily waves a hand at her men. Two of them immediately open fire. Before anyone can react,

Ruby's body is littered with bullet holes. Her body goes limp in Dolly's grip. When she lets go, Ruby falls to the floor. Dolly stares down at her, shock evident on her normally blank face. I realize she must have never actually intended to kill Ruby, let alone get her killed by the Queen. It's enough to crack her usual cool composure.

Dolly's expression turns to sheer, naked rage and she lunges forward. She fires three bullets with deadly precision, taking down the guards in front of her so she can burst out of the circle. She dodges another man who tries to grab her, slips between two coming at her from opposite directions, shoots another guard in the hand so he drops his gun. The barrel of her gun points directly at the Queen's shocked face. But before she can fire, two guards take her down. One wrestles the gun out of her hand and the other keeps her pinned to the floor.

Dolly screams. It's a wordless sound of pure hate and rage. The room magnifies it so the sound hurts my ears and echoes disturbingly in the quiet that follows.

The Queen's eyes are wide, her mouth slightly open – but she recomposes herself.

'Hold her,' she says to the guards, flapping a hand at them. 'And get the others.'

Tank rushes forward at the line of the Queen's men, trying to shove past them and get to Dolly. They latch on to him on every side and take him down. I try to cling to Pretty Boy's arm, knowing the Queen's men won't hurt him, but they yank me away. A man takes my gun and holds my arms behind my back. All I can do is wriggle helplessly.

'M-My Queen!' I turn my head to see that one of the

men who left to investigate the explosion has returned. He's clutching his side. A trail of blood snakes out the door behind him. 'They're rioting! T-They're killing us, taking the girls, looting the place . . . You need to send more men! A lot more!'

'Who?' the Queen asks, her eyes blazing and her fists clenched. 'Who dares—'

'Everyone!'

XVII
The Escape

Noise floods the room. The Queen shouts orders and her men rush to obey, some running out to rein in the chaos outside and others fortifying the doors we busted down. The Queen's orders are followed without question, but her men look nervous. There's a hesitancy to their movements, an uncertainty in their expressions. It's obvious they haven't dealt with anything like this before.

The guard holding me is distracted by the mass confusion. His grip on my arms slackens, and as he turns to look at the door I wriggle out of his grip and dart away. He shouts, but no one pays attention. They have much bigger problems; namely, the rioting is already overflowing into this room. I hear shouting at the entrance, and gunfire, but catch only glimpses of the action. Mercenaries, raiders, townies, traders, wastelanders of all sorts are fighting, taking down the Queen's men. It's no organized attack. I see raiders attacking other raiders, and the Queen's men fleeing or ripping off their incriminating emblems. Soon everyone is fighting everyone. I see the pierced-up man from last night deep in the fray, along with plenty I don't recognize. The guard really meant it when he said *everyone*. Rioting must have swept through the building like a wave as soon as people heard and saw us fighting the Queen's men.

It's the nature of the wastelands: If you smell blood, it's time to fight.

Gunfire and shouting and dying surround me. A bullet narrowly misses my head and pings into the wall. I duck behind a fake potted plant for shelter. Within seconds, a burly man picks it up and walks away with it, leaving me without cover again. I crouch down and scoot along the wall. Luckily, most people are too busy shooting someone or getting shot to notice me. I don't even have a gun, but I do have my trusty knife, which I take out for comfort's sake if nothing else.

Unable to spot the others, I move toward where Wolf was hanging. I find the Queen standing beside him. She looks remarkably out of place in her flowing dress and excessive makeup, and she doesn't have the usual gaggle of guards around her. Most of her men are already immersed in the fight. I creep closer, scuttling between potted plants and statues.

The Queen is still yelling orders like 'Contain this mess' and 'Kill them already' and 'Do something, you idiot,' but nobody seems to be listening anymore. Wolf, meanwhile, is swinging from side to side and wiggling like a very determined worm. It doesn't seem to be accomplishing much. Neither of them notices me.

The Queen starts to pace, wringing her hands.

'Idiots, idiots, all of them,' she says. There's a crazy gleam in her eyes, breaking through her grandiose attitude. 'I merely ask them to secure a few sharks, and then this mess . . . '

'Instant karma!' Wolf says cheerfully, still swinging.

'Shut up. Just 'cause I can't kill you doesn't mean I won't maim you.'

'Likely get a price reduction for missing parts, though, eh?'

'I can think of a few that shouldn't be necessary.'

I attempt a somersault to a nearby potted plant, and accidentally smack my face into the clay pot instead. I freeze there, feeling like an idiot and sure someone must've heard the noise, but nobody reacts. I duck behind the pot with a hand over my smarting nose. Once I determine I'm not bleeding, I peer through the rubbery leaves of the fake plant. The Queen's back is turned to me. None of her men are looking toward me, either. Everyone is too focused on the brawl.

I crawl out from behind the plant and toward Wolf. He finally notices me as I draw closer. He stops swinging, glances at the Queen's back and then at me again.

I check to make sure I still haven't captured the attention of the Queen's men and find them distracted by a new problem: Dolly, who somehow broke free and gained a gun again. As the nearby guards rush to stop her, I stand and use my knife to saw at Wolf's bindings. I manage to free his hands and am trying to figure out the best way to cut him down when the Queen notices me. Her eyes go wide, her thin upper lip curling back into a snarl.

'What the fuck do you think you're doing?' she shrieks. I frantically saw at the ropes holding Wolf, but before I can finish, the Queen shoves me. I stumble away from Wolf and fall to the floor. 'You little bitch. Don't interfere—'

I lunge forward and stab my knife into the trailing fabric of her dress. I expect to just tear through it and hit the floor, but instead my blade sinks into flesh.

The Queen screams. I scream, too, in surprise, and yank my knife back to find it covered in blood. Oh God, I just stabbed her in the foot.

'Guards!' she screeches.

Two men disentangle themselves from the rioting and turn to come after me. I scoot away as fast as I can on all fours and duck behind my trusty plant again, only to turn around and realize both guards are already dead.

Dolly makes her determined way toward the Queen, gun raised. The Queen, swearing and hobbling, melts back into a crowd of guards.

Dolly takes a step forward, ready to plunge in after her.

'Wait!' I yell, stepping out from behind the plant. 'Wolf needs help!' She stops, still staring after the Queen. Finally Dolly turns to face me. Her face is once again a blank slate. She looks up at Wolf and raises her gun, aiming at the rope holding him.

'Hold up,' Wolf says. 'Hold on one goddamned—'

She shoots through it, and he falls to the floor with a heavy thud. He groans and sits up, rubbing his head.

'God damn it, I hate you guys sometimes.'

I help untie his wrists. He does his ankles himself, stands up, cracks his neck, and stretches his arms. Dolly hands him my gun as he checks out the chaos around us.

'This all makes a lot more sense when I'm not looking at it upside down,' he says. 'Now, where are the others?'

Dolly raises an arm and points. Tank is clearly visible in

the middle of the chaos, towering above everyone. He has a metal pipe in hand and is swinging it wildly, taking people out left and right, guards and rioters alike.

'And Pretty Boy?' I ask. I don't see him anywhere.

'Screw Pretty Boy, let's leave 'im. He was about to finally stab us in the back anyway,' Wolf says.

'But—'

'We need him,' Dolly says. Both Wolf and I stare at her in surprise. A lightbulb seems to go off for Wolf.

'Ahh,' he says. 'I see.'

'See what?' My lightbulb remains dim. They ignore me and move in Tank's direction. Dolly pauses to shoot a few guards who take notice of us, and soon enough we're safely immersed in the insanity. I stick close behind Wolf while Dolly covers us. We don't attract too much attention. Everyone is too focused on their own goals. I see a pair of raiders playing tug-of-war with a blood-splattered painting, and a mob surrounding a screaming man who is probably one of the Queen's men, and plenty of other nasty things. There seems to be an attitude of general revelry among the rioters, while the guards are all terrified.

We hack our way through the crowd to Tank, who looks a bit too happy to be smashing some poor raider woman's head in. When Wolf grabs his arm, Tank whips around and raises his crowbar. He narrowly stops himself from hitting Wolf.

'Oh, hey there, guys,' he says, his scary war face relaxing into a smile. 'Come to join the fun?'

'Not this time. We're getting out of here.'

'Aww . . .'

'I know, I'm disappointed, too,' Wolf says. 'This is a hell of a brawl. But we gotta do the smart thing for once.'

'All right,' Tank says with a sigh. 'But ... where's Pretty Boy?'

We all pause to look around. Unsurprisingly, there's no sign of him amid all the action. He could've run to the Queen for safety, but seeing as we just came from that direction, it doesn't seem likely. Finally Dolly raises a hand and points. He's in a corner of the room outside the thick of the brawl, cowering and half-hidden behind a broken statue. When he sees us approaching, he shrinks back.

'Get the fuck away from me!'

'No can do,' Wolf says. He grabs him by the arm and drags him out. Pretty Boy fights as much as he can, trying to dig his heels into the tile and yank his arm free, but it barely slows Wolf. We head for the entrance room and have nearly made it out when a small group of guards intercepts us. There are five of them, their uniforms torn and bloodied.

'Don't move!' one says. He keeps his gun trained on Wolf. 'Didn't think we'd lose track of you, did you?'

'Nah,' Wolf says. Looking completely composed, he holds his gun to Pretty Boy's head. He stops struggling and sucks in a startled breath. 'But you're gonna let us past, or I'll blow his brains out.'

My lightbulb finally crackles to life. Of course we need Pretty Boy; the Queen wants him. The guards must be well aware of that, because they look worried.

'Not even a shark would kill his own,' one says, but his voice wavers uncertainly.

'Oh yes he would,' Pretty Boy says quickly, his voice

high-pitched with nervousness. 'He definitely would, he'd love to, please don't give him an excuse!'

Seeing the guards' hesitance, Wolf takes the opportunity to move past them. Tank shoulders a few guards out of the way as he moves by, and I stick close behind him. The Queen's men look at each other uncertainly, clearly at a loss about what to do without orders. Before they can decide, we rush by and into the entrance room. Wolf lowers his gun but keeps a tight grip on Pretty Boy's shirt.

Dolly opens the front doors to find a line of guards standing right outside. They open fire without bothering to check who's coming out, and she slams the door shut. Bullets *thunk* against the other side.

'Goddamn,' Wolf says. 'Guess we'll have to use the back way.'

'And then what? We don't have the truck anymore!' Pretty Boy says.

'Yeah, well, we'll have to figure something out.'

'But,' Dolly says, 'the only thing out the back way is—'

'Shh!' Wolf holds up a hand and everyone shuts up. From the throne room I hear the Queen's voice yelling orders to come after us. Either she's starting to gain control of the situation again, or she's decided to drop all else and follow us.

'Run,' Wolf says. He shoves Pretty Boy at Tank, throws open the door to one of the hallways, and starts sprinting. Dolly takes off after him, and Tank is soon next with Pretty Boy in tow. I follow along doggedly.

The hallway we run through looks completely different than it did last night. The place is utterly destroyed. Most doors are hanging open or ripped off their hinges. Others are closed, and horrible screaming comes from inside one of them. We run past the room where we all played cards and drank, and inside is a complete bloodbath. I narrowly dodge a bottle that flies out of the doorway, and don't pause to see who threw it. I trip over the body of a poor half-dressed woman and nearly gag when I see her mutilated face. We ignore any jeering challenges or cries for help, and just keep running.

At the end of the hallway, Wolf throws open a door and we find ourselves outside. We're behind the building now. It's completely empty, just an expanse of flat ground and then ... a cliff.

'The only thing back here is the river,' Dolly says.

'Well, shit, you couldn't have said that earlier?' Wolf says. He curses, looks around, scratches his head, and turns back to go through the door. The second he opens it, we can see the hallway inside flooding with guards. He hastily closes it again and backs toward the edge of the cliff. 'Fuck. We're fucked.'

They shoot down the first few guards to exit, but soon a crowd of them rushes through and there are too many targets. We keep backing up as they approach. Tank releases Pretty Boy to focus on shooting. After a moment's hesitation, he stays with us.

Soon we're at the very edge of the cliff. The river roars below as the Queen's men approach from the front.

Wolf swings his gun from side to side, unable to decide where to aim. I have only my knife, which I brandish uselessly. Next to me, Pretty Boy is getting the panicked look that usually means he's about to take off running. This time he has nowhere to go. He takes a step back and the ground beneath him crumbles. As earth starts sliding down the cliffside he pinwheels his arms frantically, trying not to meet the same fate.

I drop my knife and grab his arm with both hands.

'Got you,' I say, only to feel my own feet start to slip. I sit down in a desperate attempt to ground myself, and keep sliding. 'Oh shit—' I try to dig my feet in, but the dirt slips out from under me. As Pretty Boy's feet go over the edge his weight yanks me forward. Not a second too late, Tank's strong arms grab my waist and hold me up.

'D-Don't let go!' Pretty Boy yells, his feet dangling off the edge. He looks down at the river far below, and his eyes grow even wider. 'Holy shit!' I cling to him as best as I can, but I can feel his hand slipping out of mine. My injured hand hurts like hell, and the bandages make it hard to get a good grip.

'No! Pretty Boy!' I'm losing my hold. He closes his eyes, whispering what might be a prayer under his breath. 'I can't—'

A hand shoots out from beside me and grabs Pretty Boy's arm.

'I've got ya. Fucking idiot.'

I look up to see Wolf. When he nods, I gratefully release my grip and let Tank pull me back to solid ground. Panting for breath, I hurriedly pick up my knife again when I remember the Queen's men are still there. Tank and I keep them at bay while the others pull Pretty Boy to safety.

'Be *careful*,' the Queen says, looking immensely relieved to see her favorite pet unharmed. She wields a shotgun as she approaches. 'No need to panic, I'm not going to kill you.'

''Course not. Then you wouldn't get the reward, ain't that right?' Wolf asks. 'Fucking hell, so much for you being an impartial trader.'

'I told you before, Wolf. Times are changing,' she says. 'Saint is a reasonable man. Maybe he won't even kill you. I'm sure you can work out some sort of deal.'

But Wolf has stopped listening. He turns his head to look back at the river, and a thoughtful look passes over his face.

Next to him, Pretty Boy stands up, chest still heaving after his near fall.

'Thanks, Wolf,' he says breathlessly.

'No problem, buddy,' Wolf says, and shoves him off the cliff.

Silence. Everyone stares at Wolf, who looks remarkably pleased with himself.

'Man, that felt good,' he says.

'W-What just . . . ?' I ask, stunned. 'What did you—'

'After that whole mess, *now* you decide to kill Pretty Boy?' Tank says, his voice shaking. 'Jesus, Wolf, that's *fucked-up*!'

The Queen, recovering from her shock, howls in anger. Her men hesitate, awaiting a command.

I turn and peer over the cliff's edge, searching the roaring waters for any sign of him. There's nothing but water, churning white and frothy as it rushes by. Yet after a few moments, I see something: a head, bobbing downstream.

'Hey!' I shout, watching the figure flail and fight in the rapidly moving river. 'He's okay!'

''Course he is,' Wolf says. When I look up at him he has a smug grin, and the realization hits me.

'Oh, no,' I say.

'Oh, yes,' he replies. 'Here's our escape route. Hold on to your guns, guys.'

The Queen's forces, realizing our plan, begin to tighten around us.

'*Get them!*' the Queen screeches, her composure dissolving. Her men are more hesitant than she, seeing as we have weapons and a cliff to shove them over.

I move backward until I find myself on the edge. Just looking over makes my legs go wobbly. I shove my knife into my boot, taking deep breaths to fight back my panic.

'I can't,' I say. 'Wolf, I can't swim.'

The Queen smacks one of her subordinates with her shotgun in fury, and turns the barrel on us.

'Tough shit, Kid,' Wolf says, keeping a wary eye on her. 'Time to go.'

'I can't!'

'Learn,' he says, 'or die.'

He pushes me over the edge.

I scream the whole way down, though the sound is swallowed by the roar of rushing air. I remember to close my mouth just before I hit the water – and hit it *hard*. The surface smacks me harder than a thousand hands and leaves my skin screaming, but then I'm submerged and the cold water numbs me. It churns and roars, the current stronger than I could have imagined. I tumble like a rag doll. The surface is impossible to reach. I can't even tell which direction the surface *is* anymore, and when I open my eyes all I can see is murky water. Panic blooms. I flail wildly.

By some miracle, one of my hands breaches the surface and

finds open air. I fight in that direction. My lungs are about to burst. I finally heave my way up to the surface and stick my head out. One gasp of air, and I'm sucked under again.

I have to struggle not to lose my sense of direction again. A few times I find my way back to air, but it's always brief and never satisfying. In my bursts of open air I try to spot the others, but all I can see is frothing water all around me. I try to yell for help, but instead I get a mouthful of water and go under again.

The cycle continues for what feels like hours. My strength wanes away. It becomes harder and harder for me to reach the surface each time, and I feel like I'm getting less and less air. It's difficult to thrash my way upward with my arms growing heavy and my body going numb. My backpack weighs me down, but it's tangled around me so I can't cut it loose. Eventually I can't do it anymore; I have no choice but to drift underwater, letting the current carry me, fighting the urge to open my mouth and breathe in.

Just when I think I'm done for, a hand closes on my arm and pulls me upward. I open my eyes sluggishly and find, to my surprise, my head is above water – if only barely. I breathe in panicked gasps and the pain in my lungs lessens.

'I see the learning isn't going well for you,' Wolf says, grinning. His goggles are still on and his dreadlocks are slicked down with water. He treads water while keeping one hand firmly around me, holding me up with him.

I try to say something and choke up some water instead.

'How 'bout you just keep your mouth shut for a while?'

Sounds like a good plan to me. I focus on just breathing, and trying to imitate Wolf's motions to help keep us afloat.

The water isn't roaring by so quickly anymore; it's mellowed out to a slower stream, which makes it much easier to stay above the surface.

As we drift downstream, the river slows even more, and becomes shallower. Finally it reaches a point where Wolf's feet touch the ground and the current is reduced to a gentle pull. He drops me, and I splash around clumsily before realizing I can stand up on my tiptoes.

'What do you know,' Wolf says. 'We made it.'

'And the others?'

'Well, if you survived by flailing around like a fucking idiot, I'm sure they'll be just fine.'

'It's not my fault I—'

Wolf shoves me before I can finish and sends me underwater again. I come up a few feet downstream.

'What was that for?' I ask, spitting out river water that tastes like sewage.

'Get to shore.'

'Shore?'

He points, and I follow his finger. The sight of land makes my heart swell. There's an embankment here where the river gets shallow, a reprieve from the rapids. I struggle my way toward it at a painfully slow rate. Even this weak current is enough to make it hard to keep my balance. It doesn't help that my backpack is still wrapped around me and constricting my motion, either. Really, though, I'm just glad it didn't get lost in the river, even though the straps seem intent on strangling me. Wolf plows through the river at a much quicker rate. As soon as he catches up he grabs my backpack and drags me along behind him.

He shoves me onto land and I stumble and fall to my knees, grateful to have solid earth beneath me.

Pretty Boy is already sprawled out on the ground, looking as bedraggled as I feel. He looks at us, coughing up water, wet hair plastered across his face.

'Have a nice swim?' Wolf asks.

'Fuck you. You could've killed me.'

'Well, I didn't,' Wolf says. 'Though I probably should have.' He ignores the other insults Pretty Boy spits out and looks at the river. I do the same, and see Tank bobbing along. He doesn't seem to have much trouble staying afloat.

'Hey, big boy! Over here!' Wolf yells, waving a hand. Tank swims in our direction. Dolly comes right after him, moving smoothly and gracefully through the water. It looks like I'm the only one who had much trouble with the river, which makes me feel a bit ridiculous.

I struggle to disentangle my pack and squeeze water out of my clothes as the others make their way to land. I feel like a drowned rat with my clothes plastered slick against my body and my hair flattened. My beanie must have been lost in the river. I feel almost naked without it. It's something I've worn for years now. But I don't have time to feel sad.

When Dolly emerges from the water, I notice she's missing something as well: her hair.

I stare at her. Where her long, sleek, vibrant blue locks used to be is a plain black bob.

'Dolly . . . you . . . ' I point at her as she comes closer. 'Your hair . . . is gone?'

She gives me a quizzical look and raises a hand to her head.

'Oh. My wig.'

'Your wig?'

'Of course,' Wolf says, giving me an odd look. 'You didn't think her hair was *actually* blue, did you?'

'Umm.'

Wolf laughs, shaking his head.

'Oh, Kid. You never fail to fucking amaze me.' I duck my head and blush. Thankfully he shifts his attention to Dolly. 'So, time for a new color?'

She nods and bends down, opening her bag, which was tied securely to her waist, unlike mine. She pulls out, to my surprise, three wigs of varying lengths and colors. She eyes each of them critically, and holds up a bright red one.

'This?' she asks, looking at Wolf. He shrugs, and she looks at me instead. Her eyes bore into me with an intimidating intensity, as if this is an incredibly important decision. I gulp and nod quickly.

'It's a nice color,' I say, not really sure what she wants from me. She nods, satisfied, and pins her hair up. When she places the new wig over it, the combination of that and the dress makes her look like a new person.

'Are you changing out of that?' Wolf asks, gesturing at her dress. She glances down at it impassively.

'Should I?'

'It's a little bit ... well ... ' He actually sounds awkward, maybe even embarrassed, which is something I've never heard out of Wolf before. I scrutinize the dress to see what he's so bothered about, and find that the soak in the river has made the white material practically transparent. Apparently, Dolly doesn't wear a bra. I blush. Wolf looks away, and glares at Pretty Boy when he notices him staring.

'I'll change,' Dolly says, though she doesn't seem overly bothered. She unpacks her old clothing and disappears behind some nearby rocks.

Wolf clears his throat and looks around. 'Where the hell is Tank?'

'Here, boss!' a strained voice calls back. I turn to see Tank still struggling to reach land. He's practically waddling through the shallow water. When he finally reaches shore he flops down on his belly, wheezing.

'Glad you made it, fat-ass,' Wolf says.

''Course, we're all probably gonna die in a few days anyway,' Pretty Boy says. 'Seeing as we've all been soaking in radiated sewage water.'

'Aw, shut up. We've been soaking in radiation since birth. A bullet'll probably get us before that does, anyway.'

'Or an angry townie,' I say.

'Yeah, or an explosion,' Wolf says. 'See, that's the kind of attitude I'm looking for. With all of this shit to worry about, what's the chance the radiation will get us first?'

'Is that supposed to be comforting?' Pretty Boy asks, looking queasy.

'No, it's supposed to get you to shut your damn mouth.' Wolf grins and looks around at the lot of us, still sprawled across the ground and trying to catch our bearings. Dolly emerges from the rocks wearing her old wasteland garb. 'So, we ready to go?'

'Are you kidding?' Tank asks.

'Not a bit,' Wolf says. He looks up at the cliffs on either side. 'The Queen will be after us soon, and we need to find a way out of this damn canyon.'

'Just shoot me now,' Tank groans.

'Ten minutes to rest, and then we're off,' Wolf says. He sits down and starts pulling guns out of his pack, inspecting them for damage.

My backpack – I almost forgot to check it. I sit up and disentangle myself from the straps, dropping the pack into the dirt in front of me. The first thing I notice is that the zipper is open. My chest tightens. I dump out the contents, claw at the inside to make sure there isn't anything stuck, and then sit back and stare. The only thing left is my dress from the Queen's, which only survived because it tangled and caught on the zipper. My rations are gone, and my water, and . . .

'Shit,' I say, my voice coming out flat despite the hot feeling behind my eyes. 'I lost my blanket.'

'So?' Wolf asks without looking over. *So?* My chest aches. I suck in a deep breath and slowly let it leak out of me again.

'It was from my papa,' I say, squeezing the words out of my tightened throat. I press the back of my hand against my eyes, willing myself not to cry. I feel like a child. I don't want the crew to see me like this. 'It was the only thing from him I had left.'

I lower my hand. Wolf is looking at me, his expression inscrutable. I sit silently, waiting for him to tell me to stop acting like a baby, or that we don't have time for this shit right now. He sets aside the gun he's holding, sighs, and stands up.

'Five minutes,' he says gruffly. I stare up at him. 'What are you waiting for? Get off your ass and look. Maybe it got caught on some rocks or somethin'.'

I wipe my eyes, nod, and scramble onto my feet. Wolf is

already wading into the water by the time I'm up. I splash after him and straight over to the nearest clump of rocks. I crouch down and search around with my hands, prodding into every nook and cranny where my blanket could have possibly gotten stuck. I know it's a long shot. The blanket could have ended up anywhere, but that doesn't stop me from hoping. As soon as I'm positive it's not here, I move to the next possible place, and then the next. I find a crumpled tin can, and some plastic, and a soggy piece of wood, but no blanket.

My heart sinks the longer I look, as my optimism gradually fades. Eventually I'm forced to admit I'm not going to find it. I stop my search and stand still, staring at the water rushing by. It's gone. My beanie is gone. My blanket is gone. The last piece of my papa, gone.

When I look up, I see that both Dolly and Tank have come to help look as well. Pretty Boy is sitting on the shore with his head in his hands, but at the very least he isn't complaining about the waste of time. The others are all searching diligently, spread across the width of the river. The tight feeling in my chest loosens.

Maybe I don't need memories to keep me going anymore.

'I think it's been five minutes.' I cup my hands around my mouth and shout to make sure they can all hear me, because Wolf has wandered pretty far downriver. He turns back and cocks his head to one side. 'It's . . . it's gone.' I sigh out a breath and wade back to land. The others follow as I return to my backpack, shove my dress back in, and zip it up. By the time I straighten up, my eyes are dry.

Dolly's small hand squeezes my shoulder as she passes by, and Tank stops beside me as he reaches land.

'Sorry, Kid. You all right?' he asks, looking down at me. I tilt my head up and manage a smile.

'Yeah, actually. Yeah, I think I am.' I look around for Wolf, and find him back with his guns, wordlessly shoving them into his pack. 'Let's carry on, then.'

Wolf slings his pack over one shoulder and nods at me.

'Right,' he says. 'You guys heard Kid. Let's get going.'

XVIII
The Plan

We soon realize escaping isn't as easy as we thought. The river is at the bottom of a canyon, so cliffs rise up on either side of the water, with only a few rocky outcroppings on the way up.

'There's no way I'm climbing that,' Tank says, staring up at the cliffside.

'Me neither,' Pretty Boy says.

'Don't be babies. It looks easy.' Wolf climbs up on a rock to demonstrate. He grabs at the lowest outcropping for leverage, but his grasping fingers fall just short. 'You just – you just gotta – aww, hell!' He loses his balance and stumbles off the rock. Narrowly managing to catch his balance again, he folds his arms over his chest, disgruntled.

Pretty Boy lets out a snort of laughter, and Wolf rounds on him.

'What the fuck are you laughing at? You have any better ideas?' he asks, giving him a shove that sends him stumbling. 'Yeah. No. Didn't think so. But I have another one.' He jabs a finger in Pretty Boy's chest. 'Get on the ground.'

'What?'

'On the ground. Now.'

When Pretty Boy still hesitates, Wolf smacks him upside the head.

'You think I'm fucking kidding?'

'All right, all right! Ow, really, you don't—' Pretty Boy clamps his mouth shut as Wolf draws his hand back again, and obediently drops to the ground.

'On your hands and knees. There ya go. Now a bit to the right ...' Wolf positions an unhappy-looking Pretty Boy to his liking and climbs onto his back. His arms start to tremble the moment Wolf steps on. Wolf bounces up and down a few times. Pretty Boy grits his teeth, arms shaking violently.

'*Wolf!* Come on!'

'Eh, fine, fine.' Wolf grabs the rocky ledge, grasping it easily from his new height. With a grunt of effort he hoists himself onto the outcropping. It's narrow, but he manages to crouch there, leaning against the cliff wall. 'See? Easy!'

Tank, Dolly, and I glance at each other.

'Yeah, that ain't gonna work out for me,' Tank says. Dolly silently walks away, heading downriver.

'Where are you going?' Wolf shouts after her. She doesn't turn around. 'Whatever. Your turn, Kid, get up here.'

'Me?' I look up the cliff uneasily. 'I don't know about that ...'

'Shut up and get over here.'

I nervously tighten the straps of my bag and walk over. I'm about to place a foot on Pretty Boy's back, then think twice about it. Indecisive, I end up hopping awkwardly on one foot.

'Here, Kid, let me hoist you up,' Tank says, noticing my predicament.

'Nah, Pretty Boy's got it,' Wolf insists. I look up at him and he grins deviously. 'Go on, kiddo. Step on up.'

I hesitantly place one boot on Pretty Boy's back, and then the other. I pinwheel my arms before finding my balance.

'Sorry,' I mutter. He doesn't respond. I bite my lip and look up at Wolf.

'Can you reach?'

I stand up on my tiptoes and grab for the edge. My fingers scrabble at the cliff just a few centimeters beneath it.

'Uh, almost—' I try to stretch taller and lose my balance. One foot slips and lands on Pretty Boy's head.

'Ow!'

'I'm sorry!' I cringe and move my foot back over.

'Here, Kid.' Wolf extends a hand down to me. I grab a hold of it with both of mine, wincing at the pressure on my bandaged injury, and we both struggle to lift my weight. I scramble against the cliff wall for a foothold, showering dirt and rocks down. Finally I manage to reach the ledge and crouch beside Wolf, panting. I look down to see Pretty Boy covered in dirt from my ascent. He glowers up at me. Wolf is smirking. To my surprise, I feel a glimmer of amusement myself. Biting back a smile, I look away from both of them and stare at the stretch of cliff above us.

'So now what?'

'We find another ledge.'

'How does this solve anything? The rest of us still can't get up,' Pretty Boy says from below, dusting himself off.

'We'll figure it out,' Wolf says.

The next ledge isn't any easier to reach than this one was. Wolf has to help me again, giving me a boost so I can reach. Even then, I only barely manage to clamber up.

'Now help me up,' Wolf says.

'What? How?'

'Grab my hand.' He reaches out for me. I look around for something to steady myself, and grab onto a sturdy-looking rock jutting out of the cliff. I reach down with my free hand to clasp Wolf's and strain to pull him up. It's no easy task, even with him doing most of the work. Soon my arm is burning and my palms are slick with sweat. My injured hand, the one grasping the rock, starts to hurt pretty badly. It feels like the wound is tearing open again. My eyes water at the pain.

'I-I can't do this!'

'You got it. I'm almost there.' His free hand grabs the ledge, finally – and it crumbles right out from underneath us. I lose my grip on Wolf's hand and he slides downward, scrambling for a hold.

'Shit! Shit, shit!' I try to hold on to the rock as the rest of the ledge crumbles away, but I soon lose my hold and my footing and I'm free-falling. I scream, eyes closed, desperately hoping I won't break my neck when I hit the ground.

And then – *thud*. I freeze, expecting pain, but none comes. I tentatively open one eye, then the other, and find myself resting safely in Tank's arm. He grins at me.

'Caught ya.'

'Oh . . . thanks.' I let out a shaky breath. He sets me upright on the ground, and I look around for Wolf. He's sprawled across the ground on top of Pretty Boy. They're both covered in dirt but look relatively unharmed.

'So. That didn't work out well.' Wolf stands up with a grunt, leaving a groaning Pretty Boy on the ground. He turns to survey the cliff, shielding his eyes as he looks up. 'Yeah . . . that wasn't even halfway up, was it? Damn.'

'It wasn't?' I follow his eyes. He's right. And it felt so high already . . .

'Well, let's give it another go,' Wolf says.

'No!' Pretty Boy and I exclaim simultaneously. I notice him glance at me and refuse to look over. Wolf looks taken aback.

'Well, we ain't got any other plans, guys.'

'We could try riding the river downstream—' Tank starts, but I quickly interject.

'I am *not* going back in that water!'

'Then, how 'bout Wolf climbs up, gets a rope, and—'

'There ain't no way I can lift you up, fat-ass.'

'Well . . .' Tank tries to think of something else, fails, and shrugs. 'I guess that *is* our only option.'

'That's what I'm sayin', dumbasses. Now let's try this again, and try not to screw it up this—' Wolf stares up at the cliff and pauses, his mouth hanging open.

I follow his gaze. Dolly is standing at the top of the cliff, peering down at us as if confused why we aren't up yet.

'What the hell? How did you get up there?' Wolf shouts up to her. In response she points downriver.

We follow her direction to find, not very far at all, a much easier path up the cliff. It's narrow and winding and the thought of climbing it makes my legs wobble, but it's still a hell of a lot better than Wolf's plan.

'Well, shit,' Wolf says. 'I guess that works just as well.'

*

From there, it doesn't take much time to reach the top. Soon enough we find a road and we're back on track as if the ordeal with the Queen never happened.

As the heat of the day sets in, the sun soaks up the moisture from my clothes and body – all except for my boots. My feet still feel damp and clammy while the rest of me is way too hot. My feet squish noisily with every step, painfully loud in the near silence. I feel more and more ridiculous, though nobody says anything. Everyone seems subdued, or maybe just exhausted. Pretty Boy walks with his head down and his shoulders slumped, Tank is lagging behind as usual, and Dolly stays a few yards ahead and doesn't say a word. I want to speak to her, but I have no idea what to say. The atmosphere is grim; even Wolf is dragging his feet.

'So what's the plan, then?' I ask eventually, unable to take the dreary silence any longer.

'Same as before,' Wolf says. 'This Saint asshole's got Lord knows how many sharks locked up already, and we sure as hell ain't gonna join them. So we find that radio tower and explode the shit out of it.' He says it matter-of-factly, without his usual excitement.

'Really?' Pretty Boy asks, lifting his head. 'How the hell are we supposed to do that?'

'In the usual way, dumbass. With explosives.'

'Wolf, we don't *have* any explosives.'

'So we get some.'

'Oh? Just like that? We can't use the Queen anymore.'

'This is the fucking wastelands, Pretty Boy, everyone has explosives. We just need to find a town.'

'A town that will know we're coming, thanks to that broadcast.'

'Shit, you're right.' Wolf pauses for a second. 'Guess we'll need disguises, then.'

'Disguises?' I ask. 'Does that actually work?'

''Course it does. This one time, we dressed Pretty Boy up as a girl and—'

'I am *not* doing that again. No way.'

'It worked way too well,' Tank says, looking disturbed.

'Yeah, it did. He looked more like a girl than you do, Kid.'

Somehow, I don't find that hard to believe.

'Actually, that could work. We dress *Kid* up as a girl,' Wolf says, face lighting like he just came up with something brilliant.

'Uh, Wolf, I am a girl.'

'Yeah, but hardly. It still counts as a disguise.'

'What, so we send Kid in as a scout? You really think that's a good idea?' Tank asks. He says it without malice, but it stings a little.

'Yeah. Kid and Pretty Boy.'

Pretty Boy and I glance at each other simultaneously. He looks away first. I try not to let my mind wander. It makes me feel sick to think about last night, and there's something hard and bitter inside me that grows with every reminder.

'She'll fuck it up,' Pretty Boy says bluntly.

'We ain't got any other options,' Wolf says. 'I'm too easy to recognize, Tank is too scary, and Dolly is too . . . you know.'

'She'll fuck it up,' he repeats.

'Shut up. That's my decision and we're sticking with it.'

I glance at Pretty Boy again to find him adamantly avoiding my gaze, his jaw set. It takes me a moment to realize what's happening here. Pretty Boy might not trust me to do the job right, but Wolf actually does. I smile down at my boots, but at the same time my stomach flutters nervously. I hope his faith in me isn't misplaced.

'So what do we . . . do?' I ask.

'Just go in, test the waters, don't blow your cover. If things look bad, you get the hell out. If all goes well, you wait for the rest of us.'

'Why not just go in together?'

''Cause if they're gonna shoot us up the moment we step into town, then . . .'

Wolf trails off and abruptly stops walking. The others do the same. I run right into Tank and stumble back.

'What is it?' I ask, seeing nothing.

'You hear that?' Wolf asks, looking at Dolly. She tilts her head, pauses, and nods.

'What? What?' I ask, looking back and forth between them. Wolf turns to the stretch of road behind us, raising his goggles and squinting. He points.

I turn around and see it: a cloud of dust speeding down the road toward us.

'Someone's coming.'

I squint at the cloud, confused.

'Vehicles. Big ones,' Dolly says.

'The Queen?' I ask.

'Let's hope not. Binoculars?' Wolf asks. Dolly produces some from her pack and hands them to him, and he scopes out the fast-approaching dust.

'Doesn't look like the Queen,' he says. 'Or raiders. Looks like a trade caravan.'

'How do you know?' Pretty Boy asks.

'Just got a feeling.'

'Last time you said that, we ended up tied up in that crazy old woman's basement and—'

'This time will be different.' Wolf lowers the binoculars and shows that crazy grin of his. 'And screw the scouting plan, I've got something else in mind.'

XIX
The New Plan

So then I end up standing in the middle of the road and flailing my arms around as the vehicles roar toward me.

There's three of them: an open-top jeep, a big supply truck, and a pickup truck. There are a few car lengths of space in between them. They're moving at a relatively slow speed, but my heart still pounds as they bear down on me. Wolf promised they would stop. He insisted that these guys are 'bleeding-heart traders.' Probably.

As they come closer I raise my hands as high as I can get them, waving wildly to ensure they see me. A gust of wind whips my dress up, and I hastily pin my arms to my sides. Damn dress is such a pain, but Wolf insisted on it. *They ain't gonna stop for some ugly boy,* he said. *But if they see the dress before your ugly face, maybe you'll have a chance.*

They don't seem to see me. Or, if they do, they don't care that I'm here. The head jeep keeps roaring toward me without any sign of stopping. I suck in a deep breath and feel my knees start to tremble. Still, I hold my ground. I close my eyes and grit my teeth, expecting to be splattered across the road at any second.

The jeep roars past, a gust of wind buffeting me as it does so. I stumble and cringe, knowing the supply truck is next. There's no way it can pass by on this narrow road. It'll either stop or hit me head-on. I peek open one eye, unable to help myself.

And, to my amazement, the truck is stopping. It gradually slows as it approaches, brakes squealing, and stops just a few feet ahead of me. The thing is *huge*. It towers over me, making me feel like a bug about to be squished. The engine sounds like some angry beast growling and ready to swallow me whole. Legs still shaking, I manage a timid wave and a shaky smile. I can't see anything through the windshield.

A door slams. Footsteps approach. Against the sunlight, all I see is a vast silhouette getting closer. I shrink back nervously. I know the others are nearby, hidden behind a crumbling wall on the side of the road, but I still feel alone.

'Umm ... hi ... c-can I get a ride?' I squeak out, still taking tiny steps backward as the silhouette approaches.

The figure swings close, thick shoulders blocking out the direct sun so I can see. It's ... not exactly what I expected.

'Well, howdy!'

The driver, it turns out, is a broad woman with a near-blinding grin of what look like fake teeth. She wears a wide-brimmed hat and is fatter than Tank, with rolls on her arms and multiple chins. Her eyes are set a little too far apart, and her round face is all smiles. She doesn't look very bright or all that threatening. I almost feel bad about what's going to happen to her, but I stifle it. This is something I need to do for my crew.

'Umm.' I have no idea what to say.

'What's a little girl like you doing wandering around all by your lonesome?' she asks.

'Oh. I got separated from my family.' I try to pull my face into some semblance of sadness. My facial features don't want to cooperate, though, and I just grimace awkwardly.

'Aww, poor little thing.' She yanks me into a hug. I find myself with my face squished into her chest. My entire body stiffens. I can't remember the last time someone hugged me, let alone a stranger. It's . . . squishy, and uncomfortably warm and damp, and suffocating. I hold my head back as far as I can.

'Yeah – there were raiders, and – I don't know if they're – I . . . can't breathe . . . ' She finally releases me. I stumble back, blinking, and gasp for air. 'Can I get a ride to the nearest town, please?'

'Well of course, sweetie! I'd be happy to give you a lift!'

'Great!' My reply comes out a little too eager. I try to tone it down, and ask, 'Where, uh . . . where is the nearest town, anyway?'

'Just a bit up the road from here. Ain't far, hun, don't worry. Maybe your family will meet you there, if they escaped.'

'Huh? . . . Oh. Right. Yeah.' My response comes a little late, but she only grins wider.

I hear the rumble of a vehicle at my back, and turn to see the jeep has circled around. There are two men in it, each with a bandana over his head. One has a gun, which he aims at me. His eyes are dark and shrewd.

'What's the holdup, ma?' the driver shouts at us.

'Found this little one just standin' in the road!' The woman places a fleshy arm around my shoulders, squeezing me a little too hard. 'She's lost her family, poor little doll.'

'And?' the man responds. I look back and forth between him and the woman with a growing sense of unease. It's hard to tell which of them is in charge here.

'And . . . just look at her!' She beams down at me. I can feel the man's eyes on me as well, and stare down at my feet.

'I'm looking.'

'She's a little girl, Frankie!'

'*And?*'

'Do you know how much some people will *pay* for little girls?'

I'm already nodding along with her, agreeing with my defense, when her words hit me.

'Uh, pay?' I ask.

'An ugly little thing like her? Don't think so,' Frankie says, ignoring me.

'They always pay more for girls!'

'You sure we can even sell her 'round here, with this Saint guy running things?' he asks.

'Saint ain't gonna bother us. It's not like we're sharks or somethin'.'

'Still, I'm pretty sure his "law and order" spiel don't involve sellin' people . . . '

'We'll find a way,' the woman says. 'There's always some-one willing to do business.' I try to wrench free from her grip, but she clutches me tighter. 'Oh, calm down, sweetie. If your family is there, we'll try an' sell you to them first!' she says cheerfully. 'Only if they can pay the price, though. How much should we charge, Frankie?'

'Dunno. What do you think, Freddie?' He looks at the man with the gun, who shrugs without comment. 'Ehh, we'll figure it out. Fine, fine, ma, just throw 'er in with the rest of the loot.'

'No!' I struggle to break free, but the woman lifts me up off my feet. I cast a frantic glance toward where the others are hiding. No one emerges. 'Don't do that! I'm not loot!' I raise my voice pointedly. 'It would be really nice to *not become loot*!'

The woman looks down at me, raising her eyebrows and pursing her lips.

'Help! Somebody! Please! Help *now*!'

'Crazy little girl. Ain't nobody that's gonna help you,' she says with a chuckle.

'Hold up. Why's she keep looking over there?' the driver asks. I avert my eyes, feeling my cheeks redden. 'Something ain't right about this.' He reaches over and nudges the passenger. 'Go check it out, Freddie.'

The man nods silently and gets out, gun in his hands. He stalks past the woman and me, heading straight for the wall the others are hiding behind. I freeze, not even remembering to struggle. *Shit.* Oh man, Wolf is going to kill me for blowing their cover like this. But they should be fine. Just three of them here, and . . . my heart sinks as I remember there was another truck behind them. I can't even see how many guys are in that one, since it's hidden behind the supply truck. *Shit, shit*. My stomach sinks. I really screwed up this time.

I watch as Freddie approaches the wall, gun held ready, walking slowly and steadily. He pauses for a moment.

He jumps behind the wall and lets loose a spray of gunfire in one smooth motion. I squeak and renew my struggling. There's no way they could have avoided those shots! And there's no sound of return fire. The others . . .

Freddie stops, looking perplexed. He looks from the wall to me.

'Nobody here,' he calls out.

'What?' I ask, dumbfounded.

The woman lets out a snort of laughter.

'Guess she really is just slow in the head,' she says. 'Now, be a good girl and keep still.'

She walks toward the back of the truck, humming to herself as she carries me. I thrash around, starting to get seriously worried. Where the hell could they be?

'This isn't fair! I'm not loot! Definitely not loot!'

'You are now,' she says, cackling. 'And you are gonna fetch me a pretty penny, oh yes you are. A bit too scrawny and ugly, but so long as you got the right parts I'm sure someone can put you to good use—'

She rounds the back of the truck and stops when she sees the pickup truck.

The former driver is slumped in the seat, her head utterly pulverized by some blunt object. The two others aren't in much better shape. One is already lying on the side of the road, his seat stolen by a grinning Tank with a crowbar. The other is in the truck bed, and is currently having his throat slit by Dolly while Pretty Boy keeps his mouth covered.

Wolf stands triumphantly on the truck's hood, an assault rifle pointed at us.

'Hey there,' he says. 'These are some nice guns. Thanks.'

He opens fire.

The woman shrieks and drops me. I fall to the ground and roll away, wincing at the too-close gunfire, which thankfully only hit the woman's legs.

'You could've shot me!' I yell at him, climbing to my feet.

'Well, I didn't,' he says.

'And you didn't kill her, either,' I point out. The woman is still rolling around on the cracked asphalt, howling, her legs full of bullet holes and leaking everywhere. As I watch, she reaches down to a sheath on her waist and whips out a knife. She waves it wildly in the air. Wolf and I merely stare at her.

'You can do the honors.' Wolf reaches into the back of his pants, pulls out a pistol, and tosses it to me. I fumble, and it hits me in the chest with a painful *thud* and clatters to the ground. I retrieve it, rubbing at my sore chest, and only then do I realize what he said.

'Oh,' I say. 'You want . . . me to . . . ?'

'Yeah, yeah.' He gestures impatiently to the still-shrieking woman. I look from the gun to her face, with her mouth wide open and tears streaming down her round cheeks.

'I don't know—'

'She was gonna *sell* you, Kid,' he says. 'Probably to some pervy old man.'

I chew my bottom lip and nod. He's right. She deserves it. Back when I was alone, if I had gotten picked up by these people instead of Wolf, I would be dead or worse by now.

I point the gun at her head, remembering to pull back the safety. I carefully aim the sights at the center of her forehead.

'Umm.' I hesitate, trying to think of something witty to say like Wolf always does. ' . . . I'm not loot.'

Close enough.

And I blow her brains out.

It's easier than I thought. One shot, no recoil from a tiny gun like this. One shot, and her screaming stops. She stops flailing and lies very still. I can see the light go out of her wide-set eyes.

I stare at the body. My stomach churns, and I swallow back bile. My hands are shaking, the gun suddenly heavy in my hands. It shook up something in my core, seeing someone die like that. And yet, I don't feel guilty. Not at all. She deserved to die, and I killed her.

'Not bad,' Wolf says. I turn to him, a smile growing on my face. It's silly to think about at a time like this, but I'm pretty sure this is the first time Wolf has ever praised me.

'Gee, Wolf, tha—' I cut off with a shrill scream as a bullet whizzes past my head. I drop to the ground and crawl on my hands and knees to the pickup truck, seeking shelter behind one of its big tires. The sound of gunfire explodes from multiple places around me, thankfully no longer aimed at me.

Once I'm safely behind a tire I peek out. The two guys from the jeep, Frankie and Freddie, are exchanging fire with Wolf. Their bullets ping against the hood of the truck. Wolf topples off. He hits the asphalt hard, and the gun clatters out of his hand.

As the two men aim at him, I point my pistol in their direction and unload. A bullet hits one in the shoulder, and the rest of my shots miss. At least I've captured their attention. They turn their guns on me instead of Wolf. I duck behind the tire just in time as they both open fire.

The tire bursts, and the truck groans as it leans off-balance. I scramble farther underneath the now-slanted truck, clutching my now-empty gun. I frantically try to think up some way to help – but, thankfully, I don't have to. Gunfire erupts above me, coming from the bed of the truck. I wait for it to stop and crawl out from my hiding spot.

Frankie and Freddie are down. I can tell at a glance they won't be getting up again. Wolf is still lying on the asphalt.

I stand up and walk toward him, peering from side to side to make sure no other armed men are approaching us. Once I'm satisfied we're safe, I focus on Wolf and notice the blood soaking his shirt. My heart leaps into my throat and I rush over to his side. His eyes are closed.

'Oh, shit,' I breathe. The red stain is spreading from his shoulder. 'Guys, Wolf is bleeding! It looks like he got shot! Somebody hel—'

A hand pulls on my leg and sends me tumbling to the ground. I fall on my ass with a surprised squeak.

Wolf glares at me from where he's lying, and releases my leg to press a hand to his wound.

'Shut the fuck up, Kid. I'm fine.'

'You got *shot*!'

'Nothing vital.' He sits up with a grunt and a grimace, and looks down at the wound. 'It's hardly even bleeding. Jeez, don't be so dramatic.'

'Well, excuse me for being concerned!' I snap, the words jumping out before I even think about them. Wolf gives me a taken-aback look, and I feel my cheeks flush, but bite back an apology.

He stares at me for a second longer, and then looks

around at the messy scene we've created. There are bodies strewn all around us, along with blood and brains and bullets. He stands up, hand pressed to his shoulder, and heaves a sigh.

'Well, time to get back on the road,' he says. 'But first, let's eat.'

XX
Disguises

We build a small fire using wooden crates from the traders' truck. There are a lot of goods in there, food and medical supplies and such, but Wolf insists we have to save most of it to trade. Still, he lets Pretty Boy find some canned fruit as a treat. We pass the cans around the circle, eating with our hands, while Tank roasts the meat on spits of splintered wood. The reek of fresh blood makes me nauseous, but the smell of cooking meat chases that away. I watch one of the pieces slowly turning, dripping grease into the fire. My mouth waters. I swallow hard, trying to stifle the thought of meat, and resign myself to beans again.

'Mmm-mmm,' Tank says. 'Nice and fatty.'

'Which is why we'd eat you first if it ever came down to it,' Pretty Boy says. He tosses a slice of canned peach to Tank, who catches it in his mouth.

'You could try,' he says, grinning as he chews. 'Who's gonna take me down, huh? I'll take all of ya.'

'No way, you're too slow,' Pretty Boy says. Wolf, sitting between him and myself, pretends to fire a shotgun at Tank with sound effects included. He hasn't let us clean his wound yet, but it hasn't put a damper on his mood.

'All I'm saying is it would be easier to kill someone else,' Tank says, and nods not so subtly in Pretty Boy's direction.

'Well, Kid would be the easiest to kill,' Wolf says, 'but she ain't got no meat on her.'

I glance down at my skinny legs and shrug. He reaches over and grabs my face with one hand, pulling on my cheek to stretch it out.

'We-ell, maybe a bit here . . . '

I slap his hand away and stick my tongue out at him.

'She'd taste terrible,' Pretty Boy says matter-of-factly.

'Hey, what's *that* supposed to mean?' I ask. Somehow I find it genuinely offensive.

'Shame we couldn't find that finger she lost, could've had a taste,' Tank says.

'Oh, jeez, no!' I say, horrified but laughing despite myself. 'Wouldn't want to tempt you or anything!'

'Y'know, good point,' Wolf says. 'The real question is who would taste the best.' He squints thoughtfully around the circle.

'Dolly,' Pretty Boy says without missing a beat. She stares at him, unamused.

'Whoa, that was quick,' Wolf says. 'You've already thought about this, haven't you, ya sick fuck?'

'I'm the sick fuck? You brought it up!'

Wolf ignores him, and continues staring at each of us in turn.

'Yep,' he says eventually. 'It's gotta be Pretty Boy.'

'Why me?'

'Trader raised. Always taste best.'

'What?' I say, looking back and forth between them. 'Pretty Boy was a trader?' I address Wolf instead of talking directly to him.

''Course he was, look at him. He can read and he can lie, certainly ain't no dumb townie.'

Curiosity overcomes my desire to avoid him. I swallow a lump in my throat and lean forward to meet Pretty Boy's eyes.

'So you were raised in a caravan?'

'Yeah,' he says. 'Trader's son. I was only there until I was about ten years old.'

'Why?'

'Oh, here we go,' Wolf groans.

'Don't encourage him, Kid, he *loves* to talk about himself,' Tank says.

Heedless, I climb over Wolf's lap and squeeze in between them so I'm next to Pretty Boy. It makes me uncomfortable to be so close to him, but I try to push it away. It can't be all awkward glances and ignoring each other forever. I raise my eyes to his face, and resist the impulse to look away. When I swallow, it feels like there's a lump of dust in my throat.

Pretty Boy looks down at me, eyes partially closed so his long eyelashes stand out more than ever. Seeing him close up, with his beautifully crafted cheekbones and jawline, makes the old swooning instinct swell up again. I fight it down. No, no, no, I'm not going to forgive him just because he's pretty on the outside. He hurt me. He probably would've hurt me worse if Dolly hadn't shown up. I set my jaw, hold his gaze, and don't smile.

'Well, my mother owned a store before this place was a

wasteland,' he begins. He says it like he's already told the story a thousand times. Judging by the groans from Tank and Wolf, he probably has. He ignores them. 'So, post-bombs, our family went on the road as a trader caravan with the goods she saved. My mom taught me to read so I could help with inventories, to use maps so I could navigate, to talk to people and make them listen, to barter and lie if I needed to . . .' He shrugs. 'She was grooming me to be head of the caravan.'

'And then what?' I ask, enthralled despite myself.

'And then—'

'Watch out, guys, this is the tearjerker part,' Wolf interjects. I glance around to notice all the others are watching us. Pretty Boy glares at Wolf before continuing.

'And then, raiders,' he says simply. 'This was back before the wastes got real crazy, before it had really sunk in that there was no more government or law or order, so we weren't ready. The raiders killed everyone, my mom included.' His voice is tinged with sadness, as if the incident is still raw and painful for him. I stare, wide-eyed, my resentment toward him melting.

'Except for you?' I ask, my voice softening. He smirks, and the sadness is gone in an instant. *He's pretending*, I tell myself, frustrated at being hooked in so easily.

'Except for me. I was just a kid.'

'Why didn't they kill you?'

'Because I was useful.' I try to rack my brains for ways a ten-year-old could be useful to a band of raiders, and come up with nothing. He continues before I have to ask. 'I was bait. It'd usually be something like what you just did. Stand on the side of the road and wait for someone to stop. Then we'd jump 'em. I was cleanup crew, too.'

'Right,' I say. 'You didn't run away?'

'Nowhere to go,' he says. 'Anyway, I wasn't with the ones who killed my family for long. They got killed off by another crew of raiders. They kept me around when I explained what I could do. It happened like that a few times, just getting passed around over the years.'

'And that's how you got with Wolf, too?'

'Pretty much.'

'Actually his crew captured us. We cut a deal with him while he was on watch duty, and he let us slit their throats in their sleep,' Wolf says cheerfully.

'They were a bunch of assholes anyway,' Pretty Boy says without a hint of remorse. I never questioned the fact the crew didn't trust him, especially considering his cowardice, but now it makes even more sense.

'And now he's our resident scapegoat and navigator-slave,' Wolf says. 'Touching story, right?'

'Does it bother you?' I ask. Pretty Boy turns away from Wolf and looks down at me, brow creasing.

'What?'

'To kill people like your family was killed.'

The question strikes him off guard. I see the way his eyes widen before he controls them again. He purses his lips and studies my face.

'I don't need you judging me, Kid,' he says, his voice suddenly soft and dangerous.

'I'm not!' Face heating up, I backpedal. 'I didn't mean it like that.'

'Does it bother *you* to kill townies?'

'What makes you think I'm a townie?'

'You're far too stupid to be a trader, for one.'

'We-e-ell, time to eat!' Tank says overly loudly, in a painfully obvious attempt to break the tension. I stare at Pretty Boy for a moment longer, refusing to show that his comment hurt me, before turning to Tank and smiling. 'Kill was yours, so first serving goes to you, Kid,' Tank says, 'if you want it.'

My stomach flips at the thought, and I'm not sure it's a strictly unpleasant flip. Tank holds out a stick of skewered meat. I stare at it, observing how glistening fat clings to muscle and grease drips from the end. It doesn't look human; it just looks like meat. Juicy, rich, tantalizing meat that sure sounds a lot better than beans right now.

'Okay,' I say, the word practically spilling out of my mouth before I have time to consider. I reach out and take the skewer from him, twirling it in my hands and trying to pretend I can't feel everyone's eyes watching me.

Agreeing was easy, but now that it's actually in my hands I find myself hesitating. Am I really going to cross this line? Take the final step to join the rest of the crew? After the first bite, there's no turning back. Even if this is the one and only time, it'll change me forever. Brand me. I'll be a shark – the most hated thing in the wastes. Most wastelanders don't even believe in good, but they'd agree that this is evil.

I slowly raise the skewer to my mouth, inhaling the smell of warm meat. An image of the woman in her floppy hat springs to mind for a moment.

I take a bite.

Though juicy as expected, the meat is still tougher than anything else I've eaten in a while. I tear off a chunk with my teeth and chew for a full five seconds before I can swallow it. The lump feels thick as it worms its way down my throat. I suck in a deep breath.

And I take another bite. And another.

It may be chewy and thick and wrong, but holy shit does it taste good. Once I start I can't stop, eating with a relish that surprises me. It feels warm and satisfying in my belly. It's not just taking the edge off my hunger but making me actually feel *full*, something I haven't had in forever.

Only when it's halfway gone do I remember everyone is watching me. I look up, juices running down my chin, and smile.

'I cannot believe,' I say, 'I spent so long eating goddamn beans.'

Tank laughs, Dolly smiles, and Wolf shoots me a thumbs-up and his usual fierce grin.

'You really are one of us, Kid,' he says. My smile widens. 'Now, stop hogging all the damn meat.' He leans over and steals a bite before I can stop him.

'Hey!' I yank it away, laughing. Tank chuckles, reaching to grab another skewer off the fire.

'Plenty to go around, guys.'

And there is. By the time we're done everyone is full and content – except for Pretty Boy, who remains unsmiling the whole time.

Dolly ends up driving the supply truck while the rest of us pile into the jeep. We leave the truck with its blown-out tire and hood full of holes. Tank drives the jeep and the rest of us sit in the back. Pretty Boy and I are given the job of patching up Wolf's wound. Or, rather, Pretty Boy is supposed to patch him up while I hold him down, but it doesn't prove so easy.

'You better keep him down this time,' Pretty Boy says through clenched teeth, his eye already starting to swell from our last attempt. Turns out, Wolf instinctively lashes out when it hurts. Either that, or he just likes hitting Pretty Boy, even when he's trying to dig a bullet out of him. Hard to say.

I focus on holding Wolf's arms down. Trying to, at least, my skinny arms wrapped around his muscular ones.

'Okay, got him,' I say. Wolf flexes his arms and chuckles. Pretty Boy looks nervous.

'Seriously, Wolf,' he warns, 'if you hit me again, I'm done.'

'Shut up. You're done when I say you're done.'

'Well, you'll be stuck with a bullet in you until you let me do my job!'

Wolf sighs and nods grudgingly.

'Yeah. Fine. Get to it already.'

Pretty Boy bites his lip and raises the knife again. I look away as he moves it toward Wolf's wounded shoulder. The knife is the sharpest, thinnest one we have, and it's been sanitized with alcohol, but it's sure as hell no medical tool, and Pretty Boy is no doctor.

Still, I guess it's the best we can manage.

'Hold him *tight*,' Pretty Boy tells me. I squeeze my eyes shut and clutch Wolf's arms as tightly as I can, putting all of my strength into keeping them pinned.

Wolf doesn't scream when the knife goes in, but his whole

body goes rigid. His muscles bulge with the tension, straining against mine, although he doesn't pull free this time. I hold on tightly, wary of what he'll do the second he gets a chance.

'Fuck,' Wolf says. 'Fucking shit God damn *hurry up, Pretty Boy*!'

'Almost got it,' he says. 'Try to relax.'

'You're digging around in my shoulder with a fucking *knife*,' Wolf snarls. 'Tell me to relax one more time, and I'll—'

He cuts off with a low grunt. A jolt goes through his body, and his arms tremble.

'Got it,' Pretty Boy says.

Wolf hisses in a breath and lets it out in a long sigh. The tension drains out of him along with the air.

'You can let go now, Kid,' he says after a pause. I release him and scoot back, worried he's going to hit me.

Instead he cracks his neck and stretches his arms, careful not to jostle his shoulder too badly. Once I'm convinced he doesn't intend on punching me, I turn to Pretty Boy. He's holding up a small bullet, its silver surface coated with blood.

'That's it?' I ask. 'It's so small!'

'You ever been shot, Kid?' Wolf asks. I shake my head. 'Damn right you haven't. So shut up. And where the hell are my bandages, Pretty Boy?'

'Do I at least get a thank-you?'

'So now you want me to thank you for letting you knife me? Finish your job, idiot.'

Pretty Boy grabs the bottle of alcohol and douses Wolf's shoulder without warning. Wolf lets out a shout before clamping his mouth shut to stifle the noise. The sharp smell of alcohol reminds me of vomiting and other unpleasant things.

When I glance at Pretty Boy, I see the corner of his mouth tugging upward. Wolf notices it as well. Intermingled blood and alcohol drip from his arm.

He punches Pretty Boy in the jaw, the blow hitting hard enough to wipe the smirk off his face and twist his head to the side. I don't feel sorry for him at all.

'Stop looking so fucking happy!' Wolf yells.

'Lay off, Wolf,' Tank rumbles from up front. He doesn't turn away from the road, but his voice is loud enough to carry back to us.

Wolf looks rather miffed about being scolded. Nonetheless, he pulls back from Pretty Boy and drops his still-raised fist.

'Now bandage this. I'm leaking all over the place.'

Pretty Boy cradles his face, staying back.

'I *told* you if you hit me one more time—'

'Oh, stop whining and get—'

I grab the first aid kit and pull out the gauze myself, half because I want them to stop arguing and half because Wolf's still-bleeding shoulder is making me nauseous. I wrap the wound as best as I can with my clumsy hands. Wolf stubbornly sets his jaw and doesn't say anything.

'Is that all right?' I ask when I'm finished. It looks like a mess, but at least it's bandaged.

'Good enough,' Wolf says tersely. I know better than to expect a thanks. As Wolf rises to move up to the passenger seat, he smacks me on the side of the head. I look up at him, wondering what I did wrong this time, but instead he grins at me. It looks about as close to affectionate as Wolf can get. I smile back.

'Wake me up when we're getting close,' Wolf says, slumping down in the passenger seat. I silently agree and curl up in my own seat for a nap.

I wake up to a hand shaking me and an unfamiliar face.

I let out a nervous shriek and lash out, smacking the face away as hard as I can. He recoils immediately, letting out a curse, and only then do I realize it's Pretty Boy.

Suffice to say, he's not looking so pretty right now. He has a black eye, a split and bloody lip, and his jaw is red and puffy – not to mention the fresh mark from my slap. Wolf's punches really did a number on him.

'Oh, shit, I'm so sorry!' I say.

'What the hell was that for?'

'I just . . . didn't recognize you for a second!'

Wolf is cackling in the front of the jeep. Pretty Boy's shocked expression gradually changes to an indignant one.

'It's that bad?' he asks.

'No, well, it's not . . . ' I scramble, trying to think of something nice to say before remembering I have no reason to be nice to him. 'Yeah, you look awful.'

He rubs at the swollen part of his jaw, looking miffed.

'Told you it was a good enough disguise,' Wolf says, turning around to give us a thumbs-up.

'Yeah,' I say. 'I mean you certainly don't look *pretty*, so that means—'

Wolf cuts me off with a burst of wild laughter, and Pretty Boy looks even more affronted.

'So it means it's a good disguise,' I say.

He shoots me a cold look and I stifle a smile.

'Anyway, we're almost there,' Wolf says, 'so we're workin' out our disguises and the bullshit we're gonna tell the townies.'

'We're a trade caravan,' Pretty Boy explains without looking at me. 'We fought off a group of raiders on the way over, which is why we're so banged up.'

I nod. Sounds easy enough.

'And where's your disguise, Wolf?' I ask.

'I don't need one.'

'Like hell. Everyone knows what you look like,' Pretty Boy says. 'You need *something*.'

'I ain't wearing no wig or anything.'

'Then you at least need a messed-up face like me.'

'No!'

'Wolf, it's one or the other.' Pretty Boy grins at the idea. Wolf grits his teeth.

'Fine, then. The face.'

Pretty Boy leans forward eagerly, but Wolf shoves him away.

'I ain't giving you the satisfaction. Kid, you do it.'

I stare at him.

'You want me to . . . hit you?'

'Yeah.'

'In the face?'

'Yeah.'

We stare at each other. I clench one fist and stare at it, trying to imagine hitting Wolf. I can't even conjure up a mental picture of that. It seems absurd.

'I don't know if I can do that.'

'I can,' Pretty Boy says.

'Shut your mouth. Kid, man the hell up.'

I grit my teeth and nod. Balling up both fists, I try to conjure up anger against Wolf. I draw back a fist, start to swing . . . and stop a few inches from his face.

'I can't,' I confess, letting my hands drop to my sides.

'God damn it, Kid.'

'What the *hell* are you guys doing?' Tank asks, turning away from the road to look at us.

'Beating Wolf up so no one will recognize him,' Pretty Boy says smugly.

'You guys are idiots. Nobody pays attention to Wolf's face, it's the hair and the goggles people will know him by.'

We all pause to mull that over.

'What do you mean, nobody pays attention to my face?' Wolf asks. Tank doesn't answer, watching the road again. 'What the hell is wrong with my face?' He turns to me and grins frighteningly with his full set of crooked, yellowing teeth.

I gulp.

'Umm. Nothing. Nothing's wrong with your face.'

'Damn straight.'

'Well, you heard Tank. You have to wear a wig,' Pretty Boy says.

'No.'

'Or cut it.'

'No!'

'Wolf, if you blow our cover because—'

'I'm in charge here, I'll blow our cover if I want to!' Wolf says. Pretty Boy gives him an incredulous look. Eventually Wolf sighs, resigned, and turns to me.

'You still got your old shirt?'

'Umm ... yeah?' I dig in my pack and pull it out, presenting the dust-colored fabric to him.

'Thanks,' he says, and rips it in half. I stare, heart sinking as I realize I'm now trapped in this dress. I press my knobby knees closer together and try to fight back self-consciousness. I watch as he tears the shirt apart and wraps the ragged remains around his head, tucking his dreadlocks beneath it. Soon his head is cocooned, with only his eyes, mouth, and a few slivers of dirty face peeking through.

'How do I look?' he asks, and smiles. The effect is disturbing.

'Scary enough to reduce children to tears,' Pretty Boy says dryly.

'Good, that's what I always aim for.'

'What about Tank?' I ask.

'I'm not that easy to disguise. I'll just lie low and hope for the best,' Tank says. 'Heads up, here's the town.'

It's a small, barely inhabited place, all crumbling buildings and crudely done repairs. Three surprisingly tall buildings stick up among the humble little squats. They're towers of garbage, with car doors and wire mesh and other scrap metal filling the holes. The mere fact they're still standing seems to defy some law of the universe, and they look ready to topple at any second. Heaps of scrap metal and old, rusty cars decorate the town. As Tank winds between them to get inside, I stare up at the towers apprehensively. Several heads peek out from different heights on the buildings. Just the thought of being up there makes my knees quake.

'Remember,' Wolf says as the jeep stops in the center of town, 'don't call each other by the usual names.'

I glance around and notice at least three guns pointed at us from the tower windows. I gulp.

'What do we call each other, then?' I ask in a whisper.

'Huh,' Wolf says. 'I didn't think of that.'

But it's too late to solidify our plans, because we're already here and the townies are approaching. They crawl out of every nook and cranny, emerging from rusty cars and shady corners and the three towering buildings.

'Just wing it, Kid,' Wolf says, noticing my apprehension. He smiles at me, eyes glinting between folds of fabric. 'And don't fuck it up.'

XXI
Towers

Townies swarm our jeep like flies on a carcass. We're surrounded in minutes. Men, women, and children alike arrive to greet us. They don't seem afraid, not even of Wolf and his wrapped-up head, or big ol' Tank with his scary face on. It's almost strange how friendly they are. Some hold up little trinkets and trash-treasures, hoping to trade. I guess the towns this close to the Queen are more peaceful, less wary of outsiders.

Then again, maybe they're just well protected. I'm all too aware of the snipers up in those towers, as much as I'm trying not to stare at them. Instead I stare at the crowd. The amount of them is intimidating, no matter how friendly they seem.

A little girl with a dirty face holds something up toward me: a pocket watch on a rusty chain, its surface cracked. I reach out to take it, but Wolf slaps my hand away.

'No, no, no,' he says. 'Don't take anything. Then they'll want something in return.'

'Oh,' I say sheepishly. I give an apologetic smile to the girl, who blinks up at me with wide eyes. She offers the watch to

Wolf instead, but he shakes his head. She sticks it out farther, insistent. The other townies are pressing in closer, too, all trying to speak at once in an indecipherable flood of noise.

All of the sound and motion surrounding me suddenly reminds me of the mob of crazies. Nervousness hits me in a flash, and a jolt of pain goes through my missing finger. I shrink back closer to Pretty Boy and swallow hard, telling myself that these are friendly townies, not madmen. But their smiling faces now look like bared teeth, and I feel like they could turn on us in an instant and—

A hand lands on my shoulder and I jump. I turn to face Pretty Boy.

'It's okay,' he says. His face looks softer than usual, his head tilted in an annoyingly charming way, but I'm not going to fall for his bullshit.

'I'm fine,' I say, and brush the hand off. Still, I keep my distance from the townies leaning over the jeep's sides.

'Hello, hello, hello,' a very loud voice booms out. The townies abruptly stop talking and all turn in the same direction. I swivel around to do the same. They're looking at a pile of old, run-down vehicles nearby, stacked three cars high. On top is a man, only his silhouette visible against the sun. He jumps down from car to car in a series of loud crashes. When he stops a few yards away from our jeep, I realize that he's actually quite tiny. The height and his loud voice created an illusion of greatness.

The voice was an illusion, too, I see, as he lowers a megaphone.

He smiles at us. It's a slimy smile on a ratlike face.

'Welcome to Towers,' he says.

'These townies,' Wolf mutters under his breath, 'always so clever with their names.' I stifle a laugh.

The rat-man notices Wolf speaking and promptly raises the megaphone again.

'We are always very pleased to have visitors,' his voice booms obnoxiously, 'especially traders.'

He clicks the megaphone off and lowers it, face still oozing friendliness.

'But you aren't traders we're familiar with.' He speaks in a conversational tone, and makes his slow way toward us. 'And we are familiar with many traders. Where are you from, strangers?'

'Across the wastes,' Wolf says. The lie comes smoothly and easily. 'Things are bad where we came from, real bad, so we decided to find new grounds closer to the Queen.' Wolf mirrors the man's unnerving grin. 'And this Saint guy. Love what he's trying to do.'

The man squints at him as if trying to decide if he's joking.

'Saint is a very ambitious man,' he says after a pause, 'and I admire his work to make the wastes a safer place.'

'Ain't working so well this far,' Wolf says. 'We got jumped by raiders on the way over. Look what they did to our poor friend's face, the savages.' He points at Pretty Boy, who looks like he's trying very hard not to roll his eyes.

'Savage indeed,' the rat-man says, his eyes never leaving Wolf. 'It's a good thing we're all civilized people here, now isn't it?'

'Right, right. Now, about that trading business. I assume you're in charge here?'

'You assume right.'

'Let's have a chat, then.'

Wolf climbs over the side of the jeep and approaches the man. He gives him an overenthusiastic handshake and the two walk over to the supply truck, talking in low voices. I glance around at the others.

'What are *we* supposed to do?' I ask.

'Keep an eye on the townies,' Pretty Boy murmurs. I eye the crowd of townsfolk. They're no longer clustered around our jeep, but are spread out and loitering around, stealing glances at us.

'Keep an eye out for what?'

'Anything suspicious,' he says, and pointedly looks upward. I follow his gaze to one of the towers, where a sniper rifle is still aimed in our direction. It's too far away to tell for sure, but I have a nervous feeling his sights are on my head.

After a few minutes Wolf and the man return, along with Dolly, looking as porcelain as ever in her red wig. It stands out starkly in this dusty town, where almost everything, people included, is in shades of brown or gray.

'Yes, yes, we'll work something out,' the rat-man is saying. 'What are you looking for, exactly?'

'Guns,' Wolf says. 'Big guns. And explosives.'

Rat-face's forehead furrows, and his eyes narrow.

'And why is *that*, exactly? Surely traders like yourselves—'

'—have a very pressing need for self-defense,' Pretty Boy finishes from beside me. Both heads turn toward him; he smiles. 'Not to mention, there's a high demand for explosives right now.'

'Right,' says Wolf. 'Come talk to the man, Tobias, tell 'im all about this high demand.'

Tobias? It takes me a second to remember we have to use fake names. *Tobias. Right. Tobias.* I try to engrave that in my memory as Pretty Boy goes over to speak to the man.

'With Saint gaining influence and collecting sharks, raiders are getting worried that they're next. That fear makes them desperate, which makes them more dangerous than ever. People have to fortify ... ' The words become muffled as he and the townsman turn away from us. Wolf walks over and leans on the side of the jeep.

'All right,' he says. 'We're gonna stay here for the night.'

'Really?' I ask nervously. 'You remember what happened in that last town? And the Queen—'

'Ain't got a choice,' he says. 'We'll smooth over negotiations and get out of here early tomorrow. It'll be fine. Promise.'

We're given a room on the fifth floor of a tower, which is high up enough to make me avoid looking out the window at all costs. It's a cramped room, especially since Wolf insisted all five of us stay together. There's no furniture aside from three ratty cots on the floor. One is covered with stains that look suspiciously like dried blood, another is littered with cigarette burns, and the third smells like someone died on it and nobody noticed for a few days. Each of them has a blanket in an equally undesirable state, and two have lumpy pillows. Despite their condition, everyone jumps to claim one.

'Murder scene is mine,' Wolf says, indicating the blood-stained one with one hand while he removes his head-wrap. 'No arguments.'

Tank says nothing, and flops down on the burnt one with a weary groan. Sprawled out, his thick body doesn't even fit on the mattress. He lies there, eyes closed, as if daring someone to try to move him. No one does.

And so the stinky cot is left to Dolly, Pretty Boy, and me. I step away from it, raising my hands in surrender. It's not worth fighting over . . . not that I'd be able to get it if I tried. Dolly and Pretty Boy glare at each other.

'Oh, come *on*,' Pretty Boy whines. 'I was puking my lungs out all night at the Queen's, and—'

'Don't care,' Dolly says flatly.

'—and then Wolf did *this* to my face, and—'

Dolly shakes her head.

'—you *always* get the nice things, Dolly. I never get anything. And I'm a part of this crew, too. I talked to that townie for all of you today . . .'

'No,' Dolly says.

'I deserve it! It's mine!' Realizing his wheedling isn't getting him anywhere, Pretty Boy defiantly sits down on the cot. Dolly walks over, shoves him off, and takes his place.

Pretty Boy scoots away on the floor. He seems to consider challenging her again, but thinks better of it.

'Assholes,' he says, and retreats to a corner to lean against the wall.

Tank starts to snore. Apparently he fell asleep mid-argument.

'Think he's got the right idea,' Wolf said. 'Dunno what you all are complaining about. I'm the one who spent the night bein' kidnapped and shit.' He places his hands behind his head and yawns. 'Someone else take first watch. And by someone I mean Pretty Boy.'

Pretty Boy sighs but doesn't protest. Dolly walks over and hands me the pillow and blanket from her bed.

'Oh, wow, thanks,' I say with a smile. She returns to her cot.

I'm about to set up my own makeshift bed when a thought stops me. Pretty Boy *has* had a rough time lately . . . and more importantly, he came very close to abandoning us in favor of the Queen. Is it really the best idea to give him first watch? He could screw us over far too easily here. I hesitate, and then walk over to his corner and offer him the sleeping supplies.

'How 'bout I take first watch?' I say, holding out the folded blanket and pillow. He stares up at me, surprised and a bit suspicious, as if he's expecting some kind of trick. Our eyes meet, and it doesn't make me want to blush out of either attraction or embarrassment. I hold his gaze steadily, and after a moment or two he's the one to drop his eyes. He takes the offering.

'Thanks,' he says without looking up, and curls up in his corner.

I sit under the window, keep an eye and an ear out for trouble, and try not to let my mind wander to dark places. The room becomes eerie real fast once the others are asleep. The window doesn't have any glass, and the wind whistling through it reminds me how high up we are. I swear the whole tower creaks every time the wind blows, and I hear whispers and footsteps from the room above us.

I hug my knees to my chest and look over at my sleeping friends for comfort. Tank is snoring loudly, Wolf is sleeping with his mouth open and has a string of drool trailing onto his pillow, and Pretty Boy shifts and mutters in his sleep.

Dolly, I realize with a jolt, isn't actually sleeping at all. She's wide-awake, and staring at the ceiling.

'Dolly?' I whisper. She's across the room, in the cot closest to the door, but her head turns toward me. 'Is everything all right?' She nods. 'Why aren't you sleeping?' No response. She turns and stares at the ceiling again.

I move over, stepping over Wolf, and crouch beside Dolly's cot. Something must be bothering her. I search my brain for what it could be, and guiltily remember Ruby's death. That's right – I wanted to ask if she was all right, but we've been so busy it slipped my mind. Somehow it never seemed appropriate to say in front of the others, anyway.

'Umm,' I say timidly, 'I'm sorry about, um, your friend.'

'Friend?' she asks, her face a mask.

'Ruby.'

'Oh. Yes.'

I pause.

'She was your friend back from when you worked for the Queen, right?' She nods. 'So . . . that must suck. Sorry.' I'm no good at this whole comforting thing. She falls silent again, and I wonder if maybe I should stop prying – maybe she doesn't want to talk about it, and I'm just being a nuisance. But just when I open my mouth to apologize, she speaks up again.

'I didn't think the Queen would kill her,' she says quietly.

'Yeah. Me neither.' I stare down at my ragged boots. 'So . . . it wasn't your fault or anything.'

'I know,' she says.

'But it must suck, still.'

'Yes.'

We lapse into silence. The wind whistles and the tower groans around us. I can't tell if Dolly welcomes the chance to talk or resents it, but at least she seems to be opening up a little. It stirs my curiosity, and I can't help but try to get more out of her. It's such a rare opportunity to speak to Dolly like this.

'So, umm.' I try to think of the most tactful way to continue. 'Someone told me about . . . when you worked for the Queen.'

'Hm.'

'And why you stopped.'

She doesn't respond. I steal a glance at her and notice that she has, seemingly without noticing, placed a hand on her stomach.

'I had a baby,' she says after a long pause. She stops again.

'Yeah?' I say. Trying to get information from her is like pulling teeth, but somehow I get the impression she does want to talk about it. Maybe she just doesn't know how. Or maybe I'm reading her completely wrong . . . It's hard to tell with Dolly.

'She died,' she says bluntly.

'How?'

'Don't know. She was sick,' she says. Another long pause. 'Since she was born. And born too early.'

'Oh . . .'

'Radiation. She wasn't strong enough for it.'

'I heard that happens a lot,' I say. It happened all the time back in town. Lots of times the pregnancy went wrong, or the baby was born dead, or wrong, or died real young. Healthy post-bomb babies are rare. But I was born after the bombs fell, and so were plenty of others, and we lived and grew just fine. Nobody really knows why we survive while others die.

'It's strange,' Dolly says. Her voice stays as quiet and unemotional as ever. 'When it first happened I was scared. Couldn't work like that. I wanted to get rid of it. But then . . . I couldn't. The Queen let me keep the baby. She was nicer then.'

I try to picture that: the crazy old Queen supporting Dolly, letting her take off work, prepared to let her raise her child there. I can't make that idea match with the woman who shot Ruby in cold blood. I guess people change. The wastelands warp them.

'One day I woke up and she was cold,' Dolly says.

'I'm sorry,' I say.

'I never even thought I wanted her. And then she was gone and I knew I did.'

I bite back another *sorry*. It's all I can think of saying, but I feel like repeating it just makes it feel empty.

'And then you left the Queen's?'

'Yes.'

'Alone?'

'Yes.'

'So how'd you get all wrapped up in . . . this?'

'Wolf found me,' she says. 'He saved my life. I wanted to be like him.'

I know trying to get the full details on *that* story would be near to impossible, so I'm not even going to try. My imagination can fill in the blank spaces.

'Wow,' I say. 'And now you're so cool.'

'Cool?'

'Yeah. Like . . .' I scuff one boot across the floorboards. 'Like I want to be like you, the same way you wanted to be like Wolf.' It sounds so lame when I say it. I can feel myself turning red. When I look over at Dolly, though, she's smiling.

'Thank you,' she says.

'Umm, you're welcome.'

'Holy shit.' Wolf's voice nearly makes me jump out of my skin. 'This is the most awkward conversation I've ever eaves-dropped on. Can you two shut up and go to sleep already?'

Embarrassed at being overheard, I clamp my mouth shut and rise to move to the window. Dolly sits up and grabs my arm before I can get there.

'Can't sleep. I'll watch,' she says. When I hesitate, she stands up and nods to the cot.

'Are you sure?' I ask. She nods. 'Oh . . . all right.' I *am* feeling awfully tired, so it's hard to resist. I lie down on the offered cot. It's definitely not as nice as the bed at the Queen's, and the reek is pretty awful, but I'm so exhausted I hardly care. 'Good night, Dolly.'

'Good night.'

I'm asleep within minutes.

XXII
The Queen's Return

When I wake up, sunlight streams through the window. It's not the gentle glow of early morning, but the harsh light of midday. The cozy room has become a furnace; I'm covered in sweat. That discomfort, and the realization I'm alone, wakes me up.

Blinking away a sleepy haze, I notice I'm on a different cot as well. I somehow swapped to the bloodstained one – the prize formerly claimed by Wolf – and picked up a pillow and blanket. No wonder I slept so damn long. I disentangle myself from the sticky blanket and rush to the window, hesitating a moment before I stick my head out. The height makes my head swim, but I ignore the shaky feeling in my knees and search the town below. Our huge supply truck stands out among the squats and smaller vehicles. When I squint, I can make out the others clustered around it, unloading with the assistance of some townies. I spot Dolly's bright hair, Wolf's ridiculous head-wrap, and Tank carrying a hefty-looking box on each arm. Soon I see Pretty Boy as well, standing nearby and talking to the rat-faced townsman.

Hurt pricks me. I hate being left behind like this. Wolf must have really been worried I would screw things up for everyone, but like hell am I going to sit around in this room all day. I have to go out there and show them I can keep up. I head for the door, nearly tripping over a pile of stuff on the way.

Upon closer look, I realize it must be meant for me. There's a bottle of water, a tin can of food, and a pile of clothes too small to fit anyone else. I unfold them. It's a new outfit: a T-shirt and an old pair of jeans.

I change out of my god-awful dress in favor of the new clothing. The shirt is baggy and dusty, and the jeans have various multicolor patches crudely sewn on to cover holes, but it's a lot more comfy than that girly thing I was wearing. I take a gulp of water, grab the can of food, and leave to meet up with the others.

As I reach the bottom of the stairwell I use my knife to pry open the can of food, and eye the red insides before taking a cautious slurp. It turns out to be cold and slightly chunky tomato soup, not bad at all.

Outside, the town is full of midday hustle and bustle. Townsfolk are everywhere, carrying boxes of supplies to and from our truck. Everyone seems to be in good spirits, and the townies chat happily as they investigate crates of food and water and other supplies. They smile at me as I pass. My friends are smiling, too, and as I get closer I can see why: As they empty the truck of other goods, it's slowly filling up with guns and explosives. They sure have a lot of shit for such a small town. I guess towns close to the Queen really are lucky.

Even rat-face is smiling as he talks to Pretty Boy. Either his suspicions have been dismissed, or he stopped caring so much when he saw the goods we brought. I avoid the two of them and head for Tank. He's setting down two crates in front of a group of townies, who all crowd in to peer at what's inside. I nearly yell out his name, but stop myself as I remember we're using other aliases here.

'Hey!' I yell instead, and stand on my tiptoes to tap him on the shoulder. He turns around and grins at me.

'Oh hey, what's up?' He squeezes the breath out of me in a one-armed hug. 'Sleep well?'

I squirm out of the iron vise of his arm.

'Well, yeah ... but why'd you guys leave me? I wanted to help!'

He notices my disgruntled face and laughs.

'Oh, kiddo. We just figured we'd let you sleep. You've been through a lot.'

'Yeah, but ... ' It's hard to keep feeling crabby in the face of Tank's easygoing warmth. 'But so have all of us!'

'Yeah, but you're, y'know, the baby of the group.'

'I am not a baby!'

Tank laughs and heads back to the truck. I doggedly follow on his heels. The back compartment is wide open and surrounded by a crowd of people. A few men inside, including Wolf, hand off crates to the waiting townies. Every time a new box is delivered into the truck, Wolf rushes to look inside, as giddy as a little kid with sweets.

'Well, these will come in handy,' he says to one, gives the townie a thumbs-up, and dashes over to check another one. 'Is that a *bazooka*? Holy shit, I love you townies.'

I line up behind Tank, waiting for Wolf to stop drooling over his new toys and keep the line going. As soon as Tank walks off with a crate in each arm, I step up, hold out my own arms, and wait.

Wolf walks over with a box. He bends down to hand it to me, and looks surprised when he sees my face.

'You should, uh, maybe let someone else handle this one,' he says.

'No, no, I got it!' I stand on my tiptoes and reach for it.

'If you say so.' He hands it off to me and straightens up.

It's . . . a lot heavier than I expected. The wooden crate is wider around than I thought, too, and I find it difficult to get a good grip. I take a few shaky steps away from the truck, gradually leaning backward from the weight. Someone puts a hand on my shoulder to steady me.

I pause to regain my footing. Once I feel like I can stand on my own, I readjust my hold on the crate. My injured hand slips. Pain shoots through my stumpy finger. I hurriedly shift my hand, and feel the crate sliding out of my grasp.

I try to fix my hold again, narrowly avoid dropping the whole thing – and find myself falling backward. I topple over before I can even react, and land flat on my back on the hard dirt. The crate spills out its content of bandages and first aid supplies onto my face. I lie there, reeling. I can hear Wolf howling with laughter from the truck. Some things never change, I guess.

I'm too embarrassed to stand and face the stares and laughter, so instead I try to muster up some inkling of dignity. After a few seconds, Pretty Boy's bruised face pokes into my line of sight, his expression oddly caring.

'You all right, sis?'

'Eh?'

'Are you all right?' he asks, and adds with more emphasis, '*Sis?*'

Sis? It takes me a second to process. Another part of our act I have to remember. Reacting a little late, I nod. He lifts the crate off me and offers a hand. I ignore it and stand up on my own.

'I'm fine, I'm fine,' I say, brushing myself off. A wad of gauze sticks to my boot, and I try to inconspicuously peel it off with my other foot.

'Maybe you should help out with some, uh, less strenuous stuff,' he says, and laughs charmingly. It doesn't have its old effect. I can tell now he's only pretending, and it grates on my nerves to have him keep trying it on me. So I don't return his smile, and stare at my feet instead.

Unperturbed, he reaches over and grabs my arm. Before I can shake him off he turns over my injured hand and gently examines it.

'Looks like you could use some new bandages. Does it still hurt?'

Of course it still hurts. I'm missing a *finger*. I bite my lip and nod.

'Come sit down, let me have a look.'

'I can do it myself,' I say quietly.

'Whoa, somebody's stubborn today. Come on.'

He grabs my arm a little too roughly and leads me away before I can protest. We sit on a pair of overturned crates and he obtains some first aid supplies.

I can't help but be impressed by how well he can act. The

kindness he feigns is so completely different than the real Pretty Boy. If I didn't know him any better, he'd have fooled me easily. But I set my jaw and refuse to react as he tends to my wound. He unwraps the old bandages as gently as possible, and I wince at the ugly injury it reveals. There's a lot of dried blood and scabbing, and it hurts somewhere deeper than physical pain to see my finger missing.

'Well, it doesn't look infected,' Pretty Boy says. 'That's good.' He douses it in water to wash away the caked-on blood, and then in alcohol to sanitize it. My eyes tear up from the sting, and I lower my head in an effort to hide it. 'Sorry . . . it should only hurt for a second.' He touches my shoulder, squeezing lightly. I'm about to shake him off when I notice Mayor Rat-Face standing nearby and scrutinizing us. Being forced into playing this out just makes me more embarrassed, but my pride isn't worth blowing our cover.

I stare at my boots as Pretty Boy all too tenderly applies some antibiotic ointment and new bandages to my hand.

'That all right?' he asks, holding my freshly wrapped hand between his own.

'Yep.' I yank my hand away and stand. 'Thanks.'

From the side, I hear rat-face laugh. Pretty Boy and I turn to him.

'Siblings, eh?' he asks, taking a step toward us. Up close and personal, he's only a bit taller than I am, and has to look up at Pretty Boy.

'Yeah?' Pretty Boy says. His arm slithers around my shoulders. 'And?'

'You two don't seem like siblings.'

'I don't understand what you mean,' Pretty Boy says. I

decide it's best to keep my mouth shut, but the townsman turns his sharp eyes to me.

'What's your brother's name again, little one?'

I open my mouth – and freeze, racking my brains.

'Uhh,' I say. 'Well . . . it's . . . ' I can feel color creeping into my face.

Pretty Boy grimaces.

'She's, uh, the special sibling,' he says.

'Oh, cut the crap,' the townsman says. 'I know you're not siblings, and you're not traders, either. You're a good actor, kid, but she's definitely not.' Pretty Boy starts to say something, but he cuts him off. 'Did you really think those disguises were fooling anyone? It's obvious you all are trying to hide something, and I'm not so stupid I can't put two and two together, especially not after that transmission about your escape yesterday.'

Pretty Boy is starting to look trapped. I notice him glancing around, making sure no other townies are closing in on us. His hand sneaks toward his gun.

'Uh-uh. Wouldn't do that if I were you.' Rat-face juts his chin at the towers. 'Snipers all over town.' He takes another step toward us and grins his slimy grin. 'If I wanted you dead, you'd already be dead.'

'Then what are you waiting for, exactly?' Pretty Boy asks. 'You trying to cut some kind of deal with us?'

'Oh, no, no.' The townsman shrugs. 'I don't care about Saint, or the Queen, or any of this political bullshit. You're trading us essential supplies, and that's all I really give a rat's ass about. I'm a businessman. I'm not interested in making friends or enemies.'

We both stand there, not sure what to say, and the towns-man laughs.

'Just don't cause us any trouble, or I really will kill you.'

'We won't, sir.'

'Good. Then I have no problem doing business with sharks.' He gives one final unnerving smile and walks away.

I unconsciously hold my breath as he leaves, expecting the snipers to start shooting any second, but nothing happens. The townsfolk all seem as friendly and helpful as before, and continue carrying goods back and forth.

'You trust him?' I ask Pretty Boy.

'Not a bit,' he says. 'We need to get out of here. I'm gonna go talk to Wolf. You make sure we didn't leave anything in the room.'

I hate taking orders from Pretty Boy, but it's a good idea. I run back to the tower, dodging townies and trying not to attract too much attention. I slow down every time someone seems to be staring at me, and speed up again when I'm alone. Once I'm inside the tower, I try to sprint up the stair-well but run out of breath after a couple of floors. I know it didn't seem *that* urgent for us to leave, but still. If something happens, I don't want to be split up.

Once I reach the room, I hurriedly gather the stray belongings. There's nothing much, just a few cans of food, my backpack, and some half-empty bottles of water, but anything is worth saving. I shove it into my pack and, on second thought, also grab one of the blankets we used. Before heading back down I peek out the window – and notice, with a feeling of dread, a stream of vehicles approaching the town.

They're all painted black and have a design painted on the side. I squint; it's a crown.

I take off running again. The staircase moves by in a blur as I stumble down. All I can think about is how I have to warn the others before the Queen's men arrive. They'll recognize everyone instantly, and I doubt this seedy mayor is going to help us. Maybe he even called her here . . .

As I round the corner and start down the last stretch of steps, I plow right into someone heading up. He falls backward and we both tumble down a few steps before coming to a rest at the bottom. I find myself on top of Pretty Boy, both of us wide-eyed and breathing hard.

'Kid,' he says in between breaths. 'The—'

'The Queen is coming!' I blurt out as soon as I get my own breath back.

'Yeah. We saw.'

'So where are you going?'

'To hide.'

'Pretty Boy!' Of course he would run and hide. I try to get up, but he grabs my arm and holds me there.

'No, no, listen. We can't go out there; if she sees our faces it's over. Dolly's moving the truck, and Wolf said he had some kind of plan, so . . . .'

I keep struggling for a few seconds as his words sink in. Wolf has a plan. I hesitate.

'Is it a *good* plan? Is it going to actually work?'

'I don't know. He looked pretty excited, though.'

'So . . . explosives?'

'Presumably.'

He releases my arm, and I scoot off as I realize I'm still

on top of him. We move on our hands and knees over to the nearby window and poke our heads up to get a better view.

The Queen's squad of vehicles is pulling into the town. There are four big trucks, all with the Queen's obnoxious and rather poorly painted golden crown on the hood and sides. Guards pour out of the trucks, dozens of them, all with guns at the ready. And then the Queen herself emerges. Her leg has a fresh cast. Despite the injury, she moves as grandiosely as possible.

Our truck is gone, and Dolly and Tank with it. Wolf, however, is standing right out in the open, arms folded across his chest. The town's mayor is beside him, twitching nervously. Everyone else has vacated the area. I suck in a sharp breath.

'What is he doing?' I ask. 'The Queen is gonna see right through that disguise!'

'No idea,' Pretty Boy says in a low voice. 'But it *is* Wolf. He must have something batshit crazy up his sleeve. And, against all logic, his plans usually work.'

'Usually?' That's not very comforting.

'Usually,' he says firmly, and I notice sweat running down the side of his face.

I tense at the sight of the Queen approaching Wolf. All my instincts scream at me to do something, but I repeatedly assure myself Wolf wouldn't do something *this* suicidal without a plan.

I can't hear what they're saying to each other from this distance. All I can do is watch the Queen's extensive hand gesturing. The mayor talks to her, while Wolf stays where he is.

'What's happening?' I hiss at Pretty Boy.

'How the hell am I supposed to know?' He studies the scene, biting his bottom lip. I turn away from the window and creep toward the doorway.

'I'm gonna get a closer look,' I whisper. He notices me moving away and his eyes widen.

'No, Kid, just stay here—' He reaches out to grab me, but I scamper away on my hands and knees.

'I got it, don't worry!'

I rise to a crouch once I'm in the doorway. I can't see Wolf and the townsman from this angle, but I can see the Queen's escort of vehicles and several guards. I scoot out of the doorway and move toward the building across from me in a slow, awkward shuffle. About halfway there I realize there's really no benefit in doing this when no one's even looking this way, and break into a sprint. I reach the doorway and find it locked. My heart sinks, but to the side I spot a window. It has no glass, just a thin blanket covering it. It's a low window, about even with my chest, so it's easy enough to squeeze myself through it.

But the makeshift curtains wrap around me, and I end up fumbling and falling to the floor. With a loud rip of fabric, I land on my back. Only when I've managed to sit up and escape from the blanket do I realize I'm not alone.

Sitting in the corner of the dim, dingy room are two children, a boy and a girl. They're tiny and thin with eyes too big for their gaunt faces, and they're both staring at me in sheer terror. I completely forgot this little squat was probably someone's home.

I wave at them tentatively, but they only shrink farther back into the corner.

'Umm, hi,' I say, keeping my voice as quiet and soothing as possible. 'I'm not here to hurt you, so—'

Something hard and metal slams into my skull. I stumble and fall, ears ringing and brains all shook up.

'Ow! What the—' I turn around just in time to see the frying pan swing toward me a second time. I duck out of the way and scramble across the floor. The woman is skinnier than her kids, practically skin and bones, but there's a fire in her eyes that makes her scarier than Tank at his worst. She advances on me, frying pan held above her head. She pauses at a thump behind her, and we both turn to see Pretty Boy climbing through the window.

'What are you doing here?' I hiss at him. The woman looks back and forth between us, quickly determines who the bigger threat is, and flies at him.

He grabs her wrists before she can hit him and struggles to get the makeshift weapon out of her grip. Seeing their mother in potential trouble, the two kids run to her aid. The boy attaches himself to one of Pretty Boy's legs while the girl beats on him with tiny fists.

'Uh, Kid, a little help?' he says, struggling to keep them all off of him.

As amusing as it is to watch him get beaten on by little kids, I'm worried about the children getting hurt by all of his flailing around. I grab the girl under the armpits and pick her up. She struggles and yells in my grasp, so I hold her as far away from me as possible and deposit her in a corner. By the time I run back to grab the boy she's already back again, this time attacking *me* with her pitifully weak punches. I ignore her and grab the boy, prying his tiny fingers off Pretty Boy's leg. The boy reattaches to my arm and bites me, hard. I yell and recoil, but he clings to me. Meanwhile, the girl grabs me by the legs and pulls. I flail for a moment before dropping to the floor. Both of them jump on me, hitting and scratching and biting.

A loud *clang* echoes through the room, and everything stops. The mother stumbles and falls to the floor. Pretty Boy stands there, breathing hard, frying pan in hand.

'Mommy!' the girl wails, rushing to her mother's side. 'You killed her!' She starts to sob.

'Mommy?' The little boy lets go of me and sits there, openmouthed.

'*Pretty Boy!* You killed their mommy?!' I yell at him, horrified.

'I didn't kill her!' He looks baffled by the reactions. 'She's just knocked out; calm down. And what the hell are *you* freaking out about, Kid?' He walks over, pulls me up from the floor, and drags me over to a window on the other side of the room. 'We're here to see what's happening, aren't we? So stop wasting time.'

'Stop trying to yank me around!' I slap his hands away, but I know he's right. I stay low, pull the ratty curtains aside, and look out. We're a handful of yards away from Wolf now, and I can hear bits and pieces of their conversation. I can see some of the guards, too, standing around and surveying the area. As one looks my way, I duck down lower.

'Then take off the head-wrap,' the Queen says demandingly. She has her hands on her hips and looks seriously displeased. The townsman is shaking his head; he takes a few steps back from the two of them. Wolf gives a big, theatrical shrug and raises both hands to the cloth wrap. He pauses for a moment – then raises one hand and waves wildly. I'm confused for a second before realizing it must be a signal.

The Queen backs toward her guards, who are instantly up in arms. They all look around wildly, trying to find whoever Wolf is waving at.

Nothing happens.

Wolf drops the hand, then raises it and does it again, this time making the gesture even more over-the-top.

'Seriously?' he yells. 'You tryin' to make me look stupid or something?'

'Are we supposed to do something?' I whisper to Pretty Boy.

'No clue,' he whispers back.

Then I hear it: a sound like rushing air, growing louder. Those outside all hear it, too. Wolf and the townsman back away from the Queen and her guards. Some of the guards panic and run, while the rest rush to cover the Queen.

'What *is* that?' I ask, and just *barely* see something hit in the middle of the cluster of the Queen's men before Pretty Boy tackles me to the floor, just in time for the explosion.

XXIII
Queen's Gambit

The roar of the explosion is deafening. Heat leaks in through the window, followed by smoke. I pull my shirt up and cover my mouth with it. My ears buzz.

'What was that?' Pretty Boy asks between coughs.

'A bazooka, I think,' I say, remembering Wolf's excitement over finding it.

'Of course. A bazooka. Should've known.'

I look over at the two children and their unconscious mother. I can barely see them through the smoke.

'You two should stay here, okay?' I say, and move toward the door.

'*We* should stay here!' Pretty Boy protests. Nonetheless, he follows me. I push aside the dresser barricading the door, inch it open, and warily peek out the crack.

At first only the cries of the injured come from the smoke, rising up like the eerie howls of ghosts. But gradually the smoke clears away to reveal the carnage. The explosion took quite a chunk out of the Queen's escort, leaving bodies everywhere, although there's still a handful left unharmed. Mayor

Rat-Face is gone, likely hightailed it out of here the second he realized a fight was erupting in his town square. The Queen seems unhurt, thanks to a few of her men shielding her. She pushes them away and straightens up. Her expression shifts from fear to simmering rage as she sees the explosion's aftermath.

With the last wisps of smoke clearing away, Wolf finally emerges. He's laughing, of course. He tears off his head-wrap and points at the Queen.

'*Yeah!*' he says triumphantly. 'Motherfucking bazooka! That's what I'm talking about!'

The Queen turns to him, face contorted in rage, and pulls out a gun.

Before he can even open his mouth, she shoots him in the chest.

For a second I'm too stunned to move or speak. Then Wolf hits the ground, and I lurch forward.

'Wolf!' I try to run to him, but Pretty Boy holds me back.

'No, Kid, no – you'll get yourself killed.'

'She's gonna kill Wolf!'

'He's dead already, Kid! Point-blank to the chest, there's no way—'

I ignore him and try to squirm free. I break out of his hold and dash forward, only to be tackled into the dust after two steps.

'Why are you being like this?' he hisses as we fumble on the ground.

'Why are you always like *this*?'

'I'm trying to save our asses!'

'Well, you're *not* helping!'

I backhand him. He lets out a low hiss of frustration and grabs both of my wrists.

'Is this about me kissing you?' he asks, contemptuous. 'Because if it is, get the fuck over it. It was nothing.'

Even in my frantic state, that stings. Not just that he's downplaying the whole incident, but that he thinks being kissed is what I'd be upset about. I didn't even *want* to be kissed. I furiously blink back tears.

'Like I give a shit about that! This isn't *about* you! Let me go!'

After some more back-and-forth scuffling around in the dust, we realize at the same time how quiet it is. I look up to find the Queen staring at us from a few yards away. Her eyes light up upon sight of Pretty Boy.

'Get them!' she screeches. She's lost all semblance of composure and elegance. Her eyes are wild in a sweaty face, her white dress torn and dirtied. She looks crazy, and her scowl deepens when her torn-apart group of guards fails to respond immediately. She heads toward us in long, determined strides. A handful of her men straggle after her.

Pretty Boy and I scramble to our feet, tripping over each other in our hurry to get up, and run in the opposite direction. We squeeze through a narrow alleyway between two buildings, Pretty Boy shoving me forward and frantically whispering at me to hurry up, and keep running. The town is empty, all the townies holed up in their dens. We weave between buildings and piles of garbage and scrap metal. The Queen's shouting and her men's footsteps gradually fade away as we lose them. We find a small, doorless hovel and dash inside.

I drop to a crouch, panting. Pretty Boy stands near the doorway and steals worried glances outside, but it seems we've lost them for now. Even as the immediate danger wanes, I feel a deeper fear growing inside me. Thinking of Wolf brings up a raw, painful flood of emotion, but I force it down and clench my shaking hands at my sides.

'What are we going to do?' I ask, staring at Pretty Boy. Of course, out of everyone to be stuck with, it had to be him. He'll probably just run off and leave me alone, and then . . . and then, what will I do?

'I don't know.' Pretty Boy looks even more frightened than I feel, and checks every few seconds to make sure no one is outside. He fiddles nervously with his gun.

'Well, you said they had a plan, right? Wolf must have something—'

'Wolf got *shot*!' he says. I ignore him and keep babbling in an attempt to calm myself down.

'And someone had to shoot that bazooka, Dolly and Tank must be around—'

'We don't know that! And even if they are . . . with all the Queen's men, there's no way the townies will help us . . . ' Pretty Boy finally stops checking out the doorway. He slumps down to the floor with his back against the wall. 'Maybe we should turn ourselves in to the Queen.'

'Don't be stupid, she'll hand us over to Saint!'

'So we should run.'

'Of *course* you would say that,' I say. My voice comes out harsher than expected. 'That's all you ever do.'

'Kid . . . Kid, listen.' He leans toward me, eyes wide and earnest. 'You and me, we aren't like them. You know that.

We'll just get ourselves killed if we keep doing this. There's nothing wrong with running away.'

'There ain't nowhere to go, Pretty Boy,' I say. 'And we'd never last in the wastes on our own.'

'We'll figure something out!'

'No!' I take a deep breath and push my fear back, forcing up anger and determination instead. 'You know, you've had plenty of opportunities to run off. Every night, every town, the Queen . . . and you haven't!'

'That's because—'

'It's because you're too scared to even do that!' I'm practically yelling now, but I can't stop myself. 'Because you've never actually *been* on your own! You've always had a family or a crew or somebody to take care of you!'

He doesn't try to interrupt me this time, but just stares.

'You're scared of being alone because you've never been that way,' I say, 'and I'm scared of being alone because I have. So we can't run. We have to stay and find the others. We *need* them. Both of us.'

I stop, chest heaving, and realize my eyes are watering. I wipe at them impatiently and turn away from him, trying to get myself under control. A lot of feelings are stirring up all of a sudden, and I can't deal with them right now. Most of all, I'm afraid. Afraid that he'll run off and leave me, afraid that he'll stay and my choice will get us both killed.

Pretty Boy is silent. When I turn back to him, he's staring at the floor. He runs a hand through his hair, swallows hard, squeezes his eyes shut for a moment, and opens them again.

'I'm not cut out for this,' he says. 'I was never meant for this life.'

'You can learn. Even I am.'

He sighs, and is about to respond when something stops him. He raises a hand to silence me and peeks out the door. When he jerks his head back his face is pale.

'Shit, they heard us. They're coming.'

'What do we do?' I ask. He hesitates, eyes rapidly searching the room.

'Got it,' he says. 'Take this.' He throws something to me. I fumble and nearly drop it: his gun.

'What—'

'Give me your knife.'

'But why—'

'Just do it!'

I hand it over. I have no idea what he's thinking, but he seems to have some kind of plan and that's better than I can say for myself. He nods, brow furrowed.

'Now shoot the gun.'

'Huh?'

'At the ceiling. Now.'

I fire upward. A chunk of plaster falls to the ground, making me jump. I look at Pretty Boy for further instruction, but he isn't paying attention to me. Without warning, he slashes the blade across his own stomach, ripping his shirt and slicing a shallow-but-wide gash. I stare as blood starts to well up. Before I can even voice a question, he abruptly drops to the floor, clutches his stomach, and screams. I stare, baffled.

'What the hell are you—'

Guards are in the room before I finish my question. There are three of them, one nursing a wound, all with weapons on me. I drop the gun. The Queen is right behind her men, entering the room with a dramatic flourish despite her condition. She glares at me, but the look softens as she turns to Pretty Boy.

'Darling, what happened?' she coos, swooping down on him like a vulture.

'She shot me!' I hear him say as a guard grabs my arm and twists it behind my back. I stare over at Pretty Boy, my mouth hanging open, and see him looking up at the Queen with a face wet with tears. He's actually *crying*. 'I said I was going to run and she ... she tried to kill me!'

'Oh, you poor thing. Don't worry, I'm here now.' The Queen helps him up, her hand lingering on his arm. He keeps one hand pressed to his stomach, his face contorted with nonexistent pain. He smiles weakly at her, and she doesn't see the fakeness.

The Queen's guard turns me away so I can't see what's happening anymore. He roughly searches me.

'Wh-What—' I say, flabbergasted. 'But, I ... ' This is his plan? He's going to betray me and run to the Queen with his tail between his legs? My stomach twists. I never should've trusted him, never should've listened to what he said. I had him figured out at this point, I should have *known* ...

'Let her go,' Pretty Boy says. It takes a second to sink in. I turn to find him holding my knife to the Queen's throat. He has a fistful of her hair and is holding her in front of him, a meat shield between himself and the guards. The man holding my arm lets go and turns his gun on Pretty Boy, but hesitates. All three guards are obviously too afraid to fire.

'Darling,' the Queen says, her voice strained but still somehow coddling, 'what do you think you're doing?'

Pretty Boy yanks her toward the door.

'You heard me,' he says loudly. 'Let Kid go and no one has to get—' He flinches as one man takes a step toward him, and slouches down so more of his body is hidden behind the Queen. '—hurt,' he finishes more quietly, bravado cracking.

I stare at him, then at the Queen's men. They all look to her, but she's too shocked to give orders. Nobody moves.

I take a timid step away from the guards.

'Umm, so, I'm just gonna go ahead and—' Before I can finish my sentence, the nearest guard lunges at me. I jump backward to avoid him, slip, and fall to the floor hard. As soon as I hit I crawl for the door. Somebody fires a gun, and the bullet whizzes right past my head.

At the first sound of gunfire, Pretty Boy immediately loses his composure. He shoves the Queen forward and takes off, running out the door and leaving me in the dust. I scramble to my feet and follow, the Queen's furious screech sounding off behind me.

I can't see where Pretty Boy went; he got out of here way too fast. I run blindly, avoiding open ground, instead climbing fences and squeezing through tight alleyways I hope they can't follow me through. My heartbeat fills my ears. I can't tell if I'm being chased, and I'm too scared to turn and find out. The streets are all empty of life. I don't even know where I'm going or what my plan is. I just run until I can't run anymore.

Finally I stop in a narrow space between two hovels and crouch there. My chest and legs burn.

When my wheezing breath finally quiets down, I strain to hear any voices or footsteps. The town is dead quiet. Either I lost them, or they found someone else to chase. I catch a whiff of smoke and look up to see a cloud of it growing above the town. It's impossible to tell where it's coming from. I wonder who's setting fires: the Queen's men trying to smoke us out, or one of my friends spreading chaos?

Movement catches my eye. The cloth covering a window above me shifts, and a pair of sunken eyes stares out suspiciously. As soon as I look up, they disappear.

I have to keep moving. The mayor claimed he's not on anyone's side, but I wouldn't put it past him to give us up, especially with his town getting wrecked. I force myself to my feet, choose a random direction, and start moving. Once I reach the edge of the building I peer out. There's no one in sight. I hesitate, unsure what to do next, when I hear a gunshot from somewhere to my right. I instinctively head that way. I could be walking toward all the Queen's men . . . but then again, if there's gunfire, it means at least one of my friends is there.

I dash from building to building on my way, ducking behind houses and rusty piles of metal and garbage. I pass a few burning buildings on the way. The fire moves quickly, spreading around town, eating through cloth and wood and anything it touches. I pause to marvel at the blaze before continuing, and use the smoke as cover. I'm painfully careful to make sure no one sees me, sometimes crawling on all fours between shelters. I don't encounter a single person on the way. By the time I get closer to where the gunshot came from, I'm completely out of breath and feeling pretty silly about my efforts to be sneaky. Around the corner I hear voices. None are familiar, which makes my stomach turn to knots.

I make my half-crouching way over to the rusty remains of an old car and duck behind it. I hide there for a few seconds, making sure there's no change in the voices I hear, and rise up to peer over the hood.

On the other side is a wide open strip of land between two of the towers. A handful of the Queen's men are there, a ragged bunch clustered in a circle. The shadow of one tower falls across them. They look torn up already, nursing wounds and dripping blood in the dust. One's gun hand seems to be dead, but he's dutifully clutching it in the other one, limp arm hanging at his side.

At the center of their circle, tied up and blindfolded, is Pretty Boy. He's slumped onto his side on the ground, with one side of his head bloodied.

'We've got one here,' a guard says into a walkie-talkie. The response is too full of static for me to understand. 'No, he's by himself. Any sign of the others?' More static. 'Dunno where they are, but they're giving us hell.'

All I can think about is Pretty Boy trying to save me back there. I know there's not much I can do, and I really should turn my back and run . . . but how can I leave him? Even with all of the confused feelings I have about him, he's a member of our crew. Seeing him like this melts away my anger. I can't turn my back on him.

I duck behind the car again and pat down my pockets, searching for anything useful. I have no gun, no explosives, not even my trusty knife. There aren't any big rocks around to throw. All I have is my backpack, which contains a half-empty canteen and little else.

'Shit, shit, shit,' I hiss under my breath, desperately trying to think of something. I bite my lip and stand up, looking over at the guards.

As I watch, Pretty Boy rolls onto his back and groans. A guard responds with a sharp kick to the side, making me wince. Pretty Boy rolls over and tries to crawl away, but another man pins him down with a boot on his back. The circle laughs.

My stomach tightens and my fists clench at my sides. I can't just sit here and watch, not even if it's Pretty Boy. Chastising myself all the while for being such an idiot, I move out into the open.

'Hey!' I yell at the guards, hands still balled into fists. I move toward them with absolutely no idea what I intend to do. 'Stop it!'

They turn to me, guns raised in an instant. There's a confused pause as they try to figure out who the hell I am. One of them finally recognizes me.

'We-ell, you sharks are even dumber than we thought,' he says, grinning and advancing toward me. 'Just gonna walk up and surrender, huh?' The rest of the guards leave Pretty Boy where he lies and fan out, moving toward me as a unit. They close around me in a half circle, the car at my back. I hold my ground.

'We've got the little girl,' another guard says into his walkie-talkie. Smirking, he takes a few steps toward me and reaches for my arm. 'Now c'mere, and don't try anything stupid . . .'

His hand closes around my arm as I'm still trying to figure out how to react. He drags me forward and – *swoosh*. An odd sound, like rushing air.

I freeze. The hand on my arm goes slack, and I step to the side just in time as the man falls forward. He hits the ground, a chunk of skull missing. Blood and brains ooze from the back of his head.

Everybody stares.

'What the hell?' The Queen's men look as baffled I am. One opens his mouth, and before he can speak there's another soft *whoosh* and a bullet hole appears in his forehead. As the second body falls, panic breaks loose among the rest of them. One man turns in a circle, wildly firing his guns at both of the nearby towers. Another points his gun at me. The latter goes down in a second, before he even has a chance to voice a threat.

The last two promptly lose their shit. One falls to the ground and cowers, and the other, the man with the injured arm, sprints away. He falls before he makes it to the shelter of the next building.

'Please,' the last man begs, crouched in the dirt with both hands over his head. 'Please don't kill me!'

I'm the only person left standing. Bodies litter the ground around me. The only other living people are Pretty Boy and the begging guard, both cringing on the ground.

'I, uhh . . . don't really have any control over it. Sorry?' I say.

He stays on the ground, whimpering, while I stand there awkwardly. After a few seconds of nothing happening, I walk over to Pretty Boy. He's still tied up and blindfolded and is valiantly trying to squirm away from the action. When I touch his arm he flinches.

'It's me,' I say, and slip the blindfold off. He blinks up at me, breathing hard, and looks around at the bodies of the Queen's men.

'Kid?' he says, taken aback. 'What . . . what did you do?'

'Umm,' I say. 'Nothing?'

'Uhh, you sure?' He chokes out a nervous laugh. 'Thanks, I guess?'

'You're welcome, I guess,' I say, imitating his dry tone.

The whimpering of the man behind me stops abruptly. I turn around, expecting to see one of my friends finishing him off.

Instead I find the Queen.

She's an absolute mess. Her hair is in disarray, her face smeared with dirt, her fancy dress ripped and stained. She's completely alone, her usual gaggle of guards nowhere to be found. She looks more like a crazy than a queen, trailing blood and dirt in her ridiculous getup, but the shotgun in her hands demands that I take her seriously. The gun looks too big for her, and her skinny arms are shaking, but I have no doubt she could and would kill me in an instant.

'My Queen!' the man says. He crawls toward her, groveling. 'Thank God you're here, they were—'

'Shut up,' she says, and shoots him in the face. I try very hard not to look at the messy body as it falls. Instead I keep my eyes locked on the Queen as she approaches, reloading the gun.

'Well, well,' she says, in a cracked and lilting voice that makes it pretty clear she's completely lost it. I swallow hard. 'I've finally caught up with you two.'

She aims the shotgun at my head.

XXIV
Long Live the Queen

I slowly raise my hands in surrender and otherwise stay as still as possible.

'You dumb little bitch,' the Queen says. 'Do you know how *embarrassing* it is to chase a bunch of fuckup sharks like you around? This is beneath me. So beneath me.' She chews her lip and glances around the empty area. 'And where are all my men? Where? All dead? And fuck if I know how. This isn't how any of this was supposed to happen.'

'You didn't have to come here,' I say. 'And you don't have to—'

'Shut up!' she snarls. I clamp my mouth shut. Her lips twist to the side in a scowl. 'My mansion is in ruins because of you fuckers. Now the last of my men are dead. I'm not about to let you go, not when you're my last shot at securing a partnership with Saint.'

I'm really wishing my mystery sniper would step in right now, but no gunshots come. The town is silent and empty: There's just me, the Queen, and Pretty Boy, and the latter is useless. I meet his eyes and wonder if I look as scared as he does.

'Your highness,' he says, and shifts his gaze from me to the Queen. 'Why don't you just calm down for a second? She's worth nothing dead.'

The Queen whirls on him and her face contorts. She shoves the barrel of the gun in his face, pushing him flat on the ground.

'W-We!' he squeaks out. '*We're* worth nothing to you dead!'

'And *you*,' she says through gritted teeth, 'after everything I offered you, this is how you repay me?' She leans close. Spit flies out of her mouth, peppering his face. He tries to cringe away, but he's stuck between her gun and the ground. 'I could have saved you from all this.'

Her fingers twitch and tighten around the gun, moving as if to pull the trigger, then releasing again.

'But maybe,' she says, and licks her lips, smearing red lipstick around her mouth, 'maybe I should keep you around. A pretty face always has its uses . . .'

Her eyes are locked on Pretty Boy, or maybe staring through him, with the strange glazed look of someone falling apart. She seems to have forgotten I'm still here, crouched right beside the two of them.

'Or maybe I should just kill you,' she says, and her mouth stretches out into a too-wide, creepy smile. 'Yes, that would be much more satisfying.' Her fingers start to tighten on the trigger.

I tackle her to the ground. She screams, kicks, and flails, while I use both my hands just to keep the gun pointed away from me. It's a pretty pathetic fight, a ragged old woman versus a skinny little girl. We're stuck for a few seconds, her desperately trying to get a clean shot at my face and me desperately trying to stop that from happening. When she realizes neither of us is budging, she drops the gun and lashes out with her hands. Her long nails rake my face like claws. I scream, and her other hand closes around my throat and cuts off the cry. I grab two handfuls of her long hair and yank as hard as I can. We're stuck for a few seconds, both tightening our grips – she lets go before I do. But with a loud shriek and one big push, she topples me off of her. I get a face full of dirt and scramble away, kicking up a cloud of dust around us.

Through the haze I see it: the shotgun, lying in the dirt. I grab it and jump to my feet, swinging around to point it at the Queen. She's on her hands and knees still, coughing from the dust. As the cloud clears, I raise the barrel to her head.

She grins up at me. Her dress is ripped further from our fight, and her knees look bloody through the torn cloth.

'Look at you,' she says, rising to her feet. I follow her with the gun, but hesitate to shoot. 'We both know you won't pull that trigger, little girl. You're not like the others.' She walks toward me, coming just a few inches away from the gun, not a hint of fear on her face. I stumble backward, but she keeps coming closer.

'You really didn't have to come here,' I whisper.

Her chest presses against the barrel, daring me.

'You're not going to shoot me,' she says. She starts to laugh, that awful high-pitched cackle.

A few days ago, she might have been right. But not today. I close my eyes and pull the trigger.

The recoil takes me by surprise. So does the blood, a ridiculous amount of it erupting all over me. I end up on my back in the dust, ears ringing, drenched. The gun drops from my hands. I feel numb. After a few seconds of shock, I peel open my eyes. Mistake: The Queen's body is right in front of me, and it's not pretty. I squeeze my eyes shut, turn away, and take a deep breath before opening them again.

My face is warm and wet and sticky. I raise my hands to try to wipe it off and realize my hands are covered in blood as well. The smell is so thick I can taste it on the back of my tongue.

I had to kill her. She made the choice to come after us, and to try to kill me. I'm not going to feel bad about it . . . but my hands are shaking. Taking deep breaths, I scoot over to Pretty Boy and untie his hands.

He sits up and rubs his chafed wrists, with only a slight, wordless nod of acknowledgment. He recovers a lot faster than I do. He gets up, walks over to the closest body, and starts rummaging around in its pockets.

I sit down heavily. If Pretty Boy is relaxed enough to start looting, that means it's over. I strain to hear any gunshots or commotion, but there's nothing to hear. The townies are all still holed up in their homes, and the Queen's men must be either dead, hiding, or gone. Judging from the state of things, Dolly and Tank must have been busy picking them off. And Wolf . . .

Thinking about him getting shot makes me feel like something cold and sharp is poking into my chest. I suck in a breath through my teeth, let it out slowly, and force myself to my feet again. His body must be nearby. Not far away, I can see the scorched earth where the bazooka's rocket exploded, surrounded by pieces of charred bodies. But as for Wolf, there's no sign of him. I walk over just to make sure, and ignore how the smell of the burnt bodies makes me a little hungry. Wolf's body is gone. I saw the Queen shoot him right here – did the guards take the body? Or . . .

Just on cue, I hear a familiar low whistle from behind me.

'Wow, what a fuckin' mess. You do all this yourself, Kid?'

I turn around and there he is, as alive as ever.

'Wolf!' A surge of relief fills me and overflows, and I can't stop myself from running over. I slam into him, making him stumble back a few steps, and wrap my arms around him in a tight hug. He pauses, looking baffled, and roughly shoves me off. I fall on my ass in the dirt and scramble up again, still grinning. 'You're alive!'

'Of course I am, dumbass,' he says. 'You think I would go into a situation like that without a plan?' He rips off the remnants of his tattered shirt, displaying a black vest underneath, and grins. 'Bullet-proof vest, motherfuckers.'

He does a double take at me, and his triumphant grin fades slightly.

'You look like you massacred a small village with your bare hands. What the hell happened?'

'Yeah, umm. I killed the Queen. With a shotgun.' I rub the side of my head self-consciously. 'It was a little messy.'

'We-ell, look at you, Kid.' His grin is back in full force. 'Killin' people and runnin' around covered in blood. A lil' baby shark, eh?'

The baby comment chafes a little, but I still smile. He takes a look at all the dead men spread across the ground and the bloody remains of the Queen.

'I'm not even gonna ask what happened,' he says. ''Cause I'm not sure I wanna know. But I'm proud of you, kiddo.' He punches me in the shoulder. And as silly as it may be, I feel happiness welling up at his words, covering up all my shaky feelings over killing the Queen. He's *proud* of me. Hell, even more than that, I'm proud of myself. For once, I did something on my own. I smile like an idiot and can't stop, even after Wolf has walked away and started checking the bodies for weapons and valuables.

A hand claps me on the shoulder, and I turn to see Pretty Boy. In his outstretched hand is my trusty old knife. I take it.

'Forgive me yet?' he asks.

'Ain't that easy,' I say, 'but it's a start.'

He smiles a little, but then turns serious.

'I'm, uh . . . I'm sorry. About, you know, what happened. I shouldn't have done that.'

'Nope, you shouldn't have.' I stare down at my feet, my smile fading away.

'I've been a real shithead to you, and you've treated me way better than I deserve. I mean, you came and saved me even after everything, and that's really . . . ' He trails off, and when I look up at him his cheeks are turning red. 'You're a good kid, is what I'm trying to say.'

'Thanks.' I don't know what else to say. 'You . . . um . . . you've got potential to be a good guy someday. Maybe.'

He laughs, and for once it doesn't sound fake or mean.

'Thanks,' he says. He's about to say something else when

he's interrupted by a very loud and distinctly Tank-like whoop of excitement.

He and Dolly emerge from one of the nearby towers. He's lugging the bazooka with him, and Dolly is carrying an impressive-looking sniper rifle with all the delicateness of holding a child.

'Did you see me with that bazooka? Did you see?' Tank asks Wolf excitedly. 'Damn, that was fun.'

'Told you the plan would work,' Wolf says. 'We didn't even fuck anything up for once.'

'*You* guys didn't!' I butt in. 'Pretty Boy and I spent the whole time running away!'

'And getting the shit kicked out of me,' he adds. 'And you guys get to have fun with your fancy guns, what the fuck?'

'And I thought you were *dead*!' I say to Wolf.

'Aww, Kid, that's insulting. Should've known better.'

'Well, you could've let us know!' Pretty Boy nods in agreement.

'No time. You two are both pretty useless, anyway,' Wolf says.

'Hey, don't lump Kid in with Pretty Boy. That ain't fair,' Tank says with a laugh. Pretty Boy attempts to shove him, which has absolutely no effect on Tank's girth.

Meanwhile, Dolly comes up beside me.

'You have blood all over your face,' she informs me quietly.

'Uh, yeah, I know. The Queen's.'

'I saw.'

'Thanks for shooting those guards.'

'I ran out of bullets.'

'That's okay. I handled the rest.'

'Yes, you did,' she says. She walks over to the Queen's body and stares down at it. Her face not showing any reaction, she sets down her sniper rifle, pulls out a pistol, and points it at what's left of the Queen's head. I look away just before she starts shooting, and keep my gaze averted until she finishes unloading the clip. I hear her sigh quietly before walking away.

The others have started looting the bodies already. Wolf goes straight for their weapons, collecting himself quite a pile despite the fact we already have a truck full of guns and explosives. Pretty Boy is smart enough to take their walkie-talkies, which even Wolf admits is a good idea.

'All right,' Wolf says, trying to juggle a few too many guns in his arms. 'Now let's get the fuck out of here before the townies realize *I* set those houses on fire.'

For the first time in what feels like ages, we aren't running from anyone. Everyone is in high spirits as we set off, leaving Towers behind with a mess of bullet holes and blackened buildings to remember us by. I wonder if the mayor will rethink his policy on dealings with sharks.

I ride in the jeep with Wolf and Dolly, while Tank drives the big truck with Pretty Boy riding along. Pretty Boy and Wolf each have a walkie-talkie so we can communicate between vehicles. Wolf takes advantage of this by spewing vulgarities and insults at Pretty Boy whenever he gets bored. Dolly spends almost an hour meticulously cleaning her new sniper rifle, and I do my best to clean the blood off myself. Pretty Boy navigates with the help of a map from the townies, and we drive straight through the day. I drift in and out of sleep, relaxed by the movement and the warm air.

When the sun goes down we pull onto the side of the road to rest for the night. Since we didn't see any other cars and Pretty Boy judges we aren't *too* close to Saint's territory yet, Wolf lets us have a fire. There aren't any people to fry up this time, but we bust out a generous amount of canned food. There's soup, beans, and fruits. Pretty Boy reads off labels and divvies it out to whoever claims it first. I end up with some sliced pineapple and a can of chili. Fruit is always a treat. I save it for last and eat very slowly, savoring each bite with its almost overwhelming sweetness.

I sit cross-legged next to Dolly on the ground. She's proving, as usual, to be the only person in existence who can eat straight out of a can without making any kind of mess. By the time I'm done with my meal I have sauce and pineapple juice covering my hands and all down the front of my shirt. My clothes are still caked with blood, and I'm sure my combined smell of that and sweat and pineapples is pretty rank. I find myself wishing for a bath like I had back at the Queen's, but I guess that's out of the question.

Normally I wouldn't waste the water, but since we have excess right now, I use some of it to rewash my hands and face after the meal. It's quiet. Everyone is stuffed and tired and content. For a while nobody speaks, and we all sit around watching the fire and basking in the calmness. It's too dark to see anything beyond the reach of the firelight, but the wastelands don't scare me anymore. I feel safe within our bubble of light and warmth.

Pretty Boy stretches out on the ground and soon dozes off. Tank, still sitting, nods off intermittently. Dolly cleans her fingernails with a knife, and Wolf pores over one of the maps he bought. I don't know how he could be getting much out of it when he can't even read, but judging from his furrowed brows he's doing some serious thinking.

'So we're really gonna do this, Wolf?' I ask, pulling my knees to my chest and hugging them. He squints at me.

'Do what?'

'Blow up the radio tower.'

'Well, yeah.'

'But . . . ' I scuff one boot in the dirt. 'I mean, why?'

'Ain't got much of a choice, Kid, this Saint guy's after us.'

'Well, we could always run or something,' I say. 'And, I mean, from an outside perspective, isn't what he's doing kind of . . . good?'

The silence around the fire suddenly feels uncomfortably thick. I feel the tension growing with each second that passes. Wolf scrutinizes me from across the flames, and Tank and Dolly both watch him and await his response.

'Let me ask you something, Kid,' Wolf says with a hard edge to his voice. 'Do you know what happens when you give one person too much power?'

'Not really?'

'Nuclear wastelands, that's what happens.' He spreads his arms wide to show the empty stretch of desert around us. In the silence after his response, I realize how quiet it is out here. There's only the crackle of flames and the sound of my breathing. 'You know, there used to be plants here.

There used to be animals. There used to be people. You think any of them had a say in starting the war? No way. But they paid the price all the same.'

'But you don't know if Saint would be like that, he—'

'*Everybody* is like that when they get too much power. Look at the Queen: She used to be all right. She stayed neutral, her mansion was a safe place for travelers, and she treated her own people well. But once she got all big and powerful, she got addicted to it. And the second that power started to slip out from under her, she fuckin' threw away *everything* to try and get it back. She was willing to betray us, to kill Ruby. She broke all her own rules. And that's what all people are like. They'll do anything to gain power, and to keep it once they have it.' He shakes his head, grimacing. 'You post-bombers all think the world before was some kind of utopia. It wasn't. People still killed each other, and assholes didn't get the punishment they deserved. We had people in charge worse than the Queen, and the whole "justice" thing was a lot slower and a lot less reliable than putting a bullet in someone's head.'

Tank lets out an impressed whistle.

'And here I was thinking we were doing it just for fun!'

'Well, that too,' Wolf says, the corner of his mouth curving upward.

'I thought you were just a kid when the bombs fell? How do you know all this kinda stuff?' I ask.

'My parents talked about it when I was growing up. They were real smart, so it's gotta be true.' He nods to himself. 'My mom was a cop back before, y'know.'

That raises a lot of questions, like if they were so smart

how did Wolf turn out so messed up, but I figure now isn't the right time to bring that up.

'A cop? Those were like town guards, right?'

'Ehh, kind of. It just means she must've been right.'

'Oh. Okay.' I trust Wolf, so I accept it. 'My papa used to say some of the same stuff, actually.'

'Oh yeah?' Wolf looks barely interested.

'Your papa?' Tank asks, looking considerably more so. 'Y'know, you've never said . . . where did you come from, anyway? How'd you end up alone?'

'Well . . . ' It feels so far away now. Wolf and the crew have become my life. It's like I shrugged off the past and have been ignoring it ever since I got into that jeep. 'I used to live in this town . . . Bramble, it was called.'

'So you were a townie?'

'No. Well, kind of.' I never considered myself one, but I guess I did live there for a number of years. 'I mean . . . I grew up in a shelter. One of the underground ones. My papa and me.'

'What about your mom?'

'Oh, she died when I was young. Got sick or something. So it was just me and my papa for a long time.' I fiddle with my empty can, uncomfortable with everyone's eyes on me. 'But he started getting . . . sick. Not, um, physically.' I don't have the proper words to describe it. I still remember the way he looked, his eyes so distant and strange all the time, but I don't really know how to explain that. 'I think he was lonely. And we were running out of food. So we had to leave.' I force myself to set down the can, but then I don't know what to do with my hands. I pick at a hole in my jeans.

'I had never been out of the shelter. My papa was scared about radiation; he used to wear a gas mask whenever he went out. I had no idea what it was like out there, and he had no clue where to go.'

'How old were you?' Tank asks.

'Umm, twelve, I guess.'

'So where'd you go?'

'We just wandered for a while. Lucky we didn't meet any raiders or anything. We had enough food and water to survive, if barely. Finally we found a town. It was built into what my papa said used to be a school.'

'And they took you guys in?'

'They took *me* in,' I say. The answer sits there, heavy. I don't need to say anything else. Towns are wary, were warier still back then. They were all just scared, desperate survivors. They didn't trust outsiders, and only agreed to take me in because I was too young to be a threat. I remember my papa's big arms engulfing me when we said good-bye. I didn't understand why he had to go. Part of me hated that he was abandoning me; the rest of me was just grateful to have food, water, and a roof over my head.

I don't have to explain any of that. Good thing, because my tongue feels too thick to voice it.

'Sorry,' Tank says gently.

'It wasn't too bad,' I say, trying to shrug off the sadness. 'They kept me safe and fed. There were some other kids I played with. 'Course, they both died from radiation poisoning, but nothing anyone can do 'bout that . . . '

'Wow, Kid, way to dampen the mood,' Wolf says.

'Sorry,' I say. 'Anyway, it never really felt like home, so

eventually I left and I found you guys. The end.' My reasons for leaving run deeper than that, but I'm not quite sure how to explain them – the unwelcome glances, the constant feeling of not belonging, the fear they shot my papa years ago – so I leave it at that. I sit nervously, hands folded on my lap, feeling awfully exposed.

'Naw, Kid,' Wolf says. 'The beginning.'

XXV
Target Practice

When I wake up, the boys are still asleep. Tank is sleeping upright with his head leaning against a box, snoring loudly. Each of us got a couple of pillows, which Wolf was kind enough to grab along with the explosives, but Tank gave his to me. Wolf is sprawled across the open space, leaving only a tiny corner where Pretty Boy is curled up. He looks innocent when he's sleeping, handsome features relaxed and open. I don't feel an uncomfortable attraction to him like I used to, nor do I feel embarrassed or hurt or spiteful. I just feel sort of neutral, which is nice.

I sit up and stretch, cracking my shoulders and back. The crates didn't make the most comfortable bed even with a few pillows stacked on top, and there's a weird kink in my side, but I feel rested. Dolly's absence makes me curious enough to forgo more sleep. The doors are opened a tiny crack, and I can't see where she is. I slide off my crates and carefully step over Wolf. It's a challenge getting to the doors without stomping on some part of him, and I have to hop from space to space to reach the exit. I squeeze through and shut them behind me.

Dolly is just outside the truck, beside the ashes of last night's fire. Guns and boxes of ammo are spread out on the ground. She's kneeling in the middle of it all, inspecting a small handgun. As I jump down from the truck, the small sound of impact makes her instantly turn the gun toward me. I freeze and she lowers it again.

'Morning,' I say cheerfully, and take a few steps closer. I place my hands on my hips and look down at all the weapons. 'Wow, that's a lot of guns.'

'It's enough,' she says.

I crouch next to one and pick it up, handling it delicately and making sure not to point it at myself or Dolly.

'Do you know how to shoot yet?' she asks.

'Well, I mean . . . ' I shrug. 'Kind of?'

She nods, stands, and holds out the handgun she was inspecting.

'Let's practice.'

'Practice?' I repeat. 'You mean practice shooting things? I don't know, that seems a little . . . ' *Dangerous* is the first word to come to mind. *Embarrassing* is the second. I'm not exactly the best with guns. Hell, the Queen was right next to me and I still managed to goof it up, getting knocked over like that. I hesitate. Dolly doesn't budge or react whatsoever. She simply stands there, gun held out to me, until I give in and take it.

She smiles.

'Good,' she says, and grabs a pistol for herself.

*

We find a spot several yards away from the truck where there's only open wasteland and no danger of me accidentally shooting anyone. Dolly sets up the target: a pyramid of empty tin cans, the remains of our meal last night.

'So should I try to shoot it from ... what, here?' I ask, standing a few yards away. Dolly shakes her head, places a hand on my elbow, and leads me back quite a bit more. 'Seriously? There's no way I can hit that!'

'Try.'

I look doubtfully at the gun in my hand and back at Dolly. When she doesn't say anything, I sigh and plant my feet, assuming what I think is a good shooting pose. Behind me, Dolly laughs quietly.

'What?' I ask, turning around.

'Nothing. Go.'

'Right, right ... ' I turn back to the target and raise the gun. I suck in a deep breath, blow it out, do my best to steady my shaking hands as I focus on the target. Ready, and ... pull the trigger.

Nothing happens.

'Safety,' Dolly says.

'Oh, shit.' I'm turning red already and I haven't even managed to fire yet. Silently cursing myself, I click the safety off and raise the gun again. I'm already frazzled, heart thumping nervously. I don't know why it's so important to me to impress Dolly, but it is.

I fire.

I'm not sure where the bullet goes, but it's definitely nowhere near the target. A defeated sigh leaks out of me, and my arms fall slack at my sides.

'It's useless,' I say. 'I'm never gonna—' Before I can finish, Dolly places her hand on my lower back and steers me forward a few paces.

'Again,' she says. When I raise the gun, she reaches over and grabs my hands, repositioning them slightly. 'Like this.'

'Oh. Thanks.' I shoot again. The bullet dings off one of the outside cans and ricochets into the dirt.

She takes me closer, and closer. She corrects my grip and helps me aim again and again until, *finally*, I manage to knock a can off the pyramid. I let out a triumphant yell – and am promptly surprised by the sound of smattering applause behind me.

I turn around and find Wolf, Tank, and Pretty Boy sitting on the ground nearby. All the blood rushes to my face as I wonder how long they've been watching me shoot at nothing. Wolf looks thoroughly amused. I'm too flustered to say anything.

'Nice shot,' Tank says.

'Yeah, you killed the *shit* out of that can!' Wolf says, not quite as sincerely. Pretty Boy says nothing, but smirks.

Dolly pats me on the head. It makes me feel a bit better, but I'm still embarrassed. I hand the gun back to her.

'I'm done,' I tell her. Louder, to the boys, I say, 'Show's over, get outta here!'

After I stand there for a while and make it clear I won't be shooting again, they lose interest and find something else to do. I sigh, push sweaty hair out of my face, and go to pick up the can I knocked over. When it's in my hands I inspect where the bullet hit. A knot forms in my stomach. If I had this much trouble hitting an unmoving can, there's no way

I'm going to hit someone trying their damnedest to kill me. I've been trying to feel optimistic about this radio tower plan, but anxiety is creeping up on me. I can't leave the others on their own, no matter how little help I may be, but I'm starting to realize the chances of me making it out are slim. I mean, hell, they're slim for all of us, but most of all for me.

'Are you okay?' Dolly asks, jolting me out of my thoughts.

'Ahh, yeah,' I say. 'Just a little worried, I guess.'

'You'll be fine,' she says. I nod halfheartedly. 'I'll make sure of it,' she says, and places the gun back in my hand. 'Practice more. I'll watch for the boys.'

I bite my lip and look down at the gun.

'All right, all right ...' I take a few paces away from the target and stop. 'But I'm starting from here this time.'

We practice for at least an hour or two. I get better, but not by much. We take a break when the others announce it's time for breakfast, and after that Wolf decides he wants to help, too.

'If you don't hit it this time, I'm gonna hit you,' he says, leaning up too close behind me.

'What? No!' I lower the gun and turn to him. 'That's *not* helpful, Wolf!'

''Course it is. I learned like this. C'mon, just shoot.'

'Well, now I don't want to ...'

'You have five seconds before I hit you.'

'*Wolf!*'

'Four ... three ... two ...'

I raise the gun frantically and fire. It misses. I try to duck, but Wolf smacks the side of my head before I can get out of the way.

'Ow!' It didn't really hurt that much, but it's still annoying. I frown and rub the side of my head. 'I don't want to do this anymore.'

'Aww come on, don't be a pussy. I'm tryin' to help you out here.'

I fold my arms over my chest and shake my head.

'Fine, fine. How about something a little more realistic?' He leaves my side and walks over to the stacked cans.

'What do you mean a little more—' A can flies through the air toward my face. I narrowly dodge it. 'What the hell?!'

'Moving target! Shoot it!' he yells back, throwing another. It hits my shoulder this time.

'Ow! Wolf! Stop it!' I look around frantically. 'Where's Dolly? I want Dolly's training back!'

'Fuck you, I'm way better at this!'

The next can hits me in the head and sends me reeling, and I decide it's about time to change tactics. I drop my gun in the dirt, turn away, and start running.

'Get the fuck back here, Kid! That's cheating!' Another can whizzes past me. I run back to the truck and climb inside. The others are sitting there, having a conversation that stops the second I arrive. I duck behind Tank, panting.

'So I'm guessing training didn't go well?' he asks, smiling down at me.

'No. He's throwing things. He's crazy. Hide me.'

Wolf clambers noisily into the truck a few seconds later, breathing heavily. He leans one hand against the wall and spits on the floor. The spittle lands dangerously close to Pretty Boy, who wrinkles his nose and scoots away.

'Fast little fucker, ain't ya?' Wolf says. 'Knew there was a reason your dumb ass managed to stay alive for so long.' I poke my head out from behind Tank and grin at him.

'You must be getting out of shape, Wolf,' Pretty Boy says. 'Or maybe just old?'

'Shut up!' Wolf aims a halfhearted kick in his direction, but Pretty Boy dodges it. 'The only reason *you're* in shape is you're always runnin' from the fight.'

'Maybe you only stay because you can't run fast enough.'

'I said shut up. I don't need your shit right now.'

Pretty Boy shuts up, and Wolf sits down.

'All right, enough fucking around, we gotta get going soon.' Wolf takes out one of his maps and smooths the crinkled paper against his knee. 'So, there's a road leading straight up to the radio tower . . . but we ain't gonna use that, 'cause we ain't *that* stupid.' He uses one finger to circle something on the map. Wanting a better look, I come out from my hiding spot behind Tank and sit between him and Dolly. Wolf has the map angled so all of us can see it. 'Instead, we're gonna go around here.' He draws a path leading to the tower from behind.

'Right, they'll *never* expect that,' Pretty Boy says dryly. Wolf ignores him.

'Problem is, we got no idea if there are roads back there, or what the terrain is like. Might not be able to bring the big truck o' explosives around this way, which would be shitty because it's hard to blow stuff up without explosives. So, a few of us will go ahead in the jeep and scout it out first, and the rest will follow a ways back in the big truck.'

'And what if the truck can't make it?' Tank asks.

'We load the jeep up with everything we can take and pile in.'

'That sounds shitty.'

'I dunno, it would make a pretty fuckin' good entrance to charge in there in a jeep full of guns and explosives . . . '

'We'd probably blow ourselves up,' Pretty Boy says. 'Nothing ever goes right for us.'

'Yeah, why the fuck *is* that?' Wolf asks.

'I blame you. You're in charge.'

'Shut up, Pretty Boy.' Wolf folds up the map and shoves it back into his pocket. 'So, who wants to go in the jeep?'

'I guess I will,' I offer. 'I like the jeep.'

'And I'll drive,' Wolf says. 'Pretty Boy, you come navigate for me.'

'Ugh, fine.'

'Did I say you could talk?'

'Fuck you.'

Wolf only laughs.

'Tank, Dolly, you two get the truck then. One of you stay on the radio in case anything goes wrong, and watch out for other cars. We don't know if Saint has patrols in the area, and we can't get ourselves spotted.' They nod. 'All right, let's get going.'

It doesn't take long for the ride to get bumpy. Off-road, the ground is uneven and rocky. The jeep can handle it, but after a few big bumps send me a couple inches out of my seat, I decide to put on my seat belt. Wolf's driving makes it worse. I swear he's hitting big holes on purpose, not to mention ramping off uneven ground and trying to catch air. Pretty Boy keeps yelling at him to drive more carefully, but eventually he gives up and fastens his seat belt as well. If our route is so rough, I can only imagine how the big truck is faring behind us. I keep turning around to make sure they're still following us. They manage, albeit slowly. I stay in contact with them via walkie-talkie, since I don't have anything else to do.

After a few rolling hills, we reach a stretch of land that's open and flat.

'Thank God,' Pretty Boy says, relaxing in his seat.

'This should be easier,' I say into the radio.

'Aww, this is no fun at all,' Wolf says, immediately looking bored. He jams his foot down on the gas and the jeep jerks forward. After the rocky hills, this speed feels like we're flying. The wind whips through my hair and drowns out the sound of Wolf and Pretty Boy yelling at each other. I close my eyes and smile at the familiar sensation. It reminds me of the first time I was in the jeep with Wolf and Dolly, how I didn't know where I was going but was just happy to be going *somewhere* and—

An explosion.

My eyes fly open as the jeep jerks violently. My head slams into the headrest, and my body lifts from the seat. A chaos of noise and movement surrounds me, and I squeeze my eyes shut again. I lose sense of all direction as the jeep tumbles sideways, rolling over once before coming to a stop upside down. The frame of the windshield held, miraculously, and manages to prop the jeep up – the only reason we weren't crushed.

I stay with my eyes shut and my hands clenched tightly on my seat belt. I smell gasoline, hear it dripping. I force myself to take a few deep breaths and slowly open my eyes again. The world is confusing upside down. I slide my eyes from side to side.

'Wolf? Pretty Boy?' I croak out. My clumsy fingers fumble with the seat belt for a few seconds before I manage to escape and fall to the ground. I crawl out from beneath the wrecked jeep, my whole body shaking. I try to stay calm despite how disoriented I am. Once I make it a few yards from the jeep, I stop and look back. I can see Pretty Boy, just now unfastening his seat belt. Wolf isn't in the jeep or anywhere near it. I sit up and look around, and see him lying on the ground a ways away. He must have been flung from the jeep when it rolled.

'Wolf! Wolf, are you okay?' I slowly get to my feet, legs trembling, and move toward him. The walkie-talkie is sitting in the dirt nearby, and I scoop it up on the way.

'Kid, stop!' Pretty Boy yells from the jeep. I stop and turn. 'What is it?'

'Don't move,' he says. His voice is getting tight and anxious, his eyes darting all over the place as he crawls out from beneath the toppled vehicle.

'Why?' I ask, but Wolf catches my attention with a groan. I look over and see him sitting up groggily, holding a hand to his head. There's a gash on the side of his face, and he looks pretty out of it, but I'm just glad he's still in one piece, somehow.

'I really can't fucking afford to lose any more brain cells,' he says loudly, wincing. 'What the *fuck* was that?'

'A mine!' Pretty Boy says. He steps closer to me, frantically looking around in every direction as if expecting another one to jump out at him. 'This is a minefield. We are *so* fucked.'

'Oh, shit,' I breathe. I plant my feet and slowly raise the radio to my mouth while shifting my body as little as possible. 'Guys, don't come any closer,' I say into it. 'We hit a minefield.'

'That Saint fucker is way too clever,' Wolf says. 'Why isn't this on my map? Goddamn townies. We should go back and blow the place up for this.' He clambers to his feet, and I cringe at every careless movement he makes.

'What the hell are we supposed to do?' Pretty Boy asks, edging on panicky. He stands so close that he's practically on top of me, his elbows and feet invading my personal space. I'm too nervous to either move or push him off, and keep trying to stay as still as possible.

'We can go back the way we came before we hit the mine. That should be safe, right?' I say.

'Do you remember the path we took? The *exact* path?'

We all pause to look around. The silence speaks for itself.

'So what do we do?' Pretty Boy asks again.

'Why the hell are you both looking at *me*?' Wolf asks, glowering at us. His hands clench and unclench at his sides. He looks almost . . . nervous. My stomach tightens as I realize he has no idea what to do. If even Wolf is scared, that's bad news for us.

'You're supposed to be the boss!' Pretty Boy practically shouts.

'Well, fuck, I don't know nothing about no fuckin' minefield.'

'Wolf, please, *focus*,' Pretty Boy says, looking like he's desperately trying to keep a level head. 'What are we supposed to do now?'

I stand where I am and stare around me, also awaiting his answer. Wolf takes his sweet time wiping blood off his face and brushing off his clothes.

'Well . . . we gotta make it back to the truck.'

'Obviously.'

'And I guess someone will have to go first and check it out.'

'Who, exactly?'

'Not me. I'm clearly the most useful person here.'

I stare down at my feet. Out of the three of us, I know it has to be me. I'm the weakest link in the group, everyone knows it. I open my mouth to volunteer, but before I can make a sound Pretty Boy speaks again.

'Right, of course, it's me. It's always me. Who gives a shit if *I* get thrown under the bus, right?'

'Pretty Boy—' I say.

'No big deal, there shouldn't be *too* many mines in one area, right?' Pretty Boy continues, not even noticing my attempt to talk to him. I fall silent and meet Wolf's eyes. Neither of us says anything. I look back at Pretty Boy, who is chewing his lip nervously and looking at the stretch of land between us and the safety of the truck.

'What's happening?' Tank's voice crackles over the radio.

'Pretty Boy's gonna try and find a safe path to you guys,' I say.

'Tell him to be careful.'

'Tank says be careful,' I say. I bite my lip. 'And I second that.'

'Right, I'll keep that in mind.' Pretty Boy lets out a long breath and runs his hands through his hair. 'All right, all right. I'll be fine. Easy.'

He starts to walk in the direction of the truck. At first he moves at a snail's pace, taking laughably small steps and pausing to verify his safety after each and every one. Eventually Wolf shouts at him to hurry the hell up and he moves faster, pausing every so often to search the ground in front of him. I'm not sure if the mines are even visible, or if they're buried deep enough that this is all a matter of luck. I chew my dirty fingernails and try to commit his path to memory so I'll know where to go when it's my turn. It's a little difficult, because he does some strange snaking route that seems pretty random.

Every step makes me wince. Every pause lasts minutes. Every time he stops I'm *sure* something is wrong. Maybe he sees a mine; maybe he heard a telltale click of warning beneath his foot. My heart is already racing; I can't imagine how I'm going to cope with trying to cross the field myself. My eyes stay glued on Pretty Boy as he makes his agonizingly slow way toward the truck.

Something cracks. Pretty Boy and I both nearly jump out of our skins, and he freezes in place.

'My bad,' Wolf says. 'Just cracked my back. S'nothing. Go on, Pretty Boy, you're almost there.'

Pretty Boy lets out a shaky laugh.

'Okay,' he says. 'Okay.' I think he's trying to reassure himself more than anything. He's still frozen, nerves all riled up again.

'You're doing fine,' I yell out to him. 'You're almost there!'

With visible effort, he forces himself to take a step forward. And another. Another. The truck isn't far now. He starts to regain confidence, walking at a near-normal pace. I can see how eager he is to get back to safety, keeping his eyes on the truck ahead of him.

'Holy shit,' he says, looking over his shoulder at us. 'I hope you guys watched me, because I am not trying this aga—'

Boom.

I scream.

XXVI
Carry On

'Kid, look at me.'

There's a buzzing in my ears and a tightness in my chest and I can't take my eyes off the chunks of flesh that used to be Pretty Boy.

'C'mon, snap out of it.'

I've seen plenty of people die, but not like this. I guess I didn't realize that people could die so sudden, here one moment and gone the next. I didn't realize they could end up in so many pieces so quickly. I didn't realize how hard it could be to tell which pieces are which.

'Kid!'

I finally turn to look at Wolf. I stare at him, my eyes wide and watering. I realize my mouth is hanging open and snap it shut. I take a deep breath and shakily raise the radio to my mouth.

'Pretty Boy is dead,' I say. The words come out weird, flat. There's a burst of something choked and unintelligible on the other end, followed by silence.

'That stupid piece of shit,' Wolf whispers, staring out at

the minefield. 'He was almost there. Why'd he have to take his eyes off of—' He cuts himself off, shaking his head. 'Fuck. *Fuck*. Fuck everything about this.'

My hands are shaking. I clamp them around the walkie-talkie and hold it against my chest, trying to make myself still.

'What do we do?' I ask, looking out at the minefield along-side Wolf. I can't bring myself to look at his face. 'Wolf?'

The radio crackles to life, startling me.

'I'm coming to get you guys.' It's Dolly now, not Tank.

Wolf rips the device out of my hands in an instant.

'No,' he says sharply into it. 'You two stay put. We'll make it out.' He looks at me, his face back to its usual hardness, all trace of emotion gone. 'We're gonna go together.'

'Okay,' I say weakly.

'And we're gonna be fine.' He reaches out, grabs my shoulder, and gives it a brief squeeze before letting go. 'Don't lose your shit on me now, all right?'

'Okay,' I repeat more firmly. I let out a breath and nod at him.

'There we go. Now watch where I step, and follow me. Not too close, in case—' He pauses. 'Just stay back a few feet. And don't look at the mess.'

I nod again, trying not to think too hard about those last parts. Wolf sets out without anything further, his steps sur-prisingly confident given the situation. He glances back and gestures at me to follow, and I will my feet to step forward into the space he occupied a few seconds ago.

I move without thinking about it. It feels like my brain has shut down, things like sadness and fear pushed to the side. All that passes through my mind is where to step next, my eyes tracking Wolf's movements and my feet imitating them while my brain remains empty. Step, wait, step. I can do this. Soon we're halfway there, and it almost feels easy.

Then I see the arm.

Suddenly my feet won't move and neither will my eyes, staying glued on the scorched limb just a few feet to my right. It simultaneously reminds me of the arm Wolf once offered me to eat, and the first time I saw Pretty Boy. The meat I did eat, and Pretty Boy's smile.

I slap a hand across my mouth and lean over, my stomach heaving violently. Bile burns the back of my throat.

'Hey,' Wolf says from up ahead. 'What'd I tell you? Keep your eyes on me.'

I slowly remove my hand from my mouth and swallow hard. I still can't take my eyes off the arm.

'Are we just going to leave him here?' I ask, my voice coming out thick.

'We don't have a choice. Get your shit together and keep moving.'

I wipe my eyes and take a shuddery breath. I take a step closer to the arm, off of the safe path.

'What the hell are you doing?'

'Just one piece,' I say, my voice wavering. 'Then we can have a funeral.'

'It's not fucking worth it!' Wolf shouts at me. The genuine alarm in his tone gives me pause, but I take another step before I can lose my resolve. One more, and I'm able to bend down and gingerly snatch the arm out of the dirt. Ignoring the blood and the discomfiting limpness of it, I clutch it against my chest.

'Got it,' I say, making my way back to the path Wolf took.

'Good for you, you got the bloody fucking arm. Now get your ass over here before you blow yourself up.'

Through a combination of luck and attempting to follow the path Pretty Boy took, Wolf and I make it back to the truck safely. Tank is sitting on the ground in tears when we arrive. Wolf talks to him quietly while I sit with Dolly, my head resting on her shoulder. It takes me a while to remember I'm still holding the arm. Tank wants to go back for more of him, but Wolf says it's too dangerous.

We debate about leaving some sort of headstone until we realize none of us can write, and the hard-packed earth defeats our idea of a partial burial. So we settle for just the arm, a hunk of flesh that will soon be melted away by time and heat and leave nothing but dusty bones. I hope they'll serve as a warning to travelers about to cross into the minefield.

We form a half circle around the makeshift grave, and nobody knows what to do next. Tank's bulky shoulders heave with sobs. He doesn't even attempt to hide the tears flowing down his dark face. I find myself crying, too, albeit more quietly. I can't bring myself to think of the wrongs Pretty Boy did or the worse ones he might've done if he had a chance. No matter what, his loss leaves an emptiness behind.

The other two are stony-faced. Dolly's expression remains unchanged, not a flicker of emotion crossing her features as she stares at what's left of Pretty Boy. Wolf's face is unreadable, but he pats Tank on the shoulder a few times. The big man's loud sobs are the only noise besides the wind for several minutes. My mind keeps replaying the explosion over and over again, the way Pretty Boy was gone in an instant and left only a mess of guts and scattered limbs behind. A person one second, meat the next. That's the nature of the wastes.

Eventually Wolf clears his throat, looking uncomfortable.

'Well, I guess we should say something,' he says. Nobody answers. After an awkward stretch of silence, he looks over at Tank. 'You go first, big guy.'

Tank nods and takes a shaky breath. He stifles his sobs and controls himself before speaking.

'He was my friend,' he says. 'And maybe he wasn't always the most reliable friend, but he was the best I had for a long time.' He looks down at the pile and clenches his jaw, fighting back a fresh wave of tears. 'I would've taken the fall for you if I could, buddy. And I'm sorry there wasn't anything I could do.'

He stops and glances at me as if to signal that he's done. I swallow hard, trying to dislodge a lump in my throat.

There's a lot I want to say, but I don't really know how. I want to talk about how I think he tried a lot harder than anyone gave him credit for, and how he probably did the best he could to deal with a life he never wanted. I want to say he might've been a great guy in another world, but was never really cut out for this one. I want to express how unfair it is that he got blown up just when we were finally becoming friends. But the words stick on my tongue and I can't quite bring myself to say them. I don't think there's really a point in saying them, anyway. It's no good now.

'We didn't always get along,' I say, 'but you were nice, um, toward the end. So thanks I guess. And sorry for throwing up on you that one time, though you kind of deserved it.'

I shut my mouth and cross my arms over my chest. Wolf coughs in the quiet that follows, and when I glance over at him it almost looks like he's smirking.

The silence goes on for a while before we all look at Dolly.

'I have nothing to say,' she says flatly when she notices us staring.

'Aww, c'mon, Dolly. Say *something*,' Wolf says.

'I didn't like him.'

'No, something nice.'

She pauses and stares into the distance, apparently deep in thought.

'He was . . .' she says haltingly. 'Not so bad to look at.'

Wolf lets out a sound like he's choking. I slowly turn my head in his direction and find, to my amazement, he's trying to stifle a laugh. When he notices all of us looking at him, he loses it. The laughter explodes out of him like it was tired of being cooped up for so long.

'Look at this,' he says, laughing so hard his whole body shakes, 'look at this fucking mess. It's a goddamn *arm*. What kind of sick fucking funeral is this?' He pauses to gasp for breath and laugh some more.

I'm shocked by his sudden mirth, offended by the idea that he would laugh with a freshly dead friend in front of us. I don't even know what to say, and stare at him with my mouth gaping open.

But then I look at the gory arm in front of us, the meat that used to be Pretty Boy, and, oddly enough, I feel it bubbling up within me: a laugh. It bursts out before I can suppress it, the laughter coming guiltily at first but then rising in volume and shamelessness. Soon even Tank is laughing, despite the tears running down his face. Dolly gives a small smile, as if not quite sure what the joke is but sharing in our amusement anyway. We stay like that, laughing in front of a makeshift grave, for a while. And in the end, drained of my tears and laughter, I feel lighter.

'Rest in pieces,' Wolf says almost affectionately, 'you motherfucker.'

The ride is quiet without Pretty Boy. Occasionally someone tries to say something, but it's too weird. There are awkward pauses where everyone waits for one of his dry comments or jabs at Wolf, empty moments where he should be but he isn't anymore. Despite the fact he got blown to pieces right in front of me, his death doesn't hit me right away. It's like at first I don't realize he's really gone – gone forever. But as time goes on, it sinks in. I find myself expecting him to say something, and each time have to remind myself that he isn't there, and he's never going to be there again. And even though we had our issues, and even though he wasn't exactly a good guy, I find myself still missing him. I guess that's the best definition I have for death: You miss them being there, and you miss it forever.

It was the same with my papa. Losing someone doesn't hit you straight-on, it creeps up on you. Just when you think you're done feeling like a part of your life is missing, it hits you again out of nowhere and the grief is like a fresh wound. I know how it is, and I think everyone else does, too. I know Dolly has been through loss, and judging from the looks on Wolf's and Tank's faces they have as well.

But when it comes down to it, we don't have time to

grieve. The wastelands aren't going to sit and wait for us to suck it up, and neither is Saint. Every passing hour is another hour he gets to prepare for our arrival, and we really can't afford that. Before too long Wolf starts pulling out his maps again and talking strategy in a low voice with Dolly, and Tank and I start killing time by playing 'I Spy.' It's a damn slow game out in the middle of nowhere, but at least it's a distraction.

Eventually I build up the courage to speak to Wolf.

'So, uh . . . what's our plan now?' I ask. We've unanimously decided that taking a back route isn't an option anymore. We don't know how far the minefield extends, or if any other traps lay waiting for us.

'We-ell . . . ' The look on his face clearly says he has no idea. But of course Wolf would never admit that, so instead he wings it. 'We're gonna charge in from the front after all.'

'Seriously?'

'Yeah,' he says, voice growing more confident as he plunges ahead. 'We drive the big truck right in through their front door, and start tossin' out grenades. They'll never see it coming.'

'Didn't you say we couldn't do that 'cause it's too dumb?'

'Well, yeah, but that's the genius. It's so fuckin' *dumb* they're never gonna expect us to actually do it. Element of surprise.'

This is where Pretty Boy would say this sounds like a bad idea, or declare there's no way in hell he's going on this mission. Everyone is probably thinking the same thing, because nobody says anything for a while. Or maybe everyone's just thinking about what a shitty plan this is.

'Okay,' I say finally, unable to take the silence any longer. 'I guess we've done stupider things before.'

'Damn right we have!' Wolf says cheerfully. He claps me on the shoulder. 'We'll need to stop soon, divvy up the guns and grenades and other goodies. All of us load up, go in guns blazing.'

It sounds like the kind of idea that could get us all killed, but I'm not gonna be the one to say that. We don't have a lot of options, anyway.

Wolf soon declares it's time to stop and prep for arrival. We pull onto the side of the road and everyone crams into the back compartment with all of the boxes.

Wolf has sorted most of the goods into helpful piles, including guns, big guns, and 'really fuckin' huge' guns. The explosives have also been lumped together in one very dangerous-looking pile. I sit as far away from it as possible.

Wolf gives each of us a bulletproof vest and some guns to start with. My vest is way too big and looks ridiculous, but I have it better than Tank, who can barely squeeze into his. His big belly protrudes from underneath, so it doesn't really look like it's protecting anything.

Everyone else gets some big, hefty, deadly-looking guns, and I get a pistol. Wolf says he doesn't trust me with anything bigger, and I'd probably shoot myself or one of the others with anything automatic. Honestly, I'm just happy to have a gun in my hands. He gives me a new knife, too: a big and scary-looking one that looks sharp enough to slice through bone. It's definitely a lot more intimidating than my old one, but I keep that, too, just in case. It's gotten me out of a few tight spots.

'All right, so,' Wolf says. He unfurls a piece of paper with a very crude drawing on it. 'I mapped out the place so we can—'

'Wait, where's the *actual* map?'

'You insulting my handiwork, Kid?'

'Umm, no . . . ' I scrutinize the so-called map for another few seconds, and still can't make any sense out of the wobbly circles and squares. It looks like something a kid with too much radiation to the brain would draw. 'I mean, I just . . . you didn't get one from the townies?'

'They didn't have any of the inside, but they knew the basics. Are you sayin' there's something wrong with my map?'

'Er, no. It's, uh, great.'

'Damn right it is. Now keep your dumb mouth shut, I'm explainin' a plan here.' He clears his throat and points a long and dirty fingernail at a big circle. 'Now this here is the radio tower. It's not actually a circle, it's a big fuckin' tall metal thing. And, according to the townies, it's a little harder to blow up than I first imagined. So-o, with that in mind, we're not gonna go right for that one. Instead . . . ' He circles his finger around slowly and stops it on a square next to the circle. 'We're gonna go here.'

A moment of silence falls. I stare at the map, struggling to keep my mouth shut like Wolf said, until finally Tank speaks up instead.

'And what the hell is that supposed to be?'

'It's the control room, ya big dumb fuck. It's the place they've actually got all the equipment and shit for their brainwashin'.' He taps the square a few times, nodding thoughtfully. 'So we get in here, we shoot some guys, we blow the shit up. Most importantly, we kill the *fuck* out of Saint.' He looks up at us, his expression sobering for a moment. 'That's the most important bit. Remember what I said about people with power, and all the "law and order" bullshit this asshole is trying to pull. This is our entire way of life at stake. The guy's gotta go down, no matter what happens.'

'Right, boss,' Tank says, while Dolly nods. After a moment's hesitation, I nod my agreement as well. Wolf is right: Saint has to die. Especially with the Queen gone, he'll have far too much rein here if we don't pull this off.

'So what's the rest of the plan?' I ask.

'Uh . . . that's it. Then we get out. Easy.' He grins triumphantly, rolls his map up, and sticks it into his back pocket. He looks around at us as if expecting applause. Everyone stares at him.

'Well,' I say, trying to sound enthusiastic, 'I guess that doesn't sound too hard.'

'Child's play,' Wolf says confidently.

'And we're just gonna drive the truck right into the place?'

'Yup. I figure someone drives, the rest of us hide in the back, we crash through the front of the building, and – bam! All pile out and give 'em a hell of a surprise.'

'And what if we accidentally blow ourselves up?'

'Well that would be fuckin' unfortunate, wouldn't it, Kid?' Wolf grins, as unconcerned as always. He looks between me and Tank, who both look a little dubious. 'Aww, come on. Why can't you guys just be nice and quiet and follow along with the whole thing like Dolly does?'

Dolly glances up at the mention of her name, and then

returns to scrutinizing guns, which seems much more important to her.

'So this is really happening,' I say. It still doesn't feel real to me. Looting towns and the like is one thing, but this is something else entirely.

'Yep,' Wolf says. 'Don't worry, Kid. It'll be fun.'

'Yeah, fun,' Tank says, and not sarcastically. 'Plenty of people to shoot. And look how big our guns are! No way they have bigger guns than these.'

'Yeah, no way we can lose with guns this big.'

I shake my head at them, but can't help but laugh.

'Seriously, though,' Tank says. 'Don't worry, Kid. I'll be looking out for you.'

'Me, too,' Dolly says quietly behind me.

'I'll be way too busy killing people, but I'm sure you'll be fine,' Wolf says.

XXVII
The Radio Tower

Next thing I know, I'm in a truck full of explosives barreling straight at a brick building. Tank, Dolly, and I are in the back of the truck, clinging desperately to boxes for support. The truck sways and shudders. It's clearly not built to drive this fast. I'm half-worried the thing will fall apart before we hit the building, half-worried it won't. Judging from the nauseous look on Tank's face, he shares the sentiment. Dolly's face is blank. With one gun in her hand, another strapped to her back, and a belt stocked with grenades and extra ammo, she looks ready for anything. I imagine Wolf is having the time of his life up front, pushing the pedal to the floor and not giving a shit about the consequences.

'Here it comes!' Wolf shouts over the walkie-talkie. I squeeze myself in between two stacks of boxes, close my eyes, and hold on for dear life.

We slam into the building.

I feel the impact go through the truck like a wave. There's an awful crashing sound, and I can tell from the noise that we made it through the wall. Boxes topple over around me and something falls on top of my head – a can of food, I think. I ignore it and stay crouched down. The truck keeps going for a short while and slams into something else.

The engine whines like a dying animal. Everything else is silent as we all attempt to regain our bearings.

'You all right, ladies?' Tank asks.

'Fine,' Dolly says.

'I'm okay.' I realize my eyes are still closed and force them open. The back of the truck is an absolute mess, the boxes now scattered all over the floor. I stand up and brush myself off.

'All right,' Tank says. He steps over fallen boxes and supplies and makes his way to the back doors. He places a hand on the latch and turns to look back. 'Kid, you run up front and make sure Wolf's crazy ass is still alive. Dolly and I will cover you.'

'Got it.'

Tank opens the latch and pushes one door open. He pauses for a second behind the other door, waiting for gunfire, but none comes. He nods at us and steps outside. Dolly slips out after him. I follow with my pistol held ready.

The room outside is full of dust. I wave a hand as I step out, trying to get a clear look at anything, but it's impossible. I can't even tell how big the room is. I pull part of my shirt over my face to avoid breathing in dust and inch along the side of the truck, using touch to guide me. I keep my gun out. By the time I reach the front of the truck, the dust is starting to settle. The vehicle is a wreck, the hood dented in where it smashed into the wall, and the windshield is shattered. I struggle to pry open the door, and it falls off completely.

Wolf is in the driver's seat and looks relatively unharmed,

which means his ridiculous plan actually worked. He's covered from the neck down in pillows. Pillows of various shapes and colors, all strapped to his torso and limbs for protection. It makes him look like a giant, fluffy scarecrow. He has a blanket over his head, too, which kept all the broken glass off him. He got pissed at us for laughing at him while he was tying them on, so I try to refrain from laughing now, but it's hard. He's struggling to undo his seat belt. He can barely even move around in his seat, and the seat belt is stretched as tight as it can go across him.

I reach over to undo the seat belt and grab one of his pillow-arms, half-dragging him out of the truck. Once he steps down, he stumbles for a second before falling flat on his padded stomach. It releases a soft *fffshh* of air as the pillows beneath him deflate slightly. He shakes off the blanket covering his head, dispatching shards of glass with it, and I can no longer stop myself from laughing.

'Fuckin' told you it would work!' Wolf says gleefully. He sits up with visible effort, and needs my help to stand.

'Yeah, it's ... genius,' I say, laughing again at the sight of him. His arms and legs look ludicrously thick, and the padding on his stomach makes him look fatter than Tank.

With the dust all settled down, the room we destroyed becomes visible. It's small, some sort of entrance lobby. It's plain aside from a few paintings on the wall, one of which is now dangling crookedly and about to fall off. It looks like our truck smashed right through the front desk, and there are at least two mangled bodies in the wake of the tires. There's no sign of anyone alive. After sweeping the room and checking all the corners, Tank and Dolly return to us.

'This is a bit of a letdown, honestly,' Wolf says. 'I was expecting a gunfight right off the bat.'

'Yeah, what a shame, that getup would have been real intimidating,' Tank says.

'Fuck you. Safety first.' Wolf waddles over to the truck, which is releasing an alarming amount of smoke from under its hood. He grabs a sawed-off shotgun and a metal baseball bat for himself, and a heavy-looking backpack, which he tosses at me. I scramble to catch it, but it hits the ground. I bend down to pick it up.

'Whoa, Kid, watch it. That thing is full of grenades an' shit.'

'W-What!?' I nearly drop it again. 'Well don't be throwing it around like that! And why do *I* have to carry it?'

''Cause everyone else has big-ass guns to worry about. Just remember, you mess up and you'll blow us all to hell.'

'Gee, thanks.' I secure the straps around my shoulders. It isn't as heavy as I expected, but I feel nervous with it on my back. 'I feel like a suicide bomber.'

'Don't worry, that's only our last-resort plan,' Wolf says. He starts removing his pillows one by one. Before I can figure out how serious he is, or he can finish de-pillowing himself, a door near us bursts open. The three others immediately turn their guns toward it, and I fumble to get my pistol out of my belt.

A man's head pokes out of the doorway. A burst of gun-fire follows as Tank, Dolly, and Wolf all open fire. The man retreats hastily, leaving a door riddled with bullet holes.

'Oh hell no,' Wolf says. 'You ain't gettin' away so easy.' He runs toward the door, heedless of the pillows still covering most of him, and busts through. Dolly and Tank follow, and

I do the same after a slight pause. But before I can even make it to the doorway, all three of them turn and run back outside, pushing me along with them. The sound of gunfire explodes from behind them.

'Fuck, that's a lot of them!' Tank says.

'We're so fucked,' Wolf says. 'We need to find another door.'

Dolly grabs a grenade off her belt, pulls the pin, and tosses it through the open door. Everyone pulls to one side. The grenade goes off, and silence follows. We all look at each other uncertainly.

'Someone check,' Wolf says.

'Why are you looking at me?' Tank asks. 'Just 'cause I'm big don't mean I'm bulletproof. You go, pillow man.'

'Do you think pillows will help against gunfire?' I ask, doubtful.

'Shut up, Kid. You go. As most useless member of the crew, that's your duty.'

'W-What? What about that other door, we can—'

Before I can finish, Wolf grabs me by the backpack, nearly lifting me off my feet, and shoves me through the doorway. I stumble for a few steps and then freeze, looking around warily. The remains of a few bodies are splattered on the floor and walls, but otherwise the hallway is empty. The whole building looks like it's falling apart, too. I thought Saint's headquarters would have the same kind of fancy looks as the Queen's, but it's all very plain and simple.

'Nobody's here,' I call back to the others. Wolf creeps through the door cautiously, as if expecting I'm lying, with Dolly and Tank on his heels. Dolly stays facing backward, watching the door behind us as we come to a halt in the middle of the hallway.

'Well, shit,' Wolf says. 'Guess we scared 'em off, huh?'

The door behind us opens and in pours a crowd of armed men and women. They're a ragtag bunch dressed in scrappy wasteland clothing, each with a red bandana tied to their left arm. Other than that, they look more like well-equipped townies than the trained army I was expecting, but there are a *lot* of them. Dolly and the others open fire immediately, gunning them down as they try to funnel through the doorway. I panic and run forward, heading straight for another door. Just as I'm about to grab the handle, it opens to reveal another group of Saint's soldiers. I scream and slam the door shut before they can react. There's no way to lock the door, and I know I only bought myself a few seconds, so I run back to the others.

'Behind us! More of them!' I yell.

'Which behind us?' Wolf asks, turning my way. I point. The other two stay focused on trying to push back the crowd coming at us from the other side.

'Kid, you have a gun, fucking use it!'

'Right!' I steady my shaking hands on the pistol and plant myself next to Wolf. With a face of steely determination, he points his sawed-off shotgun and fires. It takes out chunks of all three men in the front of the group. While he reloads, I fire my pistol desperately, catching one man twice in the gut and another in the shoulder. It doesn't take either of them down, but it slows them enough for Wolf to be ready to fire again. But I can tell we're not nearly fast or efficient enough, and so can Wolf.

'We need to move!' he says. 'Can't be tryin' to fight in two directions!' He gestures to Tank and Dolly, and they move closer to us. Back-to-back, we make our way down the hallway and toward the door ahead of us. We start by taking it slow and steady, until I hear the dull *click-click-click* behind me that indicates someone's out of ammo. Tank abruptly turns and shoves past me and Wolf. He takes off running down the hallway and bashes into the group of Saint's men like a battering ram. Wolf jumps in after him, swinging his baseball bat and cracking skulls left and right. After a few more seconds, Dolly and I drop our attempt to hold off the ones behind us and start running as well. It's hard with this bulky backpack, but I move as fast as I can. She tosses a grenade behind us, and neither of us turns to check the result. Our crew plows through the group of men, carving a bloody path.

A bullet hits me in the back. There's a moment of blinding panic where I think I'm done for. The initial hit feels like being punched, hard, by someone a lot bigger than me – I close my eyes and wait for the worse pain to follow, but nothing comes. I look down at myself and remember the bulletproof vest. Still, being shot *hurts*. The next bullet hits me in the chest, forcing all the air from my lungs. I stumble and almost fall, but Dolly grabs my arm and pulls me up at the last second. She half-drags me along as I struggle to breathe normally again.

The hallway is lined with identical doors, no way of telling what's behind any of them. Wolf dashes to the closest one and tries it: locked. The next, also locked. Finally he finds one that opens and darts inside. He waves the rest of us in before shutting and locking the door. It's a tiny supply closet, barely big enough to fit all of us.

I sink to the floor, trying to catch my breath. It's hard forcing myself to breathe calmly when there's so much shouting and ruckus just outside the door. Trying to ignore it, I start pulling bullets out of my vest. Dolly helps with the one lodged in the back. I check myself for wounds, but it looks like I made it out fine.

The others weren't quite so lucky. Wolf's nose is bleeding heavily, making a mess of all his pillows, and as I watch he spits out a tooth. The old wound on his shoulder seems to have reopened. It amazes me that he could swing a bat with that injury. One of Dolly's arms is dripping blood, though it looks like the shot went clean through. Tank is bleeding from multiple wounds and must have at least a couple bullets in him, though he seems unconcerned.

'So,' Wolf says, wiping blood off his face, 'I'm starting to think this was a pretty fuckin' bad idea.'

'You think?' Tank says with a strained laugh.

'And we crashed our only means of escape, didn't we?'

'Pretty much,' I say.

''Course we did.' Wolf spits again, leaving a red splatter on the tile. 'Hand me that bag, Kid.' I'm eager to be rid of it. He unzips it and searches through the insides. 'Well, guess everyone should take a couple grenades. If you're gonna go down, at least take a handful of 'em down with you, right, guys?'

'Would you expect anything less?' Tank asks, taking his. Wolf shoves a couple into my hands and I stare at them nervously. I still remember that time I accidentally threw one away without pulling the pin. I'm not likely to make *that*

mistake again, but I'm sure I can find a hundred other ways
to fuck it up.

'So what's the plan now?' I ask, putting one grenade into
my pocket and moving the other from hand to hand. Tank
watches me apprehensively.

'Kill the bastards,' Wolf says.

'Yeah, well, how?'

'Still workin' on that part.' Wolf is just buying time, and I
can tell. As I wait for a real answer, the noise outside grows
louder. The soldiers are pounding on the door and yelling at
us to come out so they can blow our heads off. I guess Saint's
ideal of nonviolence doesn't apply to people who drive trucks
into his base of operations.

'All right,' Wolf says. 'We're gonna need to split up.'

'How is that gonna help anything?' I ask. The others are
already nodding, but I feel anxiety creeping up on me. I don't
want to split up. If I end up alone, I'm done for.

'We're too outnumbered, can't fight 'em head-on,' Wolf
says. It still doesn't make sense to me; wouldn't breaking up
the group just make the odds *less* in our favor? I'm pretty
sure it's a bad idea, but now isn't the time to start questioning
Wolf.

'So we split up, and then what?' I ask, still nervously toying
with my grenade.

'Well, we'll blast our way out of here and scatter. Try to
stay alive, try to pick 'em off, and try to move *up*.' He points
at the ceiling.

'Why up?'

'The control room's gotta be somewhere up there. The
building is three stories high, and I reckon it's on the top

one. If one of us makes it there, blow the shit out of it and kill Saint.'

'And what if none of us make it there?' Tank asks.

'One of us has to,' Wolf says.

Whoever ends up making it, I doubt it will be me. That means my role here has been reduced to a distraction. Once I accept that, my nervousness fades. Now *that* I can do. If I can run fast enough to stay alive for a while and get some soldiers to chase me, I'll consider it a job well done. There's a lot less pressure thinking about it that way.

'Okay,' I say. I stand up, clutching the grenade in my right hand. 'Let's do this.'

'I like that attitude, Kid.' Wolf gives me a high five. 'How 'bout everyone else?'

'Gotta die sometime,' Tank says. 'This ain't the worst way to go, I guess.'

'I won't fail you,' Dolly says.

Everyone has a look of grim determination. I can tell they must have gone through the same thought process I did. There's no way we're gonna make it out, but at least we should accomplish what we came for. We followed Wolf here, and we'll follow him to the end.

Still, it feels strange to look around and realize this might be the last time I see one of them, or even all of them. Even though I haven't been with the crew for that long, and even though things have been crazy, I wouldn't have done it any other way. Living alone isn't really living, and they're the first people I grew to love since my papa died.

'Umm,' I say, looking up at them. 'I just wanted to say . . . it's been fun, guys.'

Tank smiles.

'Wouldn't have been the same without you, Kid.'

'Yeah, things would've gone a lot smoother,' Wolf says. 'And don't go gettin' all sentimental on us, we're not dead yet.'

'Yet,' I repeat. 'Good vote of confidence, boss.' I grin at him and turn to the door.

'Now let's bash some fucking heads in!' Wolf says. He throws open the door and tosses a grenade into the crowd outside.

XXVIII
Alone in the Tower

The grenade blows a hole in the mob outside, and scatters them enough for us to burst through the door. Not even watching where the others go, I dash between two startled men and down the hall. A burst of gunfire follows me, but I dart around a corner before they can get a good shot at me. Footsteps come soon after, loud on the building's cracked tile floor. I keep running down the unfamiliar hallway. The long hall is deserted; the soldiers must have clustered around us, so there are none waiting here. I try to open a door as I hear them gaining on me. The first one is locked. *Shit.* The second also locked. *Double shit!*

They're getting closer. I refuse to look back and see just how close. I can't let myself panic; I don't have my friends here to watch my back this time. If I panic, I'm dead.

The next door is unlocked, but it's so rusty I have to struggle and waste precious time opening it. I glance behind me to see three soldiers only seconds away, two men and one woman. One has a gun, one a knife, and the last a metal pipe. Any of them would be enough to kill me.

I run inside and immediately ram into something. I stagger, catch my balance, and get a better look at the room. It's dimly lit, the only light filtering in from a broken window in the back. Desks and chairs are scattered around the room, and many of the desks have computers on them, some intact but most smashed up.

Once I have a decent map of the room in my head, I dive behind one of the desks and crawl on my hands and knees toward the back window. It's low enough for me to escape through if I need to, though the jagged, broken glass makes me hope I won't. Furthermore, the dim lighting and ample hiding spots tilt the odds slightly in my favor. It's a good spot for me to fight. The best I can hope for, at least.

I wait behind a desk and listen. I hear the three soldiers enter the room, their footsteps loud in the small space. I hear distant gunshots and the sounds of fighting elsewhere in the building, but this room is quiet besides my breathing and their footsteps.

'The little bitch is here somewhere,' a deep voice says. I can't help but be pleased people are finally getting my gender right.

'Could've gone out the window.' This one sounds female, though still gruff.

'Not enough time. She's here. Spread out, don't let her get away.'

I lean back against the desk, keeping hidden and silent. I try to quiet my breathing to hear better. I hear the crunch of glass as one moves on the other side of the room. Another bumps into something and grunts, just a few yards away.

Bang! A gunshot deafens me. I nearly bolt before realizing it

wasn't actually aimed at me; they still don't know where I am.
Crash. Crunch. More noises filling the room, coming from various directions. They're trying to scare me out. I stay where
I am, my hands curling into fists. After a few moments the
noise quiets down again. I listen intently and hear footsteps
coming toward me. The others sound farther away. Guessing
I still have a few seconds before the footsteps reach me, I look
around for something I can use to my advantage. My eyes
land on a nearby computer cord. I reach out and pull on it,
testing. It feels almost like rope, and an idea hits me. I draw
the big knife Wolf gave me out of its sheath and saw through
the cord, cutting off a section about two feet long. I slide the
knife back into its sheath and coil an end of the cord around
each hand, drawing it tight as I crawl back over to the desk.
I slip into the alcove under it and wait. The footsteps are
close, very close.

I hold my breath as the soldier steps around the corner of
the desk and pauses. I can just barely see his feet and legs. I
imagine him scouring the area – and he moves on, apparently
not seeing me. I scoot out from under the desk and creep up
behind him, moving slowly and quietly. As something else
in the room catches his attention, I jump on him. One hand
scrabbling for a hold on his shoulder, I bring the cord over
his head and around his neck. A yank draws it tight and
forces his head back. A choked cry escapes him. He stumbles
around, trying to dislodge me as I pull tighter and tighter.
He stumbles into a wall, and then a computer. I hang on
doggedly as he bangs me around. Finally he trips on another
cord and goes down; I drop to the floor and scramble out of
the way. His head strikes the corner of a desk and he hits the

ground. His gun clatters to the floor. I snatch it up and run for the door.

The other soldiers cut off my exit. The woman blocks the doorway, waiting with a cleaver in hand. The other heads right for me, wielding an iron pipe. He shoves one of the desks, sending it clattering to the floor right in my path. I freeze, trapped against the wall. Fear almost drives me into a panic, but I hold my ground and draw out the knife again. The man steps over the fallen desk and advances toward me. I glance around and find the guard I felled earlier isn't getting up. Good for me.

While I'm distracted, the closer man swings at me with his pipe. I narrowly dodge, feeling the air from its passage, and lunge forward with my knife. The blade sinks into his thigh, deeper than I expected – seconds later I realize I could've easily hit someplace more vital, but it's too late for that. The man howls with pain and stumbles back. My hands still wrapped around the knife's handle, I stumble with him, and attempt to yank the blade out. It's sunk too deep. I'm not strong enough, and the gushing blood makes the handle too slippery for me to grip properly. I let go and he falls backward over the fallen desk.

That leaves me and the woman with the cleaver. She's still standing in the doorway, and grins at me when she sees me looking. She has a dyed-red Mohawk and a face like a pig, broad and mean and ugly. I stand a few yards away from her, eye her, and pull out my gun from the back of my pants. I aim at her and she stands there, unblinking – then charges at me with a yell. Caught by surprise, I fire wildly and catch her in the shoulder right before she barrels into me. The impact sends me flying backward to slam into a desk. The air leaves my lungs. I lean against the desk for support, panting, but I only have a second to recover before she swings wildly with the cleaver. I drop to the floor and it hits the desk with a heavy *thunk*. Before she can swing again, I tackle her at the knees. She crashes down. Her head slams into the floor.

I leap to my feet, dash for the door again – and trip on a computer cord. I twist and try to right myself, but land awkwardly with my arm crushed beneath me. A jolt of pain shoots up from my wrist. Behind me, I hear the scrape of the cleaver against the ground as the woman gets on her feet. I crawl for the door on my hands and knees and force myself not to look back as heavy footsteps follow me. My heartbeat pounds in my ears. I tune out everything else, ignoring the swiftly approaching footsteps and the cries of the injured men. The door is the only thing that matters. I'm so close to escape, so close—

And I'm out the door. I scramble to my feet, turn to run, and slam into someone a lot bigger than me.

I stumble backward and into the woman who was pursuing me. She grabs my arm before I can escape, and when I look up at the other person I ran into, I find a gun in my face.

To my surprise, the soldier doesn't shoot. I stay there, trembling, waiting to die . . . but nothing happens.

'I'll kill the bitch,' the woman growls. She shoves me against the wall and grabs my throat, pinning me there. 'Fucking pain in my ass. I'll chop her into little bits.'

'Not yet,' the man with the gun says. He's a tall, lean guy with a face full of piercings and an arm covered in crude tattoos. I look at him desperately, choking. 'Saint wants her.'

'You sure? This one?' Her hold loosens slightly and I can breathe again.

'He wants 'em all. Been trying to grab 'em for a while now.' He licks his thin lips and shrugs.

'And they was dumb enough to show up for us. Heh.'

The pressure eases up as the woman backs off. I try to run, but she yanks me back and throws me to the ground. I fall on my ass and stay there, subdued. I let out a long, slow breath that makes it feel like I'm deflating. My heart slows as if accepting its fate, and I become aware of the distant shouting and gunshots elsewhere in the building. It sounds like the rest of the crew is giving them a hell of a time, which makes me smile despite my own predicament. I did what I could. It wasn't like anyone expected much of me, anyway.

A realization comes to me. The piercings, the tattoos, the scars ... these soldiers don't seem like townies. They're too big, too dangerous, too obviously familiar with their weapons. Everything about them reeks of brutal efficiency. It reeks of raiders. But why would Saint have raiders as his guards?

Instinct tells me something is wrong here. Mostly, though, I'm relieved I'm not dead yet.

'What do we do with her?'

'Take her up, I guess.'

'Take me up where?' I look from one to the other, but neither of them spares me so much as a glance.

'Knock her out, Ben,' the woman says.

'Wait wait wait—'

A sharp pain, followed by darkness.

*

I wake up groggy and confused. I look around blearily and my confused thoughts thicken as I find only unfamiliar surroundings. I'm in a dimly lit room, sitting on a rather dilapidated couch that sags beneath my weight. The walls are bare except for the off-white, peeling wallpaper. I'm alone.

Something moves behind me. Scratch the alone part. I whip around and somehow manage to fall off the couch. The tile hurts my knees, but I ignore it and crawl to hide next to the couch, as if it were all a part of the plan.

Hiding there, I can't see who or what is moving.

'She's awake,' a deep voice says. I stay where I am, heart racing as my memories catch up with me. Where did the guards take me? Where are my friends? I peek around the couch to see a rather rotund soldier opening the door. I scramble toward it and slip between his legs. He grunts in surprise and tries to grab me, but I slide under him and take off running. The hallway is unfamiliar and lined with closed doors. I try a few of them, but they're all locked. The fat soldier runs after me, huffing and puffing along as he tries to catch up. I spot the stairwell and run for it. I open the door and run into the biggest man I've ever seen in my life.

My mouth hangs open. I take a step back.

He's a monster of a man, even bigger than Tank, and made of solid muscle. Each of his arms looks as wide around as my waist, his legs thicker than tree trunks. Unlike Tank he doesn't have a big belly. In fact, it doesn't seem like he has an ounce of fat on his body. He doesn't have much of a neck, either, just a strong jaw meeting ridiculously muscular shoulders. His face is unremarkable aside from a thick scar that runs from his temple down to the corner of his mouth.

His head is shaved except for a thin strip down the middle. There's a huge ring through the front of his nose, like bulls I've seen in picture books.

I stare at him, meanwhile noting the soldiers on either side. They flood out of the stairwell after him, surrounding me and cutting off my escape. The huge man folds his arms over his chest and grins, showing yellowed teeth.

'You must be the Kid,' he says, his voice a slow and pleasant rumble. The kind of voice people would trust. The kind of voice they'd listen to.

'Um. Just Kid,' I squeak, not sure how else to respond. The man laughs, a sound that echoes through the empty hall.

'Nice to meet you, Kid,' he says. 'I'm Saint.'

XXIX
Saints and Sinners

I gape at the proffered hand and back up at his face.

'*You're* Saint?' I ask, terrified. '*You're* the guy we're trying to kill? Aw, hell!' If I ever had a slim hope of taking this guy down, it's gone now. This guy is *huge*. I kind of pictured him as a nice old man in a suit or something, not this. If I ever ran into him in the wastes, I'd think he was a mercenary, the kind of guy who would crack some skulls and eat townies for breakfast.

'That's what they call me,' he says, with a rumble of laughter at the look on my face. He lays a hand on my shoulder, turns me around, and marches me back to the room I just escaped from. I don't even try to struggle. There's no point; he's at least ten times bigger than I am. I remain helpless as he not so gently pushes me back onto the couch. He takes a chair across from it, an armchair that would be big for me but looks ludicrously small for him.

'Leave us,' he says to the soldiers behind me. I hear receding footsteps and the click of the door shutting, and gulp. I'm alone with Saint, the guy I came here to kill, the guy who looks like he could crush my skull between two fingers. He studies me and I avert my gaze, my eyes skittering around the room.

'So, Kid. Why do you think you're here?' he asks.

'Umm, because we drove a truck into the building?' My answer comes out like a question.

'No, I mean here, in this room.'

'Because your guards brought me here,' I say slowly.

He sighs. I blink at him.

'And why did they do that instead of killing you?'

'I don't know. You tell me. You're the guy in charge.' I force a smile. He looks utterly unamused.

He cracks his fingers and I'm reminded again of the power those hands hold.

'Well, umm, I guess you bring people here so you can have a trial and shit before you kill them,' I say uncertainly, and then realize 'kill' doesn't sound quite right. 'Execute them? Is that the word?'

'That's why everyone outside thinks you're here. What do you think?'

'I'm not really the thinking sort of person,' I say. 'Usually I kind of dive headfirst into things and hope it works out for the best. It, uh, doesn't seem to be going so well right now.' He waits silently. I keep looking around the room, eyes flicking back to his face every few seconds. His expression doesn't change.

What do *I* think? I haven't exactly figured it out myself. Something is pulling on the edges of my mind, some realization I have yet to uncover. The radio tower, the soldiers who look so much like raiders, Saint himself . . . it doesn't fit with the mental image I had of the man trying to unite and protect the wastelands.

'You're not who everyone thinks you are,' I say.

'What makes you say that?' He leans forward, placing his hands on his knees.

'Your men are all raiders,' I say. 'Or were.' I study his face. 'You look like a raider, too.'

He smiles.

'There we go.'

'But why would you have raiders?' I ask. 'I thought you were wiping out the bad guys.'

'Now that would be noble.' He laughs, the sound filling the room to the brim.

'So . . . you're not going to kill us?' I ask hopefully.

'No, Kid. I'm trying to recruit you.'

'Recruit us?' I repeat, not understanding at first. Something finally clicks in my mind. 'All the raiders the townies bring you . . .'

'Exactly. I'm building an army, and the townies are help-ing me do it.' His smile oozes smugness. 'By the time they realize it, I'll be too strong for them to stop me.'

'That's . . .' Pretty smart, actually. 'What's in it for the raiders?'

'Safety in numbers,' he says. 'All the reward without the risk. All the power. The only thing I ask for is loyalty, and a cut of their loot.'

My head is spinning with the idea. This is huge – and no one outside of here has any clue what he's doing. All of the towns we've been to have trusted him, listened to him, delivered him raiders like he asked them to. Everyone knows

Saint's plan is to change the wastes, but it's definitely not in the way they think. I'm not sure how to feel about it.

'So what are you talking to me for?' I ask.

'Well, Kid, you pose an interesting problem for me.' Saint leans back in the chair and folds his arms over his chest, looking down at me. I shift in my seat and find my back sticky with sweat. 'I've been tracking Wolf and his crew for a while now. They're infamous. Wolf has been wreaking havoc since he emerged from whatever hellhole he came from. Tank was one of the best mercs in the business before he went raider. Some of the fringe towns still tell ghost stories about a blue-haired woman called "the man killer." And Pretty Boy has been with various crews since he was a child.' He scrutinizes me. 'Where exactly is Pretty Boy?'

If Saint doesn't know he's dead, he might think we still have some trick up our sleeve. I stare back at him silently, putting on my best poker face. After a few moments he sighs.

'So he's dead, then. That's a pity. He would have been useful.'

He would have been useful. He says it so crisply, without a scrap of emotion in his voice. It makes my blood boil to hear him talk about a dead friend in such a calculated way. That's how he sees all of us; we're nothing more than assets to him.

'So,' he continues, 'then you show up out of nowhere. Who are you? Where do you come from? Nobody knows.' He scrutinizes me. 'And yet you survive, so clearly you're not as useless as you appear.'

Obviously, he hasn't spoken to the rest of the crew yet. I may not be the brightest girl in the wastes, but I'm smart enough to know he's measuring my value right now. I sure as hell better trick him into thinking I'm worth recruiting.

'Well, obviously,' I say, puffing out my chest and trying to act confident. 'It's not like I could've made it this far without offing a few people.' Despite my attempt at bravado, my hands are starting to sweat. I clench them into fists to stop them from shaking.

'How did you end up with Wolf's crew?'

I pause, unsuccessfully trying to come up with a good reason.

'Why should I tell you?' I retort. He lets out a snort of laughter, the corner of his lips curling upward.

'Let's not play games, little girl.' He leans forward in his chair, and I sink down in mine. 'I'll be frank with you: If I decide not to recruit you, I'll kill you. And right now, you don't seem very useful to me. So, go on. Change my mind.'

I swallow hard. My tongue feels thick and clumsy in my mouth, and the words won't come to me. I've never been very good at lying.

But then again, I'm not the person I used to be.

I'm not some helpless little girl missing her papa. I'm not the kind of girl who throws a grenade out the window without pulling the pin – I mean, not anymore. I'm a part of the crew. A raider. A killer. I've made it through a lot of shit, and like hell am I going to die like this.

'Well that's the thing, isn't it?' I start, speaking slowly. I think of my friends: Wolf's swagger, Tank's strength, Dolly's quiet badassery, Pretty Boy's silver tongue. 'I don't seem very useful. I don't look big or tough or strong. And yet here I am, in the middle of your fancy base.' I gesture to the room around me, and feel the shaking in my hands subside. 'Before I even met these guys, I was wandering the wastes alone. Completely *alone*. Do you even know what that's like?'

Saint is silent, studying my face. I swallow and continue. 'Not a lot of people do. 'Cause most people who end up alone just die, and that's the end of that. But not me. I joined a crew of goddamn sharks. I ate human flesh to survive. I learned to shoot. To kill. I blew the Queen's head off. I watched a friend die yesterday and I still came here to kick some ass.' I take a deep breath, feel my chest rise and fall, the words nearly tumbling out of my mouth now. 'And you think I'm not good enough for your mess of an army? Just 'cause I'm a little girl? Well *fuck* you. I'm worth two of your guards, and tomorrow I'll be worth four of 'em, and eventually the whole lot. Because that's who I am, and that's what I do. I survive.'

I feel the silence, tense and thick, like a noose around my neck.

'Are you done?' he asks eventually.

'Yeah, I think so.' The bravado seeps out of me, and I self-consciously raise a hand to scratch at the back of my head. 'Was that, uh, too much?'

Saint sighs deeply and shifts in his seat. He looks down on me with thoughtful eyes.

'Well, Kid—'

He cuts off. I look around, confused, before I hear what he hears: gunshots outside. Saint stands, gesturing at me to stay seated.

'Wait here,' he says, moving to the door.

I jump to my feet the second the door shuts. If I'm lucky, my friends are here to kill Saint and rescue me. But I'm rarely lucky, so I need to be ready when he gets back.

I walk along the edges of the room, searching for anything that could possibly be used as a weapon or escape route. The room is bare but for the furniture and an excessive amount of cobwebs. Still, I stubbornly circle the perimeter of the room, checking every inch. I pause by the window and look down. I'm on the third floor, so that's no good. Most of the windowpane is gone, but ragged shards of glass still cling to the edges like broken teeth. I lightly touch the edge of one. It's not as sharp as I would've hoped, but it's still the closest thing to a weapon in the room. I grab a long, thin sliver and determinedly wiggle it around, careful not to let the edges touch my skin. It's already weakened by age and abuse, and soon cracks start to form. I'm as careful as possible; I already have one injured hand, it would just be embarrassing to mess them both up.

But, hearing a scuffle outside, I wiggle more frantically. In my haste I slip, and an edge digs into my palm. It draws a line of blood and stings something fierce, but beyond the pain I feel triumphant – if it's good enough to cut me, it's good enough to cut someone else. I grit my teeth and give a final wrench to jerk it free. Flipping it in my hand so the sharpest edge is facing out, I rush to the door and press myself against the wall beside it.

Outside, the sound of a fight continues. A gunshot rings through the air. Silence follows. I wait, holding my breath as the door slowly opens. Someone steps inside.

I launch myself at the person, bellowing out a war cry, and sink the glass shard into soft flesh. It doesn't cut deeply or easily, but it does its job. I feel the skin break and the glass sink in another few centimeters. It gives me a thrill of victory – until I realize the person I just stabbed wasn't Saint at all.

He yells.

I scream.

'Did you just fucking stab me, Kid?!' Wolf shouts, looking down at the shard of glass sticking out of his arm.

'I thought you were Saint!' I say, still frozen in my just-stabbed-a-guy stance.

'How fucking dumb are you?'

'How the hell was I supposed to know it was you?' I shoot back, refusing to back down.

'Fucking shit God damn—' He grits his teeth, growls under his breath, and yanks out the glass. A gush of blood rushes to escape. Luckily it doesn't seem like I hit anything important. Wolf presses a dirty hand to the wound to stem the flow, glaring at me like he wishes it was my throat he was constricting. 'You're lucky I didn't blow your head off.'

Considering he's wielding a shotgun, I do consider myself pretty damn lucky. I give Wolf a once-over. He's looking pretty worse for wear. The pillows are gone and his shirt has been torn to shreds, leaving only the ragged-looking bulletproof vest. Scrapes and bruises decorate his arms, and there's an ugly gash across his forehead.

'You look like shit,' I say.

'So do you, but that's normal.' He scans the bare room

with growing confusion. 'What the hell were you doing in here?'

'Some guards brought me up. Saint wanted to talk to me.'

'Saint? He was here?' He turns in a circle rapidly, pointing the barrel of his gun at each corner of the room as if expecting to find him hiding.

'Yeah, he left a couple minutes ago and – wait, Wolf, listen!' I grab his arm as he turns to leave again. 'This guy, Saint, he's not at all like he's pretending to be. He's trying to recruit us for some big raider army of his.'

'Raider army?' Wolf stops and squints at me, processing the information. 'And that's why he's taking people. Huh.' He nods slowly. 'That makes sense. I *knew* one of the assholes I killed looked just like this guy Big Ben. So Saint is just tricking everyone into thinking he's the good guy?'

'Yeah.'

'Man, that's fucked-up. Knew he was an asshole.' He chews on his lip. A second or two passes, and his eyes widen, as if some big realization just hit him. 'Wait ... so Saint is actually the bad guy.' He presses his lips into a firm line, nose wrinkling in distaste. 'Does that make *us* the good guys?'

I pause, mulling it over, and slowly nod.

'Yeah, I guess it kind of does?'

'*Damn.*' He shakes his head, looking seriously annoyed. 'When this is over and done with, we better ransack the shit out of all the nearby towns so no one gets the wrong impression.'

'Good plan. But first, let's kill this guy.'

'Took the words right out of my mouth.'

Part of me wants to ask if he knows where the others are, but I know the answer will be more of a distraction than anything. If we lost someone . . . I don't want to find out now. I want to hear it later, when I have time to grieve. If I'm the only one that made it this far, Wolf needs me, and I'm not going to let him down.

XXX
The Good Guys

The building is surprisingly quiet except for the occasional muffled gunshot from below. Aside from a few bodies, presumably Wolf's handiwork, this floor is empty. It's almost eerie to be so alone after all the chaos. My body is still convinced it should be in fighting mode, my senses at their peak and my heart pounding despite the lack of action. I jump at every sound and check every corner for danger. Meanwhile, Wolf strides ahead with his typical lack of fear. We reach the stairwell without incident and start the climb to the top floor.

'You really think we can take him?' I ask. My whole body is sore, but I have to keep pushing forward. If I stop to rest, I'll crash. I can't afford to be tired or hurt right now. I wait for an answer, but none comes. 'Wolf?'

''Course we can,' he says finally. He stops and turns to face me, and I see what delayed his answer. He's breathing hard – really hard, each deep breath punctuated with a wince. Beads of sweat run down his grimy face.

'Are you okay?' I ask, knowing he's not.

'Fucking fantastic.' He clambers up the last stretch of stairs. I frown and follow more slowly. One foot slips on the stair he stopped on. I grab the handrail and look down to see a pool of blood. My gaze drifts up the stairs, following the red trail Wolf's leaving behind him.

'Wolf . . . ' I follow him to the top. He leans against the wall, struggling to catch his breath. 'You're hurt.'

'No shit. I was stabbed by a small, ugly girl about five minutes ago.'

I feel a twinge of guilt, but it's easy to see that the wound on his arm isn't the real problem here.

'You got shot,' I say. 'Where?'

He looks as if he wants to argue, but stops himself. He lifts up his shirt, wincing as the fabric peels off the wound. Breath hisses through my teeth. It's a bullet hole all right, and an ugly one, right through the fleshy part just above his hip.

'That bad?' he asks.

'Pretty bad.'

'Well, can't do nothin' about it now.' He lowers his shirt and steps closer to the door, resting a hand on the knob. 'You coming?'

I raise my eyes to his face, now recognizing the pain beneath the hard set of his jaw.

'I think you should stay behind,' I say, the words popping out before I have much time to think about them. He lets out a startled laugh, the sound echoing off the walls of the stairwell.

'You're screwing with me, right?'

'No. I'm serious. You're hurt.' I bite my lip, struggling to maintain my newfound confidence. 'And I can do it on my own.'

'We don't even know what's in there.' Despite the words, he takes his hand off the door handle and turns to face me. My heart jumps – he's listening. He's taking me seriously.

'When have we ever? And we've done pretty good up till this point.'

'That was different.'

'I can do this,' I say. 'On my own. Let me prove it.' He doesn't look convinced. 'Come on, give me a chance to be the hero for once.' I pause. 'Or . . . the villain? I'm still a little confused about where we stand as far as that goes?'

'Don't think about it too hard, you'll hurt yourself,' he says. But he isn't saying no. He takes a deep breath and wipes the back of one hand across his forehead. 'Look, Kid, you don't have to do this. Me, Tank, Dolly, we wouldn't make it in a normal world. We ain't never gonna settle down in some town and live a peaceful life. We're too fucked-up. That's why we're here, see? It's our way of life at stake here. Good guy, fake good guy, whatever he is, this Saint wants to change the wastes, and that would mean we're done for. But not you, Kid. You're different. You can still make it.'

'And just leave you guys?'

'Why the hell not?'

'You still don't get it, do you?' I ask. 'I haven't had a home in a long time. But you guys, you're . . .'

'Don't you get all choked up on me,' Wolf says, but without the usual biting tone.

'Sorry,' I say, wiping my eyes with the back of my hand. 'It's just . . . I wouldn't want to live in a world without you or

Dolly or Tank, even if it means my life is a whole lot shorter because I'm with you. I know I don't have to do this, but I want to.' Ignoring the burning feeling behind my eyes, I try to shape my face into a fierce expression. 'And I'm one of you now. I got this, Wolf.'

Wolf scrutinizes me silently. I do my best to hold it together. I know Wolf hates this kind of emotional talk, but I can't think of any other way to get through to him.

'Fine,' he says finally. 'But it ain't 'cause of that sappy shit you said. It's just 'cause I know you'll charge in like an idiot even if I say no.'

'Thanks,' I say, smiling despite my best attempt to conceal my emotions. Unable to help myself, I step forward and wrap my arms around Wolf in a hug. He stiffens, but rather than pulling away, pats me awkwardly on the back.

'Yeah, yeah. Don't go thanking me yet, you'll probably get shot up the second you go in there,' he says. I step back and nod, readying myself with my gun again.

'Time to go kick some ass,' I say cheerfully.

'Not with that gun,' he says. 'Give me that.'

I hesitantly hand over my pistol. He pushes his sawed-off shotgun into my hands.

'Much better,' he says, although I feel a bit ridiculous carrying it. 'If anything's gonna get your skinny ass through this, it'll be that baby. But remember, only two shots, all right? So make 'em count.'

'Got it,' I say. 'Thanks, Wolf.'

'Go give 'em hell.'

He opens the door for me and I step through. As the door swings shut behind me, I feel utterly alone.

The top floor is as silent and empty as the last one. As soon as I step out of the safety of the stairwell, all of my senses are on alert. Blood pumps overzealously through my veins. My hands shake, making the barrel of my gun wobble. Just because I'm willing to die doesn't mean I particularly *want* to, and despite my big words I'm scared. This is it: the final showdown. All the fighting, all the struggle, all of it has led up to this. Despite my anxiousness, I don't let my steps falter. Teeth clenched and gun raised, I swing into the first doorway – and stop. It's empty.

I break through another two doors and find both as empty as the first. The floor doesn't seem to hold anything other than old furniture and cobwebs. It makes me wonder if Saint is even up here. That's when I notice the room at the end of the hallway. The door is open, and it looks like there's a light on inside.

I guess I probably should have checked that one first. There's a very high possibility that it's a trap – but what am I supposed to do, back off? No way, not after giving that cheesy speech. I'm not gonna run back to Wolf with my tail between my legs.

I walk toward the room, barrel pointed at the doorway, and step inside.

Saint is waiting for me. He's surrounded with some kind of machinery I've never seen in my life, all alive with light and sound. Like I noticed, he even has a light on. Real electricity. I've heard some towns have it, but I've never seen it before. It's like magic. I find it hard not to gawk at the sight, but remind myself why I'm here and focus on Saint instead, keeping my gun trained on him.

To my surprise, he's unarmed, holding his hands palms out to display his lack of a weapon.

'You?' he asks, his eyebrows drawing together. 'Well, I certainly wasn't expecting you to walk in here alone,' he says. 'But that's fine. I want to talk. Work out a deal. Decimating each other's forces doesn't do any good for either of us. Look: no guards, no guns. Just me, ready to be reasonable.'

I sweep my eyes around the room, searching for any good hiding spots. I don't see any.

'Okay,' I say, not lowering my gun. The situation seems safe for the moment, but I don't want to let my guard down. 'So, say we join you. What exactly does that look like for us?'

He eyes the gun, looks like he's considering saying something about it, but then smiles instead. He leans back in his chair, arms folded over his chest, his posture relaxed.

'You'll continue working together as your own individual crew,' he says. 'Only thing that changes is that Wolf answers to me. I'll tell you what towns to hit. Sometimes you'll work alone, sometimes with other groups. You carry out raids like usual, and then give me a percentage of the loot.'

'A big percentage?'

'A fair percentage. And you can trade supplies with me or the other crews if you need something.'

I turn my attention back to his plan, and try to envision the world he proposes. An army of raiders would sweep through the wastelands easily. With the Queen gone, Saint is the only powerhouse left; maybe he even planned on her dying. The townies won't stand a chance.

'So, your army takes over,' I say slowly. 'And then you're in charge of everything.'

'That's the plan,' Saint says. 'In a way, I really will be bringing peace to the wastelands.'

'Okay, one last question,' I say. 'Is the rest of my crew okay?'

Saint leans forward, hands on his knees, and smiles broadly.

'They're all perfectly intact and alive last I heard. Now, about our deal—'

Bang.

Saint's face slowly changes from surprised to baffled to angry. He looks down at himself as a red stain spreads across his chest. I lower the barrel of my gun.

'That's all I needed to know,' I say. 'Thanks!'

His eyes are still wide open and full of hate. He opens his mouth to say something, but the attempt produces nothing more than a bloody gurgle. I wince.

'Umm, this is awkward. I thought for sure that would kill you.' I raise the gun again, point it right at his extremely pissed-off face this time. 'Well, here we go again.'

Bang.

'And that's it?' Wolf asks as we head down the stairs. His wound slows him down, and I walk ahead of him with a bounce in my step.

'Well, yeah. Then I banged up the radio equipment as best I could and left. I thought about using the explosives, but it looked pretty broken already.' I grin and whirl to look at him. 'Seriously, though, you should've seen the look on Saint's face.'

'No epic speech, no nothing?' Wolf asks, frowning. I sigh, disappointed by his lack of enthusiasm.

'Nah, I already got the speech out of my system. Figured I should just end it quickly.'

'Honestly, I'm kind of disappointed.' He shakes his head. 'All of that buildup for nothing.'

I sigh as we reach the bottom of the stairwell. Regardless of what Wolf thinks, *I* think I did a damn good job. I reach for the door, pull it open – and nearly jump out of my skin as a burst of gunfire comes from the other side. I slam the door shut, pressing my body against it to hold it closed.

'Oh shit,' I say, my eyes wide. 'I kind of forgot there's still the whole "army of raiders" issue.'

'Yep,' Wolf says, looking more resigned than startled. 'I don't really have a plan for this part.' After a moment's consideration, he yanks his shotgun out of my hands, hands me my pistol, and leans against the wall beside the doorway.

'Saint said Dolly and Tank are fine, so maybe if we meet up with them ... ' I trail off, realizing it still seems unlikely that this turns out well for us. Even with Saint gone, there are so many raiders remaining. My gut twists. Could this really be the end of the line? After we came all this way, took care of Saint and his radio, did the job we came here to do – are we just gonna die like this?

'Well,' Wolf says. 'At least we'll go out with a bang.' He faces the door with his shotgun. 'On the count of three, you open it and we go in, guns blazing. Got it?'

'Got it.' I swallow back nerves and grab the door handle with one hand, my gun in the other. I look at Wolf.

'One,' he says. 'T—'

'Wait, on three or after three?' I blurt out. Wolf sighs, lowering his gun.

'On three, dumbass. C'mon, you're killing my adrenaline rush here.'

'Okay. On three. Right.'

'One ... two ... th—'

The door slams open from the other side, smacking me in the face and sending me stumbling backward. I hit the floor on my ass. The door separates me from Wolf for a moment, and when it closes again I see three of Saint's raiders on him.

Cursing, I scramble to my feet and throw myself at the only one with a gun, sending both of us crashing to the floor in a heap. I end up on top of him – and my pistol skitters across the floor, out of reach. *Shit.* I grapple with him for his gun, struggling to keep the barrel aimed away from me. When it becomes clear I'm never going to overpower him, I free one hand and jab him in the eye with a finger. He howls in pain, and I successfully yank the gun out of his grip and turn it on him.

An arm wraps around my neck from behind. My captor lifts me up, away from the man beneath me. I struggle to break free, my feet barely scraping the ground as he pulls me off my feet, and fire the gun wildly in an attempt to hit whoever's holding me. He lets out a grunt of pain, but the arm around my neck only pulls tighter. My breath is cut off; stars dance in my vision. Desperate, I aim at the man still on the floor below us. If I can at least take out one of them, then maybe—

'Hold up!' Wolf shouts, and I stop, my finger freezing where it was about to pull the trigger. I can't move my head, but I shift my eyes to the side to get a glimpse of Wolf. He's face-to-face with the third raider. I now recognize her as the woman who captured me before, the one with the Mohawk and meat cleaver – which is currently raised above her head like she was just about to strike. Wolf is staring at her intently; she's staring at the shotgun in his hands, currently pointed right at her face. 'Aren't you Betty?' he asks. 'From Big Ben's crew?'

The woman starts, raising her eyes to Wolf's face and squinting.

'Wolf?' She pauses for a moment before grinning toothily and lowering her weapon. 'Ahh, I remember you. So *you're* the asshole crazy enough to attack Saint's headquarters. I should've guessed.'

They grin at each other, shotgun and meat cleaver both lowering. I let out a choked gurgle, since they seem to have forgotten I'm still being strangled over here. Betty glances over and jerks a hand. The pressure eases up as the man releases me. I take a deep gulp of air and glance at the guy, satisfied to see that my wildly fired bullet has taken a chunk out of his ear. I shoot one last glare at him and grab my pistol from the floor before moving over to Wolf's side.

'So,' Betty says. 'I'm hoping you guys have realized that Saint's not really Mr. Law-and-Order?'

'Yeah, we got that much,' Wolf says.

'We've been trying to tell that red-haired one that Saint just wants to recruit you guys,' the man I shot says, holding one hand to his ear and speaking a little too loudly. 'But she kills anyone who comes near her.'

'Sounds about right,' Wolf says with a grin.

'So what do you say?' Betty asks. 'Your crew gonna join up with him?'

Wolf and I exchange a glance.

'Well,' he says. 'We—'

'Saint's dead,' I say bluntly. 'I killed him.'

All eyes are on me the moment the words leave my mouth. I look back and forth between Wolf and Betty. The former looks a little concerned, his eyes flashing at the other raiders and his grip on his gun tightening once again. My own fingers twitch on the trigger of my pistol, ready in case this turns into another gunfight.

But Betty laughs, giving me a look that seems almost impressed.

'Well,' she says. 'That's that, I guess. Time to pack it up and head out, boys.' She glances at Wolf. 'You seen Ben around?'

'Nope,' he says quickly, shooting me a sharp look that I assume means to keep my mouth shut. I bite back a smile.

The other raiders grumble a bit as Betty barks orders at them to prepare to leave, and soon they trickle out of the room and leave Wolf and me behind. Outside, I hear Betty shouting the news about Saint's death to the other raiders. A chorus of groans and complaints answers her, but overall no one seems overly upset – or surprised – by the news.

Once it's clear no one is planning on hunting us down and shooting us for taking down Saint, Wolf and I walk out of the stairwell and over to the main lobby. None of the raiders we pass pay much attention to us, all prepping to head out, a rowdy mess of them taking anything they can find in the building and separating into individual crews again. There are a few tussles over weapons and other supplies, but we stay out of the fighting for once, searching for the rest of our crew instead.

We find Tank laughing and joking with a group of strangers, showing off a few new wounds he must've earned in the fighting. The moment he sees us, he lets out a whoop of joy and sweeps me up in a bone-crushing bear hug, spinning me around. I'm breathless and dizzy by the time he sets me down.

'Goddamn,' he says, grinning from ear to ear. 'I can't believe we actually pulled this off.'

'I knew it would work out the whole time,' Wolf says with a dismissive wave of his hand. 'The plan was foolproof.'

'Pretty sure it was mostly dumb luck,' Tank says. 'Plus the fact that hardly any of these raiders were actually loyal to Saint. A bunch of 'em took off the second trouble started, and a bunch of the others decided to start looting the place since Saint was busy trying to deal with us.'

Wolf lets out a snort of laughter.

''Course they did,' he says. 'Don't know why assholes like him think they'd ever be able to control us wastelanders.' He grins, fierce and proud. 'Ain't nobody gonna tame these wastes.'

We find Dolly waiting for us near the wreckage of our truck, bodies strewn across the floor around her. She's covered in an astounding amount of blood, none of which seems to be hers, and is carrying more weapons than seems like should be humanly possible.

Her face reveals no surprise whatsoever at seeing us, but

she does smile – and I smile back as she squeezes my arm, and ignore the fact that it leaves behind a smear of half-dried blood. When Wolf explains the Saint situation and his death, she merely shrugs, as if it doesn't really matter to her either way.

We leave Saint's former headquarters battered, bruised, and bleeding, but pretty damn pleased with ourselves. I can't stop smiling and feeling like a big damn hero. It doesn't last long, though. Exhaustion comes creeping up fast once the nervous energy drains out of me. Soon I can feel every little scrape and bruise and find myself wishing more than anything for a comfortable bed to sleep in for a few weeks or so. The others are quiet aside from the occasional groan or muttered curse, so I assume they're feeling much the same.

Once we make it a good distance away from the building and the rest of the straggling raiders, we stop to gather ourselves.

'So, what's the plan, Wolf?' I ask. Tank sits down heavily on the ground, and I resist the urge to join him. If I sit now, it'll just be ten times harder to get myself back up. Dolly stands next to me, quietly sorting through her various new weapons.

'Well ...' Wolf spits on the ground and looks around. Outside of Saint's grounds, there's nothing but the same old wastelands. In the distance I can see a few of the other raider crews, some on foot and some in vehicles, gradually vanishing into the wastes. 'It's gonna be a shitfest around here with all these other crews heading out again, but I've got a whole lot of killin', lootin', and eatin' to get out of my system after that whole mess.' He shakes his head, his face sour. 'Can't believe we turned out to be the goddamn good guys. What a fuckin' embarrassment.'

No more vehicle, no more goal, and possibly not even enough supplies to make it to the next town, wherever that might be. Sounds about right. Maybe the thought should be daunting, but a grin spreads across my face.

'Well, no point hanging around doing nothing,' I say. 'Let's go!'

So we carry on.

Acknowledgments

There are some people without whom this book would've never existed, so I'm going to try my best to articulate how much they mean to me. Many thanks to:

Matthew Scrivener, the best teacher I ever had, and the first person who made me truly believe in my writing.

My agent, Emmanuelle Morgen, for having faith in *Bite* ever since it was just a messy draft, and being incredible every step of the way.

Jess Rosen, for being awesome and boundlessly enthusiastic.

Susan Barnes, my fantastic editor, who fought for this book and pushed to make it the best it could be. Lindsey Hall, for being so helpful throughout the publishing process and putting up with how bad I am at answering e-mails (sorry Lindsey!). Lauren Panepinto, who designed the super kickass cover. And the rest of the amazing team at Orbit: Thank you all for working so hard to make this book a reality.

And, of course, my family. Gramma, Memere, and Pepere, who hopefully weren't too scarred by this book, for endless love and support. My mom, who made me fall in love with reading and always encouraged me to pursue my passion. My dad, to whom I suspect I owe much of my weird sense of humor. And my brothers, Todd and Lucas, whose quick wit keeps me constantly on my toes. You make my life interesting. Love you all.

extras

www.orbitbooks.net

about the author

Debut author **K. S. Merbeth** is obsessed with SSF, food, video games, and her cat, and resides in Tuscon, Arizona. You can find her on Twitter @ksmerbeth.

Find out more about K. S. Merbeth and other Orbit authors by registering for the free monthly newsletter at www.orbitbooks.net.

if you enjoyed
BITE

look out for

THE LAST DAYS OF JACK SPARKS

by

Jason Arnopp

Jack Sparks died while writing this book.

It was no secret that journalist Jack Sparks had been researching the occult for his new book. No stranger to controversy, he'd already triggered a furious Twitter storm by mocking an exorcism he witnessed.

Then there was that video: forty seconds of chilling footage that Jack repeatedly claimed was not of his making, yet was posted from his own YouTube account.

Nobody knew what happened to Jack in the days that followed – until now.

FOREWORD BY ALISTAIR SPARKS

At the centre of the house in which my late brother Jacob and I grew up, there was a black hole.

That's what we called it. In reality, it was a small room born of inexplicable architectural design. A roughly square space, right in the middle of a suburban Suffolk bungalow. No lights, windows or ventilation. No bigger than two department store changing rooms pushed together. Three doors led in and out.

Our mother made a virtue of this pointless junction box, as was her way, and hammered a coat rack to one of the walls in there. So it became the cloakroom.

Jacob, who would rise to fame and infamy as Jack Sparks, shared my instinctive fear of the word 'cloak'. Cloaks covered people, rendering them sinister, and so our dread of that room deepened. Calling it 'the black hole' had actually made it less intimidating. Something science could explain.

The cloakroom was a place we took special measures to avoid. We would take the long route around every time — anything rather than having to enter that stale pocket of black. As you hurried through, your pulse would gallop. You'd gasp or even cry out as you mistook a prickle on the nape of your neck for the cold breath of the dead and gone.

The incident happened one Saturday in the summer of 1983, when Jacob was aged five, four years my junior. As with all siblings, there was some rivalry between us, but brotherly harmony was the norm. We would climb trees, ride bikes, play football. Then we would lean against each other as we limped home, after accidents that tended to involve trees, bikes or football.

This incident was born of pure childish innocence, but feels unexpectedly relevant here, in a book to which I never dreamt I would contribute. I really feel it sheds light on my brother's nature and, I'm sorry to say, his severe downward spiral.

Most of the windows were open that day. Outside, hot air rippled. Our mother was in the garden, stretched out on a reclining lounger that occasionally broke and made her swear so loudly that our neighbours complained. She had one of her suspense novels, a pack of Silk Cut and her usual lack of suncream.

Jacob was absorbed with a toy car, whooshing it across the dining room floor, his face flushed. Seizing my chance for a bit of mutual fun, I stalked around the house and jammed all but one of the cloakroom's doors shut, dragging furniture to create blockades. The architect had at least thought to make these doors open outwards.

I peered out through the kitchen window and saw Mum dozing, the book splayed on her belly. Then I told Jacob we were going to play a game.

He, I explained, would be a ghost-hunter. And I would be a ghost, chasing him. The rules of the game were simple. I would pursue him around the house. He had to try and pass through the black hole three times without being grabbed and turned into a ghost himself.

Jacob looked uncertain. 'If I'm a ghost-hunter, why am I running?'

''Cause you've met me,' I told him. 'I'm a ghost that's too big and evil to deal with.'

He thought this over, then to my relief accepted it. The trap was set.

Jacob ran whooping ahead of me as I waved my arms about and made spooky noises, restricting my speed so as not to catch him. Making a beeline for the exact cloakroom door I'd planned, he raced across the length of the dining room and bolted into the black.

Sprinting to catch up, almost slipping over, I slammed the door shut on him. Then I gripped the handle tightly with both hands, the muscles in my arms taut with anticipation.

There was a muffled thump as Jacob tried to exit through one of the other doors, only to find it impossible. His voice was indistinct, as if piped down a bad phone line.

'Hey! It won't . . . '

His voice trailed away as he tried another door. Another thump, and this time just a bewildered cry.

The blood thundered in my head as I squeezed that door handle, ready for the assault, which began in seconds.

When Jacob wrenched it, only to encounter the percep-
tibly imperfect force of human resistance, his voice became
charged with fear.

'Ali, stop it! Ali!'

There was no chance of our mother hearing, and yet
Jacob's pitch rose along with his volume. Sometimes he
would abandon his vain attempts to open the door, only to
suddenly try again in the hope of surprising me. Or I would
hear the whumphs as he slammed himself against one of the
other doors, yelling for Mum. Still I did not relent. Since he
didn't sound terrified and was not crying, I felt confident he
too would see the funny side when I released him.

Then those calls from inside the cloakroom stopped
dead.

Biceps burning, I twisted around and leant heavily back
against the door. While watching flies chase each other, I
listened hard.

I listened for what felt like a long time.

Nothing.

The sense of fun began to fade.

'Don't worry,' I called through the thick wood. 'I'll let
you out now, okay?' I laughed, lightly.

There was no reply.

Despite standing in a room flooded with sunlight, I
began to feel uneasy.

A sly, arcane image snuck unbidden into my mind.

I pictured Jacob transformed, inside that room.

In my head, he now stood wearing a cloak, with hollow
darkness where his face should be.

I became convinced that this spectral monk who was

once my brother now stood silently waiting for me to see him. When I opened the door, I decided, he would lurch out of the room. He would tear off my limbs, one by one, laughing as he did so.

'Jakey?' I called out.

Still nothing.

'Jacob?'

My heart, which had thumped so excitedly only moments beforehand, now felt like it was banging on a door, wanting out.

I felt sick with worry about what had happened to my brother.

About what he had become in that unknowable space.

Seconds later, I saw it all coming out from under the door.

The purpose of my anecdote is certainly not to lend further ammunition to my online trolls, who nonsensically hold me responsible for the direction Jacob's life took. I merely seek to offer a glimpse of his formative years, as a child who reacted in an unusually extreme manner to an otherwise harmless prank. On that front, at least, my conscience is clear. I also felt it prudent to present my side of the story, given that my brother also includes it in this book. He will pick up the story later, but sadly tells an exaggerated version, employing far less honesty than I.

Despite the suffocating media coverage that followed my brother's untimely death at the age of thirty-six, the casual reader may be unaware of his achievements.

As a child, I had wanted to work in entertainment, but

became a scientist. Conversely, Jacob had often spoken of ambitions within science, but of course became a writer and media personality. His first step along that road was a work experience placement at the *New Musical Express* in 1996. I still smile when I think of the phone call I received from this cocky eighteen-year-old upstart, telling me, 'I'm in!' The *NME* had commissioned him to write his first published record review. Jack knew his music, even if it wasn't to my taste. Come our teens, it would be the Sex Pistols, Motörhead and The Sisters of Mercy blaring out of his den, while mine played host to a bit of Pet Shop Boys.

He quickly changed his name, thinking Jack Sparks cooler. I was snowed under with my degree in biochemistry, but was pleased that my brother was showing signs of fulfilling my own earlier dream.

From work experience onwards, Jack left Mum and myself in Suffolk to move to London's Camden Town, burrowing tenaciously into the business. During his twenties, he excelled himself, hopping back and forth across the Atlantic. While unable to catch many issues of the *NME* at the time – although I often asked Jack for copies – I gathered that his direct interviewing tecŸique and unflinching opinions generated debate among readers. This polarising effect would continue when he sought horizons beyond the musical ghetto.

His first non-fiction book, *Jack Sparks on a Pogo Stick* (Erubis Books, 2010), seemed ostensibly light-hearted, as he travelled from Land's End to JoŸ O'Groats on the titular device. But since he was unable to use motorways during his journey, it was also a fascinating study of the bygone curiosities to be found on British roads less travelled.

Jack Sparks on Gangs (Erubis, 2012) saw him dive headlong into choppier waters, perhaps as a result of the first book's mixed reviews. I had my concerns about my brother mixing with violent gangs and documenting his discoveries, but of course there was no use in pressing such points with Jack.

Gangs won the Sara Thornwood Prize. It was undeniably insightful, and broadened my own views on gang culture, in both Britain and America. Around this time, Jack established himself as a prominent atheist and began to make guest appearances on UK TV panel shows like *Never Mind the Buzzcocks*, *Would I Lie To You?* and *Shooting Stars*.

His third book was his most divisive to date. The title alone, *Jack Sparks on Drugs* (Erubis, 2014), ensured plenty of free publicity, but the concept was for my brother to try every drug under the sun and document his experiences. I was very much against him doing it, and our relationship fell on stony ground as a result of this and other matters at the time. It didn't help that drugs had made Jack more difficult and headstrong than ever. Our parting of ways – even after he entered rehab that summer – is something I shall always regret.

I am only too aware that Jack's final book, which he originally intended to be called *Jack Sparks on the Supernatural*, has been controversial from the moment its release was announced.

I have now experienced every conceivable online attack

on me, including direct threats on my life and those of my family. One troll even turned up on our doorstep one night armed with a meat cleaver. She is now behind bars.

While there has been considerable support for this book, many have called for it to be banned. To some, it must feel like a cold, cynical and rather distasteful cash-in on my part, especially as Jack had no dependants. I've stated this on social media several times, but such words are easily lost amid the deafening hubbub – a portion of my fee will be divided between prominent motor neurone disease charities around the world. I have absolutely no desire to profit from my brother's death, which I am still coming to terms with. Working on this book has been deeply cathartic. Jack's editor of five years, Eleanor Rosen, has been nothing but accommodating throughout, while standing up to me where necessary.

We are fortunate indeed that my brother always wrote his books during the process of researching them. While others might squirrel away a horde of recorded interviews, thoughts and scribbled notes, electing to deal with them all together at the end, Jack wanted to get it down. He hated interview transcription and so dealt with that workload in chunks as he went.

While co-editing this book, Eleanor and I have corrected only small, inconsequential typos and errors, while vitally retaining the format and feel of Jack's writing, especially in the book's second half, when it becomes very different. Dividing the book into two sections was our decision. To her eternal credit, Eleanor supported my push to retain Jack's written notes directed at her, which are peppered throughout his text.

I extend my heartfelt gratitude and condolences to the families of the deceased, who mostly gave permission for their loved ones' true identities to be used. Other names have been changed. Believe me, the decision to publish *Jack Sparks on the Supernatural* in its entirely uncensored form was in no way taken lightly, and I know how very difficult it is for the bereaved to read accounts of such horrendous events. Yet I also hope this book may yield some form of closure and put an end to unhelpful internet speculation – not least concerning the nature of my brother's death.

I would like to thank my beautiful wife Chloe and our children Sophie and Xanna for their incredible support.

How I wish Jack had never attended that exorcism.

How I wish he had never laid eyes on that YouTube video.

Rest in peace, my brother, and please know that I forgive you.

Alistair Sparks: 'Jack's former agent Murray Chambers has supplied me with this email exchange, which began the day after my brother attended the exorcism in Italy.'

Date: 1 November 2014
From: Jack Sparks
Subject: RE: RE: My new book!
To: Murray Chambers (The Chambers Agency)

Murray. Why the fuck would Erubis need to see 30,000 words of this book 'before going ahead'? We're still under contract with them – and eight weeks after it came out, On Drugs might as well be NAILED to the Top 10s!

Did they not actually read my proposal paragraph? An exorcist, a possessed girl, a scary YouTube video ... a fucking mystery. A mission!

Does Bill Bryson have to write 30,000 words before he can sell his latest book that he's written all about himself? Of course he doesn't, and neither should I. Sort it out.

J

Date: 1 November 2014
From: Murray Chambers (The Chambers Agency)
Subject: RE: RE: RE: My new book!
To: Jack Sparks

Jack, let me refresh your memory on a few points.

(1) While writing On Drugs, you became a drug addict.
(2) The book had to be hauled back from the brink of disaster with a ghost writer.
(3) You phoned Erubis' MD at home at 3 a.m., while coked off your face, and repeatedly called him 'a huge cunt'.

That last point in particular means there are bridges to be rebuilt. Jack Sparks on the Supernatural might well be the fourth of the four books we signed for, but Erubis (a) didn't expect a book about ghosts; and (b) need to know you're back on the straight and narrow. They're jittery. I'm working on it, but sadly we can't rely on Eleanor sticking up for you after the way you've treated her. So you need to show willing here, mate. Write the 30K.

Mx

PS Bryson's books aren't strictly speaking all about himself. Yours pretty much are. (Not a criticism, just FYI.)

Date: 1 November 2014
From: Jack Sparks
Subject: RE: RE: RE: RE: My new book!
To: Murray Chambers (The Chambers Agency)

Fuck you, Murray.

Fuck. You.

This is insane! So I had a blip. I'm still JACK SPARKS, Murray. If anything, rehab raised my profile even more and you know it.

I won't write 30,000 sample words for Erubis. I won't even write 30. Apart from anything else, I can't do any more travelling without advance cash. Get them on the phone and straighten them out.

Date: 2 November 2014
From: Murray Chambers (The Chambers Agency)
Subject: RE: RE: RE: RE: RE: My new book!
To: Jack Sparks

Okay . . . I've managed to talk them into releasing the next part of the advance. I've promised them you're fine. I've personally put my neck on the block here and I hope you appreciate that.

Just make it a great and, above all, smoothly delivered book. Also: when can I get my £500 back? It's been six months.

Mx

Date: 2 November 2014
From: Jack Sparks
Subject: RE: RE: RE: RE: RE: RE: My new book!
To: Murray Chambers (The Chambers Agency)

Ha! Knew they'd see sense. Murray, this is gonna be one hell of a book.

Let's STORM THE HILL!